THEY HAVE
OUR ATT

After a moment, the screen cleared and another video began, this time of two uniformed dark-skinned bearded men beating a young man dressed in Chassidic-style coat and hat. They beat him to the ground and continued swinging their nightsticks for some time. They eventually stopped, and straightened to walk away, laughing.

The screen of the tablet cracked and crazed. Ariel realized his hands had squeezed tightly enough that the pressure of his thumbs had broken the tablet. He laid it back on the table. "Sorry," was all he could say through his clenched teeth.

Mordechai nodded. "That second case was Jonathan Goldberg. Khamis and Sajid claimed that he was harassing them and attacked them first. He was left a quadriplegic as a result of the beating and died three months later. The state never prosecuted either case—for lack of evidence, they claimed."

Ariel's hands were tightened into fists so strongly that his knuckles were blanched white. He stared at his fists, wanting...wanting for the first time in his life to hurt someone, to cause anguish with his own hands.

He didn't know how long he sat there, seething in his anger. Finally, he looked up at Mordechai.

"So..." Ariel stopped to clear his throat. "So what's the plan?"

Mordechai nodded, with a bit of a sad smile. "They have attracted our attention, which they will ultimately regret."

BAEN BOOKS by DAVID CARRICO

The Blood Is the Life

1636: The Devil's Opera (with Eric Flint)
1636: Flight of the Nightingale

The Span of Empire (with Eric Flint)

To purchase any of these titles in e-book form,
please go to www.baen.com.

THE BLOOD IS THE LIFE

DAVID CARRICO

A Baen Books Original

Baen Publishing Enterprises
P.O. Box 1403
Riverdale, NY 10471
www.baen.com

ISBN: 978-1-9821-9291-4

Cover art by Alan Pollack

First printing, September 2022
First mass market printing, September 2023

Distributed by Simon & Schuster
1230 Avenue of the Americas
New York, NY 10020

Library of Congress Control Number: 2022024198

Printed in the United States of America

10   9   8   7   6   5   4   3   2   1

To the memory of my wife Ruth.
It's a very different story than
anything I've written before.
I think you would have liked it, even so.
Peace to you, dearheart.

And to the memory of my great friend
Rick Boatright—
raconteur, tech geek extraordinaire,
and story doctor par excellence.
You supported me from the earliest days
of my professional writing career.
I'm glad that you got to read this
before you left us. I miss you.

Acknowledgments

Thanks to Rob Hampson and Edith Maor
for being readers of early versions of the story.
It is stronger because of your suggestions,
and any errors remain my own fault.

DRAMATIS
PERSONAE

Abragam, Yakov	Friend and accomplice of Gersh Davidoff
Aharoni, Shimon	Weapons instructor for Israeli Police
Aram	Terrorist in The Grey Havens attack
Aronson, Menachem	Jewish vampire
Ashkenazi, Yaakov	Israeli official who set up Ariel Barak's identity
Benyamin, Duv	*Pakad* (chief inspector) in Israeli police
Biton, Adam	Student; classmate of Ariel Barak
Caan, Chaim (aka Ariel Barak)	Hero of the story
Caan, Bernie	Moses Caan's brother; Chaim's uncle
Caan, Miriam	Chaim's mother
Caan, Moses	Chaim's father

Caan, Rachel   Chaim Caan's aunt

Campbell, Colton   Cord Campbell's older brother;
                        died in Desert Storm

Campbell, Cord   White-supremacist Army Vet who
"Snake"   has Chaim's parents killed

Chert, Eric   Policeman and tae kwon do
                        fighter in Chattanooga

Dahan, Adam   Bartender at Shaka's club

Daud   Private guard in immigrant
                        community in New York City

Davidoff, Gersh   Sexual predator in Israel; low-
                        ranking Russian mobster

Dayan, Rivka   *Pakad* (captain) in Israeli police

Driver, Charles   Server at the hotel in Santa Carla

Elizabeth   Ethiopian Jewish assistant to Dr.
                        Mendel

Fardin   Terrorist bomber in attack on The
                        Grey Havens

Foreman, Rob   Manager/owner of Lyon Academy
                        in Chattanooga

Fridman, Leon   Friend of Gersh Davidoff

Gerson, Yonatan   Technician who works for Dr.
                        Mendel's organization

Ghorbani, Kiana   Terrorist in The Grey Havens
                        attack

Goldberg, Jonathan   Jew murdered in New York City
                        by immigrant community private
                        guards

Goldfeder, Hannah	Girl Chaim knew as a boy
Grissom, Bob	Drunk conventioneer who confronts Ariel
Gutierrez, Carlita	Admin clerk at Urgent Care
Haleva, Gil	Israeli unarmed combat instructor
Hershkowitz, Abigail "Abi"	Fellow student of Ariel; Yael's roommate
Hurwitz, Israel	Doctor leading study of Ariel's vampire metabolism
Ismail	Private guard in immigrant community in New York City
Jones, Karli	Manager of Urgent Care
Jordan, Anna	Morning-shift nurse at Urgent Care
Katz, Eleazar	Jewish vampire
Khamis	Private guard in immigrant community in New York City
Klein, Gabriel	*Samal Sheni* (sergeant) in Israeli police
Khoury, Georgia	Bartender at Shaka's club
Levchin, Arkadi	Russian mobster who emigrated to Israel from St. Petersburg
Levinson, Reuben	Rabbi of Temple Emanuel synagogue in Santa Carla; connects Chaim with Dr. Mendel
Lewis, Nick	Australian ex-pat living in Israel; manager/part owner of Shaka's club

Li, Greg	American immigrant to Israel; retired chemical engineer; owns/operates The Lucky Star
Lichtenfeld, Imi	Developer of Krav Maga unarmed combat system
Lipschutz, Hyman & Rosa	Patrons at The Dove restaurant
Majid	Terrorist in The Grey Havens attack
Malka, Yael	Student; friend of Ariel's; victim of assault by Gersh Davidoff
Martin, Bob	MMA fighter in Chattanooga
McLeod, James "Jake"	Head of The Devil's Legions chapter in Santa Carla
Meier, Josef	Israeli police officer
Mendel, Avram	Scientist and rabbi; specializes in "esoteric research"
Miller, Abraham	Jew murdered in New York City by immigrant community private guards
Montoya, Ricardo	Nurse practitioner at Urgent Care
Morgan, John	Physiology professor at UCLA
Nguyen, Tran	Nurse practitioner at Urgent Care
Olmstead, Mike	Kid who bullied Chaim Caan in seventh grade
Perlman, Marta	Technician in Dr. Hurwitz's study of Ariel
Ramirez, Elena	Chaim's best friend in high school
Ramirez, Enrico	Sergeant in Santa Carla police

Rosen, Shira	Israeli police officer
Sajid	Private guard in immigrant community in New York City
Sasson, Dvir	*Shoter* (constable) in Israeli police
Schenk, Mortimer	Maître d'hôtel at The Dove restaurant
Segel, Chana	Yaakov Ashkenazi's assistant
Shapiro, Beth	Server at the John Bull Pub
Silva Almeida, Gabriel Luis "Gabe"	MMA specialist in Brazilian jiu-jitsu in Chattanooga
Spira, Elon	*Rav Shoter* (corporal) in Israeli police
Steinberg, Joshua	Rabbi at Beth Shalom, Chaim's synagogue growing up
Tiffy	Chaim's mother's dog
Valdez, Aaron	Policeman and tae kwon do fighter in Chattanooga
Weber, Trent "Slick"	Henchman of Jake McLeod in The Devil's Legions
Weissmann, Max	Jewish rabbi and professor; friend of Reuben Levinson who helped in connecting Chaim with Dr. Mendel
Wong, Azure	California blogger at the Blue Lance blog
Zalman, Mordechai	280-year-old Jewish vampire; Chaim/Ariel's mentor

THE BLOOD
IS THE LIFE

CHAPTER 1

CHAIM CAAN WAITED IN THE SHADOW BY THE OLD
magnolia tree. The bright light of the nearby streetlight
made the shadow seem especially dark. His eyes were
focused on the man who had just exited the rear door
of the synagogue.

It was a running source of humor in the local
Jewish community that Rabbi Reuben Levinson, rabbi
of the Reform congregation Temple Emanuel, parked
his old Toyota Camry in the far corner of the synagogue parking lot to make one more spot close to the
building available for one of the elderly members of
his congregation who truly needed it. Even Chaim,
Orthodox though he was, had heard the joke, "And
don't you park in *Rav* Reuben's parking space, now."

Chaim was nervous about approaching the rabbi.
He was Reform, while Chaim's family were definitely
Orthodox. But the problem he had, he just couldn't
take it to Joshua Steinberg, the Orthodox rabbi of his
synagogue, Congregation Beth Shalom. For all that
Rabbi Steinberg was a compassionate and learned
man, Chaim was fairly certain that he was not a

1

flexible man. Rabbi Reuben, though, had a reputation for flexibility of thought. Chaim was very afraid that that was going to be tested tonight.

Keys out, the rabbi was approaching his car when Chaim moved out of the shadows. He recoiled for a moment and dropped his keys, then stood still.

"Rabbi Reuben?" Chaim began.

"Y...yes." The stutter revealed the rabbi's nervousness. Chaim could sympathize.

"I'm sorry; I didn't mean to frighten you, Rabbi." Chaim moved forward into the aura of the nearby streetlamp. He knew what the bright light would reveal—a slightly pudgy young man about the rabbi's height in jeans and a windbreaker. "I...I need to talk to you."

Reuben sighed. "Can it wait until tomorrow? I am very tired, and would like to rest first."

Chaim knew that the rabbi was probably weary. Shabbat service would put a strain on the rabbi, and he had the next morning's Torah reading and sermon to get through. But it had taken Chaim a while to screw up his courage to approach the rabbi, and he didn't want to lose the opportunity. "Umm, no, sir. I really need to talk to you now."

"Very well." The rabbi sighed again. "Let's go back into my office, then."

"No!" Chaim knew there was panic in his voice. The rabbi looked at him, quite startled. "I'd..." he continued in a calmer tone, "I'd rather talk out here, please. It won't take long."

There was a long pause as the rabbi was obviously mulling the thought over. "All right," he finally responded, "but I'm going to sit down." He suited actions to words by picking up his keys and walking over to the car to hop up on the driver's side fender. "Now, what seems to be the problem?"

"The problem?" Chaim's nerves flared as he almost giggled. "Oh, I have a problem indeed, sir, one that would test the mind of Rambam himself." The rabbi's eyebrows elevated at the reference to the medieval-era rabbi. Chaim's studies in Jewish history and culture and religion were being displayed.

He took a deep breath, and began. "My name is Chaim Caan, *Rav* Reuben. I was raised Orthodox. My father and mother were both very strict in observance, including the *kashrut* rules. We went to *shul* on every *Shabbas*." Chaim's choice of the Ashkenazic forms of the Hebrew words for sure clued the rabbi in that his family was most likely of Eastern European background.

"I went to Hebrew school after regular school for several hours a day. After my bar mitzvah, I studied Torah and Talmud. It was my father's thought that I would continue on to a *yeshiva* and study to become a rabbi."

"If you were raised so traditionally, why are you bringing this to me?" the rabbi asked. "You should know I'm Reform."

"I know," Chaim said. "And my father wouldn't be happy about this. He already thinks I'm too liberal. But this is so weird, I just don't think my rabbi at Congregation Beth Shalom can handle it."

"You think I can?"

"I have friends who attend here, and they say you're pretty levelheaded, practical, and able to think outside the box. I . . . I think I need that pretty badly, especially that last part."

"All right," Rabbi Reuben said. "I'm listening."

"Well, anyway, Dad had always wanted me to be a rabbi, but I decided to become a doctor, so I've been a premed student the last couple of years. That's something else he's not happy about."

"A worthy goal. Our people provide many of the finest doctors in the world."

"I know." Chaim put his hands in his pockets and looked down at the ground. "The thing is, once I got to school I kind of . . . started experimenting a little." A slightly bitter tone entered his voice. "I was never in trouble, growing up—never got to see much of the outside world. I was too *busy* to get into trouble. But when I started at the university, I saw that there was a whole wide world beyond the confines of my father's beliefs, and I started exploring a little."

"A not uncommon situation," the rabbi sighed.

"Not according to my father. Oh, I didn't get into anything destructive, *Rav* Reuben. I stayed away from drugs, and I don't drink a lot." Chaim sounded slightly embarrassed. "It only took one hangover to convince me that I didn't want to get drunk ever again. I not only wanted to die, I was disappointed when I didn't. But questions? Yes, I had some."

"So far I don't hear any problems." The rabbi spread his hands. "Nothing but the story of a young man exploring his universe. So why are you here?"

"The problem . . ." Chaim giggled again with a note of hysteria added that he couldn't suppress. "The problem began a week ago. It was the end of the semester, and I was with some of the guys from the dorm. I'm eighteen now . . ."

"Wait a minute . . ." the rabbi said. "You're only eighteen, but you're a couple of years into premed?"

"Yeah," Chaim said. "Elite schools, constant cramming... I graduated high school a couple of years early. I'm not a smart-ass about it, so most of the regular kids tolerate me." His voice had a very resigned tone to it. "Anyway, we went to a dance club. I don't normally hook up with anyone at these clubs." Chaim waved a hand down his front. "I mean, I'm not a party guy, and I'm not the kind of body the girls at these clubs go for. Usually I get a couple of drinks, listen to the music, and occasionally have a conversation with a couple of girls who are tired of dancing and fighting off the groping hands.

"But that night..." Chaim could hear the note of awe in his own voice. "That night... She was gorgeous. Blonde hair, long and not tied back. Green eyes that could stare into your soul. She was almost tiny." He held his hand out maybe five feet above the asphalt. "She wore white silk, and although many of the other girls had on much skimpier outfits, it was like she was naked and they were in burqas, or nuns, or something. Every guy's eyes popped when she walked in the door, and you could hear jaws dropping open all over the place. Every girl who was with a guy sank her fingernails into his arm, and if they'd had claws, those would have been out as well."

Chaim stared at the moon. There was a long moment of silence, finally broken by Rabbi Reuben.

"And?"

Chaim shook himself. "Oh ... yeah. Um, well, she kind of walked around the place, with every eye in the place following her. And when she finished, she sat down on a barstool beside me." He shook his head almost in disbelief as he remembered the experience. Chaim continued with, "Her voice ... *Rav* Reuben, her voice was indescribable. I was expecting one of those shrill soprano Valley Girl voices, but hers was dark and low, as soft and smooth as silk. It sank into my bones..."

Chaim dwindled off again. The rabbi watched and waited as Chaim stared off into the distance at the lights of the downtown district. At length, he spoke softly. "I don't remember much of the rest of the evening. I remember offering to buy her anything and everything she wanted to drink, but all she took was a little Perrier. I remember glares from the guys and evaluating looks from the other girls, as if maybe there was something more to me than they thought if I could attract and hold someone like her. I remember talking, whispering, laughing... oh, her laugh... listening to her laugh was like a sexual experience in itself. We stayed until the doors closed at 2:00 A.M., then she took me to a hotel down the street. I remember walking through the door of the room... and nothing more until the next day, when I awoke to find her gone." Another long moment of silence. "In my mind, I knew she would be gone, but my heart cried after her anyway."

"Are you sure you're not a poet?" the rabbi asked.

"There was no note, no flower, no touch of silk. None of that romantic stuff." Chaim heard the sadness mingled with hopelessness in his voice. He couldn't help it. "But she did leave me a present."

He could see the thoughts racing around in the rabbi's head. "There is a doctor in the congregation who would be very discreet..."

Chaim's laughter was laden with bitterness. "No, *Rav* Reuben, it's not an STD..." he said. "I wish it was something that simple to deal with.

"I did feel sick that day. I managed to get back

to my room, and collapsed in bed. I don't remember anything of the following three days. When I awoke on the fourth day, my world was changed."

"Changed how?"

Chaim looked away. Despair was dark in his voice as he responded, "That's the problem, *Rav* Reuben. I am fundamentally changed. I can't remain in sunlight for long. When I try to eat, even good kosher food, it tastes foul to me, and I gag."

"There is a very good gastroenterologist in the congregation..."

"And he will be of no help, either. Look at me." Chaim stepped closer, and shined the light of a key-chain LED flashlight on his face. He could see the horror on the rabbi's face as he saw that Chaim's canine teeth were longer than his other teeth.

The rabbi almost lunged off the car fender in shock. "What... what..."

"Oh, come now, *Rav* Reuben." A mocking tone entered Chaim's voice for the first time. "You've seen enough movies to know what you're looking at."

"It can't be... can't..."

"Oh, but it can." Despair returned to Chaim's voice. "I'm a vampire."

The rabbi shrank away. He said nothing, but his fear was overpowering.

Chaim turned off the light and stepped back a couple of steps.

"I won't hurt you, Rabbi. I swear by *haShem* that I will do no harm to you." Chaim's mouth quirked as he used the customary circumlocution of "The Name" to replace using one of the traditional names for the Creator of All.

Long moments passed as Chaim stood in silence, watching as Rabbi Reuben fought back his fear, until he finally spoke. "Well...well...uh...that is certainly the most unusual problem anyone has ever brought to me. Being a vampire, that is."

Bitter laughter again from Chaim.

"Oh, I've had several days to come to grips with that, Rabbi. I've determined that I can find ways to support myself by working at night. I've determined that I won't kill anyone. I've even determined that I will somehow try to break the news of what I've become to my oh-so-Orthodox parents, although they might rather hear that I'm gay or that I've become a Christian. I can deal with that. 'The Lord giveth, and the Lord taketh away, Blessed be the name of the Lord,' right?"

Chaim stepped up and laid his hands on the rabbi's shoulders.

"No, the problem I bring to you, the problem you must urgently take to the Torah and Talmud scholars, to the rabbis and *tzaddiks* and sages is this: I am a Jew. I am also a vampire, who must drink blood to live."

Chaim could see the issue finally dawn on Rabbi Reuben. He could see the horror arise in his face as the Levitical commandments ran through his mind: "...the blood thereof you shall not eat..." "...I will set my face against that soul that eateth blood, and will cut him off from among his people. For the life of the flesh is in the blood..."

"I've been claimed by a daughter of Lilith." Chaim dropped his hands as he spoke. "Help me not to lose my God as well." He slowly crumpled to the asphalt, weeping now, in harsh terrible sobs. "Help me..."

CHAPTER 2

"UMM...WELL...I DON'T KNOW ANYTHING ABOUT this kind of thing," the rabbi said after a long pause. "I didn't think it was possible, but..."

"Yeah, me, too," Chaim husked as he sat back on his heels, "but it's kind of hard to ignore the teeth." He tapped one of the canine fangs with a fingernail, producing a hard *tik-tik* sound that seemed to spook the rabbi.

"Indeed," Rabbi Reuben muttered. "Very hard to ignore."

The rabbi straightened from where he had slumped against his car. "I confess to knowing nothing about this kind of thing, or how to deal with it. Nothing in my training or experience gives me any kind of a handle on this."

"So there's nothing you can do?" Chaim's voice was dull as he rose to his feet and dusted off his knees.

"I didn't say that. *haShem* appears to have allowed for this, and even though I've never heard of it, I can't help but believe that you are not unique—you cannot be the first person to be placed in this position." He stood in thought for a moment. "Let me call someone."

He pulled his cell phone out of his pocket, queried up a number from the directory, and punched the CALL button. It rang twice.

Chaim could hear a gravelly voice respond with, "Hello, Reuben. What has you calling me so late at night?" The surrounding night was quiet, but even so, he was surprised he could hear it so clearly.

"Hello, Max," Rabbi Reuben replied. "Sorry to be calling so late, but I need some help."

"Anything, my friend," Max—whoever Max was—said. "You know that. Any time, as well. But it has to be something serious to have you on the phone at this hour on Sabbath Eve. What's up?"

"Who can you point me to who is really knowledgeable about the supernatural?" Reuben asked. "An expert."

"An expert on the supernatural?" Max's tinny phone voice had a tone of laughter even over the phone circuit. "Reuben, we're Jews—we specialize in the supernatural. Are you dealing with the burning bush, the parting of the Red Sea, the *Shekinah* glory of *haShem* filling Solomon's Temple, or something else?"

"Something else, Max."

"What, then? What is so perplexing that you call me now?"

"I need to talk to someone about vampires, Max. Specifically, Jews who become vampires."

"Oh." Max's tone went dark, and there was a long silence after that. "Why?" he said at long last.

"I've had an encounter tonight with a young man who is Jewish who presents a very strong case that he has been made a vampire by what he called 'a daughter of Lilith.'"

"Ah." Another monosyllabic response in that dark tone. "And you believe him?"

"Based on what I saw, it certainly appears to be possible."

"Oh. Well."

Chaim suspected that Max's mind was racing.

After a moment, Max said, "There may be someone. It will most likely be someone from the Ashkenazic circles, you know. It's almost going to certainly be someone of Eastern European background."

"Not a Lubavitcher, please." Chaim could hear the reluctance in Rabbi Reuben's voice. He obviously had little liking for the ultraconservative wing of Judaism.

"I doubt that," Max replied. "However, it may well be a Chassid."

Reuben sighed. "If I can get someone who can help me, I would put up with about anyone."

"That serious?"

"Yes."

Max chuckled. "All right."

"Thanks, Max. I'm totally out of my element, here."

"Most of us would be, my friend. Hang on for a moment." There was another long moment of silence before Max reentered the conversation. "Okay, the man who can probably help you is Rabbi Avram Mendel. I can't tell you a whole lot more than you would find out if you googled him. He's an old man, born in Poland in the 1930s, I think. His parents moved to Switzerland before World War II began, which is why the family survived intact. Educated in Germany, advanced degrees at Oxford and MIT. Noted scientist and researcher in genetics, but not prominent enough to win any awards. Took his life in a different direction when he decided to become a rabbi at age forty. Specializes in what is called 'esoteric research' these days."

"Which means what?"

"That it's weird stuff that some people think is bogus science."

"What do you think?"

Max was silent for a moment, then said, "Everyone I know who knows him, people that I trust, swears that he is solid, he is brilliant, and is a righteous man of faith. And every time a weird problem comes up, everyone says he is the one to talk to. He's your man if anyone is."

"Okay. I'll take your word for it," Rabbi Reuben said. "It's just this is so far out of my comfort zone, I'm leery of just about everything."

"Him you can trust," Max said. "Even more than you trust me. Should I have him call you?"

Chaim waved a hand to catch the rabbi's attention, and pointed a finger at his own chest. The rabbi nodded, and said, "No, have him call Chaim Caan at..." Chaim had his own cell phone out displaying his number, which the rabbi read off to Max.

"Got it. No promises as to how long it will take for him to decide to call, but this does sound like something up his alley."

"Thanks, Max. I do appreciate it."

"One thing about it, Reuben, you always bring me interesting problems. Now, go to bed and get some rest. Shalom, my friend."

"Shalom, Max."

The rabbi punched his phone off and returned it to his pocket.

"That was Max Weissmann. We've been friends

since high school in Chicago and in our later rabbinate studies. He's a religion and philosophy teacher at a major university, while I'm just a rabbi of a small congregation, but we stay in touch. Max knows almost everyone worth knowing in Jewish circles. That's why I called him."

"I can understand that," Chaim said. "And this Rabbi Mendel is the man he recommended?"

The rabbi looked at Chaim with lowered eyebrows. "Just how much of that conversation did you hear?"

"All of it," Chaim admitted.

The rabbi's eyebrows reversed direction. "Oh. Well. That's a bit surprising."

"I've always had good hearing," Chaim said. "It seems to have gotten a bit better since..."

"Ah." The rabbi's mouth twisted a bit. "Well, it appears Rabbi Mendel will be contacting you directly, but you might give me your phone number again just in case."

"Give me yours, and I'll text it to you." The rabbi recited his number, Chaim keyed it into his phone, and a moment later had sent the message. "That's my phone and my email address," he said. "Just in case."

"Good." Rabbi Reuben checked his phone, then returned it to his pocket. It surprised Chaim to hear the rabbi give a wry chuckle. "You know, nothing in my rabbinic studies prepared me for this. I think it is true what is said—*haShem* has a sense of humor."

"Perhaps," Chaim said. "I think He has terrible taste in practical jokes if He does."

"I won't disagree with you on that," Rabbi Reuben said. He stepped closer to Chaim and placed his hands on his shoulders. "I do not envy you what has happened. Even for a Jew, this will undoubtedly be hard to bear. You will be in my prayers, my friend."

"Thank you, *Rav* Reuben," Chaim said as he ducked his head. He was thankful, but he sounded weary and forlorn, even to himself.

Reuben dropped his hands and pulled his keys from his pocket. "I have done what I can, and I think the ball is now in Rabbi Mendel's court, but if you haven't heard by Thursday, call me, and I'll see what I can do."

"I will, *Rav* Reuben," Chaim said, some energy coming back to his voice. "And ... thank you."

With that, he turned and melded into the shadows, leaving the rabbi standing under the parking lot light by his car, with a whole lot more on his mind than he'd had when he first came out of the synagogue, Chaim was sure. He watched from behind the magnolia tree as Rabbi Reuben finally unlocked his car and drove off. Chaim hoped the rabbi would rest better than he was going to.

Chaim stood under the magnolia tree for some time, thinking dark thoughts, before he returned to his own car, which was parked across the street from the synagogue's parking lot. He had driven to Santa Carla from his apartment near the UCLA campus.

He knew he was still in shock from what had happened to him. Despite the fact that he had been living away from home for over a year, and despite the fact that he had been trying to distance himself from his family somewhat, trying to make space so he could figure out who he was as himself and not as the only child of Moses and Miriam Caan, he had a burning urge to go home. Finally he sighed, started the car, and drove there by the back streets. The traffic was light enough that it was almost restful to drive along at twenty-five miles per hour and make the frequent stops at intersections along the way.

Chaim parked on the street in front of the house. He kept his keys in his hand as he walked to the front door. A moment later he was in the house. "Mom? Dad?"

"In the kitchen," his mother called. Chaim headed toward the back of the house, where he found the two of them standing in front of the kitchen counter eating slices of chocolate cake. He wasn't surprised. It had long been their practice to have a sweet snack after Friday-night services.

They both set their plates down and proceeded to give him hugs—his mother first, then his dad. Once that was done, he looked at them both. They were each a bit shorter than his own height of five feet nine inches. His father's face seemed a little paunchier than it had been the last time he had seen them. His mother had quit coloring her hair during the Covid year, and it was showing a little more gray than he remembered. But they looked good.

"So, what's the occasion?" his father asked as he resumed eating his cake. "It's been what, three months since you last came down?"

That was his dad, all right. Never missed a chance to point out when Chaim was missing the mark.

"Moses, he just got here." His mother put her hand on his father's arm.

"What? The boy only lives twenty miles from here. He can only come home once a quarter? We're spending all that money so that he can ignore us?"

"Nice to see you, too, Dad. And I got scholarships, remember?"

His mother's Shih Tzu climbed out of her downstairs bed in the corner of the kitchen and came over to sniff at him. For a change her tail wasn't wagging. She spent her time sniffing at his shoes and lower pants legs. She looked up at him and growled.

"Tiffy!" his mother said. "What are you doing?"

Tiffy looked back at her mistress, then looked back at Chaim as he bent down and extended a finger to her. She sniffed it thoroughly as well, before giving it a desultory tongue wipe. Chaim wasn't sure what was going on, but that wasn't Tiffy's normal behavior. He stared at the dog as she waddled back to her bed and curled back up in it.

"Well, I don't care why you're here," his mother said, "it's good to see you." She gave him another hug. "Want some cake? It's Aunt Rachel's recipe."

"No, I'm not hungry right now." He placed his hand on his belt buckle. "My stomach's been a bit queasy today anyway, so I'll pass. I can't stay very long. I need to get back pretty soon. I've got night shift tonight."

"So why'd you bother?" his dad said, putting his empty plate back on the counter. "If that nothing job at the urgent care center is so important, why'd you bother coming down?"

Chaim sighed. "I came down to do a little research in the Santa Carla University library for a project I'll be doing next semester. Thought I'd get a jump start on it." He hated lying to his folks, but there was no way he was ready to tell them what was really going on. This at least was a plausible explanation. "Since I was this close, I figured I'd come by. I knew you'd be home. It's Friday, after all. And I wanted to get a couple of books from my room while I was here."

"Fine." His father waved a hand to one side. "You do what you want." He turned and headed for his study. Chaim looked after him.

His dad had never been the warmest of men—he was very formal—but they'd always had an okay relationship until two years ago when Chaim told him he was going to study medicine instead of becoming a rabbi. He'd always known his father didn't handle disappointment very well, but that event proved it to him. Overnight his father had become cold, distant, and very critical. He sighed and shook his head.

His mother was looking at him with a sad expression on her face. "It's okay, Mom," he said. He went to the cabinet and got a glass, then filled it with ice and water from the refrigerator door, so he could avoid looking at her. Setting the empty glass in the sink, he turned and brushed past her.

Chaim could see his father sitting in his chair in the small office/study as he turned to go up the stairs. He was reading something. Probably his old study copy of the *Tanakh*, the Hebrew Bible. He spent as much time with that as he ever had with Chaim.

The door to his room was at the top of the stairs, and was standing open. Chaim walked in and looked around. His room was unchanged. His mother obviously kept it dusted and cleaned, but as far as he could tell, nothing had been moved even a fraction of an inch since the last time he'd been in it.

Small desk under the window in the corner. Empty headphone stand on one desk corner. Small magnetic whiteboard on the side wall with smeared ink from the last time he had erased something on it. Dresser on the other side wall, with a few things scattered across the top. Bed against the long wall, bookcase standing next to the window.

He walked over to look at the bookcase. His Jewish study books occupied the top two shelves. He took down his two Talmud reference books from the top shelf and laid them on the bed. He hesitated, then from the second shelf pulled his copy of the *Kabbalah* that Uncle Bernie had given him, along with his copy of *The Idiot's Guide to Kabbalah*. He smiled a little at the fit his father had pitched about that. "Studying mystical trash," he'd called it, but since it had come from his brother, and since it was Jewish, he hadn't been able to bring himself to forbid it. Chaim shook his head, but tossed them on the bed as well. Maybe they could help with this mess.

Kneeling, Chaim bypassed all his Boy Scout books and the associated notebooks on the third and fourth shelves. From the bottom shelf he pulled a half dozen worn paperbacks. He had e-book copies of them, for sure, but these books were special to him. His hands brushed the covers: *Catseye*, *Star Surgeon*, *John the Balladeer*, *Lest Darkness Fall*, *Downbelow Station*, *Lord of Light*. Science fiction stories that had helped him through some dark days when he was younger. He laid them on the bed with care. They'd helped in the past—maybe they'd help now. If nothing else, maybe they'd be talismans.

Chaim stood and looked around again, then stepped back over to the desk and pulled open the top-right drawer. Lifting out a small plastic box, he opened it and took out the only thing in it. It was a small folded piece of paper that said *In Loving Memory* on top. He opened it, and read the order of service for the funeral for Elena Ramirez. Then he looked at the photo he'd tucked into the program when he'd put it in his desk over a year ago, and sighed.

He'd liked Elena—a lot. It wasn't really a schoolboy crush. They actually hadn't met until his last year, when he'd accelerated into the senior class level. Neither one of them were part of the in crowd at school. She was the oldest of his classmates, partly because her birthday was September 1, and partly because she'd lost a year of school for health reasons. Cystic fibrosis. So he was a nerd, and she was considered weird. They'd ended up being lab partners in AP Advanced Physics by default when no one wanted to work with either one of them.

None of the other girls in his class wanted to have anything to do with Chaim. The goths, the surfer girls, the skater girls, what passed for preppy girls these days—none of them. He was too young, too nerdy, and too introverted for any of them to pay attention to him. For that matter, none of the guys cared for him, either. Elena was the only one who'd taken a chance on him, and he was so glad she did.

She wasn't beautiful—certainly not like the well-tanned blonde beach girls or like the slim long-haired Asian girls. She was pudgy—they both were, actually, but she was pudgier. But she was so smart, she was quick to pick things up, and she had the wickedest sense of humor. They propped each other up all year. He taught her the secrets of Sudoku, and she taught him how to dance. They went to the senior prom together—the only dance he'd ever gone to—and she had him laughing the entire time with her running commentary on the other kids, their attire, and their dance steps.

A week after the prom, she was in the hospital. Her cystic fibrosis had flared up. A week later, she was dead from pneumonia, two weeks before graduation. He went to her funeral at the Baptist church without telling his parents, and sat in the back. He didn't understand much of what went on, and the eulogy pissed him off, because the girl the minister described was not the Elena he knew. So he spent the entire time looking at her picture up on the projection screen, trying to figure out how to say goodbye. When he came home, he put the funeral program and the little picture away. Looking at it now for the first time since the day of the funeral, he realized he still hadn't figured out how to say goodbye, but he'd gotten used to the empty space she'd used to occupy in his life—the space that no one had stepped into—definitely no other girl. He tucked the program and picture into his jacket pocket.

There was a whisper of sound behind him. He turned to see his mother standing in the doorway.

"I wrapped up a piece of cake for you to take with you." She had the crooked smile on her face she always got when she was trying to smooth things over between him and his dad. He repressed a sigh. He couldn't tell her he couldn't eat it. As much as he wanted to tell her—to tell them—what had happened, he couldn't. They weren't ready for that. *He* wasn't ready for that.

"Thanks, Mom. I'll pick it up when I leave."

She moved closer. "I don't care why you came. I'm

just glad you did." She reached up and patted him on the cheek. "I know you're trying to live your life, but I miss you. I'm a mother. I have that right."

Chaim shrugged and gave her a smile. "I know."

She frowned. "You look skinnier. You said you've been queasy. Are you sick?"

"No, Mom," he said.

"Well, you take care of yourself." She walked over to the window and looked out at the night. "So, have you met any nice girls yet?"

"Mom, I'm only eighteen. You can wait a little while to start the Jewish mother schtick, okay?" Chaim grinned at her, and she grinned back. "And no, I haven't met any girls yet. I've been busy, and most of them are still wearing masks and don't want to meet new people, even though everyone's had the vaccine." What was being called the Covid Years had really disrupted life for a lot of young singles in more than one way. Even a year later.

He walked over to the bed and gathered up the books. "I need to get going. I really do have night shift."

Chaim followed his mother down the stairs. At the bottom, she reached over to the side table and picked up the plastic plate with a huge slice of chocolate cake swathed in plastic wrap. "Here. You'll like this." She hugged him, and said again, "I'm glad you came."

He nodded, then looked in the door to his father's office. "I'm leaving, Dad."

His dad didn't look up, just waved a hand and said, "Goodbye."

Chaim's mother followed him to the door, opened it and reached up and kissed him on the cheek. "Call me later."

"Bye, Mom."

Chaim loaded the books and cake in the front passenger seat. When he started the car, he noticed the gas gauge was showing he only had a quarter of a tank, so he drove to the nearest 76 station and fueled up. By the time he got there, the smell of the chocolate cake was making his stomach churn. He noticed an older homeless lady sitting on the curb outside the building, so after he gassed up he picked up the cake and walked over to her. "You like chocolate cake?"

She looked up with a gap-toothed grin. "Sure."

"Here. I'm allergic to it."

She took it with delight, and started peeling the plastic back. He walked back to his car, musing on the question of whether that counted as a lie or not. As he pulled out of the parking lot, he decided that while it wasn't absolutely factually accurate, it wasn't a lie, because he really couldn't eat the cake. He chuckled at that, and pressed the accelerator. He needed to get to work.

It was late enough at night that the traffic was fairly light by mid-California standards. No accidents along the way, and only one road repair section that was relatively short. Chaim pulled into the parking lot a half hour before his shift began.

The lot only had four cars in it besides his, which Chaim was glad to see, since that meant things were going to be slow when he walked into the Urgent Care Plus 24/7 facility. He'd gone to work for them at the beginning of the Covid Year as a receptionist and screener because as a sophomore premed student, that was as close to real medical work as he could get. He figured the experience would pay off one way or another. He'd learned a lot, he knew—both about the realities of medicine and about people.

The strip mall UCP was in was fairly good sized, but there were only two other tenants besides the medical facility: a cannabis dispensary down at the other end of the building, which was closed, and a 24-hour doughnut shop between the two that had one customer. He had wondered more than once if the location of those two stores was planned—after all, if a cannabis patron walked out of the dispensary with a case of the munchies, wouldn't the doughnut shop benefit from it? Probably not, but he was still convinced that could be a good stand-up comedy routine. Too bad he wasn't a comedian.

The rest of the building was occupied by the UCP, and from the looks of it, there were no patients there at the moment. That was not good for the business, but was good for his peace of mind tonight.

Chaim was surprised to see the facility manager there when he walked in. She usually worked the day shift from 6:00 A.M. to 2:00 P.M. To see her there after 9:30 P.M. was very unusual. Karli Jones was a tall, energetic black woman who usually had bright eyes and a big smile for everyone. Tonight she looked exhausted.

"Karli, what are you doing here?"

She looked up from the computer she was staring at, and sighed. "Chaim. Man, am I glad to see you. Anna, our new morning-shift nurse, went home sick at 11:00 A.M., so we were shorthanded for the afternoon part of that shift, and then Carlita called in around one-thirty to say that her water had broken and she was in the hospital. That means her maternity leave's going to kick in. So yeah, I ended up covering the desk for her in the evening shift. It wasn't a horrible day, but it was extremely long. I'm beat." She stood up and moved from behind the desk.

"Wow. Sorry to hear that." Chaim sat down and logged into the computer. "Anything I need to know?"

Karli gathered her purse from a cabinet drawer and her sweater from the back of a different chair. "No. Tran and Ricardo are in the back already, and Lupe called to say she had run into a bit of a traffic slowdown but she thought she would be here on time. Other than that, just make sure the morning shift knows about Carlita."

"Got it. Go home and get some sleep."

"Yeah."

Karli walked out, and the shift began. Chaim took a deep breath. One more night to put in his time. Maybe he'd be able to sleep when he got off.

More than once in the next several days Chaim opened his Tanakh to the book *Vayikra*, which almost everyone, Jews and *goyim* alike, called Leviticus. The seventeenth chapter contained the strongest instructions not to consume blood, and he spent some time considering those. He spent more time reviewing the Talmud, looking for teachings that might be applicable to his situation. He even found an online copy of the *Shulchan Aruch*, the Jewish legal compendium. This situation was weird enough that Chaim would take help from wherever he could get it. He of course knew the rule that most laws could be disobeyed in order to save a life, but he wasn't certain that applied here. It worried him that he might not be human anymore, and if that was the case, how would any of the *mitzvot* apply to him? That kept him awake most of the daylight hours when he hid within his apartment, thankful for the heavy blinds and drapes on his windows.

Unfortunately, Chaim arrived at no conclusions. But at least, he decided at one point, he wasn't any worse off than he was before. He didn't know anything useful then, and he didn't know anything useful now. With each passing day, he looked at his phone with increasing urgency, trying to make it ring with the oh-so-expected call.

Early Wednesday afternoon, his cell phone buzzed with a text message from an unknown number, and Chaim almost sprained a finger, he punched the phone so hard to open it.

<RE: your issue. Are you available for a phone call tonight at 9 p.m. Eastern time?>

Chaim made the calculations in his head: 9:00 P.M. Eastern would be 6:00 P.M. Pacific time. Of course he would be available! He typed in *<Yes>* for a reply and he hit send.

<Good. We will call you.>

He smiled at the perfect spelling and grammar. Obviously an older person. He sighed. In one respect, his tension eased, knowing that they (whoever "they" were) were going to reach out to him. But in another, it ramped up, because he had no idea what they were going to say.

Precisely at 6:00 P.M., Chaim's cell phone rang. He'd been pacing around his living room off and on for the last several hours. He bobbled his phone pulling it out of his pocket and almost dropped it, which put a spike in his already elevated adrenaline.

"Hello," he answered in what he hoped was his normal tone of voice.

In response, the purest tenor voice he'd ever heard said, "May I speak with Mr. Chaim Caan, please?"

"Speaking."

The voice continued with mildly accented English, "Good evening, Mr. Caan. My name is Avram Mendel, and you have been forwarded to me through a chain of acquaintances beginning with Max Weissmann. I understand that you are engaged with an unusual problem."

Chaim sighed. "That would be one way of putting it." He hoped he didn't sound as despondent as he felt. He paced a few steps. "Look, I don't know what Mr. Weissmann told you, but what hit me over a week ago is absurd. It shouldn't even be possible. It's pure fantasy—except that maybe it isn't."

"'There are more things in heaven and earth, Horatio, than are dreamt of in your philosophy,'" Mendel said with a bit of a chuckle.

"Shakespeare?"

"Of course, Shakespeare. For a *goy*, he was very perceptive, and he had a definite way with words, *nu*?" Mendel gave another chuckle, then sobered as he said, "Of course, if you want to be serious, recall that *haShem* said to Isaiah, 'For my thoughts are not your thoughts, neither are your ways my ways.'" There was a brief pause before he concluded with "The Ineffable is at times inscrutable as well. But that is beside the point. Assume I know nothing. Tell me everything from the beginning."

"All right." Chaim tried to gather his thoughts. "The short version is..."

Five minutes later, he concluded with, "And that's when Rabbi Levinson called his friend Max Weissmann."

Mendel had said nothing during Chaim's recitation, but Chaim had the sense that he had been listening intently.

"Absurd. Fantasy. Those are good words for such a story, are they not?" Mendel observed. "Yet it would seem that you have decided that you are a vampire. Why?"

"I don't know that I believe—actually, I don't want to believe," Chaim said slowly, "but there are two things that have kept me from just calling myself insane and turning myself in for treatment."

"And they are?"

"First, the fangs."

"The fangs?"

"Yes, just like in the movies, those long canine teeth that seem to be standard equipment for Dracula and all his imitators. They are kind of hard to ignore."

"Ah. *Those* fangs. You do know, of course, that in this time of progressive dental technology it is possible to have prosthetic fangs implanted. I understand that it is fairly popular among certain circles of the goth culture." Mendel's voice had taken on a dry tone. "I imagine it makes things a bit difficult in eating a hamburger, but to each his own."

"Ah"—Chaim swallowed—"no, I didn't know that. None of the goths I know do that. But I'm just a suburban college kid who doesn't like to go to the dentist, so..."

"So that's likely not a factor, then."

Chaim nodded, forgetting that Mendel couldn't see him. "No. And in the end, that doesn't really matter. The second thing is, I've been changed. I can't eat, and blood smells so good to me now."

Mendel's voice was darker as he said, "Is that so?"

"*Rav* Avram"—Chaim swallowed—"the mitzvah about not eating blood, the verses say that he who does will be cut off from the congregation and cut off from *haShem*. I've had to take blood three times now. Sunlight hurts. Am I even human? Can I be a Jew now?" He knew there was panic in his voice. He couldn't help it.

"Ah. One moment." There was a sound of murmuring, and for the first time Reuben realized that Mendel was using a speakerphone and someone else was in the room with him. "Mr. Caan?" Mendel was back.

"Yes?"

"From your phone's area code, you appear to be in California. Where, specifically?"

"Santa Carla. On the coast, south of San Francisco, north of Monterey and west of Los Angeles."

There was a moment of silence, then, "Good. Mr. Caan, understand that I think there are things that can be done to help you, but I must meet with you to be certain of that. I cannot be where you are until Sunday afternoon at the earliest. Can you arrange a meeting time and place after that? A synagogue, perhaps? After dark, of course, and someplace that a stranger with a rental car GPS can locate. Would that be a problem for you?"

"Are you kidding? School's done for the semester, I work night shift for my job, and I don't have a girl-friend. Of course I'm available on Sunday evening. Not a synagogue, though. Not until I know where I stand."

"I understand," Mendel replied. "You pick the place and call this number back with the details. Someone will answer and take the information. I doubt I will be able to take your call—I have much to do between now and then—but be assured that I will see you on Sunday. I will do what I can to help, Mr. Caan."

"Thank you, *Rav* Avram. Thank you very much." The sense of relief that Chaim felt at that assurance almost had his feet stepping on air.

"It is nothing. I will see you on Sunday, yes?"

"Yes."

"Until then, may *haShem* bless you and keep you, may *haShem* make His face shine upon you and be gracious to you, may *haShem* turn His face toward you and give you His shalom. Good night, my friend."

The call ended before Chaim could speak, so his responding, "Good night," was heard only by himself. He put the phone down and stared at the wall. Could this be help? Could this rabbi really be able to address his concerns? He hoped so. Oh, how he hoped so. It might not work... "But it's more hope than I've had," he muttered. The intensity of feeling in his voice was almost frightening.

CHAPTER 3

CHAIM WATCHED AS THE VALET DROVE HIS CAR off to be parked. His older model Civic looked rather out of place among the BMW, Mercedes, and Cadillac models that filled most of the parking lot. He smiled a little, shrugged, and turned to enter The Dove. He had been here once or twice before. It was a small, very exclusive restaurant that catered to primarily a Jewish clientele and featured menus that strictly abided by the kashrut rules. It kept a low profile among the community, doing no advertising, but there were enough monied Orthodox and traditional Conservative Jewish families in the area that word of mouth gave them a steady business. Needless to say, their prices were on the high end of the scale, but his father insisted that they were worth it, and if it was good enough for Moses Caan, it had to be good enough for anyone. Chaim was rather regretful that he wasn't dining there tonight, but on the other hand, he was glad he wasn't paying for the meal, either. Getting the use of their back room for a couple of hours had not been cheap.

Chaim had dithered about what to wear, but had

finally decided to go old school with a blazer jacket—he still had one he hadn't outgrown—over a dress shirt with no tie and a pair of casual slacks. Mortimer, the restaurant's usual maître d'hôtel, looked up as he entered the door at 8:50 P.M. "Good evening, sir. Do you have a reservation, or are you meeting someone tonight?"

Chaim repressed an urge to adjust his coat-sleeve cuffs, and said, "Good evening. I am Chaim Caan. I believe I have the back room reserved at nine. Have my guests arrived?"

Mortimer checked the reservation list. "Yes, sir, that is the reservation, but you are the first to arrive. The reservation says that this will not be a meal, only drinks?"

"I won't be eating, but my guest might. We'll have to see. But please have a bottle of kosher wine available."

"Certainly, sir. Do you wish to go to the room or to await your guest here?"

Mortimer's voice had a trace of an accent that Chaim was not able to place, but his diction and use of grammar was better than his own.

"I'll wait here for him," Chaim said. He stepped to one side as an older couple appeared in the doorway to be greeted by Mortimer. "Mr. and Mrs. Lipschutz, how nice to see you again. This way to your table."

While Mortimer led that couple to their table, Chaim looked around as two more people appeared in the doorway—two men, neither of whom looked to be from the local coastal California population. He wasn't expecting two, but they had to be who he was waiting for.

The first was a blocky figure of middle height

dressed in an old-school professorial tweed jacket and gray slacks with the tasseled fringe of a *tallit* peeking out from under the coat. He pretty much had to be Rabbi Mendel. His face was framed by a gray-white square-cut beard with bushy sideburns and curly *payess* locks hanging before his ears, prominent cheekbones, and head crowned by a black homburg hat. His looks didn't surprise Chaim much, given his name. He'd done some research, and Mendel was a prominent name in Lubavitcher and Chassidic circles.

The second was a contrast in all ways: taller, very lean—almost gaunt—clean shaven with a face that reminded Reuben of the actor Basil Rathbone, long coal-black hair combed straight back, and dressed in a dark blue suit that fit him so well it reminded Chaim of Prince Philip of Great Britain before he had passed away.

He mustered up his courage and stepped forward. "Rabbi Mendel?" At the older man's nod, he offered his hand. "I'm Chaim Caan."

The older man grabbed his hand and gave it a hearty shake. "Of course you are! Pleased to meet you in the flesh, *Reb* Chaim." Mendel released his hand and jerked a thumb over his shoulder. "This is Mordechai Zalman, my associate, keeper, and occasional guardian. I tend to get lost when I travel, so I'm no longer allowed to travel alone." The last was said with a large, toothy grin.

Zalman shook his head and held out his own hand to exchange a firm handclasp with Chaim. "It's not quite as bad as all that," he said with a strong Eastern European accent. "He's simply a bit absentminded at times. We won't talk about the time he ended up in Tijuana when he was supposed to be in Toronto." That last was said with a very deadpan expression. Chaim wasn't sure how to take that, until he saw the corners of Zalman's mouth curling up slightly and heard Mendel's chuckle.

Despite also having a renowned Jewish name—even Chaim remembered that Zalman had been the surname of the Vilna Gaon—the other man didn't have the Chassidic look to him. Their voices were also distinctly different. Zalman's baritone was so deep it almost rumbled in stark contrast to the lyric tenor of the older man.

Before he could respond to that, Chaim realized that Mortimer had appeared at his elbow with an eyebrow raised. He turned to the maître d' with, "Mortimer, here are my guests, so if you could have someone lead us to the room?"

Mortimer nodded his head. "This way, if you please."

The maître d' led them himself through the smallish seating area and between the tables until they arrived at a door set far back in the right wall. Mortimer held the door open, and Chaim led the others into the room.

Once in the room they stared at each other for a moment, before Chaim kind of shook himself and gestured toward a nearby table. "Please, let's sit and get comfortable."

The round table was set with a white tablecloth and seating for two. Silverware glinted on the tabletop, and wineglasses were set as well.

Mortimer brought another chair from another table. Mendel and Chaim ended up opposite each other, with Zalman to one side. Before they sat, Mendel took off his homburg and handed it to Zalman, who laid it atop a nearby table. Chaim was not surprised to see a black kippah on the back of Mendel's head.

Mortimer stepped forward as they settled into their seats. "Will any of you gentlemen be wanting to see a menu this evening?" Chaim looked at the others, but upon receiving shakes of their heads, said, "No, that won't be needed. Wine?" he asked, looking around again.

"That would be a kindness," Mendel observed with a smile. Zalman shook his head, which surprised Chaim a bit.

"Wine for the rabbi, then," Chaim indicated, "and two waters."

Mortimer moved to a side table, returning to pour a dark red wine into Mendel's glass. A bare moment later, Zalman and Chaim had ice water in their glasses.

Collecting the silverware, Mortimer paused at the door and murmured, "If you need anything else, only ask," before slipping out.

Mendel reached out and picked up his wineglass as the door closed. He closed his eyes and recited, "Blessed are You, Adonai our God, Sovereign of all, Creator of the fruit of the vine." Eyes still closed, he took a sip from his glass, then opened his eyes with a beatific smile. "Very nice." He lifted his glass to Chaim. "Thank you, young man. I don't often get the good stuff." He took another sip, and set his glass down.

Chaim took a sip of water, setting his glass down just after Mendel did. He looked at the rabbi, who took the lead.

"Young man—Chaim—I understand that you are dealing with an unusual problem."

"You could call it that," Chaim muttered.

"Please, to refresh my memory and for *Reb* Mordechai's sake, tell me again in your own words what you have experienced." Mendel laced his fingers together across his abdomen and leaned back a bit in his chair.

Chaim laced his own fingers together before him on the table and stared down at his joined hands for a long moment before speaking. "It was a little over two weeks ago . . ." he began in a low voice, not looking up.

No one moved as Chaim spoke. No other sounds were heard other than his voice and the faint murmur of conversations occurring in the main dining room on the other side of the door. He gave his account in much the same manner and same wording as when he had confronted Reuben in the parking lot that first night. It flowed smoothly, and he thought to himself that he'd had some practice in telling the story.

After Chaim concluded, no one spoke right away. Mendel nodded a few times, a slow movement where his beard brushed his thumbs where they rested together atop his sternum. At length the rabbi looked over at his companion. "Mordechai?"

Zalman pursed his lips, then nodded. "It's true. He's been converted. I smelled it when we walked into the room. Pheromones, you know. Those changes are among the first to occur." He looked over to where Chaim's jaw hung open in a fair rendition of the expression "gobsmacked." "What, boy? Did you think you were the only one this had ever happened to?"

Chaim's head was spinning. He reached out, picked up his glass and drained it in a single swallow. Setting the glass down, he repressed a ferocious cough with difficulty. "Wha...what are you talking about? Are you saying you're...you're...a..." He couldn't get the words out.

"A vampire?" Mordechai's face carried a very thin grin—not a smile, a razor-sharp grin. "Yes. A Jewish vampire? Yes."

Chaim's mouth had closed, but he had a very bewildered expression on his face. "Are there...are there very many of...us?" He swallowed afterward.

"No," Mendel entered the conversation. "There are never many—never have been many—Jewish vampires. How many others are there?" He moved his shoulders in the inimitable Jewish shrug. "Eh, no one knows. Undoubtedly there are some, but how many? *haShem* might know, but we certainly do not."

"Actually, we do know of at least two Jewish vampires in Israel," Zalman said, "which probably explains some things about why Israel still exists and their enemies seem so feckless." He shrugged. "And there may be one in eastern Europe somewhere based on a few hints of things that have happened in the last twenty or thirty years. But yes, for the most part, *Rav* Avram is correct. We have very little way of detecting vampires, whether Jewish or other types, unless they want to be found."

"Other types?" Chaim asked, sitting back in his chair. "You mean..."

"Yes, vampires, both Jewish and goy, do exist," Mendel reentered the conversation, "though they are neither as prevalent as recent books would have you believe, nor as wantonly destructive. Evil, yes, most of them"—the rabbi spread his hands—"but not horrific, if you see the difference. It's not as easy to create a vampire as the stories would have you think, or we would undoubtedly be overrun with them. For the most part, they don't seem to survive for very long."

"Wait," Chaim interjected. "Are you one, too?"

"No." Mendel straightened and shook his head. "Not me. I'm older than I look. I was born in Gdańsk in disputed Poland in 1934, so I am well past *haShem*'s allotment of three score and ten years. But I have nothing like my friend's tally"—he gestured toward Zalman—"and I am alive solely because He has not yet sent His angel for me."

Chaim's head turned toward Zalman. "Just how old are you?"

That thin, sharp grin fleeted across his face again for a moment. "I believe I was born in 1739, but it's hard to be certain after all this time. Things that far back do get foggy in memory, as you might imagine. I was definitely born in Białystok, though." A good-humored smile appeared on his face after that.

There was a stunned silence for a long moment. Chaim's eyes closed for a moment, then reopened slowly. "You're ... two hundred and eighty years old," he said carefully, not wanting to believe this most extraordinary statement of the evening.

Zalman lifted his palms and made a scales-balancing motion. "Give or take a decade or so, yes."

"You don't sound that old. You don't sound old-fashioned at all."

"I learned English in the twentieth century," Zalman said with a smile. "My Yiddish and my German do sound funny to modern speakers. My Russian ..." He pursed his lips and shook his head slightly.

"I can vouch for that," Mendel contributed. "His

Yiddish could be smeared with a knife, and his German is old-style Hochdeutsch. He gets many funny looks when we're in Germany or Austria."

There was another pause before Chaim resumed.

"This is all very interesting—in a horrifying sort of way—but none of this addresses my concerns. Can we please get back to that?" He was kind of proud at how he had managed to hang on to his sanity long enough to steer the conversation back to its original purpose.

Mendel looked a bit abashed. "Quite right. Sorry." He folded his hands together. "The short version is that yes, you are a vampire; yes, we do know something about this; and no, this does not in and of itself exclude you from the congregation of Israel."

"But the mitzvah—" Chaim began.

Mendel raised a hand. "Mordechai, if you would."

Zalman reached a hand inside the breast of his exquisitely tailored suit and brought forth a folded paper from an inside pocket. He unfolded the paper with care, smoothed it flat on the tabletop, then turned it and presented it to Chaim.

Chaim made his way through the thick Hebrew lettering with some difficulty, and looked up. "What... what is this?"

"That, my friend," Zalman said soberly, "is a scanned copy of a ruling. Most authorities consider that the mitzvah that so concerns you is part of the foundation of the kashrut rules. There is, however, a minority opinion that it is also meant to apply to circumstances of pagan worship where blood is drunk. Regardless, it does not apply to accidentally consuming traces of blood when the kashrut rules are not adequately applied. It does not apply to times of duress or stress when blood must be consumed to survive. And most importantly for us, it does not apply to those whose only hope of life is to consume blood." He touched a finger to the page. "It is signed by the Vilna Gaon."

Chaim sat paralyzed. Yet another remarkable revelation in the evening. He was beyond stunned, surprised, and shocked. Signed by the greatest of rabbinic authorities of modern times? How?

"So just as you are not unique in being a Jewish vampire," Mendel said with gentle kindness, "you are also not unique in this concern of yours."

Chaim's finger traced the signature line. "Eliyahu ben Shlomo of Vilna." He looked up with shining eyes. "This is for real?"

Mendel nodded with a smile. "It is real, Chaim. It has been verified."

"But . . . how . . . ?"

Zalman lifted his finger from the page and held it between them. "The ruling was issued late in the sage's life, and there was only one copy of it. His family never saw it, so it was never published after his death. The man he gave it to preserved it for many years."

Chaim's mind chewed through everything he'd heard this evening, and arrived at what would have been an unthinkable conclusion at the beginning of the conversation. "You?"

Zalman nodded. "I guarded that piece of parchment as if it had been written by the finger of *haShem*. It was my sole protection, my sole justification, my sole explanation and defense of my life from 1793 until I met *Rav* Avram." He lowered his hand. "It is why afterward I took his surname for my own. I was not born Zalman."

Chaim released a deep sigh. "I guess I can understand that." He looked back and forth at the two men. "I want a copy of this."

"Take that one," Zalman said.

Chaim folded the page along its crease lines with care, and put it in his inner jacket pocket. "Thank you," he said. "This"—he touched the breast of his blazer—"means a lot to me."

Before he could continue, Zalman spoke. "Not to be rude," the older vampire said, "but I have a couple of questions to ask." He looked at Chaim. "First, if you were converted over two weeks ago, how have you fed in that time? You're conscious, alert, articulate—you've had to have fed at least four times in that period. What did you do?"

Chaim looked down at the table. "I . . . uh, I . . ." Chaim began with a stutter, "I . . . would go down to one of the homeless areas, find someone who seemed healthy, and . . . I'd buy them a meal, then I'd buy them a bottle of their favorite booze. Once they were unconscious, I'd . . . feed from them, but only enough to quiet the hunger. I never took more than probably half a unit. And I'd leave them more food for when they woke up."

"Where did you feed from? The neck?" Zalman's tone was dispassionate; his face was expressionless, almost as if it didn't matter.

"No." Chaim shook his head, still looking down. "From the lower arm and wrist." He looked up, almost pleading. "I didn't know what else to do! But I made sure that I went to different areas, and I made sure I only used each one once. I tried to be careful, and not create more of me!"

Zalman held up his right hand. "Peace, child. You did as well as anyone could have done. And it takes more than one contact to create a new vampire. Be at peace about that."

Chaim's look of shame slowly transitioned to one more of relief. He sat in silence, and the others gave him that moment.

At length, Chaim looked up again. "Why do I feel like there's more to your agenda? You could have handled this much with a phone call and a fax machine."

"Because you are a good man filled with wisdom and a discerning spirit," Mendel replied with a smile. "My young friend, as you may have guessed from some of our earlier conversation, Mordechai and I are part of a small organization. It's not a clandestine group, by any means, but we don't go out of our way to publicize it, either. Our purpose is to investigate and collect information on what some people call the paranormal."

After a moment, Chaim nodded. "And vampires are part of that work?"

"Indeed," Mendel said. "Now, with the help of Mordechai and one or two others over the years, we have gathered some knowledge, but we have never been able to work with or examine a new vampire. We would greatly appreciate it if you would return with us to our place of study and allow our doctors to examine you. Getting a baseline of what a new vampire is like will greatly help us understand the process by which we arrive at one like, well, Mordechai, for example."

"They'll pay you for that, by the way." Mordechai's grin was back, and his tone was dry enough to suck all the humidity out of the room's air.

"Of course we will," Mendel said, waving a hand in

dismissal at his friend, "and pay you well. Did you say you were a premed student?" Chaim nodded. "Then you may find our facilities and our work interesting. We'll fly you out and fly you back, of course."

"Private jet," Mordechai added. "No ticket necessary, no security searches. Only way to travel." His grin grew a bit sharper. "If you like, you could fly back with us tomorrow night."

"Umm, let me think about it tonight. Can I call you tomorrow?"

"Of course."

There followed a long moment of silence, then the rabbi placed his palms flat on the table. "Well, I think perhaps that is enough for a beginning. I have your phone number. Shall I call you tomorrow afternoon?"

Chaim nodded, still somewhat in a daze from everything he had heard that evening. Mendel stood, and the others followed suit. The meeting was apparently over.

Chaim's head was spinning. "I don't think I'm going to believe all this tomorrow," he muttered.

"It doesn't matter if you do or don't, *Reb* Chaim. You've been part of a very good thing tonight, and I thank you from the bottom of my heart." Mendel threw his arms around Chaim, who discovered that although the man was over eighty years old he could still hug like a bear. He staggered a bit after Mendel released his clasp.

"Thank you, Rabbi," Chaim said with a smile and shining eyes. "Thank you so much for meeting with me. I think you've saved my life."

"This is only the beginning," Mendel replied. "We'll speak again tomorrow."

The rabbi picked up his hat and headed toward the door. Zalman looked at Chaim with his head tilted to one side. "You going to be okay, young friend?"

Chaim thought for a moment, then nodded. "I think so. I've just had my understanding of the universe expanded considerably."

Zalman smiled. "Contact with Rabbi Avram can do that." He chuckled. "Remind me to tell you some day of my first meeting with him." With that, he turned and followed the rabbi.

Chaim was left in the empty room, the door standing open, feeling absolutely washed out. After a moment, he sighed, picked up his water glass and moved to the side table where he refilled it from a carafe. The maître d' stepped into the room as he was taking a slow sip.

"All done this evening, Mr. Caan? They didn't stay long."

"All done, Mortimer. Thanks for hosting us. It didn't take as long as we thought it would to settle our business."

"Our pleasure." Mortimer gave a small smile, turned and exited the room.

Chaim finished the water, set the glass down carefully, and headed for the door himself.

"I'm still probably not going to believe this tomorrow," he muttered.

Once the valet brought his car around and he got out on the street, Chaim focused on driving to work. Halfway there, he realized he'd made his decision, apparently without consciously thinking about it. He was going to take Rabbi Mendel's offer. That meant he needed to tell Karli about it, though. Better to get it over with, so at the next stoplight he pulled out his phone and said, "Call Karli."

The phone dialed out and linked up with the car's Bluetooth systems. He heard it ring once, twice, then...

"Hello, Chaim. What do you want?" Karli didn't sound very happy, but then again, if he was getting a phone call at 10:00 P.M. after a long day, he probably wouldn't be happy either.

"Hi, Karli. I hate to be calling you at this hour, and I hate to be bringing you bad news, but there's no way around it. Tonight's going to be my last shift."

"What? Are you kidding me?"

"No. I got a chance at a position with a really significant medical research project, but I had to tell them yes or no right away and I have to report right away. I'm going to take it. Sorry. I really am, but this is a big opportunity for me that I can't pass up." Another statement, he realized, that wasn't totally factual but was in essence true.

There was a long silence, then Karli said in a very controlled tone, "It's a good thing you're not in arm's reach of me right now." Her sigh sounded heavy even over the phone. "Okay, I understand you didn't have any time to give notice, and I understand it's a good opportunity for you. But you can tell your new boss for me that he's a rat bastard." Another pause and a sense of Karli being distracted. "Crap. I've got a conference call with corporate first thing in the morning, so I won't be in until about 9:00 A.M. Just leave me a resignation letter in the desk. I'll deal with it when I get there."

"Okay," Chaim replied.

"And Chaim?" Karli's voice was softer.

"Yeah?"

"Good luck."

"Thanks."

Late Thursday afternoon Chaim's phone rang.

"Hello."

"Chaim, this is Rabbi Mendel. Have you reached your decision?"

"Yes, I have." He took a deep breath. "I'm in. And I'm packed. Where do I go?"

CHAPTER 4

Two days later

CHAIM SAT IN A SMALL CONFERENCE ROOM, WAITING for someone—he wasn't sure who. He'd been brought here to a small town in Tennessee after agreeing to come with Rabbi Mendel. When he'd arrived they'd given him a suite of rooms, complete with a seventy-inch state-of-the-art television and a mini-fridge stocked with a couple of bottles of whole blood. Not quite five-star-hotel quality, but still rather posh and very comfortable. And since the suite was on a floor that was totally underground, there were no annoying sunbeams oozing through the cracks and gaps of blinds and drapes, which Chaim appreciated.

The television had one of the most advanced game consoles Chaim had ever seen tied into it. It made him kind of wish that he was more of a gamer, but he never had been. He realized that was partly because he'd never been very interested in them. He'd never cared much for animated movies, either, and he wondered if the similarities of the mediums might have been a factor. Add to that the fact that he'd never had the time available to play games enough to get very good at any of them. Between his extra studies in Torah and Talmud, which his father had insisted he do, and his time with the Boy Scouts, which his mother had insisted he do, the concept of "free time" never really existed for him. About the only time he'd been able to squirrel away for himself was when he'd lock himself in the bathroom and read science fiction novels on his phone.

Yeah, life for Chaim might have been easier if he'd been a gamer. He'd still have been a nerd, but at least then he'd have been part of a group of nerds. But instead, he'd been a solo nerd. Not much fun there.

Chaim had to wonder if this whole being a vampire thing was going to be a variation on that theme—if he was going to be the ultimate solo nerd. Despite the evidence of Mordechai Zalman, who'd ever heard of Jewish vampires?

Every day when he woke up from restless slumber, Chaim awoke with the hope that the last few weeks had simply been a bad dream—that this whole experience had been some kind of viral infection or weird disease or maybe a mental aberration, but that his body would throw it off and let him go back to his real life. It hadn't yet, but he kept hoping. That hope was growing more forlorn with the passing of each day, but it still lingered in his mind.

The door to the room opened just as Chaim heaved a big sigh. Mendel chuckled as he entered. "Yes, you are tired of waiting for an old man. I apologize for the delay. Sit, sit." The rabbi waved a hand as Chaim scrambled to his feet. Mendel was smiling as he took a

seat across the table from the young man. Mordechai
Zalman grinned as he took his own seat, and a third
man, an older man with thinning gray hair, took the
seat at the end of the table. Mendel gestured to him,
and said, "Chaim, this is Dr. Israel Hurwitz, who is
directing the team that will be conducting the studies
we will be running. Dr. Hurwitz?"

"Chaim, thank you for coming here and putting up
with our poking and prodding you. This work should
give us some invaluable data for a baseline of vampiric
beginnings. We've never had this before—have never
been able to get this. What little reliable data we have
is from studying Mordechai and one or two other very
older vampires. We are all incredibly excited about
this opportunity. Thank you." Dr. Hurwitz absolutely
beamed at Chaim. Hurwitz was a genial fellow, and
it was hard not to feel good around him.

Chaim smiled back in response. He still wasn't
sure he should be doing this, but if it could give
him a better understanding of who and what he was
now, or if by some divine miracle they could figure
out how to reverse it, he needed to be a part of this
work. "Nice to meet you, Dr. Hurwitz. I'm here to
do what I can. Can you tell me what I can expect to
be involved in?" He listened carefully as Dr. Hurwitz
began to explain the team's plans and protocols.

"For all intents and purposes, you can think of
the next few days as being a super-physical exam,"
Hurwitz began. "We'll begin by measuring all the
normal body metrics that your family doctor would
check if he was giving you a physical: height, weight,
body fat measurements, cholesterol, blood sugar and
blood chemistry, lipids, and a few others like EKG

and EEG. Then we'll do full-body CT scans and MRI scans. After that, a few more specialized tests: thyroid, liver panels, prostate exams. While we wait on those results, we'll do some gross physical tests like run a cardiac stress test, how fast you can run, how far you can run, some weight-lifting measurements. After we review all those results, we may come up with a few more tests."

"Are you considering doing biopsies?" Chaim asked.

"Not at this time," Hurwitz replied, "but we're not going to absolutely rule them out. If we decide we need to, though, we will discuss it with you first. Muscle-density measurement, for example, may require it."

Chaim winced at that one. He nodded. "Yeah, whatever that takes, I guess. So, when do we get started?"

"How about in an hour?" Dr. Hurwitz raised his eyebrows hopefully.

Chaim stood. "I'm game. Let me go change into some shorts and a T-shirt and you can have at me."

Later that day, Chaim was again back in the same conference room, waiting. He looked up as Rabbi Mendel and Mordechai Zalman entered. Zalman closed the door and flipped a switch on the wall, which lit up a small sign that said SECURE, then they settled side by side across the table from him. Zalman was carrying an attaché case, which he set on the table long enough to open and take out a recorder, which he also set on the table, along with three microphones, of which one was placed in front of each of them. He closed the attaché case and set it on the floor under the table.

Chaim looked at the recorder, raised his eyebrows, and looked at the other men. "Umm, what's this about?"

Rabbi Mendel folded his hands in front of him on the table. "Before you get too immersed in Dr. Hurwitz's testing regimen, Mordechai and I want to interview you about your experience in becoming a vampire. We want to record it, so we don't have to take notes and risk being distracted. We will have a transcript prepared afterward. The transcript itself will remain sealed, but data will be extracted from it in a report. Not a redacted transcript, but an anonymized summarized report."

"Okay," Chaim said slowly. "But why? I already told you what happened."

"We are not so much concerned about what happened," Mordechai said. "What we want to develop are as many details as you can recall about the woman— rather, the female—who changed you."

"And to some extent what she did." Mendel's voice was quiet. "You are the first vampire we know of who was 'converted' in recent years. There are almost certainly others"—he waved a hand palm up—"non-Jews, of course, but we have never been able to find one just after the event. The majority of them don't last long. Mental deterioration, we think, combined with internecine conflicts. There are some old, old stories that can be found in mythologies and obscure folktales, but sifting them for the real truths behind them is almost impossible. So not only do you represent perhaps a treasure trove of information on the physiology of a new vampire to Dr. Hurwitz, you also represent valuable data about vampire behavior and predation. We need to develop and capture as much of that information as we can before it becomes stale in your mind and starts fading."

"Oh." Chaim sat back in the chair, and mentally

called himself an idiot. Of course they would want to know that. In fact, now that the subject had come up, he was surprised they hadn't jumped on him about that at that very first meeting at The Dove. "I'm... not sure how much help I'll be. Most of that time is very foggy in my mind."

"We'll work with you," Mordechai said, "and I'm sure you'll get tired of hearing questions asked in different ways, but we think we can help you recall more than you realize you know."

"Okay, I guess." Chaim shrugged. "What do you want to know about this vampiress?"

"Too romantic," Mordechai said. "Think of her as a disease vector."

Chaim looked at him wide-eyed for a moment. "Huh. I never thought of her like that, but I guess you're right." He placed his hands on the table before him and interlaced his fingers. "So where do you want to start?"

"Don't mention any names in this," Mordechai cautioned as he reached toward the recorder. "And"—he pressed the RECORD button—"begin." He paused a beat, and presented the first questions. "You told us at the restaurant that she was 'almost tiny,' had long, blonde hair, and green eyes. Correct?"

"Yes."

"Can you elaborate on that? Provide more detail? What age she looked, for example? Shade of blonde, and was it dyed?"

Chaim thought back to that night, to the time she entered the club and made her slow progression around the room. He remembered how he hadn't been able to look at anyone else, and the shock that he'd felt when he'd realized she was coming his way and eventually took the stool beside him at the bar. He took a deep breath. "Okay, I'm five foot nine, so I'm not very tall—at least, not by California standards. But I was almost a head taller than she was, and she was wearing four-inch sandal-strap heels. Without the shoes, she couldn't have been much taller than four foot ten—if that." He paused for a moment. "Her hair . . . I'd have to say honey blonde, and I don't think it was a dye job. The color was even; there was no hint of shade differences, even at her roots, and her eyebrows were the same shade. It was perfectly straight and hung to at least the bottom of her shoulder blades when she was standing. No hint of curl or wave. It looked like it had been cut recently, because the ends were even."

"Do you recall anything about its texture?" Mendel spoke for the first time.

Chaim shook his head. "Nothing unusual. It was smooth and soft, but it wasn't little-kid fine and wispy. Not superthick or coarse, either. Just . . . nice." His voice trailed away, and he stared between the other two men at a spot on the wall behind them.

"Was she petite? Stocky?" Mendel asked. "What was her frame like? Was she well-muscled? Hard? Soft?"

Chaim looked down at his hands for a moment, then back up. "I remember her as being very petite. She almost looked like she was fourteen, except for her face. Not soft, but not an athlete, either."

Mordechai spoke up. "You said her eyes were green. Are you sure about that?"

"Yes, I . . ." Chaim began, but before he could continue the picture in his mind wavered. "I . . ." Suddenly Chaim wasn't sure of anything. "I don't know. I thought they were, but . . . now I'm not sure."

Mordechai leaned forward, tension in his frame. "What shape was her face? Round? Long? Heart-shaped?"

Chaim held his hands up to stop the flow of words. His head was starting to spin. "Stop. Please . . . just stop." He put his head in his hands and rested his elbows on the table. Taking deep breaths, he closed his eyes and pressed on his temples, trying to hold onto himself and bring himself back to solid ground. After some moments, the whirling sensation slowed and stopped, and he opened his eyes and lowered his hands.

"That was weird," Chaim muttered. Mordechai raised a hand palm up and beckoned with his fingers, obviously encouraging him to keep talking. "I thought I remembered what she looked like, but while you were talking, I got dizzy all of a sudden. Now, it's like I'm seeing two pictures at once: what I had described to you before, and now someone different, but my mind keeps telling me it's the same person."

"So what does this other person look like?" Mendel was the one leaning forward intently now.

"About the same size, still small and petite. The hair is still straight and long, but it's a dark blonde that's almost brown. Her eyes are not green—they seem to be so dark a brown they're almost black. And her face—she reminds me of Hannah Goldfeder, a girl who used to go to our synagogue before they moved to Colorado a couple of years ago."

"Was this Hannah Goldfeder a beautiful girl?" Mendel was still intent.

Chaim shook his head. "No. Distinctive, but some-where between handsome and cute. Of course, at fourteen, that could describe a lot of girls. But both of them had somewhat triangular faces, except this woman's face reminds me of a fox—only prettier." He suddenly started furiously rubbing at his nose with his right hand, then grabbing it between the thumb and forefinger and twisting it back and forth. "And now my nose is itching like crazy!"

When the itching finally stopped, Chaim settled back in his chair, and cautiously released his now tender nasal appendage. "Wow." He looked at the others, noting that they were sitting in a relaxed manner, in stark contrast to the tension they had been showing just moments before.

Mendel looked at Mordechai. "Pheromones?"

Mordechai nodded. "Pheromones. If we can prove it, we may find they bind to the histamine blockers, and when they finally fade away..."

"Itching," Mendel said.

"Exactly."

"What do you mean, pheromones?" Chaim asked, resisting the urge to rub his nose some more.

Mendel touched his fingers together before his chest for a moment, then pointed at Mordechai. "He has always said that all vampires exude changed pheromones, but that some of them could act almost like drugs to normal humans. It seems he may be right."

Chaim frowned, then nodded as he recalled, "That's right. You said that I had vampire pheromones when we met at the restaurant." His eyes widened and he snapped his fingers. "Tiffy!"

The others looked puzzled. "Tiffy?" Mordechai tilted his head in a bit of an angle.

"My mother's dog. She growled at me when I was at home for a little while a week or so ago. She almost never growls at anyone, and she's never growled at me." He looked at Mordechai. "Pheromones?"

"Almost certainly. Most dogs and almost all cats object to the presence of a vampire, even if they knew him before the change. You're lucky she didn't bite you."

"Heh. She might have been able to nibble a few skin cells off the end of my pinky." Chaim smiled as he stuck out the finger in question. The smile faded as he sobered. "So you're saying I was for all intents and purposes drugged?"

Mordechai nodded. "There have been some vampires who have very strong control over their pheromones. It might not surprise you that the ones I've known of or followed over the generations were female."

Chaim shook his head. "No," he said bitterly, "that wouldn't surprise me at all. So it was a setup?"

Mordechai shook his head. "No, I would judge you were simply a prime opportunity. The fact that you were converted means that if she wasn't looking for you specifically, she was looking for someone like you. How many times did she feed off of you?"

"I ... I don't know for sure. Once ... twice ..."

Mordechai stood. "Take off your shirt and shoes," he ordered.

"What?"

"Just do it. We need to verify something."

Chaim took a deep breath, but didn't say anything. He toed his shoes off his feet, bent over and pulled off his socks, then stood and removed his shirt. Mendel offered a flashlight to Mordechai, who clicked it on and approached Chaim. The light was bluish, and he shined it on the sides of Chaim's neck.

"Confirmed one"—he touched the left side with a fingertip—"and two." He touched the right side. Mordechai's voice was matter of fact. "Hold your hands out in front of you, palms up."

Chaim did so. Mordechai shined the light across his wrists. "Confirmed three," he touched the left wrist, and shook his head. "That was enough to convert you, right there. But she wasn't done." He touched the right wrist. "Confirmed four."

Mordechai moved back a couple of steps. "Sit down and raise your feet."

"What? What are you looking for?"

"You're the medical student," Mendel said. "How much of your blood is in your legs?"

Chaim sat down slowly as that realization dawned on him. He lifted his feet and placed them on the table. Mordechai shined the light on the instep and ankle of each foot. "Confirmed five," he said, touching the inside of the left ankle. "Confirmed six"—touching the inside of the right ankle. He turned the light off and handed it back to Mendel. "Get dressed, lad." Mordechai sat and tented his fingers before his lips while Chaim restored his clothing and resumed his own seat.

"What was that about?" Chaim demanded, tension flooding his own body.

Mordechai sighed. "That light reveals slight differences in skin temperature due to injury or trauma resulting in subtle scarring. Once I can see them, I can feel them. Contrary to popular fiction, it takes more than one feeding to generate a new vampire. Everything I've heard and seen over the generations would indicate it takes at least three feedings in close succession. You were smart in your feedings in the wild, so to speak, to take only a single feed from each subject. She took six."

Chaim shook his head, trying to fathom what Mordechai was leading up to. "What . . . what does that mean?"

"It means," Mordechai said grimly, "that your conversion was not an accident. You were not a mistake. Your conversion was not happenstance. And your conversion had nothing to do with sex. You were a project."

Chaim shook his head, bewildered. He opened his mouth, but nothing came out.

Mordechai continued in that same grim tone. "She came to that club that night for the express purpose of creating another vampire. One of the reasons the world is not awash in vampires is because most of them cannot control their urges. By the time they get to the third feeding, they've almost drained the subject, and death rather than conversion is inevitable."

There was a pause before Mordechai resumed. "But she, whoever she was, controlled herself enough to feed six times. I repeat—you weren't an opportunity—you were a project. She crafted you with intent."

"Why?" Chaim's mouth was so dry that he felt like his teeth were pebbles and his lips were sunbaked leather.

Mordechai shook his head. "I have no idea. I've not heard of something like this being done before. The odds of finding her aren't good, but we will look for her. And if we can find her, and more importantly, if we can hold her, maybe we can discover what her goal was."

Chaim sat, staring between the men at the wall behind them. He shook his head. "But why the feet?"

"There is a sizable vein that runs across the top of the inside ankle," Mordechai said. "She was almost certainly aiming to make sure and certain that you converted. Three infection sites minimum, four to be sure. Six? I'd say overkill, if it wasn't a bad joke."

Chaim stared at him, a memory rising to the front of his mind—the sensation of her small hands holding each foot, while her tongue laved them, arousing sensations that fired neurons in strange ways that were almost unbearable. A sudden wave of nausea washed through him, and he bolted to the large rectangular trash can in the corner and bent over it. He didn't vomit—quite—and he was glad he didn't because he wasn't sure he could anymore. But it was a near thing, and the quivering of his arms and legs and the tension in his back and neck drove a spike of pain through his head.

He didn't know how long he hovered on the edge of that disaster, but he finally was able to step back from it, uncurling his fingers, taking a deep breath, and straightening before he turned around to face the others.

"If we find her," he said in the coldest voice he had ever produced, "she is mine. You can drain her of information first, but afterward . . . she is mine."

The next day about noon, Chaim's phone rang. The only reason he knew it was close to noon was from his watch. He hadn't seen outside daylight for quite some time.

From the ringtone, he knew it was his mother. He started to walk out of the room, hesitated, and went back and picked up the phone.

"Hello, Mom."

"Chaim? Is that you?"

"Yes, Mom," Chaim said, suppressing the long-suffering tone that was trying to get out. "Who else would call you Mom?"

"Well, you never know."

Chaim rolled his eyes, glad that she couldn't see him. "Mom, I..."

"Chaim," she interjected, running over what he had started to say, "what kind of work is it you're doing?"

"Mo-om!" Chaim's frustration bled through and produced the two-toned two-syllable word that used to get him in trouble a few years earlier. "I can't tell you that. I told you guys, I signed a nondisclosure agreement. That agreement says I can't tell anyone what I'm doing. It doesn't say I can't tell anyone except my mother and father—it says I can't tell anyone. So stop asking—please!"

Chaim heard a matronly sniff over the phone, followed by, "Well, all I can say is that a company that won't let a boy tell his mother what he's doing is not so much of a company. All mysterious, and everything. It makes me wonder if they're involving you in something illegal."

And there was the difference between his mother and father, Chaim thought. His father's first reaction about Chaim's job would be, "Is it righteous?" His mother's concern was more practical: "Is it legal?" Similarly, his father had insisted Chaim study Torah and Talmud, while his mother had pushed him into the Boy Scouts. Chaim had to admit, it had added a certain diversity to his growing-up years. He shook his head.

"No, Mom, they're not doing anything illegal. In fact, what they're doing is very important, but they can't talk about it until all their research is completed. I promise you, when they finally announce what they're working on and go public with it, I'll let you know."

"Hmmph." That graceless syllable meant that his mother was going to change the subject, but Chaim knew she had not given up on it. He knew it would come back up again in later conversations. "So, are there any Jews where you are now?"

"A few," Chaim said in a resigned tone.

"Any girls?"

Chaim sighed. "Mom, if you don't stop with the prying and the matchmaking, I'm going to start calling you Yente. You're not a *shadchanit*—you're not a matchmaker. So stop with it, already."

"Any mother wants her son to be happy, to be married, to have children." Her voice was serious, now. Chaim's head tilted to one side as he considered that. "You've already moved out at such a young age. We hardly see you. I hardly get to talk to you. Don't begrudge me my hopes and wishes and dreams."

There was an almost plaintive note in her voice, but Chaim didn't think she was trying to guilt-trip him—this time. His mouth quirked a bit.

"All right, Mom. But you have to leave that up to *haShem*, all right?"

There was silence from the other end of the connection, but Chaim knew she was still there, still listening.

"I've been meaning to ask you," he said, forcing a change of topic, "do you remember any old folktales or stories from Lithuania? Would Great-Grandma and Great-Grandpa have told any stories about weird stuff?"

"What do you mean, 'weird stuff'?" his mother asked, her voice a bit wary.

"Oh, like vampire stories, and stuff like that."

"Pfft! What makes you think of trash like that?"

"Oh, some of the guys here were talking about vampire stories and movies the other day, and how Dracula came from Transylvania, and it made me wonder if there were things like that in Lithuania."

"No, not that they ever said. But if vampires were real, I think the old stories have it wrong."

Chaim's eyes widened. This was unexpected. "What do you mean?"

"According to the Tanakh, those few places that mention the awful, evil night demons, lamias, or Lilith, they were always female. So they got it wrong when they give the power to males."

"Um," Chaim said. "I hadn't thought about that."

"I was sure you hadn't."

He heard the smug tone in his mother's voice. He shook his head again. It was time to draw this to an end before she said anything else to upheave his worldview.

"Listen, Mom, I have a meeting in a couple of minutes. I need to go. Thanks for calling, and tell Dad I'll try to call again soon."

"All right. Be careful."

"I will. Love you. Bye."

"Goodbye."

Chaim thumbed the button to end the call, and heaved a big sigh.

Hmm. A feminist view of monsters, and from his mother. Who'd have thought it? But it bore thinking about, now that it had been drawn to his attention. Wow.

CHAPTER 5

One week later

CHAIM WAS BACK IN THE CONFERENCE ROOM. THE last week had been more of a challenge than he'd expected. The list of tests the doctors wanted to run had kept growing. He'd found some of them interesting, from what he knew so far about physiology. A few of them mystified him, including the DNA tests. He wasn't sure why that would be important to a study of vampires, but then, he was neither a doctor—yet—nor an expert on vampires, despite being one. But the last of the tests had been wrapped up that morning, and he'd been asked to wait here. So he was waiting. Bored, but waiting. He couldn't even pull his cell phone out and read, because he'd left it in his bedroom.

The door opened, and Rabbi Mendel walked in, followed by Dr. Hurwitz and Mordechai Zalman. They all seated themselves, Mordechai at one end of the table and the other two across the table from Chaim.

"To begin with, Mr. Caan," Dr. Hurwitz said, "let

me thank you again for agreeing to participate in our study. The data we've collected in the last few days gives us more insight to the vampiric condition and how it comes about than anyone has ever had before. We still don't know what the actual cause is, but once it begins, we can trace its effect and changes with much better understanding now because of you."

Chaim quirked his mouth a bit. "Call me Chaim. Mr. Caan is my dad. And for what it's worth, you're welcome. I learned a little bit through this exercise, too, although certainly not as much as you apparently did."

Hurwitz smiled. "We're still working on the final reports for Dr. Mendel and his group, but I think they will be pleased by them." He sobered. "I almost hate to ask this, but is there any chance you could stay with us for a few months and let us do additional tests and take additional measurements as you continue to develop?"

Chaim blinked. He needed to get started on figuring out how he was going to continue school, he thought. Not to mention how he was going to support himself.

Before Chaim could say anything, Mendel spoke up. "This may help you make a decision." He opened a folder and slid something across the table to Chaim.

He found himself looking at a check made out to him in the amount of five thousand dollars. His eyes widened and he looked up at the rabbi.

"That is your stipend for the last few days."

"I told you they'd pay you," Zalman reminded him with a grin.

Chaim looked at the check. "Well, that should make my father happier when he finds out about it."

"You will receive that much every month that you

remain in the testing program, plus room, regular clothing expenses, and...ah...sustenance," Mendel concluded with an awkward substitution for "food" or "board."

Chaim shrugged. "I'm sure that sixteen ounces of human blood every three days isn't cheap."

"Roughly sixty dollars per liter," Mendel said. "Not outrageous. About the price of a good bottle of wine, actually." He smiled. "We've been doing this for a while, and we have reliable sources of supply."

Chaim looked down at the check, shrugged, and looked up again. "I'm okay with this. Frankly, I'm going to need the money. But I need something to do. I can't just sit in windowless rooms all day when I'm not being tested, and your cable TV selection sucks."

"I agree," Mendel said. "We'll see if we can do something about that. Israel"—he looked at Hurwitz—"you have your agreement. Go tell your team to start designing that long-term protocol."

"Indeed!" Hurwitz got to his feet and leaned over to offer a handshake to Chaim. "Thank you, again, Chaim. We'll talk to you in a few hours about what we'll be doing." With that, he bustled out of the room.

When the door closed, Chaim sighed and looked at the other two men—if one could use that word for Zalman the vampire. "All those tests, and I still don't know any more about me or what's going to happen with me."

Zalman leaned forward and laced his fingers together on the table before him. "We've read the preliminary report summaries. I can give you the highlights."

Chaim looked at him. "So, give, already."

"What data they have from you after the last few

days bears out that becoming a vampire, whatever the actual cause, does trigger some metabolic changes. That's been understood since they first examined me some time ago. But now, they get to see it happen.

"For example, you've lost a noticeable portion of your body fat just in the time you've been here. Now"—Zalman held up a hand to forestall Chaim's obvious retort—"part of that is undoubtedly due to your significant change in diet." He grinned. "But part of it is metabolic in nature. You'll notice that I'm not exactly pudgy." He poked a finger into a very lean cheek. "The other vampires we know of are much the same. So they kind of expected to see that, and were gratified to observe it."

"Okay, so I'm going to be skinny. I'm okay with that," Chaim said. "What else?"

"Despite the body fat reduction, you haven't lost any weight," Zalman continued. "In fact, you've gained a bit."

Chaim thought about that. "I'm not noticeably larger. Muscle density?"

Zalman nodded. "That, and bone density as well. The minerals from the blood you consume are optimized for your development, especially iron, potassium, and calcium, so your new metabolism is rebuilding you from the inside out, as they say. That's one of the reasons they want to have you stay, so they can track that. I'm guessing it will take at least three to four months if you get regular blood supplies, maybe a bit longer."

"So all those stories about superfast, superstrong vampires are true?" Chaim was grinning. He couldn't help himself.

Zalman snorted. "Faster, yes. Stronger, yes. But not a superman." He shook his head once.

"How much faster and stronger?"

"I can run fifty meters in about four seconds," Zalman stated. "Closer to three if I really push myself. That's almost half the current world record. I have run a full marathon distance in less than ninety minutes, which is twenty-five percent faster than the current world record. I weigh a bit over ninety kilograms, and I can regularly bench-press four hundred kilograms. That's a bit over ten percent over the current world record, which was set by an absolute ox of a man. I haven't tried for a maximum. And I know from personal experience that small-arms fire doesn't produce serious damage. Shotguns don't even penetrate."

"Wow." Chaim was impressed. "They'll have to invent whole new Olympic categories if you—we—ever go public."

"That said"—the older vampire directed a stern glare at Chaim—"that does not mean that I am immortal. Cut my head off, I'll assuredly die. Blow a twelve-centimeter hole through my chest with a cannon, I'll die. Douse me in gasoline and set me on fire, I'll likely die, and I'll certainly feel the pain. Strap me to a biggish bomb and blow me up? I'll die." His thin-edged grin appeared again. "But other than that, I am very hard to kill." He sobered. "On the other hand, the oldest vampire I know of was about my age or a bit older, and I don't know of any vampire who died of old age or its equivalent."

Chaim nodded. "That makes sense, I guess." He thought for a moment. "Stake through the heart? Holy water? Cross? Silver? Sunlight? Turn into a bat? No mirror reflection? Can't enter a building without being invited? That the standard list?"

Mendel pursed his lips and nodded.

Zalman echoed the nod. "I think that's the one. Okay, in order." He held up his left index finger.

"Stake through the heart: remember we said we're observing increased muscle density. The heart is already one of the toughest muscles in the body. With what we're expecting to see, a standard stake, even if it was pushed all the way through the chest and out the back, would very likely just push the heart up and out of the way, not even really bruise it. A diamond or monomolecular point and edge might slice the heart, but the odds are high that even that wouldn't penetrate the heart through and through. Did I mention amazing recuperative powers? Yeah, that part is almost true."

Middle finger was next raised. "Holy water? We have no definite proof that that has ever been effective. Personally, I think it's either wishful thinking on the part of the Catholic Church or psychological susceptibility on the part of the oldest vampires."

"Big words for a guy born in the eighteenth century." Chaim smiled.

Zalman made a universal hand sign in his direction and continued. "Certainly holy water has never worked on Jewish vampires. On the other hand, I'm not discounting what would happen if powerful acids were thrown on us. Even water well-laced with quicklime would be unpleasant, especially if it got in our eyes."

Ring and little fingers up together next. "Same story for silver and crosses, either together or separately. Doesn't work on us, don't know if they work or not on other vampires."

"What about other holy symbols?" Chaim asked.

Zalman grinned and used his other hand to hook a necklace out from under his shirt collar. Chaim saw a silver Magen David pendant with Hebrew writing inlaid in the middle of it hanging from a silver chain. "That answer your question?"

Chaim nodded.

Three fingers on the right hand raised. "Turn into a bat, no mirror reflection, and having to be invited. All appear to be nothing but assimilated folklore. All I can say is that I have never turned into a bat or any other creature, and neither has any other vampire I've ever known. Likewise with the invitation to enter and the lack of mirror reflection things, both of which—even for folklore and old wives' tales—are just ridiculous."

Zalman dropped his left hand and raised his remaining right finger. "Now we get to the sunlight issue. There is some evidence that there is something to that."

Chaim's eyebrows raised and he sat up straight. "No kidding? What gives?"

Zalman gestured with palm up to Mendel. "Your turn, Rabbi."

Mendel grimaced before speaking. "The change does some things to your body beside the metabolic shifts and structural changes. Your whole system becomes more sensitive to radiation, and that's one of the things that Dr. Hurwitz's team wants a better baseline on, so you'll be dealing with a lot more tests in that area."

"Huh." Chaim pursed his lips for a moment. "That probably explains why the MRI tickled and the full-body CT scan made me itch all over."

"Undoubtedly. And after the first time you made

those comments, you wouldn't believe the arguments they sparked among the team in private." Mendel's mouth spread in a big grin which lifted up the fringe of his beard. "I love to see scientists arguing about what primary observations mean. It means they're doing real work."

His smile faded away. "So an increased sensitivity to sunlight or radiation could cause a number of problems, especially in deserts and lower latitudes." He tapped a finger on the tabletop a few times. "The other thing is that there appears to be a mutation that happens in the eyes."

"Mutation?" That was an alarming announcement to Chaim. "What mutation? Why? How?"

"If he is a yardstick to go by"—Mendel waved a hand at Zalman—"your eyes are going to change. You're a premed student, so I'm certain you know of the rods and cones in your eyes."

"I've had the beginning physiology class," Chaim said. "There are about twenty times as many rods in the human eye as there are cones, and there are millions of cones. Rods provide low-light-level vision, fine-detail vision, and no-color vision. Cones activate at higher light levels, provide color vision, but not as much detail. They work together to provide spatial acuity. Professor Morgan was an eyeball fan," he said with a grin. "We spent an entire month on the eye and the optic nerve."

"Indeed." Mendel nodded, then continued with, "This is something else the team really wants to study. It appears that some of your rods are going to shift to a third state, something in between rods and cones. They don't have a word for it yet. They're just calling the original rods Type A rods and calling the new ones Type B rods. It appears that the Type B rods will greatly expand your night vision, providing much better detail and at least some color vision at lower light levels. And if you follow Mordechai's pattern, you will see a little deeper into the infrared part of the spectrum as well."

"Dr. Hurwitz's comment after they observed me was that I was an excellent design for an apex nocturnal predator." That thin, slicing grin was back on Zalman's face.

"A reasonably astute assessment," Mendel said as he combed his fingers through his beard. "However, there are drawbacks—one big one, anyway. Exposure to really bright light for extended periods of time is literally painful, and it appears it might serve to permanently degrade vision after a certain amount of exposure."

"So a vampire left in the desert would fry from the radiation and go blind from the light?"

Mendel spread his hands. "Quite possibly. And it certainly would be one factor to explain why vampires are not the overlords of Earth."

"Yet," Zalman said with a grin.

"So how do you deal with it?" Chaim turned to face Zalman, who shrugged.

"First, don't go out in the daylight unless you absolutely have to. Second, if you have to, wear long sleeves, full length trousers, gloves if you can get away with it, and wide-brimmed hats. These days, there are radiation-resistant fabrics, as well. Third, SPF 50 or higher sunscreen applied liberally and often. And finally, if you have to go out, very dark wraparound sunglasses and, if possible, very specially designed polarized contact lenses."

"Wow." Chaim set his elbows on the table, interlaced his fingers, and rested his chin on his thumbs. "I was hoping the sunlight thing would be bogus, too. Guess not. It does sound like I'm definitely going to have to adopt a nocturnal lifestyle."

"Yes," Mendel said. "I'm sorry."

"Why? It's not your fault. If it's anyone's fault, it's that blonde bitch that converted me." Chaim snorted. "'Converted.' That certainly has new meaning and import compared to what it usually means when we talk about Jews converting. I still haven't figured out how I'm going to explain this to my parents. Or if. They weren't real happy about my leaving home for a few weeks of 'helping run some tests.' I can't imagine how they'll react to finding out there really are vampires and their number one and only son *is* one."

"If—when—the time comes," Mendel said gently, "let me know and I will give you what help I can."

"Thank you."

There was a long moment of silence, then Mendel said, "One last thing. We would like a copy of your college transcript just to show some evidence of general intelligence and education. It will be anonymized, of course. Would you be willing to sign a request for it?"

Chaim shrugged. "Don't need to. I have a copy of the transcript and my last few grade reports on my laptop. I was getting ready to start sending applications out for internships for next summer, so I already requested one. You want it sent to the email address you already gave me, or somewhere else?"

"That would be fine," Mendel replied. "Enough for now. You've had a long day, Chaim, and I expect Dr. Hurwitz's team will have you up bright and early tomorrow—for certain values of bright and early. Get some rest."

"You're probably right, *Rav* Avram." Chaim sighed. "Or actually, I'm sure you're right. I know I'll have other questions, but it's not like there's a deadline, now, is there?" After a moment, he grimaced. "No pun intended."

Both the older men smiled. "Good night," they chorused as they stood and trooped out of the conference room together.

Chaim remained in the conference room. For a long moment he just stared at the wall opposite him, not really seeing it, just thinking.

He realized he'd mostly been going through the motions the last few weeks—that although the front of his mind had seemed to accept and understand how he had changed, how he had been changed—the back of his mind, his subconscious, whatever it was, had not. It had been rolling along ignoring all of the changes and just assuming that things would get back to normal sooner or later.

But tonight—tonight had gotten through. The kind of changes Mendel had described were permanent—were irreversible. It sank into the core of Chaim's mind and being that he wasn't a normal guy anymore. He would *never* be "normal" anymore. Never be Orthodox anymore. Never again. *He was a vampire* . . . with everything that implied. He'd done it to himself. He'd betrayed himself—betrayed his Orthodoxy—for a one-night stand. And with that, his guilt broke free.

Chaim stood and went down the hall to the restroom. He stood there, staring at himself in the mirror over the sink. He could see outward evidence of the changes.

Hell, even his mom had. His face was leaner, the facial bones were more prominent. He looked like a different person.

That thought caused him to laugh bitterly. It was appropriate that he look like a different person—because he was. Inside and out, he was different. Not Chaim Caan any longer, no matter what he called himself. No longer the confused kid who was questioning what he had grown up with but still clung to the Orthodox label, but someone who he still wasn't absolutely certain could or should even be called a Jew.

A sudden surge of anger flooded through him and rocked his mind. His fists balled, his teeth gritted so strongly he heard them creak. As he stared at himself, his anger mounted, again, and again. Disgust and self-hate poured through his mind.

"You punk bastard," he muttered. "You were so desperate for a girl to like you, you let this happen. You pathetic excuse for a man."

The next instant, before he was consciously aware of it, Chaim drove his fist into the center of the mirrored image's face. The mirror glass shattered from the force of the blow and cascaded into the sink bowls and onto the floor.

That shocked Chaim, and he was still standing just staring at the results of his angry blow when the door to the bathroom opened and Dr. Hurwitz and one of the male team members looked in. They looked at Chaim, then looked at where the mirror used to be, then back at him, surprise and shock on their faces.

"I, uh, broke the mirror," Chaim muttered, cradling his bleeding hand against his chest. "Sorry."

❖　　❖　　❖

It was the next evening when Zalman caught up with Chaim. He walked into the little infirmary room where Dr. Hurwitz had finished taking the bandage off his hand. The cuts on the hand looked almost healed to Chaim, based on his pre-conversion experiences. But those experiences didn't apply anymore, Chaim reminded himself.

Marta, one of the techs, was taking photographs of the wounds while Dr. Hurwitz was dictating notes to his phone about accelerated healing. Chaim looked down at the top of her head as she bent forward to focus the digital camera on his hand. Her hair was short, black, thick, and just a bit the other side of wavy without being really curly. He was tempted for a moment to try and run his hand through it, just to see what it would feel like. The temptation disappeared as she straightened.

Chaim had Marta pegged at maybe thirty years old—enough older than him that he wasn't attracted to her much. Her intense focus on her job may have had something to do with that as well. She was a couple of inches shorter than Chaim, not quite stocky—what Elena would have called "curvy" instead. Just kind of a "face" face, with heavy eyebrows and dark brown eyes that lit up whenever she exhibited one of her occasional smiles. Pleasant to be around, but all business.

Zalman stopped in the doorway and leaned against the doorframe, arms crossed, expressionless face in place, waiting. Dr. Hurwitz finished his dictation, turned off the recording, and directed his gaze to the older vampire. "Do you need something, Mordechai?"

Zalman's mouth quirked. "I need to have a talk with Chaim as soon as you are finished. Don't let me rush you."

Marta finished clicking pictures, looked up to receive a nod from Dr. Hurwitz, and walked over to plug the camera into a docking station. While she was uploading the pictures she had taken, Dr. Hurwitz took Chaim's hand in both of his, turning and twisting it under the bright examination light. After a minute or so, he released it and looked at Chaim. "This is not a test we would have tried to make, and I can't say that I'm glad that you injured yourself. But we are getting some interesting information about vampiric healing out of this event, so we can't say it was all bad." He gave a strained smile. "From the looks of it, you'll probably be completely healed in another day or two. I'll be very interested to see if you develop any scarring. But please, can we not do this again? We don't need any additional excitement in our work, trust me."

Chaim nodded, and said, "I'll try."

Zalman straightened. "Are you finished with him now?"

Dr. Hurwitz waved a hand. "He's all yours. Can you have him back in an hour?"

Zalman smiled faintly. "Probably." He beckoned to Chaim. "Let's go find some privacy."

A few minutes later they were outside. It was after 10:00 P.M., there were only a few wisps of low clouds, and the night sky looked almost like spangled velvet. They were far enough away from Chattanooga that there wasn't much light pollution, and Chaim stopped for a moment to just stare upwards.

After a moment, he sighed. "I love the night sky. It always impresses on me just how much *haShem* as creator is an artist."

"Indeed," Zalman said. "Your first time outside since arriving?"

"Nah," Chaim said. "I come out at night a couple of times a week. I'm discovering that doing the whole underground thing all the time gets a bit old. I'm not—quite—claustrophobic, but after two or three days I start getting a bit 'antsy,' to use one of my dad's words. So I come out during a break in the tests, get a bit of fresh air, stare at the skies, remind myself that the universe consists of more than concrete walls and air-conditioned air."

They both stared at the night sky for a long moment, then Chaim sighed, and said, "I guess you want to talk to me about last night. I'm sorry. I'll pay for the mirror."

"The mirror's not a problem." Zalman put his hands behind his back and started walking. Chaim fell in beside him and mirrored Zalman by tucking his own hands behind him. "To get you for a test subject, they would have allowed you to break as many mirrors as you wanted." He chuckled for a moment, then sobered. "No, I'm more concerned about *why* you broke the mirror."

Chaim sighed again. "I'm stupid." Zalman looked at him, and even in the dim light in the parking lot Chaim could see his eyebrows raised. "Seriously. I'm stupid. I've just been running on automatic pilot or cruise control or something since..."

"Since your encounter with the vampire that changed you." Zalman offered after a moment of silence.

"Yeah. Ever since then. I mean, I knew what had happened, I knew the changes I was feeling and seeing, but somewhere in my mind I was still believing that I was still the same guy, and things were going to work out and I'd go back to who I was . . ." He swallowed.

"Who you were before."

"Yeah."

"And last night?"

"Last night it sank in that this"—Chaim passed his hand down his front—"this is real. This is real. This is forever. And I got really mad at myself for hooking up with that chick and doing this to myself, so . . ."

"You punched yourself."

"In the mirror. Yeah."

They walked in silence for a long moment, circling around the parking lot.

"I've been expecting something like this," Zalman eventually said.

"Glad to know that my freak-out happened on schedule," Chaim said with some bitterness.

Zalman chuckled. "Actually, you've been doing rather well. Better than I did, as far as I can remember. But a 'freak-out,' as you put it, is rather to be expected, you know. For all that the conversion doesn't seem to be as physically destructive as some of the other things that you might have experienced, it is perhaps the most traumatic thing I can think of for one person to experience. Your entire body is being changed underneath you, so to speak. Your entire perspective on life is being wrenched askew. For all that you have the memories of Chaim Caan, you're not that person anymore. You can't be. And all of your relationships . . . well, the chances of them surviving aren't good."

"I know," Chaim whispered. He looked over at Zalman. "What was it like for you?"

Now Zalman sighed. "I don't remember much of

that time. Very foggy memories of feeling lost, of feeling confused, of being driven away." He stopped and turned to face Chaim. "The one clear memory I have is my father telling me that I was dead, and my brother trying to stab me with a pitchfork."

Zalman's face was stark in Chaim's sight. He could see it clearly, even in the dark. It finally dawned on him that his vampire night vision was giving him that.

"That's what I'm afraid of," Chaim said in a low tone. "How can I possibly explain this to my parents? And if they believe me, as religious as they are, could they somehow accept that?"

"I don't have an answer for that," Zalman said. "Except, I haven't seen that kind of acceptance often in my over two centuries of life, not even from parents."

"That's what I'm afraid of." The following silence was stark.

After a moment, Zalman turned back and they started walking again. "The other thing I need to impress on you is that you are changing mentally as well. The anger that you felt last night, a good part of that was because your emotional matrix changes as a vampire. Think of it as a post-trauma change. You will most likely find it a little more difficult to connect with people."

"Not that I was ever very good at that before," Chaim muttered.

"Regardless," Mordechai continued, "you'll find yourself feeling somewhat distanced from people that you see and even meet. You will definitely find your anger quicker to flare than before. You will need to learn to suppress that if you're going to move among regular people. Save your anger for important work, not for dealing with everyday irritations. Trust me, there will be times when that anger can and will be valuable. Learn to use it wisely, and don't give in to it readily, because that way leads to self-destruction."

"That sounds like the voice of experience," Chaim said.

"Indeed," was all Zalman said in response. They continued walking in silence for a time. "Have you talked to your parents recently?" Zalman asked.

"Mom called a few days ago. I need to call Dad."

"Indeed," Zalman said. "Don't leave it too long."

Chaim tried not to sigh. Zalman was right, and he knew it. He just didn't want to do it.

CHAPTER 6

FOUR DAYS LATER ZALMAN ENTERED THE WORKOUT room where Chaim was standing next to a treadmill having monitor electrodes pasted all over his body. "Ah. One of the endurance tests, I presume, Marta?"

The tech nodded as she applied the last electrode and handed the wireless unit to Chaim for him to hook to his belt.

"The marathon? The steeplechase?"

She looked up at Zalman. "The hill climb."

"Oh," Zalman said, "that's not so bad." He gave an evil chuckle. "For certain values of not so bad." For a change he was in sweats, and climbed up on the treadmill next to Chaim's.

"Thanks," Chaim muttered as he shifted the unit to the back of his waist. He looked over at the other man. "You going to watch?"

"No," Zalman said as he settled his feet onto the track. "I'm going to pace you."

"What?" Chaim was perplexed at that. "Why?"

"Partly for something to do," Zalman replied. "I get just as bored as you do. And partly because they asked me to." He nodded at the tech, who nodded back and left the room.

After a moment, her voice came over the intercom. "Okay, if you will take your places, we'll start things up in a moment."

Chaim stepped onto the treadmill and settled his feet fairly close to the front of the belt, placing his hands on the side rails in preparation for the initial lurch that always caught him off guard. It didn't seem to matter how much warning they gave him, the first movement of the belt staggered him. And as usual, when the belt started moving a moment later, he lurched and it took him three steps to find the rhythm.

"I hate these things," he muttered.

"Why?" from Zalman, who was pacing smoothly on his machine.

"I'm a bit of a klutz, and these things just seem to make it worse."

Zalman chucked.

"What are you laughing at? I bet the first time you used one you tripped over your own feet." Chaim let go of the rails and stepped up his pace as the treadmill increased its speed. The readouts of the machine were blanked out, supposedly because they didn't want him reacting to them rather than the sensations of the run.

"That's the first time I've heard one of your generation use that word."

"What, klutz? Ha. Growing up around my parents, I heard it almost every day. 'Chaim, don't be such a klutz.' One of the joys of moving out of the house was not hearing that word."

"Well, I doubt you'll hear it anymore," Zalman said, his stride lengthening as the belts sped up again. "I suspect you'll find your balance and agility are improving."

"From your mouth to *haShem*'s ear," Chaim said with earnestness. "I'd love to be able to walk down a block and not trip over a crack in the sidewalk or even worse, my own shadow."

Zalman chuckled again.

At first it bothered Chaim that their steps weren't in synch as they ran, but he figured out soon that since the other vampire was taller than him, his pace would be different, so he mentally shrugged and quit thinking about it.

After the treadmills both elevated to introduce a grade to their run, Chaim looked over at Zalman. "Can I ask you something?"

"Sure."

"What do you do?"

"What?" Zalman looked at him with a quizzical expression.

"What's your job? If I wasn't here, what would you be doing? Are you Rabbi Mendel's deputy director, or something?"

Zalman laughed. "No, not hardly. I'm here right now because you're here. I can help you adjust, and they use me for a baseline of what you're going to probably become."

"Okay, I can see that." The treadmill ratcheted up another couple of degrees. "So what would you be doing if I wasn't here?"

"Hard to say," Zalman replied. "I don't necessarily do just one thing. I'm kind of an independent contractor, going from place to place and doing whatever people need me to do."

"Uh-huh." Chaim leaned forward a little as the grade increased yet again. He could feel the tension in his leg muscles, but they weren't burning like they used to when he ran hard. Interesting. "So what's the most important thing you do?"

Zalman looked over at him. "You really want to know?"

"I asked, didn't I?"

"All right." They ran several steps before Zalman said, "I'm a *magen*."

Chaim translated the Hebrew word in his mind. "A shield?"

"No, or not exactly. More of a . . . a protector."

"What's that? Like a bodyguard?"

"No. I belong to a . . . group, let's call it, that occasionally can be called on to deal with . . . situations . . . involving Jews."

"Like Mossad, or something like that?"

"No, no," Zalman said with a grimace. "Not part of the Israeli government, or any government, for that matter. We're not a large group, nor are we militant, and mostly we work behind the scenes to convince those causing the problems that they need to stop."

"So like James Bond, or Rambo?"

That produced a laugh, followed by, "Not usually. More like the IRS, much of the time."

"Okay, now *that* is scary."

"There are occasional times, though, where we need to be a bit more . . . direct."

Chaim waited, but Zalman said nothing more along that line. "So how did you get into this line of work? That's not exactly something I would see a vampire doing." The treadmills ratcheted up another degree, and Chaim was starting to feel the effects of it. It took him a moment to realize that Zalman hadn't responded. When he looked over at him, he saw a very hard expression, a fixed gaze like he was staring off into a far distance. "Um, Mordechai?"

Zalman looked over at him, and grimaced. "Sorry. Old memories."

"You don't have to tell me."

"No, you probably need to know anyway." After a deep breath, Zalman continued with, "I was in Warsaw in 1944. Me and Menachem and Eleazar."

"Who are they?"

Zalman looked surprised. "Didn't I tell you there were two other vampires in Israel?"

"Yeah, but you didn't say their names."

"Ah. Sorry. But we were in Warsaw."

It clicked in Chaim's mind. "The Ghetto Uprising." One of the most famed events involving Jews in World War II, after the Holocaust and the concentration camps.

"Yes. The Ghetto Uprising."

"How did you . . . stupid, you're vampires. Of course you survived."

"It was hard. Bad. Menachem and Eleazar managed to escort some mothers and young children out early on. I stayed through the end." Zalman's expression was grim.

"Umm, what did you do?"

"Whatever I had to do. And I made sure the besiegers paid in blood for their victory. The official German casualty list is off by at least a factor of ten, maybe more. They buried—no pun intended—the rest of them in the Eastern Front casualty lists. That wasn't all my doing, but enough of it was."

They ran in silence for several minutes, before Chaim again mustered enough courage to speak. "So, is that why you're a protector now?"

"Partly. Maybe mostly. Even for me, who had witnessed pogroms and oppression for over two hundred years, that was extreme."

"Eye for an eye part of that?"

Mordechai shook his head. "No." His face closed in again and set like granite. Chaim looked at him once, then looked forward without saying anything further.

He figured they'd run at least a mile before Mordechai spoke again.

"The rabbis say that an eye for an eye is not a formula for justice. It would, if implemented literally, leave a world full of blind people. It is instead to prevent oppression by the strong and cruel. And it is to teach us that revenge is not our right, not our mission, not our prerogative, and certainly not our passion. And despite that, it is a hard-fought lesson to learn, especially for such as us."

"How so?"

"Even more than regular humans, the adrenaline"— Mordechai slapped his chest twice with his right hand—"the anger"—he tapped his temple with the first two fingers of his right hand—"the power and might"—he raised a right fist clenched so tight that Chaim could see the tendons in his arm and hand standing out—"all make us—we vampires—susceptible to that fault, that breakdown. And to be a *magen*, to be a shield, you cannot do that. You cannot be that. You must not. You can channel your adrenaline and your rage to fuel your strength, but you cannot unleash it, you must restrain it and only do what is necessary, no matter how wrong those who face you are. And oh, but how the Nazis pushed me to that limit over and over and over again."

"But wouldn't they have deserved the worst?"

"Undoubtedly," Mordechai said in his deepest, raspiest tones. "But it wasn't my place to do that to them. And if I had descended to their level, I would have become them, and that I refused to do." He looked directly at Chaim. "That we cannot—we *must* not—do. We are not . . . Hebrew doesn't have a word for this . . . like what the Russians would call *nekulturny*. Vampires though we are, we are still part of Adonai's chosen people"—Mordechai's use of one of the actual Names of *haShem* made it clear to Chaim how deeply the older vampire felt this and how holy he considered it to be—"and we cannot bring disrepute on His Name."

Chaim bore his gaze for a long moment, still pacing on the treadmill, before he nodded slowly. Mordechai faced forward again, and they ran for a distance without speaking. Finally, Mordechai spoke again. "Do you know of *tikkun olam*? What does it mean to you?"

It was Chaim's turn to not speak for long moments as they ran. When he finally had his thoughts together, he said, "Repairing a broken world. I know some use it to justify their political causes. Others use it as a platform to launch mitzvot of good works—women's shelters, food banks, free medical clinics."

"But what does it mean to you?"

"Honestly, I don't know. I would like to make life better for people. That's why I started working to be a doctor. Does that count as *tikkun olam*?" They ran for a while longer. "Turnabout's fair play—what does it mean to you?"

Mordechai sighed. "I am not a Kabbalist, not a mystic. But in this, I do find some merit in the teachings of the Lurianic strand of Kabbalah, for whom *tikkun olam* was the gathering of light and souls. To repair the broken world is to preserve and separate what is holy until it is all reclaimed in the Godhead." He shook his head. "To me, the fragments of light, the souls to be gathered, are those of our people. And for them to be gathered, they must first be preserved. So for me, *tikkun olam* is first and foremost the protection of Jews, wherever they are. Only then can other aspects be brought into play."

"And so you are a *magen*?" Chaim asked.

"And so I am a *magen*."

There was another interlude of silence, eventually broken by Chaim. "So who is this group you work with?"

Zalman pulled the necklace from around his neck that he had shown Chaim back in their meeting and handed it to Chaim. He held the medallion in his hand. "The *magen* shield," he murmured, "and"—he parsed out the Hebrew word גיבורים inlaid in the center of the shield—"the *Gibborim*. King David's Mighty Men." He handed the medallion back to Zalman, who placed the chain back around his neck as he continued running. "So is your group thirty and three, then, like David's?"

The older vampire's mouth quirked. "No. In fact, it's barely three. But it helps me remember what I should be about."

A few more minutes of silence passed.

"I think I might like that," Chaim said quietly. "If I'm not going to be a doctor and healing people, and if I'm going to toughen up like you say I will, I might be able to do that."

"Well, don't give up on the doctor thing just yet. The old man wants to talk to you about that," Zalman said. "But if you're serious, there is no reason why you couldn't do both."

"Seriously?"

"Seriously."

Just then both treadmills clicked and began slowing and lowering to their starting positions. Chaim was surprised. "We're done already?"

"You're done." Marta had reentered the room. She motioned Chaim down off the treadmill and started removing the sensors.

"Are you sure? It doesn't seem like we did that much."

"You ran sixteen kilometers at mostly a twenty-five percent grade, all the while holding on a lengthy conversation. Yeah," she snorted, "you're done."

"Wow."

Chaim looked over to Zalman, only to receive a sardonic grin.

It was a couple of days later when Chaim stepped out of the most recent testing room to find Rabbi Mendel and Mordechai Zalman both waiting on him. Mendel looked his professorial usual and Zalman wore one of his London bespoke suits. "Come, my boy, we need to talk." He followed them to their normal conference room, wondering what was going to happen now.

Once they were seated. Chaim looked at Mendel and jerked a thumb at Zalman. "He said you had something to talk to me about. Something about my being a doctor."

"Yes, I do." Mendel was serious, Chaim saw. His

usual good humor seemed to be not in view today. "But to do that, we need to talk about something else first."

"Fine," Chaim said. "What's that?"

Mendel laced his fingers together on the table before him. "You're Orthodox, correct?"

"Uh-huh. Not Lubavitcher, but Orthodox otherwise."

"And since your family is Eastern European in background, then you are Ashkenazic in background as well, *nu*?"

"Of course. My great-grandparents were from Lithuania."

Mendel shrugged. "You will be able to work that out, I'm sure." Before Chaim could work through that in his mind, Mendel continued with, "You are aware, I am certain, of the recent work in genetics that has established the genetic almost-uniquity of the *Kohanim*, the priestly lineage."

"Umm, yeah," Chaim said. "But what does that have to do with..." His brain caught up with his mouth and his jaw snapped shut.

After a moment, he said, "Does this have something to do with the vampire thing?"

Mendel nodded.

Chaim looked at Zalman. "What was your surname before you took the Zalman name?"

"Kaplan."

"One of the priestly names," Chaim murmured.

"As is yours," Mendel said.

"As are those of Menachem Aronson and Eleazar Katz in Israel," Zalman added.

"And this is important why?" Chaim wasn't sure where this was heading.

Mendel sighed. "Every Jewish vampire that we have been able to trace who has lived for more than a few years was male and of the Kohanim—was of the priestly lineage."

There was silence while Chaim worked through that in his own mind. At length, he laid his hands palms down on the table before him. "You think this may have something to do with this Y-chromosomal Aaron thing they found."

Mendel spread his hands out to each side. "May. May. But the fact that we have found no trace of long-lived female Jewish vampires and the only long-lived male vampires we've found are of the Kohanim does kind of make us wonder, you might say."

"I can see that," Chaim muttered, staring down at his hands. After a moment, he lifted his head. "All right. What does this have to do with me?"

"You wanted to be a doctor," Mendel said, clasping his hand together and leaning over them. "How about if you became a geneticist?"

Chaim pursed his lips. "I had thought about cardiology or neurology, but I wasn't anywhere close to making—or needing to make—that decision yet." He thought about it. "Knowing this, the thought intrigues me. But what's in it for me?"

"The group I am associated with will pay your way through university and medical school in Israel if you'll give us several years of service after you graduate," Mendel said. "Tuition, fees, books, room and—well, not board, but sustenance. Add in a moderate monthly stipend. Tel Aviv University is probably top of the list, but we have more than one good school, so you can take your choice. And from your grades and transcript so far, they would almost certainly love to have you. We have the connections to get your visa and enrollment fast-tracked, get you on the lists for the programs you would need, and to get you enough night classes and labs and independent study sessions to make it easier on your schedule."

How did they get... of course they had his transcript. He'd given it to them. Stupid. "What about residency?"

Mendel snorted. "Night shift in a big teaching hospital with a busy emergency room. No problem. In actuality, you'll most likely work shifts around the clock, but since you won't be outside, it shouldn't be a problem. Postgrad study, probably at Weizmann Institute of Science."

"So why me? There's got to be other geneticists out there."

"Of course there are," Mendel admitted. "But we can't just advertise for someone to research the genetics of vampires."

Chaim snorted. "Yeah, I guess I can see that."

"The good ones are all signing up to research well-funded common and popular issues," Mendel said. "No one wants to link up with a small group who won't even tell them what they want researched without a major-league nondisclosure agreement being signed first. So if you want in on this, you're our first real hope for this work. Plus, it won't hurt that you have a personal stake in it."

Silence for the space of three breaths.

"How long?" Chaim asked.

"How long to make your decision? Fairly soon, I'm afraid."

"No, how long would I have to work for you afterward?"

Mendel's eyebrows lifted a little. "Ah. Well, we would hope you would work with us for quite some time, but the minimum would be a year for every year or part of a year that we support you."

"Fair enough," Chaim replied. After a moment, he asked, "So who *is* your group? The *Gibborim* that Mordechai belongs to?"

"No." Mendel smiled. "A very limited partnership with no name funded by very long-sighted people concerned about the future and welfare of the human race in general and the Jews in particular. It's not open to investments from the public. We're not related to or officially connected with the *Gibborim*"—he grinned at Zalman—"but we acknowledge each other exist and we do cooperate upon occasion."

"Like with me?"

"Like with you," Zalman acknowledged.

Chaim looked at Mendel. "You're not just a rabbi, are you?"

Zalman laughed. "I told you he'd figure it out." He looked at Chaim. "Undergraduate and graduate work at the University of Heidelberg, another degree from Oxford University, and a PhD from MIT. All before age forty, which is when he decided to do his rabbinical training."

"Wow," Chaim said, impressed. "I thought I was an overachiever."

"Neither here nor there." Mendel waved a dismissive hand. "Mordechai, how much longer are you going to be with us?"

"A few days, maybe, but I'm probably going to have

to leave soon. There's a problem heating up in New York that I may have to look into."

"Past time for that one," Mendel said with a frown. "Past time." Zalman shrugged.

Mendel looked back at Chaim. "You don't have to decide on the offer tonight, but the sooner you can decide, the sooner we can put things in motion if you say yes."

Chaim shrugged. "I want it. I just have to figure out how to explain to my parents that I'm not going back to school at UCLA and that I'm moving to Israel. On the one hand, Dad will probably be excited about it, especially the parts about Israel and full tuition and expenses coverage. But Mom...she is a Jewish mother, with everything that that implies. She'll immediately start worrying about terrorists." He sighed.

"Have you talked to them lately?"

"I started calling them every Saturday night. That's enough for Dad—more than enough, usually," he said with a twist to his mouth. "Mom"—he pursed his lips for a moment—"Mom usually finds excuses to call me at least twice during the week. She keeps trying to find out what I'm doing, even though I told them I signed a nondisclosure agreement. She seems to think that because she's my mother she's not subject to that. She's started trying to find out where I'm at, trying to get at it that way somehow. I had to disable my GPS locator on my phone."

"A not uncommon problem with mothers," Mendel murmured.

"Yeah, well, she also manages to ask at least once a week if I've met any nice Jewish girls where I'm at." Chaim shook his head. "I made the mistake of telling her I had, and now she wants names and what they do. Mothers." He shook his head. "I'll figure out some way to explain this."

"So you're going to agree?"

Chaim took a deep breath. "Oh, I'm in. This sounds like the best deal possible in my new existence, and as you say, I do have a personal stake in the matter."

Mendel smiled, rose up from his chair and stretched his hand across the table. "Good. Very good. You won't be sorry."

"Yeah, well, that remains to be seen," Chaim muttered as he shook hands with the rabbi. He frowned at a pang in his abdomen.

"Hunger?" Zalman spoke in a quiet tone, all humor gone from his face.

"Yeah." Chaim laid a hand on his stomach. "They don't want me to take too much blood at a time or too frequently, for more than one reason. I understand, but it does mess with me when I'm getting close to the next time."

Mendel looked over at Zalman. "Give it to him."

"You sure about this? Does Hurwitz know?"

Mendel nodded.

"All right." Zalman pulled something out of his pocket and slid it across the table to Chaim. "Here. Try this."

Chaim picked it up. "A sports bar? Or rather," he said, looking at the wrapper, which had a Star of David prominently featured on it alongside Hebrew lettering, "a *magen* bar? Really?"

"It's not a sports bar," Zalman said. "Or not just a sports bar. Try it."

He peeled the wrapper back, then looked at Zalman.

"Try it."

He lowered his head and took a cautious sniff.

"Huh. It doesn't smell bad." Eyebrows lowered, he looked up at Zalman again.

"Try it."

Chaim took a cautious nibble of one corner, chewing the bite carefully. He felt his eyebrows climb in reaction to the surprise of the taste.

"It...it doesn't taste bad." Chaim tried another small bite, and chewed it thoroughly before swallowing. "It doesn't taste great...it's actually kind of blah...but it doesn't taste bad." He took a larger bite. "What's in this thing?"

Flattening out the wrapper, Chaim read the ingredient list. "Figs, ground and whole roasted sesame seeds, sesame oil, barley, native honey, and...manna?" He swallowed and looked up, remembering the narratives in Exodus. "Honestly? Manna?"

Mendel smiled at him. "Honestly. It's produced in Israel from native products. Manna is a type of edible resin originally produced by several types of bushes and trees in the Sinai area. A researcher managed to adapt it to horticulture. It's become surprisingly popular."

Chaim looked down and realized in surprise he had eaten the entire bar. "I thought vampires..."

"Remember, how much is truth and how much is myth is part of what we're trying to discover." Mendel's smile broadened into a momentary grin.

Zalman nodded. "We don't know if it's because you—we—are all Jewish, or if it's because the ingredients are all raised and processed in Galilee, or both, or if it's something altogether different."

"Not ignoring the possibility of the divine, either." Mendel's smile had faded to a most sober expression.

"I don't care," Chaim said. "Just having something to actually eat will be great." He looked over at Zalman with a fixed stare. "You got any more of those on you?"

Zalman's sly grin appeared once more, and he took another bar out of an inside pocket and slid it across the table to Chaim.

CHAPTER 7

CHAIM WAS COMING OUT OF ONE OF THE TESTING rooms the following Friday morning, and found Zalman standing in the hallway. "Hey. Waiting on me?"

"Yes." Zalman fell in beside him as he walked down the hall. "Just want to make sure—are you serious about wanting to be part of the *Gibborim*?"

"Yeah, I am." Chaim looked up at Zalman out of the corner of his eye. "Why?"

"Have you done any karate or judo or anything like that?"

Chaim snorted. "If it wasn't in Torah or Talmud or school, I didn't get to do it. No, I didn't have anything involving martial arts, and not a lot of athletics in general other than swimming in Boy Scouts. My father didn't allow room in my schedule for things like tennis and basketball and karate. He barely made room for Scouts. Why? Am I going to have to pass some kind of fitness exam or something?"

"No. On the other hand, while your body is getting harder and tougher from the conversion, you need to learn how to use it."

"Makes sense, I guess," Chaim said. "I hate exercise, though."

"This won't be exercise as you think of it," Zalman said. "Think of it more like an odd dance."

"So what, when, and where?"

Zalman stopped where another hallway crossed the one they'd been following. "I'm leaving in a couple of hours."

"That New York thing?" Chaim remembered that coming up in the conversation with Rabbi Mendel.

"That New York thing. I'm not sure how long it will take, so I'm bringing in someone to train you. His name is Gil Haleva, and he's an Israeli arms master. I'd have probably brought him in anyway, but this works out best for right now."

"Does he know you?"

"Yes, he and I have worked together before."

"Does he know about . . . us?"

"He knows that I'm unusual, but he doesn't know that I'm a vampire."

"So don't let the secret out."

"Right. Don't say anything about that. In fact, he's smart, and he's been around me before, so try not to talk about anything odd at all. He can put pieces together pretty well."

"Uh-huh. Just play dumb and do what he says?" Chaim let a little sarcasm creep into his voice.

Zalman shook his head. "If he asks questions, you can say that we're related. Anything else, just tell him that you're not authorized to talk about it. The only other thing is to not out-perform him. Just do what he says, the way he says to do it, and ignore any side comments."

Chaim nodded. "Got it. When will he show up?"

"He should be here Sunday morning." Zalman pulled something out of his pocket. "Here. You'll want this."

Zalman draped a silver chain around Chaim's neck and put another of the *magen* medallions in Chaim's hand. He stared down at the *Gibborim* inlaid in the center of it. Suddenly the seriousness of it all transfixed him like nothing else had since the night he met the blonde. He didn't know how long he stood there, staring at the medallion, but finally he closed his hand around it and closed his eyes. It took him a moment to find the right Hebrew words.

"Now if I have indeed found favor in Your sight, Adonai, let me know Your ways, so that I may know You and continue to find favor in Your sight."

Chaim felt that *haShem* would not mind him paraphrasing the prayer of Moses from Exodus 33. After all, at that moment if anyone was as much a stranger in a strange land as Moses had been, it had to be him.

He tucked the medallion inside his shirt and opened his eyes. It did not surprise him that Zalman was gone.

It was Sunday afternoon when Haleva made his appearance. After the early afternoon's blood tests, which were becoming more of a trial due to the increasing toughness of Chaim's skin, Chaim had taken over one of the visitors' offices which was equipped with a moderately powerful computer and three monitors, browsing the information available about the various universities in Israel, trying to get a feel for what they were like. He'd already committed to Mendel's suggestion, after all—he might as well start trying to get on board.

There was a tap at the open door. He looked up to see a grim-faced stranger in sweats looking at him.

"Yes?"

"Are you Chaim Caan?" The stranger's voice was a dark tenor with some rasp to it. Chàim's neck hairs stirred.

"Yes. You?"

The stranger smiled, which transformed his face. He entered the room and held out his hand. "I'm Gil Haleva, and I'm here to get you started on training."

Chaim stood up. "Hi. Yeah, I'm Chaim. Glad to meet you. Have a seat. I thought you were going to be here this morning." At least he was wearing a decent set of sweats himself, so he looked somewhat presentable.

Gil pulled up a side chair and they both sat. "Bit of a weather delay in the flight, but I'm finally here." Chaim blinked. He hadn't paid attention to the weather in weeks. "So, tell me, do you have any kind of training or martial arts experience?"

Chaim shook his head. "No, sorry. Nothing."

"Actually, that's good." Gil was obviously earnest about that response. "It means you don't have anything to unlearn, and we can start with building the right foundation right away." He leaned forward in his chair a little. "What are your goals? What do you want to accomplish? Strength? Speed? Self-defense? Competition?"

Chaim considered that. "I'm not sure that I know enough to answer that question."

Gil's eyebrows contracted a bit at that. "Okay, why did Mordechai call me in, then?"

"Oh." Chaim pulled his *Gibborim* medallion out from under his shirt and handed it to Gil. "That's because I want to do the same kind of work he does."

Gil's eyebrows went the other direction. "Ah." He tilted his head and looked at Chaim. Chaim could just see him wondering what the prep-looking American kid was bringing to the table for Mordechai to want this kind of training for him. After a moment, Gil shrugged and handed the medallion back. "Okay. If that's true, that will simplify things."

"Why?"

Gil's mouth quirked at one corner. "Because if you're going to work with or for Mordechai, you won't need any of the competition stuff or any of the civilian nonlethal self-defense stuff. We'll focus on the real hard stuff. This will be all about turning you into a lethal killing machine." His face was sober and his eyes bored into Chaim's.

Chaim kept his face still. He'd come to that conclusion himself after hearing Zalman's account of being in Warsaw. Still, it was a bit of a shock to hear it so bluntly expressed.

After a moment, Gil continued with, "I mean, you do know the kind of work he does." That wasn't a question.

"Some."

"Okay." Gil leaned forward a bit. "Just so you'll know, I'll teach you a foundation of Krav Maga, the Israeli Defense Force fighting system, then we'll move on to those techniques that you will most need to know and figure out what will work best for your size and strength and skill." He leaned back. "When do you want to start?"

Chaim looked at his watch. "How about now?"

Gil grinned. "Yeah, no time like the present. Got an exercise room?"

"You could say that." Chaim shut down the computer and led the way to the workout room.

Looking around the room, Gil whistled. "Not very big, but at least one of everything necessary, and state of the art. Nice. What about one with space to spar?"

"Next door," came from behind them. Marta had entered the room. She had what looked to be a shirt in one hand, which she tossed to Chaim. "Here. We're going to want readouts from your sessions, and the sticky electrodes won't work. This has the monitors incorporated into it, so you can work out and not worry about them getting knocked off. Just don't mess it up. Those things are expensive. Hi, Gil."

"Marta."

So they knew each other. That was good. Probably.

Chaim held the shirt up and whistled. "Looks tight. Spandex?"

"Spandex's successor. Stretches easier, breathes better, and it doesn't bind." Marta walked over and opened the connecting door to the other room.

"Ha." He looked at Gil and gestured at the door, following him through.

The room they entered was a bit over twice as large as the workout room, with mats covering most of the floor. Gil looked around. "Yeah, this will do. So," he turned to Chaim, "you wearing trunks under that?"

Chaim had to make a mental shift of trunks = shorts before he understood the question. "Yeah."

"Well, let me see what I've got to work with." Gil spun his hand in a forward-looping circle a few times, then set his hands on his hips as if he was waiting. Chaim stripped off his jacket and sweatpants and tossed them on a nearby table.

"Shirt," Gil said. Chaim peeled off his T-shirt and added it to the pile. He stood in place while Gil walked around him. "Hmm. Pale. You could use a little sun." Chaim managed to not frown as Gil chuckled. "Very low body fat. Less than five percent if I judge it right." He looked at Marta.

"About three percent, the last time we measured it."

"Height?"

"Five foot nine," Chaim responded.

"One and three-quarter meters," Marta added.

"Weight?"

"One hundred eighty pounds," Chaim said.

"Actually a bit more than that now," Marta said. "Eighty-six kilograms."

Gil's eyebrows rose. "Must be dense structure, then."

You have no idea, Chaim thought, suppressing a smile.

"You're very lean and you look fit. Do you run?"

"Yeah," Chaim laughed.

"What's so funny?" Gil said with a quirk to his mouth. "Let me in on the joke."

Chaim waved a hand at Marta, who had a smile on her face.

"He runs a fifteen-k on Sundays, Tuesdays, and Thursdays. The last two weeks he's been running a twenty-five percent grade." She dropped the smile and shrugged. "He's not world-class, but there's nobody in my running club that could keep up with him."

Not world class yet. Chaim kept that thought behind his teeth, suppressing another smile as he did so.

"Weights?"

"Not a lot," Chaim said. "I do some free weights and leg presses on Mondays, Wednesdays, and Fridays."

"Bench press?"

"One hundred twenty kilograms," Marta responded. "We haven't been pushing that."

Yet another smile suppressed by Chaim as he noticed Marta didn't say how many reps he did the press.

"I can see that," Gil said. "You've got a greyhound here, not an ox." He stepped up to Chaim, squeezed a bicep for a few seconds, then slapped the back of his hand against Chaim's abdomen. "Hard." He held his hand out to Chaim. "Match my grip for as long as you can."

Chaim took the grip, and started to squeeze as hard as he could, but remembered in time Mordechai's instruction to not outperform Gil, so he slowly ramped up his own compression until it balanced with Gil's. The Israeli held the grip for almost a minute, which surprised Chaim, but he maintained his own grip to match. At last, Gil nodded and released. Chaim followed suit.

"Good. Good strong grip." He looked at Marta. "Can I see copies of his physical baseline?"

She shrugged. "That's up to Chaim. Privacy laws, and all that."

He thought about that for a moment, taking into account everything Mordechai had told him. "Gross physical condition and attributes, yes," he finally responded. "Bloodwork, scans, and other details, no. If in doubt, no."

Marta grinned and looked back at Gil, whose mouth was a bit twisted. "And I was told to remind you at this point that the nondisclosure agreement you signed earlier when you got here covers everything you see, hear, experience, or do while you're here, as well as any observations or conclusions you might arrive at while you're here or after you leave. You can think about it. You just can't talk about it, communicate, make any kind of electronic or physical notes about it, or in any way cause those thoughts to leave your head and be transmitted to someone else except Chaim and the staff here. Clear?" Gil said nothing—his frown deepened. "Else you'll be dealing with Dr. Mendel—or Rabbi Avram, whichever persona he would present to you that day."

"Oh, no," Gil said. "Anything but that. I'll be good." The frown was replaced by a look of concentration. "When can I see what I can see?"

Marta grinned again. "Now. We expected your request and anticipated his directive."

Gil looked back over his shoulder. "I need tonight to think about this . . . tonight my time, that is. I'm eight hours ahead of you, so . . ."

Marta interrupted. "He's living a night-shift schedule right now, so he's not too far off of what you're on."

"So, meet for breakfast?"

"After breakfast," Chaim said, avoiding the whole issue of food and eating.

"Nine hundred hours Tel Aviv time, then." Chaim nodded. "Great." Gil turned to Marta again. "Lead me to it." They left the room together.

Chaim moved over to the table to reclaim his T-shirt and sweats and put them on. He stood there with his hands on his hips, wondering if this was such a good idea. After a time, he shrugged. One way or another, he'd get through it. He suspected there'd be some unpleasant moments in the next little while, but his life was already such a sterling example of shit happens he couldn't see how a few lumps and bruises could make things any worse.

Gil scrolled through the report. "I don't see his body temp in here, but from what I felt out there when I was touching his arm and hand, it's probably way low. What, thirty-five Celsius?"

"Close. Resting, it's usually around thirty-four point five Celsius."

Gil scrolled back up. "So, resting blood pressure usually around eighty over fifty, resting pulse around thirty-four, resting temp around thirty-four point five Celsius." He shook his head. "This guy is a calendar model for low-key low-stress, right?" Marta didn't respond. "What's he like when he's worked up?"

Marta reached over and clicked on another tab on the screen. "These are the readings from his last fifteen-k, right at the end of the run before we shut it down."

"Hmm." Gil frowned. "No change in the temp. Pulse forty-one, blood pressure ninety over sixty. Hmm." He toggled back to the previous screen. "Didn't you tell me he was running these at a twenty-five percent grade?"

"Yeah."

"Hmm. Way under all the norms." He toggled back to the second screen. "What happens when he's exhausted?"

Marta shrugged. "Nothing. Same numbers."

Gil looked at her. "No drop-off when he's physically exhausted?"

"We haven't been able to get him to that state without starving him, and that skews our tests."

"Right-handed or left?"

"Right dominant," Marta said, "but pretty good usage with his left. Not ambidextrous by any means, and I don't think you'd want to give him a complex detailed minute assembly project to work left-handed, but he eats left-handed a lot, and works a computer stylus left-handed just fine." She shrugged again. "I think you'll find he's both flexible and adaptable." She grinned. "Those aren't exactly the same things, you know."

Gil shook his head. "I think I'm beginning to see why Mordechai wants me to train him."

"Mordechai has said nothing to us about what he expects to develop from this, but between him and Dr. Mendel I'm sure there are multiple expectations, and wheels within wheels."

"Heh. Not only do I expect that, I'd be disappointed if that wasn't the case." Gil stood. "Okay, I've seen enough for now. I need to think about this. Is there some food available without leaving the complex?"

"Some sandwiches in the break-room refrigerator. Kosher, of course. Roast beef with Grey Poupon tonight, I think."

"Great. Show me the way."

"Forget the idea of martial *arts*," Gil began the next morning with a sneer. "Krav Maga is a combat system, especially the way the Israeli Defense Force uses it. There is no art to it. It is a brutal approach to combat whose sole purpose is to at least incapacitate your opponent—your enemy—in very short order, if not outright destroy him."

He was walking around Chaim in slow steps as he spoke. Chaim didn't turn his head to watch him, but he did track him by his steps.

"Krav Maga is to other combat systems what English is to other languages. Just as English is a mongrel language that will mug other languages in back alleys to take and assimilate words and expressions and concepts, so Krav Maga is a mongrel combat system that will adopt, pilfer, and outright steal anything from any other combat system that it thinks might be useful. And this is why I was glad when you told me that you hadn't had any training, because it really will speed things up if you don't have any old habits or muscle memory to get in the way of what I'm going to teach you."

Gil stopped in front of Chaim, maybe two steps away. "Can you touch the floor?"

Chaim didn't say anything, just bent at the waist with his knees straight and placed his palms on the floor in front of him.

"Good. How about the other direction?"

Chaim brought his hands up and straightened, then kept moving slowly as he bent backward in an arch and ended up with his fingertips touching the floor behind him.

"Uh, yeah. That's good. Straighten up, please. My back hurts just looking at you."

Chaim straightened with a small smile. No need to tell Gil that the scientists had been testing his flexibility since his first day there.

Gil had his arms folded across his chest once Chaim was able to look at him again. He was slightly taller than Chaim. The older man's face was neutral, and Chaim tried to match that as he returned his gaze, eye to eye.

"Right. First of all, every Krav Maga instructor has

his own way of teaching. We're not very formalized...
not like some of the karate schools. The one thing
we all have in common is this is a very aggressive,
very hard combat system, so our teaching is much the
same. Even in defense it's aggressive. Everything is
done hard and fast. My preferred method is to teach
a few of the defensive moves, then teach you how to
spring into offensive moves from those. Then repeat
with other moves.

"Second, despite what I just said, training in a
gymnasium or dojo is not the same as combat. There
will be rules—maybe not very many, but there will
be rules. Combat doesn't have rules. Training and
sparring can last for a fair amount of time. Combat
is fast, hard, and brutal. In combat, the first man
who makes a major strike will usually win. So you
won't get the feel of combat from training or sparring.
You'll get the moves, but you won't get the feel. And
that's why a lot of trainees don't survive their first
real fights—because by the time they break past their
training experiences and figure out how they have to
go all out, their opponent has made that major strike
and they're down and probably out.

"Third, you can start out training in trunks and
tees and barefoot, but before long I want you working
out in street clothes and the heaviest shoes you have."

"I have a pair of Doc Marten boots," Chaim said.

"Good. Great." Gil dropped his hands to his hips.
"The idea, obviously, is that fights and combat don't
happen in gymnasiums—they happen out on the street,
out in the fields, so you need to be used to fighting
in street clothes or uniforms.

"Any questions?"

"How long will it take me to become good?" Chaim asked.

"At least you didn't ask about becoming a master." Gil got a thin smile on his face. "The answer is, how long have you got? The philosophy is, if you're not learning new stuff every time you fight, you're probably not doing it right. The question you should have asked is, how long until you're competent? That depends on how hard you want to work. My contract here is for three months. If you focus and work hard, you could have the basics pretty well incorporated by then. After that, it's just practice and experience."

Just practice and experience, Chaim repeated mentally. Somehow he didn't think it would be that simple.

"One final point," Gil said. "We're both going to be tired and sore and cranky most of the time before this is over. This is going to be hard for both of us, although in different ways. Doing this kind of intensive training is almost as hard on the instructor as it is on the trainee.

"I haven't overstated the fact that this is a hard and rough and aggressive combat system. We'll try to minimize damage, but accidents happen in training, especially when we're going to be moving as fast as we are. I think I can promise there won't be any major broken bones, but no guarantees. We will certainly have a fine collection of bruises, you probably more than me. If this bothers you, now is the time to walk away."

Chaim shook his head. "I'm not any fonder of pain than the next guy, but I need this. If this is the only way or the best way to get it, so be it." He shrugged. "It is what it is."

❖   ❖   ❖

Two weeks into the training, Chaim was still struggling with the workouts. It wasn't the physical aspect of the workouts that bothered him most. He was actually doing okay with that, from what he could tell, which surprised him somewhat. No, it was the mental aspect that was plaguing him. Hitting someone and being hit was hard for him at first, especially the hitting someone part. He just wasn't comfortable at trying to be violent. He'd never been one to stick up for himself in conflicts. He'd always been the one to turn away, even when he knew he was in the right, or more importantly, even when he knew the other guy was wrong. He was finding it more difficult to overcome a lifetime of habit and conditioning than he had thought it would be.

And tonight was a case in point. Even after two weeks, he still felt a reluctance to lash out at Gil. He knew the moves, but it felt like his mind was dragging weights. By the time he would start a strike or a kick, Gil would be at least one move beyond it, if not two. It was starting to frustrate him.

Anger flared in his mind and flowed through his body. His shoulders tightened, his hands lifted a fraction of an inch, his eyes narrowed. Gil danced in and threw a straight left. Chaim didn't think—he just reacted, throwing his left hand up to block the punch to the side while he ducked and turned in to hammer his right fist into Gil's left side between his hip and the short ribs. An instant later he brought a kick around with his right foot, aiming to take out Gil's left knee, but Gil had already started to lift his leg, so he only kicked the calf muscle. It was a good hit, though, and Gil winced as it landed. The instructor backed off and held up both hands, grinning like a madman.

"Finally!" Gil said, holding one hand to his side as he reached down to rub his calf with the other. He spat his mouth guard into one hand. "Finally, you throw a punch like you mean it. And the kick was solid, too. Glad today wasn't boot day. Good job, man." He straightened. "Whatever it was that got you to do that, remember that. That's what I need from you every time we face off, okay?"

Chaim nodded.

"Good. Now, do it again to prove it wasn't a fluke." Gil put the mouth guard back in and raised his hands. Chaim raised his own hands and began moving. The anger still flowed, and he felt lighter than usual.

It became easier the next couple of weeks for Chaim to call up the anger. Toward the end, he wasn't even feeling the anger. It just jazzed his body, but left his mind clear. So maybe it was just adrenaline.

He mentioned it to Dr. Hurwitz, and ended up regretting it almost immediately, because the doctor and Marta interrupted his next practice session to draw blood. By now his skin was getting tough enough that it was hard to get the needle through, even with the larger-bore reusable titanium needles they had had to start using. They were more painful than the usual one-use disposable kits, as well. Those kits were a topic of dark humor in the lab now.

The frequent anger—if that was what it was—was leaving him edgy. Or at least, he thought it was the anger. But maybe—maybe it was just part of becoming a vampire. Maybe it was just how he was going to be as he continued his "conversion." Maybe . . .

That thought didn't give him much comfort. Despite

Mordechai's assurances that he didn't have to become a monster...despite the example that Mordechai set before him...despite Rabbi Avram's assurance that he would not lose his place among the sons of Abraham because of what he had already become, what he was continuing to become, that fear still lurked in the dark corners of his mind. And it seemed like the dark corners were growing, and becoming darker.

What caused Chaim to turn a corner was a chance discovery. He stepped out into the hallway after a session with Gil, and something teased his nose that he hadn't smelled here before. "What's that?"

"What's what?" Gil replied, massaging the left side of his rib cage where Chaim had landed a solid blow a few minutes earlier.

"That smell." Chaim started down the hallway. "It smells like...chlorine." He started trotting, leaving Gil and Marta behind. He paused at the cross-corridor to sniff, turned to his left, and kept moving. That corridor ended in a T-junction with another corridor, where another sniff took him to the right for about twenty feet. He stopped in front of a double door, and took a deep breath. "Water...and chlorine." He opened the door.

Marta and Gil found Chaim standing on the edge of a large swimming pool. "Why didn't you tell me this was here?" he said, not turning from the water.

"It was shut down when Covid hit," Marta said to his back. "It's been empty for almost two years. It wasn't approved for reopening until right before you came, and it turned out one of the circulation pumps had to be replaced. They finished filling it with water yesterday, and started the chemicals this morning. It should be swimmable..."

"Now," Chaim said, stripping off his shirt. A moment later his shoes and slacks joined his shirt on the concrete and he made a near splashless dive into the water.

"Well, I was going to say tomorrow, but it's probably okay now," Marta said to Gil.

"At least he wasn't commando under the slacks."

They watched Chaim swim for a couple of laps. "The kid's a pretty good swimmer," Gil said.

"He's from California," Marta said. "What did you expect?"

Gil laughed. "I'll see him tomorrow." He turned and left.

Chaim did three more laps before stopping, exulting in the feeling of knifing through the water. When he had finished, he came up to the side of the pool and rested his forearms on it to look at Marta. He had what felt like the biggest smile he'd ever had on his face.

"Boy, that feels good," he said, shaking his head and flinging waterdrops all the way to where Marta sat on a bench against the side wall. "I wish I'd known this was here. I'd have been down here nagging the workers along. Olympic sized?"

"Olympic length," Mara said, "but only half the width—five lanes instead of ten." She smiled at him. "I forgot until just now you're from California. Between the ocean and every other house having a pool, I imagine you lived in the water." Her voice sounded a little envious.

Chaim shook his head. "Not in my neighborhood. There were usually only one or two pools on each block, and I didn't do the ocean thing."

"Why not?"

"First of all, no time. Between a full load at school

and then Torah studies and later Talmud studies, I didn't have the time for the ocean."

"And?" she said.

"And?" Chaim repeated, looking at her. She frowned at him, and he relented. "Let's just say I wasn't a good fit with the ocean crowd: too short, too pale, too plump, too big a nerd, and last but not least, too Jewish. Saturday was prime beach and surfing time, and I'm Orthodox, so I didn't get out then."

"Ah. But there's got to be more to it than that. You're too good at swimming for it to be just an every once in a while thing for you. My cousin did competitive swimming. I know what good looks like. You're good."

"Yeah, well, that would be my mom,"

"Your mom?"

Chaim's mouth quirked. "Yeah. A Jewish mother, right? Well, around fourth grade she got all worried that I wasn't developing correctly and I needed more socializing, that school and shul weren't enough. I'm sure she got it from Oprah's Book Club, or something like that. She talked to her friends, to our rabbi, and to her therapist, and somehow arrived at her own consensus that Boy Scouts were the answer. So she told my dad to get me in Boy Scouts."

He placed his palms on the surface and pushed up, almost shooting himself out of the pool to land on his feet. "Dad refused, saying that I didn't need it and I shouldn't waste time on it." A sort of grin crossed Chaim's face. "I remember when that happened. I think that was the first time Dad had told Mom she couldn't have something she was serious about. It was January when she asked, and for the next three weeks it was like Idaho was camped in our living room. Just cold, man."

Chaim shook his head. "You know, I thought my dad was a smart man, but taking that long to give in was pretty stupid on his part. You don't mess with a Jewish mother in full-bore mama mode. Even I know that. So he finally gave in, and I started Scouts. It was a troop made up mostly of Jewish kids sponsored by one of the synagogues in town. The high school swimming coach was our assistant scoutmaster, and every single one of us got a merit badge in swimming. Most of them got drafted for the school swim team."

Marta laughed. "Did you like Boy Scouts?"

Chaim shrugged. "It was okay. I made almost all of my merit badges on science and technology stuff, and some urban topics. Think I only did one campout, and was thoroughly miserable the whole time. Made Eagle Scout at fourteen."

"Wow," Marta said. "That was fast. Didn't that used to be something only older scouts did?"

Chaim shook his head. "Nah, not these days. The Eagle Scout thing is still the premium rank, so they want as many kids to get it as they can. So they have started telling parents to get their kids to Eagle by the time they're fourteen, because after that they discover girls, and too many of them lose interest."

Marta laughed again, and shook her head. "Darned girls, messing everything up." She grinned at Chaim. "So, did you make your Jewish mother happy?"

"Not really. I learned to work and cooperate with others, sure, but I can't say I made any close friends. I'm connected with a few of them in social media, but I don't hang out with any of them now. Haven't since I made Eagle and left the program." He bent over to pick up his clothes and shoes.

"Wet underwear is no substitute for a pair of swim trunks, you know," Marta said with a deadpan expression.

Chaim looked over at her in surprise. Marta was ordinarily all business, and the comment was a little more personal than she usually made. He felt a bit of a blush on his face, which surprised him. He'd not felt that kind of emotional reaction much in the weeks since his life-changing encounter. "You've seen more of me than this," he tried to joke back. It left him a bit uncomfortable.

"You do realize you've opened a new door, don't you?" Marta asked. He looked at her with raised eyebrows. "I mean, Dr. Hurwitz is going to develop a whole new battery of tests for this, you know."

Chaim groaned. "He will, won't he?" He shook his head again, then looked up with a gleam in his eyes. "Good luck with getting the EKG patches to stick to my skin in the water, though."

Chaim didn't care if the team came up with more tests or if they wanted him to swim with EKG sensors glued to his body. Just being able to swim frequently helped him level out. It was something he had done well before the "conversion," and the fact that he could still do it well helped him feel like maybe things would be okay.

After a couple of assessments of his metabolism and exertion during swimming, the team decided to not pursue those any further. The results mirrored those from tracking his running, and the waterproof wireless sensors were not inexpensive. Chaim was just as glad. The adhesive for the waterproof sensors made his new-model vampire skin itch. The team actually did more tests about that than they did for the swimming. There was a running joke about "vampire repellent" for a few days.

After that, things settled to a form of normal, except that Chaim wasn't quite as tense as he had been. And now, if no one could find Chaim, they looked in the swimming pool first.

Chaim replayed the last part of his initial conversation with Gil in his mind many times, usually just after a grueling workout. It wasn't particularly satisfying that Gil turned out to be a fine predictor of the near future. Tired-sore-and-cranky pretty well described Chaim's state of being most of those days—even with the vampire-adjusted body and metabolism—because it turned out that Gil hit like a mallet. He didn't seem to be pulling his punches any in the training, and Chaim just had to absorb it and take more. The reminder that "It is what it is" became Chaim's mantra as he started counting down the days to the end of the contract.

The last two weeks of the training were just in street clothes: Docker-style slacks and athletic shoes or the Doc Marten boots. With his natural strength, Chaim had no problems with the extra weight, and by that time he'd had enough practice to adjust to the feel of the clothes and shoes. Even with the new calmer Chaim, he still had plenty of anger and adrenaline to fuel his practices. He was still having to restrain his reactions, even so. Apparently he was doing a good enough job of that, since Gil never said anything.

Chaim's countdown was at four days when he neared the open door to the usual conference room one night. He stopped several steps down the hallway, because the room was occupied, and they were talking about him.

"We've gotten a baseline about exertion and duration from your workouts that really extends and enhances our datasets." That was Dr. Hurwitz. "That is almost invaluable to us."

"I'm glad to have been of help"—that was Gil—"but I'm not sure you know what you have, here, Dr. Hurwitz. Can I give you my perspective?"

"Sure."

Chaim leaned against the wall in the hall. He wasn't going anywhere until this was over.

"First, once I got him engaged, this kid's ability to focus is incredible. I've had very few students like him, and I've taught some of the best in Israel. He learns fast—I show him a move, and in three days it's committed to muscle memory. He makes mistakes—he can't help but make mistakes at this stage of his training—but he doesn't repeat them. He's dangerous now. When he has more experience, he'll be lethal. When he has a lot more experience, he'll be Death on two feet.

"Second, I don't know what you've done to him. He's hard, physically, but he's as fast as anyone I've ever worked with. And I can't find his limits. I've tried to wear him down, but he wears me down instead.

"Third, I don't know what you're doing with him, but whether you realize it or not this kid could be a super soldier. I'm sure you have plans for him. If Mordechai is involved, I'm not sure I want to know or should know what those plans are. But please, if something like that is possible, please tell Israel about it. If he can be cloned, or if his training can be duplicated, whatever. Because the IDF would pay any amount to have even a company of that kid's equivalents. It might actually keep the nation alive for a few generations.

"Fourth, whatever comes of this, I hope someone instilled ethics and morality in that kid, because I really don't want to think about what he'll be capable of if you didn't."

Chaim swallowed at that. And what Gil didn't know probably made the observation even more pointed.

"Dr. Mendel and Mr. Zalman haven't discussed any plans with us," Dr. Hurwitz said.

"Of course they haven't said anything . . . yet." Gil's sarcasm was thick in his voice. "But the kid showed me a *Gibborim* medallion like the one I've seen Mordechai wearing, and Mordechai arranged the training. I've worked with Mordechai. I've worked with people who worked with him during the Six-Day War and the Yom Kippur War. I've talked with people who worked with him during the 1956 Sinai War and the first Arab War in 1948 and 1949. And I've heard stories about what he supposedly did in World War II. So I'm absolutely certain that Mordechai has a plan. That man wouldn't sneeze or fart without a plan. Whether he's even told himself yet that he has a plan, I don't know, but he has a plan. Count on it."

Chaim suppressed a rueful chuckle. Mordechai had said that Gil was sharp and would pick up on even the tiniest pieces if given an opportunity. He was right.

"How much longer will you be with us, Mr. Haleva?"

"My contract is for three months, and it's just about up. I could stay a few days longer if someone was willing to pay my rates, but I have to be back in Tel Aviv absolutely no later than ten days from now. So one way or another, I'll be gone soon. And I really need to talk to Mordechai at least once before I leave. Do you know if or when he'll be back?"

"He was supposed to be back to check on things a couple of days ago." That was Marta. "We haven't had a word from him."

"But that's not too unusual," Dr. Hurwitz said dryly. "He and Dr. Mendel both tend to have very fluid schedules, you might say."

"I can imagine." Gil's tone was even drier.

"So is the training finished?" Marta again.

"Basically," Gil responded. "He's learned the techniques and the drill. Now he just needs experience, and I can't give that to him. I can't stay that long, and you're not paying me enough for that. But tomorrow night I'm going to give him his graduation exercise."

Chaim's forehead creased at that statement. Gil's tone indicated he wasn't smiling when he said that, so somehow Chaim doubted that it would be what his dorm buddies would have called a party.

CHAPTER 8

THAT THOUGHT WAS STILL RUNNING THROUGH Chaim's mind the next evening when Gil came by the office he was using.

"Time to go."

Chaim shut down the computer and finished his bottle of Perrier. "So, what's on the agenda tonight?"

"Something special." Gil led the way down the hallway and around a corner. "Something off campus, so to speak."

Before Chaim could respond, they entered the main foyer to the building, and Gil halted so suddenly that Chaim had to dodge to his right to avoid running into him.

"Zalman!" Gil exclaimed. Chaim could hear the surprise in his voice.

Mordechai straightened from where he was leaning back against the wall by the outside door with his arms folded across his chest. "Haleva. Chaim." He nodded to both of them.

"What are you doing here?"

That sardonic grin appeared on the older man's

face. "Oh, I was coming in today anyway, and when Dr. Hurwitz mentioned something about you throwing a graduation exercise for Chaim, I just moved a little faster. Knowing the kinds of parties you throw, Gil, I can't miss this."

"Okay, but I don't think my little rental car will fit all three of us," Gil said. "The back seat isn't much more than a package shelf."

"My car will," Mordechai said.

"Fine. You drive. Lead the way," Gil waved at the door.

Mordechai's grin broadened, and he turned toward the door. Chaim followed, and once outside took a deep breath of the outside air. It was the first time he'd been outside in close to two weeks. Gil had been keeping him busy.

Once they were all in the car, Chaim in the back seat, Mordechai looked over at Gil. "Where to?"

"Lyon Academy. You know it?"

For answer, Mordechai started the car and put it in gear.

The research center was some distance outside of Chattanooga. Chaim watched the trees go by in the darkness. It didn't take too long to get to I-40, where they headed for town. He didn't pay attention to street names, but in maybe a quarter of an hour they took an exit and went down a side street to a freestanding building next to a retail strip building that featured a used book store and a comic book shop sandwiched in between a Korean BBQ restaurant at one end, a sushi place at the other, and a mom-and-pop taco shop in the middle. He smiled at the thought that the shops were closed but the food places were busy.

The sushi place in particular pulled at him. Good sushi was one of his favorite foods—or it had been. It was popular enough in California that there were places that were certified kosher. Since he'd been changed, it wasn't possible for him any longer, and it was one of the things he missed most about eating.

There were a few other cars in the parking lot in front of the building, but Mordechai was able to park in front of the main entrance. The sign mounted above the door announced LYON ACADEMY in big white letters on a blue background with heraldic lions in white on each end. Chaim got out of the car, still not sure what was going on. He followed the others inside, and it immediately became clear that he was in a dojo or training facility. Mats were scattered around the floor and in some cases hung from the wall. Several things clicked in his mind.

His thought was confirmed when Gil handed him a set of fighting gloves. "Here. You're going to need these." Chaim pulled them on, flexing his fingers where they protruded from the leather.

There were several other men grouped near a counter at one side of the room, a couple dressed in sweats but most in shorts and tees. Gil walked up to one of them, a blocky middle-aged but fit black guy in a red polo shirt and black shorts, and stuck out his hand. "Hey, Rob, thanks for hosting this."

"No problem, Gil." They shook hands. "So, introduce us to your boy, here."

Gil waved a hand at Chaim. "This is Chaim Caan. I've been working with him for three months now. Chaim, this is Rob Foreman, owner, manager, and teacher here at Lyon Academy."

Rob offered his hand. "Good to meet you, Chaim," he said as they shook hands. "Let me introduce you to the rest of the guys.

"First, this is Bob Martin." Bob was a burly white guy who wasn't a whole lot taller than Chaim. He had a rather crooked nose. "He's the local light heavyweight MMA champ for the area." Bob flashed a grin and they shook hands.

"This is Eric Chert"—another muscular white guy, this time a couple of inches over six feet with a shaved head—"and his partner Aaron Valdez." Aaron was built much like Eric, and likewise had a shaved head, but his skin was light-coffee colored. Both men looked to be hard as nails, but were pleasant as they shook hands. "They're both cops, and both do tae kwon do.

"And last but definitely not least," Rob said with a smile, "this is Gabriel Luis Silva Almeida."

The final guy was not much larger than Chaim, with pale skin, coal black hair, and an infectious grin. He didn't wince as Rob recited his name, so he must have gotten it close to right. "Just call me Gabe," he said with a slight accent as they shook hands.

"Finally, someone close to my own size," Chaim responded with a grin of his own.

"As you might guess from the name, Gabe teaches Brazilian jiujitsu here in town," Rob concluded. He looked over at Gil. "Gil, you called this meeting. You want to get it started?"

"Right." Gil moved forward a step or so. "I said a minute ago that I've been working with Chaim for about three months now. What I've been teaching him is my own version of Krav Maga." A couple of the others' faces stiffened a bit at that. "This isn't the

US street version of Krav Maga. I'm an instructor for the Israeli Defense Force, and I teach mostly their special ops people. So what he's been learning is a bit different from what the average Krav Maga school here teaches."

Chaim looked around. The men by the counter now looked more interested than they had when Gil had started.

"Chaim's done pretty well..."

Chaim almost snorted at Gil's statement, given what he'd overheard the previous day.

"...but he's short on experience, especially against other combat systems, so I asked Rob if he could find a few guys to work out with him tonight to give him a feel for what it's like to come up against other styles. He's good, but like I said, he's short on experience. Did Rob tell you the deal?"

Heads nodded. "Five hundred dollars each for a two-hour gig," Aaron said. He shrugged. "I'm up for it." Heads nodded again.

"Five hundred each, plus medical expenses if anybody needs it," Gil confirmed. "This won't be contest rules. This is street rules, except no throat punches or eye gouging, and preferably no broken bones."

"Yeah," Eric said. "We've got to remain fit for duty."

"Speak for yourself," Aaron said with a grin. "I start my vacation tomorrow. That five hundred will come in right handy. You just make sure your cup's on right." He placed his hand on his groin and pulled up.

Eric punched him in the shoulder. "*Hijo de puta.*"

"*Tu madre.*"

Even Chaim was smiling. Spanish invective was common in California, after all.

"Right." Gil reclaimed their attention. "Five-minute rounds. Two cycles of them. Then we'll see what's what after that. Bob, would you take the lead?"

Bob's grin returned. "Sure." He stripped off his tee and stepped onto the mat, knocking his fists together.

Chaim was wearing a close-fitting black tee and black slacks, so he didn't have anything to remove. He kept his athletic shoes on. He looked over at where Mordechai was standing with a bag next to his feet, to see him hold one hand flat at waist level for just a moment. *Right. Restraint is called for.* He sighed before slipping in his mouth guard and stepping up on the mat himself, opposite the big man, settling his weight above his feet, waiting.

Gil stepped between them. "Remember: no throat punches, no eye gouging, no broken bones." He put his hand out, held it for a moment, then dropped it with, "Begin!" and stepped back.

Bob tried a bull rush while looping a roundhouse right. Chaim slipped to one side, ducking, and hammered a punch under the short ribs as Bob went by. He was almost tagged by a high kick that Bob launched into out of the spin he made after Chaim hit him, but backpedaled to avoid that as well.

Chaim's adrenaline had been rising from the moment he had entered the room. By now it was sizzling in his system. He felt it as an almost electric charge. He could have stood and traded punches with the bigger man, but Mordechai's instruction was restraint, so he ducked and slipped around the mat, blocking punches when they got close enough and throwing enough punches of his own to sting the other man.

Twice Bob tried to take him down. Chaim managed

to block both of them, the second time receiving a punch to the side of his head as he broke away that made even his head ring a bit. He heard some of the other guys talking about it, but his focus remained on Bob. He began to get a feel for Bob's patterns, especially after he tried another one of those spinning kicks. The second one was so fast it almost nailed Chaim. But the five minutes ran out before he could move on it.

There was no break. Bob stepped off the mat and Eric Chert stepped on, moving forward methodically. Chaim blocked three punches and a kick before he could throw his own first punch.

Eric was all strikes with fewer kicks, with the occasional elbow thrown in for good measure. No grappling. More of his hits landed than Bob's, but that was at least partly because he was more precise and had a longer reach. Chaim was reduced for this first round to hammering his arms and legs while he tried to figure out how Eric moved. His frustration began to mount. He took more hits than he landed, but nothing as hard as that hit to the head Bob had made. He wasn't sure if Bob was just that much stronger, or if Eric wasn't punching to his max.

Five minutes passed. Eric stepped off, Aaron stepped on. He just stood there, hands up before him, and waited. Chaim circled him. Aaron just turned in place, waiting.

Finally Chaim threw a punch, stepping forward as he did so, only to run into a front kick to the chest that stopped him cold. Aaron's height differential and longer legs were obviously going to be a problem.

Aaron proceeded to give a tutorial on the art of

kicking. High, low, left, right, front, side—they came from every direction, with enough punches added to the mix to complicate matters. Chaim was spending most of his focus and energy blocking, and his frustration continued to grow because way more kicks were getting through than he wanted, even with his toughness. Toward the end of the time period he abandoned the dodging gambit and started absorbing the kicks so he could get close enough to begin throwing punches at Aaron's thighs, not so much to block the kicks as to punish him. It gratified him to see signs of a limp by the end.

He took that gratification into the final first round. Gabe bounced onto the mat as soon as Aaron's period ended and rushed Chaim before his attention had fully shifted. His next conscious thought was that fighting Gabe was like fighting a hybrid of an insane monkey and an angry octopus. It didn't seem to matter what he did, there was a hand holding on to him or a foot wrapped around a knee or an ankle. Gabe managed three takedowns in the first two minutes, which was three more than the other guys combined. Chaim managed to keep moving and break free of them, but it wasn't easy. None of his techniques worked. None of his strikes were landing. He almost felt useless, he seemed to be having so little effect on the other fighter. His mouth guard was being punished by the clenching of his teeth in anger. By the end of that five-minute round, he was breathing hard, which was something even Gil hadn't managed to do to him.

"Five-minute break," Gil announced. Chaim froze for a moment, then lowered his hands and stepped off the mat. He stood to one side and rolled his head around in circles and shrugged his shoulders back and forth, taking stock of his bruises. Even as a vampire, he had more than a few, the worst of which was the headshot Bob had given him. He spat out his mouth guard and ran his tongue around behind his teeth, checking for looseness and soreness. Nothing, so the mouth guard had done its job. He looked at the others, standing there talking to each other and swinging their arms and bouncing on their toes to keep loose. He felt his eyebrows draw down and his lips press into a thin line. The tension—the compression—the overload of emotion and adrenaline—whatever it was—had him feeling like two pounds of dynamite being forced into a one-pound mold.

Mordechai stepped over beside him and turned to face the wall they were in front of. "Not bad," he murmured. Chaim shot a sidelong glance at him, but said nothing. "But having to choke everything down is killing you, isn't it?"

"Yeah," Chaim responded, shifting his feet.

"I thought so." Mordechai sounded almost smug to Chaim's ear. "Release the aggression."

"What?" Chaim turned to look at the older vampire. "I thought I . . ."

"No, don't release the speed or the strength. Release the aggression. Go on the attack. Take the hits and wade through the kicks, but take the fight to them. You can be a touch faster, maybe, but that's all. But that will be enough."

Chaim had turned to face forward again, but a quick glance at Mordechai showed that thin-lipped, cutting smile. Okay. Mordechai wanted aggression? He'd get aggression.

Bob stepped onto the mat again, this time without the rush. Chaim had an idea what was coming, so he traded a few punches with Bob, then backed up a step or so. Sure enough, Bob launched a roundhouse kick with his right leg, but this time instead of ducking it Chaim turned into it and drove a knuckle-punch into the arch of the foot.

Chaim felt a flash of satisfaction when he saw the wince cross Bob's face. At that same moment he swept Bob's left leg out from under him before he could regain his balance. He pushed Bob so that he headed face-first for the ground, instantly following with a knee between the shoulder blades that forced Bob to the mat. A split second later Chaim hammered a fist into the back of Bob's head. The solid *thump* resounded in the room and forced a grunt from Bob with echoes of sympathy from the others.

Bob slapped the mat twice and Chaim rolled off of him, only to see him rise with blood flowing from both nostrils. Rob tossed a rolled-up towel to Bob, who grabbed it and applied it to his face, holding a thumb up to Chaim while Rob took another towel to clean the mat. One down, three to go.

Chaim's head felt like it was fizzing as he pivoted to face Eric. Eric was moving a little bit slower, perhaps trying to adjust to what he had just seen. Chaim didn't even think about it, just moved forward like a machine, ignoring Eric's punches to step forward fast enough to get inside Eric's guard and hammer his abs relentlessly. His lips peeled back in a snarl when he felt Eric flinch back, and he hooked Eric's ankle and sent him down. Two and a half seconds later he had the arm bar set on Eric's right arm. He felt Eric try to power out of it, but just pulled a little harder on the wrist he was holding. Eric slapped the mat on the other side, and Chaim released it, rolling to his feet to face Aaron.

Aaron must be a good poker player, Chaim decided, because his face didn't show anything of what he must be thinking. Chaim, on the other hand, felt like he was grinning like an idiot even with the mouth guard filling his mouth. He was almost trembling; he wanted to charge straight ahead and just overpower Aaron, but he couldn't show his hand yet. Not yet.

Chaim forced himself to do a changeup. He didn't charge right away, instead dancing in and out to throw punches, and catching a few in return, including a hard right hand to the face that left him blinking tears for a moment.

After several exchanges like that, Aaron reacted with a front kick as Chaim dropped a shoulder like he was going to step in again. Chaim ducked under the kick and pushed off hard to come up underneath the leg while at the same time throwing a punch into Aaron's groin followed by a fist to the head. He pushed away and Aaron collapsed to the mat. He kind of felt bad about what he had done, but he was already spinning to face Gabe.

Gabe was rushing toward Chaim, right hand leading the way. Chaim moved forward, turned a bit and did an arm-wrap takedown, following around behind as Gabe started turning. He was just that bit faster to snake his left hand under Gabe's left armpit and up to clamp on the back of his neck as he wrapped his legs around the other man's waist. Gabe rolled hard to his right to try and break free, but Chaim went with the roll and in the process ran his right arm up under Gabe's right armpit and brought his hand up to lock in the full nelson, ending up on his back as he did so. A split second later his heels pushed down and separated Gabe's thighs, splitting his legs and reducing his leverage.

"Your neck breaks," Chaim said in a loud tone as Gabe strained against the hold, "in five . . . four . . . three . . ."

CHAPTER 9

"YIELD!" GABE YELLED HOARSELY, UNABLE TO SLAP the mat.

Chaim released his holds and helped push Gabe to his feet, only to be grabbed in a fierce hug by the Brazilian. "Good fight, man," Gabe said as he pushed back from him. "You're the first person to put me in a full nelson since I was fourteen. I've got to figure out how you did it to see how to get out of it."

"Thanks," Chaim said, grinning in triumph. "You gave me more trouble than anyone else."

Gabe beamed at the compliment and turned away as Bob pushed forward, still holding a bloody towel in his left hand as he held out his right. "Great fight, man," the bigger man enthused. His already misshapen nose was definitely pointing in a new direction.

"Sorry I broke your nose," Chaim said as they shook hands.

"Nah, not to worry. Not the first time, obviously." Bob grinned and laid a finger on the abused appendage. "Besides, I'm officially retiring this week. Getting married in a few months, and my girlfriend wants me to get my nose fixed. Now I've got an excuse to do it without looking like a wuss."

Gil pushed forward long enough to hand Bob a card. "Send your bills here. We'll take care of them."

"You don't have to," Bob said with another grin, "but I'm not going to argue with you. Great fight," he said again to Chaim as he turned away.

Aaron was next, smiling as he held out one hand and held the other over his groin for a moment. "Good fight, man. You're like Mr. Machine out there. But I know one thing—if I spar with you again, I'm wearing two cups."

"Sorry about that," Chaim said, taking his hand for the shake.

"No, you're not. And it was within tonight's rules." Aaron's face was serious now. "Always push the envelope, man. Always take it to the edge."

"I told you not to depend on those flashy kicks, dude," Eric said as he pushed forward with a backhand to Aaron's shoulder.

"Yeah, *pendejo*, you just keep telling yourself that," Aaron said as he moved back toward the counter.

"Some righteous fight, there," Eric said with a solid handclasp. "Dynamite moves, that second round. From what I saw tonight, you may not always win your first fight with someone, but you'll damn sure take him the second time. And you," he said, turning to Gil, "if you can take a grass-green newbie to this in three months, it's no wonder the Israeli army kicks ass. Seriously, if you ever get this way again, I'd pay good money to sit in a masters' class under you, or even take some private lessons."

"Not this trip," Gil said. "I'm flying back to Israel shortly. But if I'm this way again, it could happen."

"Seriously," Eric said, shaking hands with the instructor. "Please. Call Rob. Any day, any time, even if it's only for an hour. I really want to work with you."

"We'll see," Gil said.

As Eric headed back over toward the counter where the rest of the guys were gathering their stuff, Gil looked around. "Any chance I could get a couple of you to do a two-on-one with Chaim? Just for a few minutes?"

Aaron looked back. "If he promises not to hit me in the balls again."

Gil looked at Chaim with a grin. Chaim nodded.

Aaron looked at Eric. "You up for it?"

"I am if you are."

"Let's do it."

The two of them set their bags down and walked back to the mat. They took up positions at the far end of the mat with Eric at twelve o'clock and Aaron at three o'clock and stood waiting.

Chaim looked at Mordechai, but didn't get a sign, so he shrugged his shoulders, flexed his hands a couple of times, and stepped onto the mat at about the eight o'clock position. Immediately the others stepped forward together side by side, shuffling not in unison, but enough together that they presented a consistent front to him. He stepped back in reflex, then realized that they had almost forced him into the corner of the mat. He stopped in place, but before he could move again they were on him.

Eric was throwing left jabs at his face in rapid-fire mode. None of them hit his face; most of them glanced off his glove or shoulder, but they were always there. Aaron was alternating heavy punches at his gut and his head, all of which were landing somewhere, and all of which hurt. It was impossible to focus on two at once, he decided in distraction, and his eyes shifted as he prepared to deal with Aaron first, as he was getting tired of the hard hits. Just as he was about to launch off, Eric delivered a right-hand bomb to Chaim's head. He caught it coming out of the corner of his eye. He wasn't able to duck it entirely, so he did get hit hard, but it didn't hit square on. It did, however, about tear his left ear off his head—or that's what it felt like. And it knocked his head into the path of one of Aaron's punches, so he got rocked twice in less than a second.

Feeling something akin to desperation, Chaim launched forward and burst between them, probably showing more speed and strength than Mordechai wanted, but he had to get out of that corner. He reached the other end of the mat and spun on the ball of one foot to face the others.

With a quick headshake, Chaim started back toward them, trending toward Eric. Two steps away he darted toward Aaron, only to shift back to Eric next step. He ducked one punch, slapped another aside, and drove his right hand into Eric's solar plexus.

Feeling Aaron behind him, Chaim threw his left hand behind his head as he ducked and spun, feeling a punch glance off his hand.

There were several seconds of flurried movement and punches as Chaim drove inside. He managed to hook Aaron's ankle and send him down. There were several more seconds of movements that ended with Chaim on Aaron's back, legs around his waist and left arm wrapped around Aaron's throat like he was going for a rear naked choke hold. As Aaron's hands both tried to grip Chaim's arm and pull it away, Chaim brought his right hand up and over and hooked the tips of his index and ring fingers in Aaron's orbital ridges, pulling Aaron's head back.

"You're blind," he said in Aaron's ear. Aaron froze, then reached out and slapped the mat. Chaim released his holds and pushed the bigger man off of him, then rolled to his feet, breathing heavy himself, and walked over to where Eric was on his knees, one hand pressed to his sternum.

Chaim reached out and touched the knuckles of his right hand to Eric's larynx. "You're dead," he said. Eric said nothing—he probably couldn't—bur raised his other hand in acknowledgment. Chaim stuck an arm under Eric's armpit and hauled him to his feet, helped by Aaron on the other side. "Can you breathe?"

After a moment, Eric nodded. "Yeah," he husked. "Didn't quite pass out, but God, that hurt."

It was another minute or so before Eric's breathing evened out and he dropped his hand. He turned slowly and moved over to the counter to pick up his shirt and put it on. The others made way for him.

Aaron looked at Chaim. "No offense, man, but forget what I said about sparring with you again. You're scary."

That wasn't an easy thing to hear, but Chaim just nodded. There really wasn't anything he could say in response. The fact was, he wasn't really comfortable with what he had just done. The sheer violence against multiple people for the last hour had his composure broken, and the fact that he had actually done fairly well, from what he could tell, was perhaps even more disturbing.

Gil had moved over to Eric and handed him one of

the medical cards like he'd given Bob, quietly urging him to see an orthopedic doctor soon just to make sure there were no lasting effects. Then he stepped back a few steps.

"Thank you, gentlemen, for your time tonight. It is very much appreciated. Even though we didn't go the whole two hours, we've decided to pay you an additional five hundred dollars apiece. Rob will have your checks tomorrow. Again, thank you for participating, and have a good evening."

Four very solemn faces had lit up a bit at the mention of the additional money, but the only one who smiled was Bob Martin. The rest just nodded, and they gathered their stuff. A minute later, Rob, Gil, Chaim, and Mordechai were left in the gym.

"Well," Mordechai said, pushing away from the wall he had been leaning against for the last hour, "that was an interesting exhibit. But let's see what you're really capable of." He picked up the bag at his feet and tossed it to Chaim. "You should probably put that on." The older man stripped off his windbreaker to reveal a sleeveless black tee that clung to him like paint. "You're going to need it."

Chaim looked at Rob and Gil, then at Mordechai. "You sure about this?" Receiving a nod in return, he unzipped the bag and pulled out what proved to be a weighty black vest. "Armor?" he guessed.

"After a fashion," Mordechai said as he moved to the mat. "More protection than that T-shirt, anyway. Have you worked with it before?"

"No," Chaim said.

"I don't drill with armor," Gil interjected. "You know that. As far as I'm concerned, pain is a teacher."

Mordechai nodded, turned to face Chaim, and beckoned to him with one hand. Gil and Rob looked at each other, and moved over to lean back on the counter.

Chaim figured out how to put the vest on and fasten the straps. He shrugged his shoulders a couple of times to settle the weight, and swung his arms to check his freedom of movement, then stepped onto the mat.

"In the words of a certain movie"—Mordechai reached up and mimed pulling on a rope—"ding, ding."

Chaim never was certain about how long that bout lasted. He really didn't have very many concrete memories of it—just the sense that he was in the center of a storm that was battering him from every direction. Fists, knees, feet, they seemed innumerable, flicking in and out, impacting like a sledgehammer, then moving on to let the next one in.

He did know that toward the end of it, he began to develop a sense of the ... rhythm, one might say. He began to feel a bit more ... effective, maybe. The only clear memory he had came at the end, when he drove a fist past a block and put a scrape on Mordechai's cheek.

Mordechai stepped back and held up both hands. "Enough. That's good enough. Well done, Chaim." Chaim stood still for a long moment, fists still raised, eyes boring into Mordechai's, chest heaving as he fought for air like he hadn't done in months. "Well done," Mordechai repeated as he lowered his hands.

Chaim lowered his own hands and stood, still breathing hard. He began to catalog the aches and pains he was feeling. There were definitely more than he'd had when he'd started. He wasn't sure that Mordechai had left any part of him untouched except for the soles of his feet and the top of his head.

When his breathing had slowed to close to normal, Chaim looked at Mordechai. "Was that necessary?"

"Yes." Mordechai walked over to his windbreaker, picked it up and put it on. "We both need to know what you're capable of, and you need to have some idea of what your limits are."

Chaim shook his head. "Right. Let's not do that again any time soon, okay? I haven't felt like this since Mike Olmstead beat me up in seventh grade."

"Wow." That came from Rob in a quiet voice. They both looked toward the counter to see Rob standing there wide-eyed contrasted with Gil's narrowed eyes glaring at them above his folded arms.

The Israeli said something in rapid Hebrew that Chaim didn't catch.

"Speak English," Mordechai replied.

"So he's another you," Gil spat. "You knew that, and he knew that, and you didn't tell me. I don't appreciate the joke, old man."

"No joke, Gil." Mordechai shook his head. "Serious business."

"Right. If you knew he could do that, why did you have me train him like a rank newbie? And why did he hold back?"

"Because he was a rank newbie, as you put it. He wasn't lying when he said he had no training or experience. And he held back on my instruction, partly to avoid hurting you, and partly because you have no experience in training someone like him ... or me. If he'd tried to train all out, you wouldn't have known what to do and most likely would have been hurt in attempting it. No, we . . . I . . . decided to have him train at a nominal level, and then try to figure out how to ramp it up from there. Which he managed nicely toward the end of our little bout." He pointed his razor grin toward Chaim.

"So what are you? Space aliens? Fallen angels? Homo superior? The next great mutation?" Gil's voice was dark, and his expression wasn't any lighter.

"None of the above," Mordechai answered evenly. "If you need a label for a group of two, how about *homo insolitus*, which carries the sense of unusual, extraordinary, uncommon, or odd." He grinned. "Personally, I like that last one. Odd Man."

The grin switched off and the voice got serious again. "And in case there was any doubt in your mind, Gil, the events of this evening are definitely covered by the nondisclosure agreement you signed."

"Who would I tell?" Gil said bitterly. "Even the IDF wouldn't believe this. 'There are two supermen in the world, both of them Jews, but I don't know where they came from, I don't know how they got that way, and I don't know how to make more of them.'" He snorted. "I'd lose my security rating and be assigned to be a security guard at a bakery."

"Ironically, the men who created the Superman story were both Jewish," Mordechai said. "Nice story, but a bit unreal."

Pot calling the kettle black. Chaim's lips quirked.

"Regardless," Mordechai forged on, "you and Rob knew a little bit before this, and you both know a little bit more now. And neither one of you can say anything about it to anyone else, but at least you know you're not alone in that."

Gil looked over at Rob. "So where do you know this maniac from?"

Rob laughed. "He's my business partner. I always knew he was weird, but I guess he's a little weirder than I thought."

Gil's eyebrows lifted. "So how did that come about?"

"Long story, man. Long story, but if you want to hear it, I've got Kentucky bourbon, Tennessee rye, some Canadian scotch, and even some local white lightnin' back at my place."

Gil looked at Mordechai from under lowered eyebrows, then returned his gaze to Rob. "If you'll let me crash the night, I think I want to hear that story."

"Deal. It's a bachelor pad, but it's clean. Come on." Rob clapped Gil on the shoulder. "I'll get you to work tomorrow."

Gil glowered at Mordechai and Chaim one more time. "Deal."

Mordechai grinned again. "Come on, Chaim. We can tell when we're not wanted."

Chaim stripped off the vest and threw it, his gloves, and his mouth protector back in Mordechai's bag as he followed him out the door. He climbed in the front seat, but said nothing as Mordechai backed up and then drove out on the street.

The ride back to the center was quiet. Chaim was still processing the evening's experiences, and it seemed Mordechai was going to respect that. Chaim didn't stir until Mordechai parked his car and turned the engine off.

"We need to talk."

"Tomorrow," Mordechai said. "Rabbi Avram wants to give you the latest details on the tests, and there are some decisions that need to be made. So bring your questions and issues then. They may overlap with some of his and mine."

Chaim followed the other vampire into the building and made his way to his room. He stripped off his clothes and showered, even though he didn't feel dirty or sweaty. Something else the conversion had changed, it appeared. But the act of letting hot water run over his body from head to foot seemed cathartic or cleansing, and after the evening he'd had, he definitely needed that.

He'd intentionally hurt people tonight. That thought circled through and through his mind as the water poured over him. He'd never in his life expected to do that. First following his father's wishes that he become a rabbi, then his own wishes that he be a doctor...it had never been part of his thinking that he'd intentionally try to injure someone. Oh, sure, he knew that was the intent behind the training. He'd seen enough martial arts bouts on YouTube to understand that. But somehow it had all been one big kung fu movie in his mind, full of leaps and hits and people flying through the air and bouncing back up again. Until tonight.

Tonight it was his hands and feet that had made the hits and hurt Bob and Eric and Aaron. Tonight it was his mind that directed his actions. Tonight it was his will that had basically said "Do it."

He lifted up the *Gibborim* medal that hung around his neck, that never left his body anymore, and touched the *magen* to his lips. If the God that said "Let there be light"; if the God that created Adam and Eve; if the God of Abraham, Isaac, and Jacob; if the God who delivered Moses and the Hebrews from Pharaoh in the waters; if the God of David, Solomon, and Daniel—if that God had made him to be a Protector like Mordechai, then he would accept it.

"*Sh'ma, Israel, Adonai elohenu, Adonai echod.*"

Hear, O Israel, the Lord our God, the Lord is One.

Chaim touched the *magen* to his lips again, then let it drop to the chain as peace filled him.

CHAPTER 10

CHAIM LOOKED UP FROM HIS TANAKH AS RABBI Mendel and Mordechai Zalman entered the conference room. Mordechai closed the door behind him and took a seat across the table from Chaim while the rabbi sat at the end of the table.

"Catching up on your *parsha*?" The rabbi's round face had a gentle smile as he mentioned the regular Torah readings.

"Meditating on Judges, actually," Chaim said, closing the book and setting it to one side.

Mendel's eyebrows rose. "Indeed? And which passage has caught your attention?"

"The third chapter."

"Ah." Mendel's eyebrows lowered, and his smile returned. "Let me guess: Ehud ben-Gera?" His smile broadened at Chaim's nod. "A worthy subject of meditation. Let me ask you why you consider him?"

Chaim grinned a little. "The first time I read this, years ago, I thought he was kind of like James Bond." Both Mendel's and Zalman's eyebrows went up. "I mean, look at the story—he comes in with the tribute party to meet the king, he presents the tribute, and does reconnaissance on the palace. He has an assassin's dagger strapped to his right side under his cloak where no one would expect it, because he's left-handed. He comes back to the palace alone, tells the king he has a secret message for the king's ears alone, gets the king alone, stabs him, escapes, and then leads the Israelite army to victory over the Moabites. Like I said, kind of like James Bond—but it also reminds me of what Mordechai has done." He sobered for a moment, then grinned again. "And I thought it was cool that he was left-handed. I tried for the longest time to make myself left-handed. I can do a lot left-handed now. I'm not ambidextrous, but I can do a lot."

"Hmm," Mendel said. "A worthy subject of meditation, indeed—and a worthy protector. I commend you for your studies. But"—he opened the folder that lay before him on the table—"we have things both practical and personal that need to be discussed now."

Chaim said nothing, simply waited as the rabbi sorted through the pages in the folder.

"Here we are." Mendel selected a page, and held it before him. "So, Dr. Hurwitz and his team are confident that they have a better understanding of what vampirism does in a human body as a result of being able to study you these last three months. They have decided that it does not fit the classical model of a disease. Their current analogical model is that of a computer virus that invades a system and reprograms it."

"Great," Chaim muttered. "My life is a bad science-fiction movie."

"Perhaps not so bad as that," Mendel said gently.

He looked at the paper again. "In addition to the metabolic and functional changes we talked about in our last discussion, they have determined that significant changes happened in the hormones and enzymes of your body.

"First, the easy stuff. Your hair color and eye color appear to be unchanged. Your fingerprints and footprints still match your records. On the other hand, your testosterone levels are significantly higher. This is apparently connected with your body's rebuilding itself to be harder and tougher. This may or may not be connected with the anger issues that I understand Mordechai spoke to you about. Dr. Hurwitz and his team say that the consistently higher testosterone levels would be expected to have a consistent emotional effect in all areas of a personality, not just in sporadic anger spikes. What you demonstrated and what Mordechai has told them about does not seem to be the emotional effect that high testosterone levels produce in norm—that is, regular men."

"You can say 'normal,' sir. I've accepted that I'm now abnormal in just about every way." Chaim's voice was level. He was actually a little proud of how calm he felt.

"As you say. So there may be a connection there, but they can't define it or prove it if there is. At least, not yet.

"In comparison, however, your production of estradiol—estrogen, in other words—has reduced somewhat in actual amount and a lot in comparison to the rise in testosterone. They're not sure yet what effect this will have, either, other than affecting your body fat levels."

Mendel put that page down and picked up another. "They've determined that much of the reason for the shift in diet requirement..."

"Drinking of blood, you mean?"

"Yes... much of the reason for the shift to consuming blood is because your body's generation of dietary enzymes has significantly changed. The enzymes that break down fats and proteins have almost disappeared from your system. This is probably related to the fact that your body fat has dropped below measurable levels." Mendel looked at him. "Long term, they're not sure of the implications of that, but looking at Mordechai, you can see it's not necessarily going to be an issue." After a moment, he resumed. "And the enzymes that break down carbohydrates are much, much lower than normal. Your body now needs your nutrition to basically be predigested into very simple forms: glucose and hemoglobin and associated minerals. It's very efficient in using those once it takes them in, but it can't take much of anything else."

"Except the *magen* bars."

"Except those, and don't ask the good doctor about them," Mendel said with a small smile, "because he does not have an explanation for them, and that irritates him."

"Heh." Chaim returned the smile.

"This means that your liver has changed what it does, because it now produces no bile."

Chaim sat up. "So my gall bladder..."

"Has shrunk to the size of a single peanut, and may well atrophy altogether. And as a side note, your appendix seems to have disappeared.

"Related to that," Mendel said, picking up a third

page, "the sunlight sensitivity is now suspected to be at least related to—if not caused by—changes in liver function. The liver normally breaks down excessive amounts of hemoglobin, and when it doesn't, normal people develop jaundice, which usually expresses as yellowish skin and light sensitivity."

Chaim raised his hand and looked at it, then at Mendel. "No jaundice."

"It's a theory at the moment, Chaim. They'll need more time and more samples to verify it. But it does fit with the fact that you're taking in a lot more iron, which is probably going to your bones, cartilage, muscle, and skin. But it's not all going to your structure. Hence, your urine."

"Yeah. I look like I'm pissing liquid rust."

"Not far off," Mendel acknowledged. "And your feces will no longer float."

"No kidding," Chaim said. "I swear the last bowel movement I had went *thunk* when it hit the bottom of the toilet."

Mendel smiled at that. "Remind me to tell you some time of the nurse who had to administer barium enemas."

"Heh. But it's weird only doing a dump every three days or so. Is that going to be normal?"

"Two samples doesn't give us much of a baseline, Chaim, but from what Mordechai says, probably. Remember, you're not taking in the mass quantities of fiber that you used to ingest."

"True. And it still stinks, but it stinks differently."

"They noted that at the bottom of the page," Mendel said with a mischievous grin.

Chaim snorted. "So what else?"

Another page. "Your pancreas is still functioning, at least partially. Production of pancreatic lipase, one of the fat breakers, has pretty much ceased, but production of deoxyribonuclease and ribonuclease, the DNA and RNA breakers, is still up. And it's still producing at least trace amounts of insulin, although you metabolize the glucose from the blood so quickly they're really not sure it comes into play."

Page five. "The thymus gland appears to actually be functioning a little above the normal human level, but they're not sure if that's a new normal or if it's an effect of all the other changes and it will settle back down after all the changes are done. If it remains elevated, you may well not have to worry about cancers in your new existence."

A glance back down at the page. "The thyroid gland appears to be functioning normally. They're not sure why." Mendel smiled a bit. "Another topic to avoid with Dr. Hurwitz. As I mentioned, he dislikes not having answers."

"Got it."

"And adrenaline appears to be a bit higher than normal but otherwise unchanged." Mendel nodded at that, and laid the page down.

"Could that be connected to the anger?" Chaim asked.

Mendel looked at the page. "No comments about that one way or the other. We'll ask." He jotted a note down.

Sixth page. "Last but not least, the prostate."

Chaim sat up straight. Any male would be concerned about this information. He waited, but Mendel took his time to address the subject. Finally, he sighed, which caused a knot to form in the pit of Chaim's stomach.

"Major changes have been and perhaps still are taking place in the prostate."

Mendel paused again.

After a moment, Chaim said, "What? Is it still there? Does it still work?" He was sure that it did. He had produced sperm for them, after all. But Mendel's manner was beginning to frighten him.

"It . . . is still there," Mendel said, staring at the paper, "if somewhat smaller than before. And it does seem to still produce testosterone, semen, and sperm. But the last two . . ."

More silence.

"Am I sterile?"

Mendel shook his head. "They don't know. They do know that your spermata now appear to uniformly feature the Y chromosome. No X chromosomes have appeared in their tests. And they do know that the sperm, while reduced in number, are very active—*very* active—to the point that they fear that any one of the sperm will rupture any egg cell it penetrates."

Chaim swallowed. He opened his mouth to ask another question, but Mendel held up his hand to forestall him.

"In addition," Mendel said in a low tone, "your spermatic fluid had changed markedly. It . . . has changed composition to the point where it appears it will create an allergic reaction in any woman whose vagina it comes in contact with. The odds are strong that it will produce a severe allergic reaction in many—if not most—women. Dr. Hurwitz uses the word . . . toxic . . . in his report." Mendel cleared his throat, still looking down. "This all together means that while you could, with proper precautions, make love to a woman—a wife—without harm, you will almost certainly . . . never have children."

Mendel at last looked up. Chaim, grappling with his

own shock, saw a tear tracing its way down the old man's seamed cheek, to lose itself in his beard where others glistened in the light. "I am so sorry, Chaim." The whisper carried a world of sorrow.

Grief almost crushed Chaim. To become a vampire—to suffer through that "conversion"—to realize that his relationship to his parents was forever irrevocably changed—and to now fully realize that he would never know the blessing that God gave husbands and fathers—a loving wife, and children to follow after him—that was almost more than he could bear.

He pulled the medallion from under his shirt, touched it to his lips, and whispered, *"Sh'ma, Israel, Adonai elohenu, Adonai echod."* He clung to that thought, letting it echo in his mind over and over again.

At length his mind slowed. He kissed the medallion again, and returned it to its place inside his shirt, and looked up at the other men, dry-eyed. "So," he said in a rough voice, "something else that the modern myths didn't get right. There won't be any sex-maniac half-breed vampires running around." Both men shook their heads, Mendel still sorrowful, but Mordechai with a slight upturn of his lips to acknowledge the strength it took Chaim to make that pathetic joke.

Chaim heaved his shoulder in a deep sigh. "It is what it is. Anything else in the report?"

Mendel shook his head as he gathered the papers together in a neat stack and returned them to the folder. "No. I suspect that the good doctor has some further ideas, but he seldom talks about anything if there is not at least some physical evidence to support it."

"I can appreciate that." Chaim clasped his hands in front of him on the table and stared at his thumbs.

"I have finally accepted that normal will never be part of my life again. The reports, especially this most recent one, make that clear. I cannot continue floating along expecting that things will somehow work out and I'll be able to resume the life I had before the *conversion*." His last word was loaded with vitriol. "So we—or rather, I—need to make some decisions."

"What do you have in mind?" the rabbi said, clasping his own hands in mirror image of Chaim.

"You and I have talked about how I can break this to my parents." Chaim's voice was low. He was still gazing at his hands. "I...don't see how I can do that." He raised his head, and his eyes looked haunted— widened, pupils large and black, and seemingly sunken in his face. "This would crush them. And there's no way to hide it. Look at the obvious external physical changes. My mother would be all Jewish-mother-on-steroids as soon as I walked in the door, wanting to know what happened and insisting I go to the doctor to be checked for AIDS or something worse. My father would know something was wrong, and would grill me like a detective. I'd have no peace.

"There's no lie that would satisfy them, and the truth...they'd never accept it. Not being able to eat with them? They would never buy that. It's part of who we are, we Jews, that we eat together. That would almost certainly be the last straw. They'd probably end up trying to have me committed for psychiatric observation.

"And if they did, somehow, accept it? That would be even worse. The no-grandchildren thing would crush them both, and even if they started out trying to understand and trying to be supportive, they would never understand the reality, and would eventually start to blame me for it."

"I doubt that," Rabbi Mendel murmured.

"You don't know my mother." Chaim's tone contained more than a hint of bitterness. "I love her dearly, but when she gets disappointed big time, she could teach graduate level seminars in passive aggression and smile while she was doing it. No, this would poison them, and the end result would be it would poison me as well. I don't think you want to deal with what I would be like at the end."

"But..." Mendel began, only to pause when Mordechai lifted a hand.

"He's right, *Rav* Avram."

Mendel sat back. "Explain, please."

"From my own experience, and the few I have met along the way who would talk about their pasts, families never understand, never accept what has happened. And the more religious the family, the more they are torn apart by the taint of demonism with which such as we must so often deal."

"But..." Mendel tried again.

"Trust me, Avram. He's right. There are no good solutions."

There was a moment of breathless silence, then the rabbi sighed.

"All right. I don't like it, but all right." He looked at Chaim. "Then what do you intend?"

"I'm not sure," he said, looking back down at his hands. "I'm still working this out in my own head. But just thinking out loud, if there aren't any good solutions, as Mordechai says—I certainly can't see any—then the only thing I know to do is make a clean, sharp break as quickly as possible so I can quit living a lie for them.

"So"—Chaim looked up at the others—"I still want to take you up on the study program. With that in mind, I need to be in Israel as soon as possible. I'm not even going to call them. I'll send them a letter telling them that because of my work this summer I've been offered a work-study position in Israel, but I have to take it right now to get it. That's even got a little bit of truth to it."

Mendel nodded. "I sorrow for the position you are in, but I understand why you feel you need to do this." He looked at Mordechai, who nodded. "We can make this happen, and quickly. You may need to sign some power of attorney forms, but we can make it happen."

"I'll sign anything," Chaim said. "Second"—he swallowed hard—"once I'm in Israel, I'll need to disappear."

"Disappear?"

"Chaim Caan will need to vanish. I'll need to become someone else." He stared at Mendel. "You've hinted at the strings that you can pull to get me into the country and into school. Do you have access to the strings that can get me a new identity?"

Mordechai spoke up. "If they do not, I do."

"Good. Once I am provided with that, I need to drop off the face of the earth as far as they're concerned. Cut off all contact, so they're not connected to me and won't be touched by..." He brought his hands up to his chest. "...this."

Mendel was shaking his head. "No, Chaim. No. You would simply be replacing the pain and torment and nightmares of your metamorphosis with the pain and torment and nightmares where they imagine that you died, or were kidnapped, or became a drug addict, or had become a Muslim, or any other nightmare your 'Jewish mother on steroids,' as you put it, could dream up. No. You would simply trade one heartbreak for another equally as bad. Find another way."

"And to make it worse, they would most likely continue to search for you," Mordechai said. "They would certainly petition the government to find you, and there are private investigators in Israel, you know, that they could hire to search for you. If they are as you say, they would persist, would they not?"

"Crap." Chaim's voice was bitter. "Yes, that's exactly what they would do. They would never give up. They would never rest. Damn."

There was a long moment of silence. Chaim looked up when Mordechai cleared his throat. "There might be a way..." the older vampire began.

"How?"

"You've obviously thought about this. Let it begin as you lined out. Once you are in Israel, however, send your parents some emails over the course of a few weeks. Then, the next time there is a terrorist event, your name gets added to the casualty list, and your parents are shipped a tin of ashes. It will still be a lie. But it will be a lie that permits the clean, sharp break you asked for. It will still be a grief to them, but it will be a lie and a grief that permits them closure, permits them a healing of sorts, which neither of the other alternatives would allow."

Chaim tried to think, although the clamor in his head was not conducive to clear thought. "What... what happens if there isn't a terrorist attack?"

"Although things have been more peaceful since the various Arab peace accords, there are still attacks. One will most likely happen soon enough. If not..." Mordechai shrugged. "Then one gets manufactured." Chaim looked at him aghast. Another shrug. "These things happen from time to time, sometimes to make a point. But you wouldn't be the first who came to us who needed to disappear."

Chaim looked at Mendel, who was nodding slowly despite the moue of his mouth indicating he wasn't happy with the idea. He turned back to Mordechai, who simply stared back at him. He looked down at his hands where they clasped each other in white-knuckled ardency. A moment later, two tears trickling from his own eyes, he nodded.

"Do it."

CHAPTER 11

Dear Dad and Mom

By the time you get this, I will be in Israel. Because of the work I've been doing this summer, I was offered a position in a work-study program at Tel Aviv University in the field of genetics. It's a wonderful opportunity, but the window for acceptance was very short, so I basically had to decide today whether or not I was going to take it. I accepted the offer, because I have found a passion for working in genetics and hopefully will be in a position before long to do research into new cures for diseases.

I did not call you, Dad, not only because of the short time frame I had to make the decision, but also because I knew you would try to talk me out of it. This is what I have decided to do with my life, Dad, to explore the complexity of human life as created by haShem. I ask that you please respect that.

Mom, I know this probably upsets you, but just take some comfort in the fact that I'll be

*among millions of Jewish girls. Perhaps I'll find
one for me there.*

*I am taking my cell phone with me, so I will
call you soon. You'll be able to call me and I'll
be able to call you. Just be aware that this will
be an international call and won't be covered by
your US phone plan. Expensive, in other words.
Email will be easier and cheaper.*

*I've already made arrangements to dispose
of my apartment and my stuff, so don't worry
about that. I'm sending a notification to UCLA
that I won't be back to school, so that will be
taken care of also.*

*This isn't a big secret, so you can tell your
friends and our family about it. And greet Rabbi
Joshua at Congregation Beth Shalom for me.*

*Again, I'm sorry this is so sudden and undoubt-
edly comes as such a shock, but I really did
have to make the decision in like 30 minutes.
This is what I want to do. This is what I feel
called to do. Please understand that.*

Love you both.
Chaim

Dear Rabbi Levinson

*I want to take this opportunity to thank you
for everything you did to help me deal with my
situation. You went way out of your way to try
and find me help, and the help that you found
me turned out to be very good, very helpful
indeed. Again, thank you.*

*I can no longer return home, for various
and many reasons which you might be able to*

imagine. Likewise, for essentially those same reasons, I am relocating to another country. This is related to the work I have been part of for the last few months. It is important and meaningful work, but it is likewise work that would not be available to me if it weren't for my situation and those you put me in contact with. So thank you a third time.

Because of my situation, it is most unlikely that we will ever be in contact again. I will remember you with great fondness, however, for what promises to be a very long time. Please continue to be the wise and compassionate man that you are, and please continue to help those you can help, even if they are as weird as I was—am.

It is possible that you may hear something of me in the future. Remember my situation, and recall that haShem does upon occasion take his chosen ones to strange and unexpected callings.

In closing, let me offer to you and for you this prayer from the siddur and from Torah:

    May the Lord bless you and keep you
    May the Lord make his face shine upon
        you and be gracious to you
    May the Lord turn his face toward you
        and grant you peace
           Shalom
           Chaim Caan

Karli—

Just a note to fill you in on what's happened with me. That job that I left you at the last minute to take has turned into a gold mine. I'm enrolled at a work-study program in Israel, can you believe it? I'll be studying genetics, which I've decided is very cool and should be my life's work. But my deadline to decide to take it was just as short as the deadline to take the job with the medical research project, so I'm already in Israel. Where things are just a bit different than they are in California. Funny how that works.

Anyway, tell everybody hi for me, and that I'm thinking about them. I'll try to drop you another line later.

Ta.
Chaim

Chaim looked at his face in the hotel-room mirror, then compared it to the photo on the California driver's license he held in his hand. Even making allowance for the abysmal quality of the photo, there was a definite difference in appearance, even more marked than he had noted in the past. The picture showed a pudgy, round-faced boy with a goofy smile. The mirror reflection showed a face that was anything but pudgy—still kind of round, but with sharp edges to cheek and jaw, and a nose that reminded Chaim not so much of his father or grandfather but of his great-grandfather— almost hawkish. He could see a family resemblance, but even he, knowing the truth, wouldn't have said the one image was the same person as the other.

He sighed, then turned back to the small table that was in the room. It was a nice hotel room. Spacious enough for a king-sized bed, a small desk, and a small round table with four chairs. The TV that hung on the wall was larger than his parents' fifty-inch TV, if not quite as nice as the TV he'd had at the study facility, and it overpowered the rest of the room. Chaim left it off most of the time, preferring to use his laptop to stay connected to reality.

Tucking the license back into his wallet, he was shoving that into his jeans hip pocket when there was a knock at the door. He stepped over and looked at the security panel, which showed what he expected—Mordechai Zalman with a small bag in his hand and what looked like an older government functionary of some kind with an attaché case. He opened the door, and they entered.

"Chaim"—Mordechai waved his hand at the other man—"this is Yaakov Ashkenazi. Yaakov, this is Chaim Caan—at least for the next little while."

"Pleased to meet you." Yaakov's English carried a thick accent.

"Likewise," Chaim said.

"So, let's sit down and get this over with." Mordechai pulled out a chair and sat at the table. Yaakov and Chaim followed suit.

Yaakov set his attaché case on the table and opened it long enough to take out a folder. Closing the case, he placed the folder on the table before him and rested his folded hands on top of it.

"Are you certain you want to do this?" Yaakov's face was set in serious lines. But from the looks of his face, that was probably his default expression.

"Yes." Chaim nodded.

"This is an irrevocable step," the other man warned. "Once taken, it cannot be undone. Think very carefully before you go any farther."

Rising in Chaim's mind were the memories of the

phone calls he had had with his parents, and the emails they had exchanged—the confusion and anger in his father's voice, and the confusion and histrionics from his mother. If that was how they reacted to him leaving California and moving to Israel, how would they react to the truth of his situation? He shook his head, then looked up. "I have thought about it. This is the best thing I can do."

Yaakov looked at Chaim, glanced at Mordechai, then looked back. "Very well, then."

He opened the folder. "You are now the person Ariel Barak."

Chaim absorbed that. Ariel, meaning Lion of God. A fairly common name in Israel today, he thought. It was well-thought of, having been the name of a popular prime minister. And Barak, meaning Lightning, a name from scripture—the name of a famous general in history, as well as being the surname of a different prime minister. Ariel Barak. He liked the sound of that. He gave a definite nod.

"First, you are now a recent immigrant. Here is the background you need to know about your identity. It is, by nature, somewhat sketchy, so it would be best if you don't get into many conversations about your history. We did make you American, so that your cultural background and associations and speech patterns should still work for you." Yaakov passed a single piece of paper to Chaim. "There is no way you could pass for a sabra, a native-born, but since about twenty-five percent of all Jews living in Israel today are immigrants, you will not attract attention. You will be just one more among millions, many of whom are reticent to speak about their past.

"Second, here is your Israeli ID card. Keep that with you at all times. If you're asked to present it and you don't have it, things could get awkward and unpleasant.

"Third, here is your Israeli driver's license. This is not your ID card, so keep the two straight. Since both your actual and your new backgrounds are American, if you drive, you shouldn't have much trouble. Just keep to the right."

Chaim looked at the two cards. He knew it would feel a bit weird to not produce the driver's license as ID, but he suspected it wouldn't take long to get used to it. The picture in both was the same and was very recent, showing his new leaner look. It still took him aback to see that hawkish face looking back at him. Both seemed to have biometric data included.

Yaakov slid a small blue folder across the table. "Fourth, here is your Israeli passport."

Chaim—Ariel—picked it up and opened it. It used the same picture as the ID card, and it also contained biometric data.

"Fifth," Yaakov said, "here is your new mobile phone." Yaakov opened his case again and placed a phone in a plastic bag on the table. "It is a similar model to your previous unit.

"And last but not least, we will open an account for you with a branch of Bank Leumi. It will have the equivalent of one thousand US dollars in it to begin with." Yaakov slid a card across the table. "This is your signature card for the account. Please sign it, Mr. Barak."

Ariel—he was going to have to get used to the new name—took the proffered pen, thought about it, and carefully signed *Ariel Barak* in the appropriate space on the card. As he pushed the card and pen back across the table, he made a note that he needed to practice his new signature.

Yaakov placed the card in his folder, then pulled out his own mobile and tapped an icon before holding it up to his ear. After a moment, he said, "Chana? Yaakov. On the matter of Ariel Barak—go." He terminated the call and put the mobile back in his pocket.

"Your account will be active in twenty-four hours," Yaakov said. "Here is the account information"—he passed over a small card with numbers on it—"and here is your debit MasterCard to access the account." The colorful piece of plastic slid across the table and stopped against the passport. "Your salary from whatever work you end up doing will be transferred to this account automatically."

Yaakov placed his folder in the case, and folded his hands on the table.

"Do you have any questions?"

Ariel shook his head. "I'm sure I'll think of some later, but none now."

"My number is in your phone. Call me if you think of anything. Meanwhile, I need to collect your old wallet and contents, your US passport, your old phone, and your watch, please."

Ariel stood, pulled his wallet from his hip pocket. He pulled the US currency—a few hundred dollars— from his wallet and held it up, raising his eyebrows.

"Keep it," Mordechai said. "We'll also get the funds from your US bank account and put them in your new account."

Ariel nodded, pulled his new passport from his shirt pocket and stashed the cash there, then laid the wallet and old passport on the table. He stepped over to the dresser, gathered up his phone and his watch, and added them to the pile.

"What about my laptop?" he asked.

"I'll take care of that," Mordechai answered.

Ariel shrugged, and watched Yaakov place all the components of his old life in a plastic bag.

"Do you have anything else with personal information on it?" Yaakov looked up. "Plane ticket? Bus card? Jewelry? Car rental contract or receipts?"

Ariel looked around. "No. No plane ticket. The credit card receipts I have are in the wallet. Other than that, nothing."

Yaakov sealed the bag, placed it in his case, and closed it. He looked at Mordechai. "Call me if you find anything else." Mordechai nodded but said nothing. Yaakov took his attaché case in his left hand and held the right out to Ariel. "I hope things go well for you, young man. Blessings on you. Shalom."

A moment later, Ariel was alone in the room with Mordechai, who smiled a gentle smile at him. "Right or wrong, you've done it. You've taken the step. How do you feel?"

Ariel shrugged. "Honestly, I'm numb and weary. Ask me tomorrow."

"Fair enough."

Mordechai stood and put his bag on the table. Opening the top, he handed a wallet to Ariel. "That's as close to what you had as I could find."

Ariel looked at it. "That's fine." He felt it. "That's good leather—better than my old one." He reached out and slotted the new cards into the wallet, added his US cash, then laid it back on the table by the phone.

Next out of the bag was a watch. "Again, as close as I could find to your old one. Pretty inexpensive."

"I don't wear expensive watches," Ariel said. "Every good watch I've ever been given stopped running inside of four months. Every single one of them. But a cheap Casio or Timex will last me for five years or more." He slipped the watch on his wrist. "Hmm. Eight-thirty... or should I say twenty-thirty?"

"Either one," Mordechai said. "Official Israeli time is 24-hour, but a lot of people still talk the 12-hour clock." He stuck a hand into the bag, then pulled it out and handed the bag to Ariel. "Here. Go change into these."

Ariel came out of the bathroom a few minutes later and threw the clothes he had been wearing on the bed. New Adidas on his feet, black slacks, dark blue polo shirt, black windbreaker. He used that moment of action to slip Elena Ramirez's picture and funeral program out of his old windbreaker pocket and into his new one. "I haven't felt this preppy since tenth grade," he said with a grin. "I am going to have to learn how sizes work over here, though. None of the labels made any sense to me."

Mordechai chuckled. "One of the joys of setting up housekeeping in a new country. I'm sure you'll manage. The shopkeepers are used to it. Now, gather up your laptop, and let's go."

Ariel slipped the laptop into its backpack, storing the charger and cords in a side pocket and looping the headphones around his neck. Once that was on his shoulder, he stuffed the wallet and passport in his hip pockets, the phone in one of his front pockets, and folded up the paper and put it in the other front pocket.

He picked up a pair of boots and looked up at Mordechai with a hint of defiance. "I'm taking my Doc Martens. They're all broken in, and I don't want to start over with a new pair."

Mordechai smiled. "Fine. They're generic enough that no one will notice."

Ariel picked up the empty bag and tucked the boots into it. He looked around. "Do we need to do anything with the rest of this?"

Mordechai shook his head. "Someone will be by in a few minutes to clean up. I assume there's nothing else here you'll miss greatly?"

Ariel shook his head in turn. "No, not really."

"Good enough. Let's be on our way, then."

Ariel followed the older man out the door, letting it close behind him with a pang as it shut on his old life forever.

CHAPTER 12

THEY WENT DOWN TWO FLOORS AND INTO A DIF-
ferent wing of the hotel, arriving at a nondescript door
by itself near the end of the hallway. Mordechai placed
his thumb on a small metal plate on the door, a *click*
sounded, and he opened the door, waving Ariel inside.

Inside was a glass barrier, behind which was a
desk with a tough-faced young woman in a business
suit seated at it.

She looked up. "Yes?"

"Zalman for Dr. Mendel." Mordechai held a card
up to an outline on the glass. A green light flashed,
and a door opened in the barrier.

"Room 4," she said as they stepped through. Mordechai made a motion like a salute, and stepped through
a door at the back of the space. Ariel followed him,
and found himself in a short hallway with two doors
on either side. Mordechai opened the last door on
the right.

Once inside the room, Ariel wasn't surprised to
find Rabbi Mendel waiting. There was a young man
with him, though, that Ariel hadn't met.

"Rabbi," Mordechai said, "meet Ariel Barak."

"Nice to meet you, Mr. Barak. Please hand your laptop to Yonatan, here. He will archive it and then scrub it. Is there anything on the hard drive you absolutely need to have?"

Ariel frowned for a moment. "I should keep the school work and study folders. I'll miss most everything else, but I don't need it. Except...would it be possible have the family photo folder stored somewhere? I don't need it now, but in a few years..."

"Yonatan?" Mendel looked over his shoulder.

"I will go through your study files and anonymize them," Yonatan said as he stepped up beside the rabbi.

"Even the PDFs?"

"Even the PDFs. We're good at this, Mr. Barak." Yonatan smiled at him. "When you get your new laptop next week, they will be in a hidden folder that you will be given a password for. As to the pictures, we can store those in a time vault here and release them to you in, say, ten years. Would that be long enough, Dr. Mendel?"

Mendel held Ariel's gaze. "Ten years should be adequate, Yonatan."

Yonatan gave a sympathetic smile to Ariel, and held out his hand.

Ariel hesitated for a moment. "What about the emails I need to be able to send for a few more days or weeks?"

Yonatan handed him a small tablet. "That is a sanitized unit. The only thing it can do is handle your email account. Do not send emails to your family from anything else. Once that need is done, you'll turn the tablet back in to us."

Ariel took the tablet. He was reluctant to let the last link to his old life go, but after a sigh he slid the backpack strap off his shoulder and handed it to Yonatan.

"Headphones, too," Yonatan said, holding out his other hand.

Ariel pulled them off his neck where he'd forgotten about them, and handed them over as well.

"And the picture of the girl," Mordechai said.

Ariel stiffened, then slowly pulled Elena's picture and the funeral program out of his pocket. He looked down at them and didn't move.

"We will put these in a physical vault," Mendel said softly. "In five years, you can have them back."

It took Ariel a long moment to accept that, but he did eventually hand them over to Yonatan. Yonatan nodded at him, then turned and left through a door at the back of the room.

"Please, sit," Mendel said.

Mordechai sat, and after a moment, Ariel followed suit.

"So, the first phase of this transition is done." Mendel folded his hands before him. "Now we have to figure out what to do for the next phase."

"I thought I would be going to school," Ariel said. He titled his head as a knot formed in his stomach. "You said that you had things lined up for me."

"We did," Mendel said. "But that was before you insisted on an identity switch. We could make those arrangements quickly for an American student who had a transcript at a major university. Now you're a brand-new person with no official US records to draw on. We can still do it, but it's going to take a while to create all the pieces, much less pull them all together.

Although we work with the government, we are not the government. We don't have their resources, and we can't just say 'Shibboleth' and make things happen."

Ariel stared at the older man, whose face was showing most of his age right then. "All right. I guess I can see that. I wish you had said something about that earlier, though."

Mendel shrugged. "We can do it, or rather, we can see to it that it gets done. But it will take some time, and we will have to call in some favors. It's not going to be as easy as we had hoped."

Ariel's mouth quirked in a sour expression. "All right," he repeated. "It is what it is. So what do we—I—do now?"

Mendel switched languages. "How is your ability to speak Hebrew?"

Ariel gulped. "Not very good," he began. "But my teacher in shul made us talk with it. He made us do more than just read scripture. And last summer I got bored and got one of the language learning apps"—he used the English term—"and played with it most of the summer. I can probably get around the city with it, but I doubt I could have an educated conversation."

"How about writing?" Still in Hebrew.

Ariel shrugged. "I do better there, but my written vocabulary is very scripture oriented."

Mendel looked to Mordechai. "Well?"

"I think that will work," he responded in English. "Ariel"—he shifted a shoulder back and looked directly at him—"we need to find something for you to do while *Rav* Avram, here"—he jerked a thumb back across the desk—"is running all the behind-the-scenes things to get you into a school. So, here's what I propose.

"As an *oleh* . . ."

"A what?" Ariel asked.

"An *oleh* . . . an immigrant who has made aliyah to Israel," Mordechai explained.

"Ah. I know what aliyah is, but I hadn't heard the *oleh* term before."

"Well, we've already established that your Hebrew needs some work." Mordechai's smile was a warm one, not his cutting razor smile. "Anyway, as one of the *olim*, you won't be conscripted and you are not obligated to make the service commitment to the IDF that sabras are. However, if you volunteer, it would provide some opportunities you might not otherwise have available to you, or not as easily."

Ariel said nothing; just waited for Mordechai to continue.

"To do the work I do as one of the *Gibborim*, you need some additional training. This is as good a time for it as any."

"So, I need to be a soldier?"

"You need some of the same training as a soldier, but actually, it would make more sense for you to serve with the Israel Police, at least for a time."

"What, be a cop or a sheriff?"

Mordechai shook his head. "No. Or not exactly. You need to remember that Israel is not much larger than America's state of New Jersey both in geography and in population. In America, they have at least three levels of local police organizations: the city police, the county sheriffs, and the state police, which may or may not include the highway patrol troopers and the state investigative body. Then at the national level there is the FBI, and several other agencies with various

levels of policing authority. So America has an absolute
smorgasbord of policing available. Israel is too small to
allow that amount of duplication, dilution, and misuse
of resources. They can't afford it. There is one civilian
police agency: the Israeli Police. Granted, they handle
everything from traffic control to street policing to crim-
inal investigations to counterterrorism, but they are one
agency. There is a certain amount of overlap between
the police and the IDF in the Border Police, which has
police command officers but a lot of IDF conscripts in
their ranks, because the Border Police works in parts
of the country where open combat can occur.

"So not army, and not what you're thinking of as
police. No, the counterterrorism and hostage rescue
group, the Special Police or Yamam, would be who
I would align you with first."

Ariel thought seriously about that. Is this what he
wanted to do? Is this what he really wanted to do?
Did he want to commit a Methuselah's lifetime to
violence, to death, even? What would it do to him?
On the other hand, given what had already happened
to him, would it be so bad? He didn't know. But then,
how could he know?

He looked Mordechai in the eye. "Is this righteous?"

Mordechai nodded. "How can it not be righteous
to protect *haShem*'s chosen ones—His children—from
the evils that men do?"

"No," Ariel said. "Is this righteous *for me*?"

Mordechai paused for a moment. "I can't answer
that for you," he eventually said. "I can tell you that I
would not have permitted you to set your feet on this
road if I didn't believe it is fundamentally righteous
for you. We do not use the word *Gibborim* lightly."

Ariel considered that, then made a choice that he knew would be irrevocable. He also knew he would probably regret it from time to time. He nodded. "All right. Can I do this without having gone through the army?"

"Ordinarily, probably not, but there are occasional exceptions. I've already laid the groundwork for it."

"Is that who you work for?"

Now Mordechai's razor smile appeared. "Not as such, no. I am actually paid a consultancy retainer by Mossad, the foreign intelligence agency, and most of my commissions come from them. They do upon occasion lend me to either Yamam or to Shin Bet, the internal security organization, usually for some kind of counterterrorism operation."

"So the Special Police?"

"Eventually, yes." Mordechai tilted his head. "I had thought of signing you up first with the IDF and running you through their initial training, but the dietary issues—both your need for blood and you not eating with the company mess—would just cause too much difficulty. So, I think what we'll do is get you the firearms training you need by way of the police, which will probably take you between four and eight weeks. Then at roughly the same time we'll probably run you through a concentrated language school to get you up to some level of conversational ability, at least to the point where you can give and receive orders reliably. That might take another couple of months beyond the firearms training time. That will keep you busy while Rabbi Mendel is working to get your college program straightened out. If it takes him longer than that, a few more weeks or months in police service wouldn't hurt you any."

Ariel started to open his mouth to complain about the waste of time, but then he remembered how old Mordechai really was. He closed his mouth without saying anything, but an upturned corner of Mordechai's mouth told him that Mordechai probably knew what he was thinking.

"Fine," Ariel said in Hebrew. "So when do I start?" His speech was slow, but he thought he had the words right.

"Soon," Mordechai replied in Hebrew. "Soon."

CHAPTER 13

AND IT WAS INDEED SOON. TWO NIGHTS LATER Ariel trailed behind Mordechai as he entered an anonymous government building in northeastern Tel Aviv. Tonight they were both wearing dark clothing. For a change, Mordechai was wearing a turtleneck shirt and a blazer, but he still carried himself as if he was wearing one of his Savile Row suits. Ariel felt a little underdressed by comparison.

The building wasn't extremely large, but unlike most of the buildings around them was set in a large cleared space which had more parking space than usual. Ariel looked around as they passed through the doors and through a security scanner. The walls the doors were set into seemed awfully thick. Mordechai caught his glance, and smiled. "Reinforced hardened polymer concrete, extra thick. The windows were originally thick armor glass. They replaced them with the new transparent aluminum last year. It would take one of the Americans' bunker busters to take this building down."

"Why?"

Mordechai snorted. "You don't need to know. Just assume that there are good reasons. Come on."

After passing through the security checkpoint, where Ariel was reluctantly admitted by the grim-faced guards only on Mordechai's authorization, they went to the single elevator that was behind the checkpoint. Ariel was surprised to see more subsurface numbers than aboveground floors. Mordechai pushed the button for the bottom floor and looked over at Ariel.

"You . . ."

". . . don't need to know. Got it."

Mordechai grinned and nodded, then turned to face the doors as the elevator slowed to a stop. The doors opened to an unremarkable hallway with surprisingly few doors along it. Mordechai led the way to the right and opened the only door on the right side of the hall. Ariel followed him into a very large and long high-ceilinged room where they were met by a short, stocky older man with short, grizzled hair and beard.

"Mordechai, you old rascal! How long has it been?"

The two older men embraced. Mordechai laughed, and said, "Only about six months, old friend."

"Bah! When you get to be my age, six months goes by like the blink of an eye. But it's good to see you."

"Likewise, Shimon. Likewise." Mordechai turned and beckoned Ariel forward. "Shimon, this is my friend and protégé Ariel Barak. Ariel, this is Shimon Aharoni, whom I have asked to teach you firearms."

Shimon offered his hand. "Good to meet you, young man."

"My pleasure," Ariel said as they shook hands. The old man's grip was very firm.

"So," Shimon said, turning back to Mordechai, "does this have anything to do with the package you sent me?"

"Indeed. That's the pistol I want you to train him with, that he will carry after you pass him."

"A Glock 40?" Shimon looked doubtful. Ariel caught a glimpse from the corner of the man's eye. Shimon shifted to Hebrew. "Are you sure he can handle a ten-millimeter? He's not very big."

Mordechai smiled and laid his hand on his friend's shoulder. "Trust me, Shimon, he can handle it."

Shimon's doubt did not decrease. "If you say so."

The older vampire turned back to Ariel and pulled something from his pocket. "This is your weapon license." Mordechai shifted back to English. "Carry this at all times, especially when you have the weapon with you. If you're caught with the gun but don't have the card, there will be serious consequences. And unlike America, Israeli weapon licenses are weapon specific. This license is only for the pistol that Shimon will be training you with. Don't lose either one of them."

Ariel took the license. It looked to be fairly similar to his Israeli ID card. He pulled his wallet out, tucked the license away, and put it back in his pocket. "Don't lose it. Got it."

"Okay. Shimon will get you started tonight. I have a meeting upstairs, but I'll be back for you in a couple of hours."

A moment later, Ariel was left with Shimon, who looked at him with a wry smile. "So, how good is your Hebrew?"

Ariel shrugged. "I can read and discuss Torah and Talmud with some success. Not so good at getting or giving directions on the street yet."

"Eh, not so bad, then. It will come to you. But we'll begin with English. Come over here, please."

Ariel took off his windbreaker and joined the older man at a counter that ran across the back of the room. Shimon pulled over a black case with a big G impressed on it and flipped it open to reveal what looked to Ariel to be a very large pistol.

"This," Shimon said, "is a Glock model 40, their best ten-millimeter pistol, which makes it one of the best and most powerful handguns in the world. Treat it with respect. If you don't, it will probably kill you."

Ariel shifted his gaze from the gun to Shimon's face, and saw that he was deadly serious. A moment later he had a mental wince at the turn of phrase in his thoughts, but a moment after that realized it was appropriate for the subject. He nodded to show he was following.

Shimon nodded back. "Good. Now, listen to me. I have four rules that you will obey at all times, understood?"

Ariel nodded again.

"Good." Shimon raised his left hand and lifted his index finger. "Rule 1: Do not point a weapon—pistol, rifle, shotgun, machine gun, it doesn't matter—do not point a weapon at someone unless you intend to shoot them."

Middle finger was raised to stand alongside the index finger. "Rule 2: Do not put your finger on the trigger unless you are about to shoot someone."

Ring finger was elevated to join the others. "Rule 3: Never assume that any weapon, whether yours or someone else's, is unloaded, even if the magazine has been removed. Always verify by removing the magazine and working the action to clear the chamber. Understand?"

"Don't point a weapon at someone unless I intend to shoot them," Ariel recited. "Don't put my finger on the trigger unless I'm about to shoot someone. Never assume a weapon is unloaded. Got it."

Shimon nodded and lowered his hand. "Good. Remember that."

The old man's face looked like granite in that moment. Ariel nodded. "Understood."

Shimon raised his hand again with all four fingers now extended. "Rule 4: This is not a rule of the gun so much as it is a rule of what you do with the gun. First, understand that a ten-millimeter pistol will often shoot through a person."

Ariel swallowed. "Seriously?"

"Seriously. Sometimes that's not a problem—like when you're in a combat situation with multiple foes. But sometimes it can be a problem—like when you've got a target who is holding a hostage in the middle of a group of hostages. So you can put a bullet into your target, but if it will travel through him and come out the other side, you might hit one of the hostages as well. Sometimes you don't have any choice, you have to take the shot, but sometimes you can wait a few moments and see if whoever is behind him will move."

"Wow." Ariel thought for a moment. "So be aware of what's behind your target."

"Yes. That's part of the fourth rule. The other part of the rule is to be aware of the difference between cover and concealment."

Ariel was confused and tilted his head a bit. Cover? Concealment? What was Shimon getting at?

The older man grinned, walked over to a nearby

closet, opened the door, and stepped behind it. "Can you see me?" Shimon's voice had a trace of humor in it.

"No," Ariel replied.

"So I'm concealed, right?"

Ariel nodded, then flushed as he realized that if he couldn't see Shimon, Shimon couldn't see him. "Sorry, right."

"But am I covered? Would this door stop a bullet?"

Ariel snorted. "If it's just a standard hollow interior door, not a chance."

"Right," Shimon announced as he came out from behind the door. "So most interior walls, most interior doors will not provide cover, only concealment. And a lot of exterior walls aren't much better. But concealment can still get you killed. You have no idea what's behind a concealment. You don't know if it's a chair, if it's one unarmed man, or three men with knives, or five men with submachine guns. You just don't know."

Shimon leaned back against the counter that ran the length of the back wall and crossed his arms. "I can't tell you how many movies and TV shows where I've seen a character shoot through a door or a wall to hit the bad guy. But a real-life cop almost certainly won't do that. Do you know why?"

Ariel thought about it. "Because he doesn't know what's on the other side?"

"Correct! What if there's a hostage on the other side? Or what if there are three girls who know nothing about what's going on thirty feet away?"

Ariel sighed, and nodded.

"That said"—Shimon's voice lowered in pitch—"sometimes you have to shoot anyway. Sometimes the man or woman you're after is so dangerous you have to take the chance to keep them from getting away. And you pray with all your heart that no one innocent will be hurt. And sometimes those prayers are answered."

Ariel understood the unspoken message—sometimes those prayers are not answered.

"The problem with cover," Shimon resumed with his regular voice, "is more ricochets than anything else. And you have no control over that, other than not shooting at all, which if the cover is good, is not a bad idea, so you don't waste ammunition. Again, you can't go by the movies. Unless your name is John Wick, you don't carry a dozen loaded magazines around in your pockets or in belt packs. You just don't. So if your situation lasts more than five minutes—and even outside of combat they occasionally do—making your ammunition last is a consideration.

"And finally, think about all this from your side of the table. If you take shelter behind something, is it good cover, or is it only flimsy concealment? That can be the difference between life and death for you—as it too often has been for our police and soldiers. Learn to look around you and be aware of your surroundings. Is a car concealment or shelter? Is a bus stop concealment or shelter? Is a restaurant table turned up on its side concealment or shelter?" He looked at Ariel with his eyebrows raised for a moment, but continued before Ariel could form a response. "Concealment only, and not good concealment at that."

Ariel nodded soberly. Shimon nodded back.

After a moment, Ariel asked, "How many different types of ammunition are there for this pistol?"

"Good question." Shimon smiled a little. "There

are some special or unusual loads you'll most likely never use, but there are three common types of ammunition." He opened a drawer and pulled out three boxes of bullets that he set beside the pistol case. "Frangible"—he touched one box—"expanding or hollow point"—he touched the second box—"and full metal jacket." He touched the third. He then pulled a bullet from each box and set them on the counter. "A frangible bullet breaks up on impact, leaves a serious wound but almost certainly doesn't pass through the body and come out the other side. An expanding bullet will mushroom to maybe twice its original diameter on impact, which will slow it down some. It will leave a nasty wound as well, but in the right circumstances still might pass through and exit the body to strike someone or something else. A ten-millimeter full metal jacket bullet will almost certainly pass through the body and exit to hit someone or something else, especially if it's an armor-piercing bullet."

"Sounds like I need to use the expanding bullets."

Shimon smiled again. "You'll be training with hollow point loads. They're not risk free, but they're less risky than the full metal jacket loads for the kind of work the police do." He put the frangible and full metal jacket bullets back in their boxes and then put them back in the drawer, but left the hollow point box on the counter.

Shimon sobered and looked at Ariel. "Okay. Now, because it's Mordechai who brought you to me, I assume you're going to be working with him." Ariel nodded. "And it looks like he's already pulled some strings since he's already got you your weapon license. You don't normally get that until after you've had the full training and had the weapon assigned to you. So I'm going to assume that you will be either working with the IDF, the police, or one of the secret agencies under Mordechai's direction."

Ariel didn't respond to that. He didn't know what Mordechai would want him to say.

"One last comment, and then we'll get started." Shimon's mouth kind of quirked. "Despite all the movies and television programs, guns are not toys and are not carried for fun. Always remember that you are not Dirty Harry, you are not Rambo, you are not John Wick. When you carry that weapon, you will do so as a representative of the State of Israel and in defense of the Israeli people. If you will be working with Mordechai, the odds are very high that you will have to use that weapon for its designed purpose and shoot someone—probably several someones, over time. I can train you to use the weapon, to use it properly, to use it well, but when it comes down to it, you will be the one who will have to make the decision to pull the trigger. Make sure you do so for the right reasons."

There was a moment of silence, then Shimon smiled. "Well, let's get started." He took the pistol out of the case. "The first thing I'm going to show you is how to disassemble and clean..."

By the time Mordechai returned, Ariel could routinely disassemble and reassemble his pistol in short order; he knew how to clean it; and he knew how to load the magazine and insert it in the pistol. Shimon had drilled him on that last several times, to make sure he could do so quickly and smoothly. All of that had taken less than an hour. Since then he had been shooting at human-outline targets on the back wall. Shimon had showed him a two-handed grip and had coached him through sighting and slowly squeezing the trigger. He thought he was getting the hang of it.

He heard Mordechai come through the door as he loaded a fresh magazine and chambered a round. "How's he doing?" he heard Mordechai ask as he lined up the sights. He pulled the trigger as Shimon responded.

"Not bad for a first-timer. His last couple of magazines have all been in five-inch groups."

Ariel continued his measured shooting until his last two shots. He raised his sights for the fourteenth shot, and lowered them for the fifteenth. The action locked back, he lowered the pistol, ejected the magazine, made sure the chamber was clear, laid both on the counter before him, and pushed the button to have the target reeled back up to the counter. He smiled when it arrived and hung before him. The first thirteen shots were in a three-inch grouping in the center of the chest, the fourteenth shot was a hole in the center of the forehead of the figure, and the fifteenth was a hole just above the line that marked the bottom of the trunk between the legs. He turned to the others and raised his eyebrows, still smiling.

"*Klugscheißer*," Mordechai said in German as they came up on either side of Ariel. Shimon chuckled, and Mordechai's mouth quirked up at one corner. Ariel didn't know much German, so he didn't know what the term meant, but from the context he had a pretty good guess. His smile broadened.

"Nice shooting," Shimon said. "Nice tight grouping on the chest. The one to the head, good placement, but that's a shot you don't take unless you don't have any choice. Even one of these"—he tapped the pistol—"can have a shot ricochet or skate off of the bone. Not very likely, but it does happen. This one"—he pointed at the groin shot—"his wife or girlfriend would curse you for ruining his sex life, and most likely it would be lethal, but not immediately so, so that's another shot you wouldn't take unless it was the only one available. If you can make that shot, you'd be better off to shoot his knee out from under him, because when he dropped you could put another shot into his chest. But not bad. Now, even though modern alloys and modern gunpowder formulas have reduced the problems of corrosion, it's still a good idea to clean your pistol after shooting it. Go do so while I talk to Mordechai."

Ariel picked up the pistol and the empty magazine and moved to the back counter. He stood with his back to the others while his hands disassembled the pistol to its component parts and he picked up the cleaning tools, but his hearing was focused on the others' conversation.

"So what do you think?" from Mordechai.

"Eh, he's not a genius with a pistol, but he's the best first-timer I've seen in a long while. He listens, you don't have to tell him twice, and he doesn't argue. His first two magazines were rough, but after that, he seemed to catch the knack. I wouldn't send him into a shooting contest just yet, but in a few months, with regular practice, could be."

"Good to hear. Not surprising, but good to hear. How soon can you run him through the combat range?"

"You insist it has to be at night?"

"Yes."

"First opening is in two nights. You remember this usually is at least a week in duration?"

Mordechai chuckled. "Yes, I remember. I used to teach it, if you'll recall. But he might surprise you."

"How do you mean?"

"Ariel was raised Orthodox in the US. He went to public school, then to a parallel Hebrew school. His life was very focused, and he did well under it. He graduated from high school a year and a half early, then matriculated into university in a science program and did extremely well for a couple of years before an unplanned-for event blew his life apart. He focuses well, he learns quickly, which you've already noted, and he's a lot tougher than you think he is. He may surprise you."

"If you say so." Shimon sounded a bit skeptical. "Regardless, I can't start him until night after tomorrow."

"Here?"

"No, the north range. It's going to be shut down soon, and the classes have already moved to the new range. We should have it to ourselves."

"Good."

By now Ariel had cleaned and reassembled the pistol and was inserting bullets into the magazine. The last bullet clicked in, so he laid the pistol and magazine on the table before turning around to face the others.

"You ready to carry that for real?" Mordechai's face was solemn.

That brought Ariel's mind to a stop. Was he ready to carry a weapon? Was he ready to shoot someone if he had to, if the situation called for it? His mind circled back through the thoughts he'd had when he

chose to come to Israel. If he was going to be one of
the *Gibborim*, this would be part of his life. He took a
deep breath, then released it. If this was what *haShem*
had called him to do, then he had to be prepared to
do it. He pulled the medallion from under his shirt,
kissed it, and put it back. He looked up.

"Do you carry?"

Mordechai opened his blazer to show a large pistol
tucked into each armpit.

Ariel's mouth quirked, and he nodded. "Yes."

Mordechai acknowledged that statement with a nod
of his own as he buttoned his jacket. He looked at
Shimon. "What kind of holster would you recommend?"

Shimon looked at Ariel, looked him up and down
as if seeing him for the first time. "You're right-
handed." That was a statement, not a question, but
Ariel nodded to confirm it. "So, behind the back,
right hip, left cross-body, or left shoulder. Do you
have any preferences?"

Ariel shrugged. "I've never worn a holster before,
so I don't have a clue."

"Not behind the back," Mordechai said. "Too easy
to be disarmed by someone behind you."

"Agreed," Shimon said. "Although you'd be surprised
at the number of fools who insist on carrying there.
Well, maybe *you* wouldn't, but most would." He crossed
his arms and leaned back against the front counter.
"I'd say either right hip or left shoulder. Hip will give
a faster draw, shoulder will give better concealment."

Mordechai pursed his lips. "Shoulder," he finally
said. "For now. We can always change later. Do you
have a rig he can wear?"

"Might." Shimon stood and moved to a locker in the

far rear corner of the room. "I keep a few things in here. Let me see what I've got." He rummaged around for a few moments, then pulled out what looked to be a balled-up mess of black leather straps. "Here it is. Let's see if it fits."

Shimon moved to the back counter and unrolled the bundle. "Yes, what I thought. This should work if it will fit." He held it up. "Turn around, lad, and hold your arms up."

Ariel did so, and felt the harness dropped over his hands and slide down his arms to land on his shoulders. He dropped his arms and shrugged, trying to get it to settle into place.

"Rule 5," Shimon said. "You don't carry your pistol with a round in the chamber. You can have a fully loaded magazine in the pistol, but you don't chamber a round until you're ready to shoot. Understand?" Ariel nodded. "You will hear arguments from gun owners and gun carriers from around the world about whether or not you should carry with a round in the chamber. We don't, here in Israel. In fact, carrying with an empty chamber is often called the Israeli carry. Now, put the magazine in the pistol."

Ariel picked up the pistol, closed the slide, and inserted the magazine.

Shimon nodded. "Put the pistol in the holster." Ariel did so with a bit of difficulty, forcing the gun to slide into the stiff leather. "Relax." Ariel tried to, letting his shoulders drop a little. He felt Shimon's hands on his back adjusting the harness. "There. Try moving around in that."

Ariel shrugged his shoulders and moved his arms around. "Seems okay," he said.

"Draw the weapon," Mordechai said.

Ariel reached up and pulled the pistol out of the holster, keeping his finger off the trigger. It came out easier than it had gone in.

"Again," Mordechai directed.

Ariel restored the pistol to the holster, then drew it out again.

"How does that feel?"

"I think okay," Ariel said. "But I've never worn one of these before, so how would I know?"

Mordechai's mouth quirked. "Fair enough. Put your jacket on and try it again."

Ariel walked over and picked up his windbreaker. After putting it on, he left it unzipped and drew the pistol. It came out easily. He put it back and looked at Mordechai.

"No hang-ups, nothing binding?"

Ariel shook his head. "Not that I can tell."

"So you're ready to carry?"

Ariel nodded.

"Good enough." Mordechai turned to Shimon. "Extra magazine?"

Shimon returned to his corner cabinet and came back with three more magazines and a belt holder for them. "You put this on, left side." While Ariel struggled with that, Shimon loaded the magazines, rapidly clicking the bullets in one after another. He had them done by the time that Ariel had the holder settled. A moment later they were in place. Ariel pulled one out just to get the feel for it, then put it back in. Shimon nodded.

Mordechai clapped Shimon on the shoulder. "Thank

you, old friend. We'll see you Tuesday night at the north facility."

They shook hands, and then Shimon shook hands with Ariel. "Good luck, young man." There was a certain hint of *you're going to need it* in the old man's expression. Ariel didn't disagree with him.

CHAPTER 14

ARIEL WALKED OUT AT MORDECHAI'S SIDE. NEITHER of them said anything until after they got in Mordechai's car and were out in traffic.

"So what does *Klugscheißer* mean?" Ariel asked.

Mordechai laughed. "Smart-ass," he replied a moment later.

"What? That was the best you could come up with?"

"I can curse in six languages and insult your mother in eight," Mordechai said, keeping his eyes on the road. "Be glad that was all I chose to say."

Ariel chuckled at that. "So, how many languages are common in Israel? Hebrew, of course, and I assume Arabic and English. What else?"

"Hebrew is the official language, spoken by most everyone in the country. Arabic is next most common, spoken by maybe twenty percent of the residents. Right behind it is Russian."

"Russian?" Ariel was surprised by that.

"Yes, there was a mass migration of Russian and Ukrainian Jews to Israel in the eighties and nineties. Almost as many people speak Russian as speak Arabic."

"So where does English fall?"

"Many Israelis can speak English to one degree or another. It's a required second language in the schools, and it's widely used in the commercial business and banking sector and in the government. It's also fairly common among the military, especially the officers. But the number of citizens for whom it's their birth language has dropped a lot over the last generation or so and is pretty small now. Mostly immigrants from Canada, the US, and the British Commonwealth. German, French, Yiddish, also more common years ago, but small numbers now. Amharic from the Ethiopian migration. A few others."

"Huh. So when do I start my Hebrew classes?"

"Soon. Next week, hopefully. I think I've found a tutor who can meet with you at night."

Mordechai negotiated a difficult turn, avoiding oncoming traffic. Ariel waited until they were through the maneuver and traveling down a quiet street before he said anything else.

"I know you fought in the wars, but how often have you had to use weapons otherwise? I would have expected our speed and strength to be enough to take down anyone we'd face."

Mordechai sighed. "There are times where speed and strength and stealth are all that are required to deal with a situation. But there are also times where the ability to kill at a distance, or to kill many rapidly, is what is needed. Recall that Israel is beset by enemies."

"How often?"

"Twice in the last six months."

"Wow." Ariel absorbed that. "So you think I . . ."

"You may be called on. That is possible. But the

odds are not high. Our counterintelligence and counter-
terrorist groups are very good, and *we* don't ordinarily
get called in that often."

Ariel heard the emphasis on *we* and understood what
Mordechai was saying. "Am I going to meet the other
two of us? What were their names—Menachem . . ."

"Menachem Aronson and Eleazar Katz," Mordechai
replied. "Yes, but not just yet. They . . . it's hard to
explain. They don't deal well with modern times, so they
choose not to meet it any more than they have to. They
have small, very isolated residences, with very well-paid
housekeepers and a lot of books. They seem to be content. We don't call on them very often—the last time was
in 1995 when Prime Minister Yitzhak Rabin was assas-
sinated. They were added to Shimon Peres' bodyguards
for several months, and it's a good thing they were. They
quietly stopped several follow-up assassination attempts."

"Quietly?"

"Menachem and Eleazar tend to be very . . . direct,
one might say, but they are very good at stealth—
better than I am, in truth. So good that the news
organizations never heard or said anything about them."

"Huh."

"And the organizations that sponsored the assassins
were left wondering what happened, which is not a
bad state of affairs."

Mordechai turned off on a side street and parked
near a bar with the sign JOHN BULL PUB flashing
neon from the window. "Come on. They claim to be
an English-style pub. They're not, but not even the
English have many real English-style pubs anymore.
Besides, we're not here to eat."

Ariel followed Mordechai into the pub. The lighting

was dim inside, although brighter than outdoors. It was late in the evening on a weeknight, and there weren't many people there.

Mordechai looked around. "There," he said, and led the way to a small isolated table in a back corner. They settled into chairs so that they both were looking back out over the seating. A petite waitress appeared in the next moment.

"Hi, I'm Beth, and I'm your server tonight," she announced in accented English. "What would you like?"

"What do you have in the way of a single malt scotch?" Mordechai asked.

Confusion crossed her face. "I don't know. I'll have to go ask."

"Do, please."

She scurried off.

"Scotch?" Ariel asked.

"Wait and see, my boy."

It took a long moment, but eventually Beth reappeared. "The bartender says that we have Glenlivet." She pronounced the last word carefully.

"Ah, well, I had hoped for Glenfiddich, but Glenlivet will be acceptable. I'll have a small Glenlivet and water, and my friend here will have a Perrier."

"Right away, gentlemen." Beth scurried off again.

"Scotch?" Ariel repeated.

Mordechai grinned. "Dr. Hurwitz's report left out a couple of things."

"Like what?"

"Like the whole thing about everything but blood tasting nasty."

Ariel thought back. "Yeah. And I forgot to ask about it. So what gives?"

"Whatever causes the vampirism, one of the first things it does is it changes the sense of smell."

"Smell?" Ariel thought for a moment. "Oh, right. Most of what passes for flavor is actually scent driven. I knew that," he said in a disgusted tone. "I should have already figured that one out."

"Right," Mordechai said. "The basic tongue sensations of salt, sweet, sour, and bitter still seem to work fairly well for us. But the perception of scents, to use Dr. Hurwitz's analogy, gets reprogrammed very quickly, at least partly to ramp up our ability to smell. So in addition to everything else, the vampire thing crosses the blood-brain barrier almost immediately to do that."

They paused to allow Beth to set their drinks on the table, which she did with facility, then returned to the bar.

"So, scotch?" Ariel repeated, nodding at Mordechai's glass.

"It turns out that besides water we can actually consume other non-blood-based liquids."

"You mean besides the *magen* bars?"

"Yes, besides them. In a pinch, if you're really desperate, you can drink a glucose and water mixture and survive on that. You won't feel great, but you can survive on it for a while. It's best if you get the hospital glucose bags or bottles if you have to do this, though, in order to get the best purity. Not the more common dextrose solutions, mind you. It has to be glucose. Dextrose will make you sick, and other sugars like fructose or maltose or table-sugar sucrose are even worse. It has to be pure glucose, understand?"

"Got it. Glucose. Good to know. But what does that have to do with scotch?"

"Bear with me. Our bodies don't metabolize alcohol after the conversion. It usually passes through the liver and kidneys and right out of the body. But enough of it might damage the kidneys, so avoid it. Beer and wine, even kosher, have so many extra carbohydrates and other compounds that they will make you very, very sick. Don't even try them. You're not geared for vomiting anymore. But oddly enough, a highly distilled high-proof alcohol can be pleasurable in one sense."

Mordechai lifted his glass, sniffed it, and smiled.

"It smells good?" Ariel was surprised.

Mordechai shrugged. "It's an acquired 'taste,' so to speak. It has to be highly distilled. This"—he lifted the glass again—"is at least eighty-proof, at least forty percent alcohol, with the balance being water and the flavor esters of the whisky. I don't drink it, I literally inhale it." And he proceeded to do so.

"So vodka, gin, stuff like that..."

Mordechai shook his head. "Those can be high alcohol and high proof, but they just don't have the flavor esters of a good scotch whisky. And it has to be a good single malt scotch. The blended scotches just smell like piss to me." He lifted the glass again and inhaled. "Ah."

"May I?"

Mordechai slid the glass across the table. "Be my guest."

Ariel gingerly lifted the glass below his nose and sniffed. The odor was strong, was almost overpowering to his senses, in fact. It made his nose tingle, almost like hairs in the nasal passages were stirring around. But the scent...he couldn't describe it, and he wouldn't want to experience it a lot, but it was almost...almost...it almost reminded him of what a good steak smelled like when it was being charcoal grilled. The smell hung in the back of his throat almost begging to be swallowed.

"Wow." Ariel took another sniff, then dared to touch the glass to his lips and take a tiny sip. It was disappointing. Little flavor, no burning in the back of his throat, no sensation of heat as it trickled down his throat. "Wow," meaning something entirely different from the first time.

Mordechai reclaimed the glass and took another sniff. "Indeed, wow."

Ariel sat and drank his Perrier, playing with the bubbles, while Mordechai sniffed his scotch. As he neared the bottom of the bottle, he looked over at Mordechai.

"So, you have two licenses for your pistols?"

"Yes." Mordechai sniffed the scotch again. "And a Mossad ID, a Shin Bet ID, and a Special Police ID, none of which allow me to carry guns. Only the licenses do."

"Can you shoot with both hands?"

"I can, but I shoot better with the right than the left, so if I need to shoot I usually use the right. I carry the extra pistol after having one jam and break on me in an operation."

"So you don't shoot with both hands at the same time?"

"Forget the movies, Ariel. Any kind of firefight or battle is an exercise in multitasking, and there are very, very few people in the world who can carry two guns and select separate targets for each of them in that kind of situation. That is the ultimate in multitasking, and most people who try it end up getting distracted, which then ends up with them getting dead. Yes, you are strong enough that you can reliably shoot that pistol you're carrying one-handed with a little more training and experience. Yes, you can undoubtedly learn to shoot at least fairly well left-handed, again, with more training and experience. Yes, with combat training you can undoubtedly learn to carry two pistols and use them to shoot at the same target fairly well. But forget about being able to carry two guns and having the level of situational awareness to be able to target them independently. That's a one in a billion skill. Even Dirty Harry and John Wick only used one gun at a time.

"That said, what Shimon said is the truth: in a firefight, in a battle, you take the shot you have at the moment, because that may be the best shot you get. The only time you wait for a better shot is if you're on a sniper mission, which I doubt you will ever be."

At that moment, Mordechai's phone sounded. He pulled it out of his jacket pocket and looked at the screen. "Trouble." He stood and pulled a money clip out of his pocket. "Come on, we're leaving."

He dropped a bill on the table and headed for the door. Ariel gulped down the last of his water and hurried to catch up.

CHAPTER 15

THE RIDE THAT FOLLOWED HAD ARIEL BRACING his feet on the floor and hanging on to the door handgrip with all his might. Mordechai seemed to have been transformed into a Formula One driver, shifting gears rapidly, feet dancing between the three pedals, weaving around cars and the occasional pedestrian. There were blue and red lights flashing from the front of the roofline, so it gave some warning to everyone ahead of them, but there was no siren.

As he drove, Mordechai made time to further Ariel's education.

"Pay attention for a moment. There's a risk with the shoulder holster you should know of because we're walking into a hostage situation . . ."

"We are?" Ariel jerked upright.

"Yes, now listen. Shimon never brings this up. If you draw from that holster—when you draw from that holster—just be aware of the fact that unless your target is standing to your left, when you pull your pistol and swing it around to sight on your target, you're going to cover quite an arc of space—somewhere between ninety and one hundred eighty degrees usually—before your muzzle and sights will point at your target. If there are people in that arc, you are endangering them. This is where Shimon's Rule 2 is very important: Do not put your finger on the trigger until the pistol is sighted on your target. Keep that very much in your mind tonight."

"Got it." Ariel nodded.

Mordechai tapped a switch on the console and the lights died about a block before he pulled to a stop behind a van at the side of the road. Ariel saw several figures in gray uniforms.

"Special Police?" he asked as Mordechai turned the ignition off.

"The Yamam, yes. Come on."

Mordechai got out of the car, took off his blazer, and tossed it onto the driver's seat. Then he opened the trunk of the car, pulled out an armored vest and tossed it to Ariel. "Put that on." He pulled another one out for himself.

Ariel followed him toward the van. They walked past several figures in uniforms and combat harnesses with rifles.

"Oh, shit," Ariel heard from behind them.

"What?" another voice said, this one female.

"Shit's about to get real," the first one replied.

"Why?"

"Because that's Zalman, and he only shows up when things are bad."

Mordechai halted by the van where a burly man in uniform and a helmet was talking to a couple of other officers. He turned to them as they arrived.

"What do you have, *Pakad* Benyamin?" Mordechai was speaking Hebrew, but Ariel knew enough to follow that much.

The *pakad* pointed down the street. "South on the cross street, halfway down the block on this side of the street is a techno club called The Grey Havens. Thirty minutes ago a terrorist entered through the front door wearing an explosive jacket. Once he got inside, someone spotted it, but for some reason he didn't explode it. Most of the crowd left in a panic, especially after someone outside started shooting at them. Two men with rifles pushed their way into the club right after that—we don't know why, but we know there are still people in the club, including a number of women."

Mordechai looked up. "Drone deployed?"

"Tracking four suspects outside the club. No obvious vehicles. Nothing in the air." The captain's voice was grim.

"Anyone on the roofs?"

"Not that we can see. No mobile heat sources, anyway."

"People down?"

"Looks like as many as seven wounded outside, two or three bodies. Unknown inside."

"Any demands or public notices yet?"

"Rosen?" Benyamin looked to the woman on his right.

"No, sir. Not as of yet."

"So we don't know who this is or what they want?"

"No, sir."

"Something went wrong with their plan, then. At a guess, the explosives didn't work. Do we have a plan of the interior of the club?"

"Meier?" Again Benyamin referred to one of his officers.

"They remodeled before they opened a year ago,"

the third officer said, "so no, we're not sure the plans we have match the current interior."

"Pity." Mordechai stared off in the distance, obviously thinking. "They have a back door?"

"Yes."

"It's possible they have more people inside than three. We need to contain this now. Can we shut down the power to the club?"

"Maybe," Meier said. "If we can get to the back of the building without being seen. Depends on how the power comes in and where the main boxes are."

"I'd prefer to shut down power at the nearest transformer," Benyamin said. "That should black out the club and the street outside."

"Agreed. How long?"

"Already in the works," Benyamin said with a thin smile. "Ten minutes, Meier?"

Meier looked at his watch. "About that long."

Mordechai looked at Benyamin. "You're prepared to sweep the street?"

"Already staged."

"Good man." Mordechai pointed at a dark spot across and slightly up the street. "That the alley to the club's back door?"

"Yes, sir," Meier said.

Mordechai thought for a moment. "Give me a headset and a couple of *Rav Shoters* for backup." Corporals, Ariel's brain translated. "My associate and I will enter the back of the club. You sweep the street and watch the front of the club. Give us fifteen minutes to position ourselves and then cut the power."

What? What did he just say? Ariel wasn't sure he believed his ears.

Benyamin barked something into the van, and a few seconds later someone stepped out to hand a headset to Mordechai. He settled it on his head and put the earpiece in his ear. "Test," he said, nodding at the response he heard. A moment later, two police joined up with them, one male, one female, both carrying short-barreled automatic weapons. They nodded to Zalman, he nodded back, beckoned to Ariel, and moved across the street. Ariel shook his head, but followed after. A few feet down the alleyway, Mordechai stopped and wrapped his hand around the microphone of his headset.

"Are you crazy?" Ariel hissed before he could say anything.

"No," Mordechai said in an almost whisper. Ariel could see his sharp grin on his face. "With only three in the building, I could take them all myself, and probably will. You stand back and watch. Once I clear the back, stay there and watch and listen. No gun. No shooting. This will give you a taste for what this is all about. Think of it as either an initiation or as a last chance to change your mind. Just move quietly from here on, and stay right behind me until we get there."

With that, Mordechai released the microphone and turned to move down the alley, staying in the pools of shadow from the few lights burning on the backs of the buildings. Ariel did his best to follow him, but he was sure he wasn't moving as smoothly or as unobtrusively as the older vampire was. On the other hand, he was at least as quiet as their escorts were.

It didn't take long to arrive at the back of the club. Mordechai stopped some distance back in the last big shadow pool and spent some time looking around, looking up, examining the walls and protrusions. Finally he slipped to the door, Ariel in his wake. The two police followed a few feet behind, spreading out a little bit.

Ariel looked at the graphic painted on the back door, all flowing lines and what looked sort of like a tree and flowing letters that didn't resemble any alphabet he knew anything about. "What is that?" he whispered.

Mordechai chuckled and whispered back, "Didn't you read *The Lord of the Rings*? That's right out of *The Fellowship of the Ring*."

"No, just saw the movies."

Mordechai turned and stared at him. "You poor, deprived child. You must not have gotten the import of the club's name. We shall have to remedy that—but later." He looked back at the wall. "Ah, there it is. Come here." Ariel stepped up as Mordechai pulled a very slim light from a pocket—not much more than a long wire with a small knob on one end and a small hooded LED on the other. The light was surprisingly bright, and he shined it across a numeric keypad box on the wall next to the door. "Tell me what you see on the keys." He was still whispering.

Ariel focused on the box. The light was shining from the side, washing across the keys. It took a moment, but he did see something different about them. "3, 4, 6, 7, and the hash key are silver and dull. The rest are silver and shiny."

"Right. First piece of data: even though almost all security systems allow the creation of multiple individual passcodes, over ninety percent of the homes and businesses that install them only create one code which they give to everyone to use."

It didn't take long for Ariel to reach a conclusion. "That's dumb."

"Indeed. Second piece of data: when they create that passcode, between forty and sixty percent of the time it will have four to seven digits, and it will be in low to high sequence."

Ariel thought about it, and whispered, "So if we know what keys they hit..."

"We have about a one-in-three chance of knowing what their passcode is."

"But where does the hash key go?"

"That depends on the system software, but almost always at the end."

Mordechai shifted the light to his left hand and reached out his right index finger. "3, 4, 6, 7, hash." He flicked the light off as he pressed the last key. Nothing. No sound from the lock, no movement of the door.

"*Scheiße!*" Mordechai muttered as he turned the flashlight on again. "Maybe they ran in high-to-low sequence. Let's try 7, 6, 4, 3, hash," he said, pressing the keys as he spoke.

Nothing. No sound from the lock or door.

"Maybe they used random order or used keys more than once."

"Obviously," Mordechai hissed. "But we don't have time to think of all the variations. No, they must have done something they thought was clever. But what?"

Mordechai looked around the alley, then turned back to the club's rear wall, looking at the utilities and the doorframe. Suddenly he froze. After a moment, he lifted a hand and traced part of the graphic of the tree with a finger. "Surely they didn't," he murmured.

"What?" Ariel was confused.

Mordechai didn't respond but bent over the keypad again. "3, 7, 3, 4, 6, 3, hash," he whispered as he tapped the keys. There was a click from the door.

"Those silly bastards." Mordechai smiled broadly as he grasped the door handle and pulled the door open just enough to prevent the door locks from reengaging.

"What?" Ariel whispered insistently.

"Later." Mordechai lifted his left hand and looked at his watch, then lifted his index finger and cocked his head as if waiting. At almost that moment the lights in the alley went off.

"Do a slow ten-count, then follow me," Mordechai whispered.

"What about them?" Ariel jerked a thumb at their escorts.

"They get to watch our backs out here. Start counting."

Without waiting for an acknowledgment, Mordechai opened the door enough to slip in. Ariel swallowed and started counting, "One...two...three..." When he reached the end of the slow count, he opened the door just enough to slide inside, immediately stepping to the left and putting his back against the wall, letting the door close silently while he let his vision adjust.

That didn't take long. With the shutdown of the regular power supply, a handful of emergency lights had apparently activated. There was one in the room where they were, which appeared to be a kitchen. There was a sound. Ariel looked over at Mordechai to see him lowering a body to the floor. He swallowed again. Mordechai looked up, held up a hand to stop him where he was, and moved soundlessly out of the kitchen through the archway on the opposite wall.

The emergency lighting wasn't blindingly bright, but Ariel could see very well with it. Whether any others could was a question he couldn't answer yet. After several long moments of hearing nothing, he started moving around the perimeter of the kitchen's work area, glad he had athletic shoes on for the quiet factor and hoping they wouldn't squeak on the concrete floor.

Ariel's fourth step didn't go very far before it hit something soft. He looked down to see the body of a young man in dark slacks and a white T-shirt with dark blotches on it. He swallowed again, and his stomach knotted. The policeman's comment flashed through his mind: "Shit just got real." His hands fisted for a moment, then relaxed as he bent down and touched the man's forehead almost in benediction before he straightened and moved on.

Three more soft steps took Ariel to the end wall, where he turned and moved along it. At the other corner there was a partially open door. Ariel pushed the door open gently, freezing when the hinges made a slight creak. After a moment, he stuck his head through the door. There was no emergency light in the room, but enough light came through from the kitchen that he could tell it was a very small office, and no one was in it.

Ariel ghosted along the far wall until he came to the central doorway. He looked through it to see a short masking wall that blocked vision of the kitchen from the rest of the club with doorways on each side of it. To the right was a server station with a couple of terminals and a drink station for coffee, tea, and soft drinks. It was unoccupied. To the left was a short hallway toward restrooms. He listened, and heard a few mutters of a language he didn't know coming around the masking wall. He didn't think it was Arabic. He stepped back and slid past the doorway to the club area with his face turned away from the doorway, trusting in his dark clothing and dark hair in the uncertain light to mask him from the view of anyone who might see him.

As he neared the restroom doors—three of them, for some reason—Ariel could see no light leaking under the doors or around the door frames. He paused to slightly open each door enough to reveal total darkness in each of the restrooms. Assuming that no one would willingly be in the dark, Ariel let each door close softly and moved on.

There was a doorway into the club area. Ariel peeked around the edge of it, moving slowly to pan his gaze across more and more of the club. It was mostly an open area for dancing and milling around, with a few tall tables scattered around the perimeter, a bar at one end and a DJ station on the far street side wall. The entrance door was at the north end of that wall.

There were two emergency lights in the room, one above the DJ station and one opposite it on the other side of the room. They created deep pools of shadow near the corners of the room. Ariel slipped out of the hallway and into one of them.

There were a group of people seated on the floor under the second light with a man standing near them aiming an automatic rifle in their general direction. Ariel thought it looked like an AK-47, or at least what he thought one looked like. Another man stood closer to the entrance to the club. He had stripped off his tunic and was frantically wiggling wires and connections on the belt of explosives wrapped around his body. He was the source of the muttering and occasional louder word that Ariel was hearing. Apparently Mordechai's guess that something had gone wrong was correct.

Ariel thought about drawing his pistol. In fact, his hand was on the butt of the pistol. But given that the overwhelming majority of the people in the room were hostages, and given Mordechai's little mini-lecture on the drive over, he decided to be prudent, and slowly withdrew his hand.

At that moment Mordechai burst out of one of the shadows. He moved so quickly Ariel could barely track him. In what seemed to be less than a second the gunman was lying on the floor, neck broken, and Mordechai was a step away from the bomber. In another second, the bomber was lying on the floor with two broken arms, and Mordechai was looking around.

Kiana Ghorbani had crouched among the infidel hostages when Majid and Aram had come in the entrance with their weapons. After they got the patrons who hadn't escaped grouped together and seated on the floor, Majid stood guard over them while Aram went to the back rooms of the club. The plan was for her to mingle with the hostages to be a wild card if something went wrong.

Something did go wrong, obviously, when Fardin started struggling with the bomb he was wearing. That wasn't supposed to happen. She stayed in her place, watching, eyes darting around to try and see if anyone was going to rush him, prepared to help Majid if necessary.

Some moments passed, until she caught a hint of

movement out of the corner of her right eye. She turned her head and watched in horror from where she crouched as Majid was killed before her eyes. His killer had come from the back corner, so he must have come in through the back, which meant that Aram was already dead. Her hand was already drawing the tempered glass knife from the sheath strapped under her left sleeve as she thought that, and she reached out to grab the heavily pregnant infidel woman she had sheltered behind, dragging her up as she stood up.

"Stop!" she shouted in English as she nestled the edge of the blade against the side of the woman's throat. The killer paused as he was reaching down to grab Fardin where he lay on the floor groaning in pain. The killer's head and eyes tracked toward her.

"I'll—"

Before she could utter another syllable of her threat, she felt the bones of her hand and wrist shatter and the knife begin to drop as they were suddenly crushed. She felt someone yank her away from her hostage, and she came face-to-face with a scrawny, bony infidel whose teeth were longer than normal. He had a bit of a grin on his face as she thumped up against his chest.

Her left hand dipped into her pocket, and she returned his grin through the curtain of pain as she pulled out the grenade, feeling the tug as the pin was pulled out because it was safety-pinned to the inside of her pocket. Her grin broadened and she showed teeth of her own as the spoon flew off.

Ariel had moved into motion with the intent of taking the woman prisoner, but he abandoned that idea as soon as he saw the grenade, blurring into motion to slam her to the floor and trap her arm under her body with his weight holding her down. A moment later there was a muffled *whoomp!*, and her body surged against his as a spray of blood flew out from under her.

He raised to his hands and knees and shook his head, then slowly climbed to his feet. He started to brush his chest off, but after looking down decided not to. His armor was speckled with blood, and a couple of fragments had somehow made it around or through the woman's body and were lodged in the armor.

"You all right?" Mordechai said as he approached.

"Yeah." Ariel looked around. "I think so."

"Okay." Mordechai reached up and adjusted his headset microphone. "Yamam, Zalman. Inside terrorists are neutralized. We have . . ." Mordechai's eyes shifted around quickly. "Looks like fourteen civilians in here, and one wounded terrorist. Please call for the explosives unit to come take care of this bomb. Also, come escort the civilians out." He listened for a moment. "No, what you heard was not the bomb, it was a grenade. The bomb is still here, so we need the bomb disposal people immediately. Right. And turn the lights back on."

A few moments later, just as the entrance door opened to admit several of the gray-uniformed Special Police, the main power came back on and the emergency lights shut down. Ariel blinked a few times, as the emergency lights were actually a bit brighter than the main lights, but they weren't spread as evenly.

Ariel took a deep breath, then stepped over to where the pregnant woman was standing, shaking, hands at her mouth. "Let me help you out," he said gently, placing his arm around her shoulder and guiding her toward the entrance. A policewoman met him there and took over getting the woman outside. He turned and went back to stand beside Mordechai by the moaning bomber.

"How many dead and wounded outside?" Mordechai was saying into his microphone. "Terrorists, four dead. Good. Civilians? Two dead, seven wounded. All right. Inside, three terrorists dead, one of which ate her own grenade and will need to be cleaned up with a shovel and a sponge, one terrorist wounded. He's the one wearing the bomb, so where are the explosives people? Well, tell them to hurry." There was a pause, then Mordechai resumed. "Civilians dead inside, one cook in the kitchen."

Ariel held up two fingers. "Two cooks."

"Correction, two cooks dead in the kitchen. One of the terrorists is in the kitchen as well. All the hostages seem to have survived this time, praise *haShem*. Right. Done."

While Mordechai continued his conversation, Ariel walked over and toed the glass knife with his shoe. So clean, so clear, so hard, so deadly.

"Leave that," Mordechai said behind him. "Evidence. You sure you're all right?"

Ariel continued to look at the knife. "Yeah, I think so." He looked up with a tilt to his head. "You ever had to kill a woman? Like this, I mean?"

"Not with a grenade, no, but a terrorist? Yes. They're becoming more common, I'm afraid. Their leaders appear to be running out of gullible young men. Darwinian selection in operation, perhaps."

"I expected to have to deal with...taking someone down. But..."

"But not a woman."

"No."

Mordechai sighed. "Welcome to the twenty-first century and true equal rights." He stepped closer and lowered his voice. "You did a good job, even though you disobeyed me. That grenade probably wouldn't have killed you, but it certainly would have hurt or killed some of the hostages, especially the pregnant woman who was close. Good job," he repeated.

Pakad Benyamin came in the entrance then, and Mordechai stepped over to talk to him. Ariel shifted his gaze to where the female terrorist lay facedown in a broad pool of her own blood. It struck him as somewhat ironic and even a bit darkly humorous that although he was a vampire, and he was due to feed very soon, he wasn't even tempted to taste her blood. He wasn't sure if that said more about him or about her.

CHAPTER 16

BY THE TIME THE BOMB CREW ARRIVED, EVERYONE had cleared out of the club. The bodies had already been removed, so it was just the bomber who was left inside with the crew. By that point, Mordechai had wrapped up his discussions with Benyamin and his officers and turned in his headset, so he beckoned to Ariel and they walked back up the street and around the corner to where Mordechai's car was parked. They threw their armor in the trunk, Mordechai moved his blazer to the back seat, they got in, and moments later were moving down the street again.

Mordechai touched a button on the console. "Call Mendel," he said.

The sound of a phone ringing filled the car. It rang three times, then Rabbi Mendel's voice said, "Hallo."

"Rabbi, Mordechai Zalman here. I have young Ariel with me, and we have had a somewhat intense evening. We both need about a half-liter of our favorite beverage. We will arrive in about twenty minutes or so."

"Ah. I understand. It will be waiting when you get here."

"Very good. Shalom."

"Shalom."

There was a click and the call ended.

They were a couple of kilometers closer to their destination when Ariel looked over at Mordechai. "Why does blood taste different?"

"What?" Ariel could see Mordechai's head move as he glanced over at him.

"Why does blood in Israel taste different than blood in America?"

Mordechai chuckled for a moment. "I don't know. Genetics, maybe. Diet, maybe. American blood banks mostly process their donations and separate red blood cells from platelets and plasma, but I think Israel is like most of Europe and they store whole blood with much less processing."

Ariel snorted. "Kind of like the difference between low-fat milk and whole milk?"

"Maybe. I don't know. I don't think I've noticed."

"There's a difference," Ariel said. "I don't know what it is, and I don't know why, but I know it's there."

"Does the difference in taste make any real difference to you? Is it like different wines, or something like that?" Now Mordechai sounded amused.

"More like the difference between Coke and Pepsi. Not huge, but there. It just makes me curious."

"Add it to the list of things you can research after you attain your degrees."

Ariel snorted again.

Although he was driving reasonably, it still wasn't long before Mordechai steered his car into the underground parking associated with the anonymous building where Dr. Mendel's group had their facilities.

Ariel waited while Mordechai took his jacket out of the car and locked it, then they walked together to the elevator. Mordechai's thumbprint sufficed to summon it. He caught Ariel watching. "Remind me to remind *Rav* Avram to have you added to the security list."

Ariel was surprised when the elevator took them down rather than up, but the doors opened before he said anything, so he followed Mordechai out and down a short hallway. Mordechai again presented his thumb to another of the small metal plates, and a door opened before them. Ariel noted there was no handle on the door. After he walked through and the door closed behind them, he noticed there was no handle on the inside either.

"How do we get out if the power fails?" he asked.

Mordechai shrugged. "Battery backup for a couple of hours or so. Generator should automatically start after a few minutes. If it doesn't, and the batteries run down, you don't."

"Remind me not to stay long, then," Ariel muttered. "I'm still not very fond of spending a lot of time underground, you know, which is weird, considering what I am now."

Mordechai chuckled.

They were in what appeared to be a small break room: refrigerator, microwave, counter with sink, a couple of small tables with chairs. Mordechai pulled a chair out and sat at one of the tables, waving a hand at another chair. Ariel sat as well, sagging in a bit of relief as the tension of the last couple of hours began to flow out of his body.

A moment later, a door at the other end of the room opened, and Rabbi Mendel walked in, followed by a young black woman carrying a tray with four bottles, two that from their coloring had to be blood, and two of water. "Over there, if you would, Elizabeth," the rabbi said.

She delivered her tray to their table, smiled at Ariel, then turned and left.

"The silent type," Ariel said.

"The techs don't let me carry anything anymore after I dropped a bottle of blood a few months ago and it shattered on the floor," Mendel said with a sigh. "Elizabeth says an old man shouldn't have to carry things anyway, so if she's around she makes sure I don't."

"One of the Ethiopians?" Ariel asked.

Mendel nodded as he settled in a chair between them.

Ariel read the labels on the two bottles of blood. "O positive and A positive," he said.

"The two most common blood types in Israel," Mendel said.

Ariel rested the tips of his right-hand index and little fingers on top of the two bottles. "May I?"

Mordechai made a permissive gesture toward the bottles. "Glasses in the cabinet," he said.

Ariel went to the cabinet, found five glasses and brought them back to the table. He twisted the cap off the O bottle, poured a little into a glass, and lifted it to his mouth. He tasted the blood, considered it, held it in his mouth, then swallowed it. Mordechai had by then opened one of the water bottles, and handed Ariel a glass of water which he drank, swished around in his mouth, and swallowed. He then repeated the process with the A bottle and a clean glass. After finishing the second drink of water, Mordechai said, "Well?"

"There's a definite difference in taste between the two," Ariel said.

"How so?" Mendel asked, his eyebrows raised.

"The O positive seemed to taste a little bit sweeter than the A, which seemed to have a bit stronger metallic taste. Not a big difference between them, but there."

"Interesting," Mendel said. "And you did this why?"

"We had a conversation coming in," Mordechai said. "He said the blood in Israel tastes different than the blood he had in the US. Seems like the difference causes may be more than just location."

"Interesting." Mendel opened his notebook and jotted a note. "I'll have to pass that on to Dr. Hurwitz. I don't think we've investigated that before. Do you sense the difference?" He looked at Mordechai, who shook his head. "Interesting," Mendel said the third time. He waved his hands at them. "Go on, drink it."

Mordechai repeated his permissive gesture, and Ariel took the A positive bottle. The two of them filled their glasses, and sat sipping. Ariel concentrated on the sensations: cool from the refrigeration, kind of like sipping a thick soup. He felt his body reacting to it as it slipped down his throat and into his stomach, almost like a hungry child grabbing for his favorite sweet. Ariel didn't gulp it down or try to guzzle it. It needed more respect than that, he felt. The divine commandment about blood weighed on his mind.

They finished about the same time, and both took a drink of water to rinse out their mouths. "A word of advice," Mordechai said. "Brush your teeth. The aftertaste of old blood does not make for pleasant breath."

"Yeah, I figured that one out back in Chattanooga,"

Ariel said. "I caught a whiff of my breath once the next day after a dose." He shuddered. "That should be part of Vampire 101: Brush your teeth after a meal."

Mordechai laughed, and even Mendel smiled at the lame joke. Then the smile faded away.

"So what happened tonight?" Mendel asked.

Mordechai sobered and leaned forward, clasping his hands on the table. "You should see the report from Yamam before long. A fairly standard attempt at a bombing, except the bomb fizzled. This group had a Plan B—which they don't, always—which was to have two or three others in the club and some more outside, both groups with weapons. When the bomb didn't go off, some of the club patrons escaped, but the rest were taken as hostages. Ariel and I came in the back—me to work, him to observe. I terminated two of them. We would have had two prisoners, but one of them—a woman—pulled a grenade and Ariel put her down on top of it. So, three dead terrorists, the bomber injured but captured, and a few civilians killed or wounded outside the building but most unharmed." He shrugged. "Not the greatest of successes, but it could have been much worse."

Mendel closed his eyes and shook his head. "Will they never learn? Will they never stop?"

"Doubtful," Mordechai said.

"So this was impromptu?"

Mordechai shrugged. "Yes, to a degree, but once you're inside of a building, everything becomes impromptu. Recall that 'no plan survives contact with the enemy.'"

Ariel heard the quotes in Mordechai's voice. "Was that Clausewitz?" he asked.

Mordechai turned to him with raised eyebrows.

"Right period, wrong German," was his response. "That was originally said by Helmuth von Moltke, called the Elder because he had a nephew who used the same name. A stuffy, snobbish, arrogant man, but probably the greatest general between Napoleon and World War II. I've often thought that if he had been commanding the German General Staff in World War I instead of his nephew, the Germans would have won that war, and there would have been no World War II. That might have been better for us." He spread both hands across the table, palms up, and Ariel understood him to mean Jews.

"Did you know him?"

Mordechai nodded. "I did meet him not long before his death in 1891. We had a couple of conversations. I didn't like him, but I learned some things from him." Mordechai nodded a couple of times before he said, "That was a paraphrase of the original saying. The paraphrase is what you usually hear quoted. The original is somewhat longer." His smile flirted with his mouth for a moment. "Moltke was a Prussian aristocrat, and like most of that lot would use three words where one would do."

Ariel sat back, impressed again at Mordechai's age. It was so easy to overlook that the man who was driving the car tonight was over two hundred eighty years old. After a moment, he realized that Mendel had said something to him.

"I'm sorry, would you say that again?"

"I said, how do you feel after tonight?"

Ariel thought about that. How did he feel? "Stressed. Frazzled. Glad I survived. Sorry that any of our people were hurt or killed, but glad I had a hand in keeping it from being worse."

"I gave you an instruction to remain in the back," Mordechai said in a level voice. "You disobeyed me."

"You also told me to watch and listen. I couldn't see anything in the back, and I couldn't hear anything understandable. I didn't plan to do anything—I was just trying to see—but when I saw the female terrorist holding a knife to the woman's throat, I couldn't let that stand."

Mordechai's mouth quirked. "So you took it on yourself to deal with her. You were actually farther away from her than I was. I would have taken her down in the next instant."

"Maybe so," Ariel said, "but I was there, and this is why I was there—to protect our people. Or in this case, to protect one very pregnant mother and the life she was carrying."

Mordechai looked at him for a long moment, then nodded. "Agreed. And what you did was both right and righteous. However, understand that this was not a videogame or an action movie. Real lives were at stake, and a single mistake on your part wouldn't have ended in Game Over, it would have ended in blood and death."

Ariel said nothing in response.

Mordechai leaned forward. "You were stupid lucky. You did something stupid, and it worked out. You cannot take that chance. You cannot take your own path in any operation, because almost inevitably someone will die. It might even be you. There's a reason why young vampires don't survive long. But being who and what you are, most likely it will be some of those you are supposed to protect. You take orders from your leaders, you follow the plans, because that will almost certainly produce the most survivors, including yourself and any possible teammates."

After a moment, Ariel nodded. "Fair enough. I'll try to do better, and try to learn from you." He smiled. It was a small smile, and a bit thin-lipped, but it was a smile. "You know, that line about this not being a videogame would have more impact if I was actually a gamer."

Mordechai chuckled in return, and drew a line in the air as if counting score.

Ariel picked up his water glass and drained the last of the water, then sat there slowly turning the glass in his hands. Mendel stirred, and Ariel looked at him.

"It did not bother you to kill someone?"

"I've come to grips with that already, Rabbi," Ariel explained. "When I decided to take this road, I had to deal with that. I'm not happy to be involved in that death, but really, she took her own life when she pulled that grenade out of her pocket. All I did was make sure that she didn't hurt anyone else in the process."

He gazed steadily into Mendel's eyes, until the rabbi nodded in response.

"Well said," Mordechai replied. "And tonight will provide your ashes. Your parents will receive closure."

Ariel was startled by that. It hadn't occurred to him yet that that was a possible result of tonight's action. His mind was suddenly filled with the sight and sound of his mother crying hysterically. This would rock her world to its foundations, but . . . it would still be kinder and gentler than the truth of what he had become. He closed his eyes and clung to that.

He heard Mordechai stand up. "I've got something to do. I'll be in touch. Would you see to it that Ariel gets home?"

"Of course, old friend," Mendel replied softly.

Ariel heard the door open and close.

The room stayed quiet for a long time. Other than Mendel's breathing, all Ariel heard was the mechanical sounds of the ventilation fan and the refrigerator.

Finally, Ariel opened his eyes. "Mordechai said that I should be added to the security list."

"Indeed. We'll do that before you leave tonight," Mendel said.

After a moment, Ariel looked around. "Where did Mordechai have to go? Or is that need-to-know territory?"

Mendel shook his head. "No, no security involved there. Tonight and much of tomorrow he'll probably be at the Western Wall, praying. He always does that after one of these episodes."

"Huh. I didn't have him pegged as being all that religious."

Mendel frowned. "He has more spiritual depth and understanding than the two of us put together, boy. He has been a vampire for over two hundred years, Ariel. Let that sink into your bones. He has known your fears and feelings and problems for ten times your lifetime, for a hundred times your experience as a vampire, and yet he still prays to *haShem*. He has survived over two hundred years of oppression, pogroms, and the Holocaust itself, yet his faith in *haShem* is still real and solid.

"Mordechai was personally acquainted with the Vilna Gaon. He is of the priestly lineage. Think about the implications of that. He has meditated on Torah and Talmud for over two hundred years. You should ask him what he believes. His insights are incredible. You should do so well when half his age you have."

Mendel's anger and passion rocked Ariel. He couldn't

speak for a long moment. He couldn't find the words. "I'm . . . sorry," he finally said. "I didn't understand."

"No, you didn't," Mendel said. "But you're young. You've been through a difficult time these last few weeks, and everything you thought you understood about the world has changed, but you're still very young. You're very smart, you learn quickly, and you will be a valued part of our work before long, assuming you survive, but you are very young. You lack experience. Knowledge can come from training and study, but wisdom only comes by experience. Our job is to help you survive long enough to get that experience. That is why Mordechai has disarranged his schedule and his operations to spend as much time as possible with you. That is why he has called in two lifetimes' worth of favors to ease your way and smooth your path. If you survive and become half the man he is, it will be because of him. Never forget that. And he prays for you. You might spend some prayers for the consolation of *his* soul."

Ariel considered that, staring across the room at a blank wall. At length, he sighed. "'Is not wisdom found among the aged?'" he quoted. "'Does not long life bring understanding?'"

The rabbi's eyebrows raised. "You've studied Job," he said with an approving tone.

Ariel shrugged. "One of my father's favorite verses."

"Then your father is a man of wisdom."

Ariel nodded, a lump in his throat. That relationship was soon to break.

Mendel seemed to sense the emotion, and stood. "Come. Let us get you entered in the security lists so that you no longer have to rely on Mordechai's thumb to gain entry."

CHAPTER 17

Nine months later

"I'M DONE," ADAM BITON SAID, SETTING HIS EMPTY beer glass on the table. "See you all in class tomorrow."

"Good night," Yael Malka said. Ariel echoed her, lifting his Perrier bottle in salute. As Adam walked away, the two of them looked at each other. "Last men standing," Yael said with a grin.

"For certain values of men, anyway," Ariel responded. She laughed and took a swig of her own beer.

Yael was older than Ariel by several years, but they were sharing classes together because she was a sabra and had spent time in the Israeli Defense Force before she started school. She didn't hold it against him that as an immigrant he wasn't required to do the same.

Ariel liked Yael. She was smart, pert, and very funny to hang around with. She was also, if not pretty, rather handsome, being at least a couple of inches taller than Ariel with warm brown eyes and wavy brunette hair. She reminded him somewhat of Elena, for all that she didn't look anything like her. He was comfortable in her presence, which wasn't something he could say about many girls. In another life he would have considered asking her out, but given his situation, he didn't think that was a good idea right then—and probably not ever.

They'd hit it off fairly well at the beginning of the class session. They shared two different classes and a lab, all evening classes. She was consistently friendly with him, and didn't seem to be put off by his quirks about food and drink, unlike some of his other classmates. She also had picked up on the fact that he understood almost everything the instructors presented the first time around, and she wasn't shy about asking for help or note-sharing.

"Your Hebrew is getting better," she said as she put her half-empty glass back on the table. "Your vocabulary is increasing, and you sound smoother."

"Thanks," Ariel said as he turned his water bottle around in his hands. "I've been working on it. I've had a couple of nights this week where I remember dreaming in Hebrew, so I think I'm finally getting there."

"Your accent is shifting, too. Another couple of months or so, and you'll probably sound like a sabra."

Ariel shrugged. "That I don't care so much about. But I need to be fluent as fast as possible, given the program I'm in."

Yael nodded, then picked up her glass and took another swig. She set the glass down and turned it around and around in her fingers. "Can I ask you something? Personal, I mean? Feel free to tell me to get screwed if you want to."

"Ask. Worst I can do is say no."

She reached out and tapped his bottle. "You only drink water with us. You never eat with us. Is there a reason? Something besides just being weird? Are you pulling a Daniel on us? Or are you an android or cyborg?" Her smile lit her face up, but he could tell she was serious.

Ariel sighed. He had known this would come up sooner or later. At least it was Yael, who he thought would be pretty easy to talk to about it.

"It's not a religious or philosophical choice, Yael. I've got some medical issues. My digestive tract has some real abnormalities. I'm on an extremely limited diet, and I basically can't find anything that's safe for me to eat at any restaurant. It would make me sick as a dog. I avoid alcohol for the same reasons." That was the truth...it just wasn't all the truth.

He reached into his windbreaker pocket and pulled out a *magen* bar that he happened to have on him. "This is one of the few things I can eat." He peeled it open and bit a big chunk out of one corner. "See?" he said, mouth full, "you can tell everyone now that you've actually seen me eat something." He chewed, swallowed, and grinned.

Yael reached over, took the bar from his hand, and bit the other corner off. She chewed it, eyes thoughtful, and nodded after swallowing. "Not bad. Bland, but not bad." She took another swig of beer, and set her nearly empty glass down. "Okay, that I can understand. And that certainly explains your ultra-lean appearance. How low is your body fat?"

"Under three percent," Ariel admitted.

"I'd die for your metabolism," Yael said, grabbing a handful of waist on her right side.

"Be careful what you wish for," Ariel said. "You wouldn't want the problems that come with it." His voice darkened noticeably.

"Ah, right." Yael turned her glass around a few more times before looking up again. "'Nother question?"

"Sure." Ariel lifted his bottle to take his own drink.

"Are you gay?"

Ariel choked on the water coming into his mouth. It took a few moments of spluttering and coughing to get his throat cleared enough to talk. Yael had her hand up to her mouth, obviously suppressing a laugh.

"No," he finally got out. "I am genetically and in gender a hundred percent male, and I am absolutely hetero in my orientation. So I can say with assurance that I'm not gay."

"Well, that will disappoint a couple of guys in the class," Yael said with a smile.

"Who . . . never mind. I don't want to know."

She leaned forward a little and looked into his eyes. "But that leads to why, when I or any of the other girls in the class flirt with you or strongly hint that we'd like to get together with you, you don't respond?"

Ariel closed his eyes, and sighed. When he opened them again, Yael was still staring at him. He looked down.

"Yael, first, I . . ." He hesitated for a long moment. "First, I'm seriously introverted. The words 'geek' and 'nerd' could have been invented for me. Because of that I . . . don't have a lot of experience with girls. So, I don't . . ." His voice trailed away.

Yael touched a fingertip to the back of his hand. It almost burned. "I wouldn't mind."

Ariel forced himself to look up, remembering what

Dr. Mendel had told him in that last conversation. "Well, secondly, let's just say that digestive and metabolic problems aren't the only issues I have. I'd... appreciate it if you didn't spread that around."

Despite his own turmoil, the look on Yael's face almost made Ariel laugh—a mixture of horror and disbelief. She looked down and there was a moment of silence.

"Who do you work for?" she finally said, looking up again.

Ariel was a bit confused. "What do you mean?"

"You're carrying a weapon..."

"How do you know?"

She looked at him with her eyebrows lowered. "Ariel, I was in an IDF combat squad for two years and I'm still in the reserves. I know what a pistol being carried looks like. You're carrying a weapon, so you must have a weapon license. No one your age would have a weapon license in Israel without working for someone." She raised her eyebrows.

Ariel's mouth quirked. "I can't tell you," he responded.

Her eyes lit up. "But you are working for someone?"

"Yes." He figured it wouldn't hurt to admit that, since she'd basically figured it out anyway.

She sat back, satisfied. "Okay. I won't bug you anymore... about any of it. No promises for the rest of our friends, though." She held out a fist.

"Fair enough." Ariel grinned at her, and bumped fists with her.

She grinned back, then took a pull at her glass. Ariel had his bottle halfway to his mouth when his mobile buzzed. He looked down to see a message from Marta. He tapped the screen.

DON'T FORGET APPT WITH DR HURWITZ
ON THURSDAY.

Ariel sighed. "Yes, I know," he muttered as he
thumbed the Delete icon. He looked up to see Yael
with her head tilted and one eyebrow raised. "Reminder
for an appointment day after tomorrow," he said with
a grimace.

"Ah." Her grin reappeared. "Mobiles—can't live
with them..."

"And can't live without them," completing the quote
with a laugh.

One week later

ARIEL TAPPED *SAVE* ON HIS WORKSTATION, AND
watched as his data was stored. He closed the app,
logged off, and stood up with a sigh, looking around.
He was the last one in the lab, which didn't surprise
him. He'd been late getting in, and then he'd made
a false start on the exam because he'd misread and
misunderstood the Hebrew wording of a question, which
ended up costing him some time before he realized
his error, backtracked, and started over. Fortunately
he realized it before the first commit point in the test,
so he was able to redo from the beginning rather than
making corrections after the commit.

He gathered his notes and stuffed them in his
backpack, making sure his mobile was in his jacket
pocket. Taking a deep breath and releasing it, he
stood up and made his way to the lab exit, turning
the lights off as he walked out.

"Hey, Ariel!" He saw a group of his classmates
gathered down by the exit. One of them beckoned, and

Yael broke away and trotted toward him. They used English a lot, partly as a courtesy to him, because his Hebrew, while much improved, was still not second nature to him, and partly so some of them could practice their own English.

He watched Yael move toward him. He still enjoyed watching her, but then his attention was attracted by something else: Mordechai leaning against a hallway wall on the other side of the exit.

"Hey," she said as she bounced to a stop. "We're going to go to the Parallels Club to drink some beer and brag about how we think we did on the test. You want to come?"

Ariel shook his head. "Ordinarily, yeah, but I've got a prior commitment tonight."

"Well, we'll be there a while, so if you get done early, come check us out."

"Got it."

Ariel watched as she trotted back to the group, shared the response, and several of them waved at him as they headed out the doors. After they cleared out, he walked down to face Mordechai.

"Haven't seen you in a while," Ariel said in Hebrew.

"Had a commission in Turkey," Mordechai replied.

"All done?"

"Done enough. There are some things that need to develop before I go back, but once they do, it shouldn't take long to finish."

"Good." Ariel slung his backpack and stuck his hands in his jacket pockets.

The two men walked out the door together. Once they were well into the open space between the buildings, Ariel stopped and looked up at the night sky for a moment, where a sliver of the moon was riding high.

"Need to decompress?" Mordechai murmured.

"No," Ariel responded in a similar tone. "Just...still trying to put the mosaic tiles in place to show the big picture, I guess. I'm committed to this. I know I am. But I still wonder sometimes if this is right for me...if this is *righteous* for Ariel Barak. Still wishing that *haShem* would give me a bit more of a clue if I'm in the right place."

"My experience has usually been that that is something you learn by looking backwards."

"Huh. In other words, I can see where I've been in the right place in the past, but the immediate moment is never certain because I'm in it? Kind of a Heisenberg kind of thing?"

Mordechai shrugged. "My experience."

Ariel tilted his head for a moment. "Never thought of it that way, but you could be right." He straightened. "John Bull?"

"Sure, if you want to take the chance." Mordechai's eyebrows lifted. "You do recall what happened the last time we went there."

"I'll take my chances. You drive."

Mordechai chuckled as he straightened from the wall, and they walked out together. When they got to the car, Mordechai held his hand up. Ariel paused as Mordechai looked around, then put a hand in his jacket. What he pulled out he handed to Ariel.

It was a knife in a black leather sheath. Ariel pulled it out of the sheath. It was a glass knife. His eyebrows rose, and he looked at Mordechai. "Yes, it's the knife the female terrorist had at The Grey Havens. It's specially tempered glass, almost unbreakable, and almost unde-tectable by any security scanner in the world."

"So why is it in my hands?"

"I thought you might like a memento of your first operation."

"Doesn't this constitute evidence?"

"If there was an investigation going on, certainly. Given that they were caught in the act, and all but one of them are dead, not really. It's a legal curiosity. A legal problem as well, as it would be cluttering up an evidence room for no good purpose. So I claimed it for research purposes, signed it over to Rabbi Mendel, and after they did their tests, he gave it back to me. It's now yours, free, clear, and legal."

Ariel looked at the knife, inserted it back in the sheath, and put it in his inside jacket pocket. "Thanks, I guess. It will give me something to think about." Mordechai smiled, made a small hand gesture, and opened the driver's door to the car.

The ride to the so-called pub was uneventful, with conversation mostly centered on Israeli politics because of an upcoming election. This continued until after the young man who was serving the tables that night brought their order to them, setting a bottle of Perrier matter-of-factly before Ariel, but presenting Mordechai's Glenlivet to him with a certain amount of what appeared to be respect.

Mordechai took a deep sniff of the scotch, and smiled. "Was that your last exam of the term?"

"Yeah."

"How do you think you did?"

Ariel took a pull at his bottle and played with the bubbles in his mouth a bit before he swallowed.

"Honestly? I'm sure I aced it. There may be a question or two I didn't answer the way they wanted, but my answers are right."

"So, you wrapped up your term, then?"

"Yeah, I believe so." He took another pull at his bottle.

"Good. You feel like making a trip back to the US with me?"

Ariel frowned. "Why?"

"There's an issue in New York I might like your help with."

"Science issue, vampire issue, or *Gibborim* issue?"

"The last."

Ariel took another drink, this time holding the water and letting the bubbles fizz for a long moment. He swallowed it bit by bit, letting the sensation die away slowly until the last bit of it was gone.

"Why me? Why not someone else?"

"Because I can't be in two places at once, and the action needs to happen at the same time."

"Ah. Is this righteous?"

"Very. Ehud ben-Gera would approve."

"Then yes."

Ariel drained his bottle and waved at the server for another. "How long will it take? The next term begins in three weeks."

"Plenty of time. Shouldn't take more than a week."

"Good. Spar with me tonight?"

Mordechai nodded. "Sure."

The second bottle of Perrier arrived, and Ariel took a big drink of it.

"You thirsty today?" Mordechai looked at him with a raised eyebrow.

"Hunger, mostly."

"Ah. Well, after we spar, you can feed."

"Yeah."

"So tell me, how do you feel about your weapons training?"

"What, Shimon didn't give you a report?"

"Of course he did," Mordechai said. "But I want your report."

Ariel shrugged. "Last round of target shooting, 99 score with right hand and 85 score with left hand. Last round of combat shooting, 95 score with right hand and 81 score with left hand. He introduced me to the M16 last week. He said I'm 'adequate' with that so far."

"Not bad," Mordechai said. "From Shimon, not bad at all. I'm sure he gave you his four rules." That wasn't a question.

"Oh, yeah. I got those the first night, and he's repeated them at least twice since then, as well as the lecture on the difference between cover and concealment."

"Good. He's right about those rules, but he does go on and on about them sometimes." Mordechai took a deep sniff of his scotch. "Have you decided what ammunition you will usually carry?"

"He's let me shoot all the common loads. Right now I'm following his suggestion and carrying hollow points."

Mordechai nodded. "That's why Shimon has been training you with them. Not risk free, but less risky than the full metal jacket for our work."

"Huh." Ariel took another drink.

"You keeping up with Dr. Hurwitz?"

"Saw him last week. He says I'm developing along

the expected parameters, whatever that's supposed to mean."

Mordechai chuckled. "No researcher likes to release information before the research is done. The only reason he told Rabbi Mendel and me anything is because the rabbi's group is paying the bills."

"I'll have to keep that in mind for when I'm on that side of the table," Ariel quipped.

"Speaking of which, school okay?"

"Yeah. Glad the term's over, though. I need a break."

"Your friends seem to like you."

"Most of them, most of the time. I've got the reputation of being a bit weird because I won't eat with them or drink booze with them. Had a couple of older guys try to bully me because I was new and was an immigrant. That didn't last long." He smiled a little before he took another drink from the bottle. "Biggest problem is holding off the girls that want dates."

"To be expected, I suppose." Mordechai lifted his glass for another sniff.

"Yeah, whatever. It would have made my mother happy." Ariel frowned a bit at that thought.

"I saw the announcement in the local newspaper."

"Yeah, I got a copy of that, too. Kind of weird seeing your own death announcement. Even weirder seeing the space in the mausoleum with my name on it. I'm halfway tempted to fly over and get a selfie of me standing next to it."

"Probably not wise," Mordechai murmured.

"Yeah, you're probably right. If someone saw me, it might cause questions." Ariel sighed. "But at least they're able to move on. If I was still there, things would have blown up by now."

"Even so," Mordechai said.

"Yeah."

They sat together in silence, occasionally lifting either the scotch glass or the Perrier bottle. They lifted together when Ariel took his last sip of Perrier, and set them down at the same time.

"Shall we go spar?" Mordechai asked.

"Let's. I've got some angst to work off."

Mordechai left a bill on the table, and they walked out together.

Two days later Ariel relaxed as their plane's wheels left the runway at Ben Gurion Airport. They were flying in a corporate model jet, a Bombardier 8000, which as far as Ariel was concerned was the lap of luxury compared to most commercial airlines, even in the post-Covid era.

"Here." Mordechai dropped a folder on the table between them. "Read through that, then we'll talk."

It didn't take long. It was mostly newspaper articles about how an immigrant group had settled in a north Brooklyn neighborhood and slowly taken it over, then had started its own community patrols "for the safety of the neighborhood." After a time, they even acquired a few cars to patrol in and had them painted in a uniform style that to some extent mimicked the police-force cruisers, complete with old-fashioned light bars mounted on the roofs.

The neighborhood in question was situated just north of a major Jewish neighborhood, a map informed him. His mouth twisted at that. And subsequent articles described the beginnings of a pattern of harassment of Jews along the boundary between the two neighborhoods, beginning with speech and progressing up to various physical accostings, frequently aimed at the elderly. A burning began to grow in Ariel's stomach. He flipped through the rest of the pages in the folder, seeing the pattern continue to develop.

He closed the folder and gently laid it on the table, then swiveled his gaze to where Mordechai sat. "Well?"

"Well, what?"

"There must be more to it than this if we are flying in."

Mordechai laid a tablet on the table. "Watch this."

Ariel picked up the tablet and pushed the PLAY button. He watched, teeth clenched, as a dashcam caught the image of its car running into what appeared to be an older man, Chassidic by his clothing, crossing a street at night. The car came to a halt. There was no sound, but the dome lights came on from the doors of the car being opened and two figures appeared in the headlights of the car, laughing and slapping hands together. They continued to laugh as they looked down at something in front of the car, almost certainly the pedestrian. The picture froze after a couple of minutes, and two thumbnail-type photos of two bearded men appeared in the upper corners of the tablet. After a moment, the screen cleared and another video began, this time of two uniformed dark-skinned bearded men beating a young man also dressed in Chassidic-style coat and hat. They beat him to the ground and continued swinging their nightsticks for some time. They eventually stopped, and straightened to walk away, laughing. Again, the picture froze, and two more thumbnail photos appeared in the upper corners.

The screen split, and both final pictures appeared a moment before the screen of the tablet cracked and crazed. Ariel realized his hands had squeezed tightly enough that the pressure of his thumbs had broken the tablet. He laid it back on the table. "Sorry," was all he could say through his clenched teeth.

Mordechai nodded. "The first man was Abraham Miller, a resident in the Jewish neighborhood out for a walk at night because he had trouble sleeping. He made the mistake of walking through the boundary street. Daud and Ismail ran him down with their patrol car, then stood and watched as he bled to death from a severed femoral artery because of a compound fracture of the right femur. They called it in to the city police, said they found him in the street.

"The second case was Jonathan Goldberg. Khamis and Sajid claimed that he was harassing them and attacked them first. He was left a quadriplegic as a result of the beating, and died three months later. Both of them were in the wrong place at the wrong time. The state never prosecuted either case—for lack of evidence, they claimed."

Ariel's hands were tightened into fists so strongly that his knuckles were blanched white, and his breath was moving in and out of his nostrils almost like the wind of a storm. His teeth felt like they should be shattering, his jaws were clenched so hard. He stared at his fists, wanting . . . wanting for the first time in his life to hurt someone, to cause anguish with his own hands. He felt as if his head was going to explode from the pressure he was feeling in it. One part of his mind was horrified at what he had seen, one part of his mind was horrified at his reaction to it, and both those parts were overwhelmed by the rage that he felt.

He didn't know how long he sat there, seething

in his anger, starting to tremble from the intensity of it. At some point, his breathing began to slow down. He felt his jaws begin to loosen a bit, and his hands began to relax. It took more time before the trembling stopped and he was able to rest his hands on his thighs and look up at Mordechai.

"So..." Ariel stopped to clear phlegm out of his throat. "So what's the plan?"

Mordechai tilted his head a bit, then gave a slow nod. "Are you ready for this?"

"I...think so. It's just hard to believe this could happen in my own country."

"Ah, but it's not your country anymore, Ariel. You're not a citizen of the United States of America any longer, so what happens in its territory and within its borders shouldn't be of concern to you."

It took a moment for Ariel to fully absorb that. "But..."

His retort was stilled by Mordechai holding up an index finger. "But...you are still a Jew. And things that affect American Jews affect all of us. Never again."

The Holocaust remembrance slogan struck Ariel as it never had before. "Never again," he repeated.

Mordechai nodded again, this time with a bit of a sad smile. "The plan, as you call it, is to simply make these four men disappear." He leaned back in his seat and steepled his fingers below his chin. "Their leaders were smart enough to make them vanish for a time, but they have recently returned to the patrol's staff rotation, albeit only at night so far. They are still paired together." He shook his head. "Short-sighted of their leaders, but still, if they were very smart, they wouldn't have allowed this to happen at all. They have attracted our attention, which they will ultimately regret."

"So how do we know this? We have people watching them?"

A hint of a smile appeared on Mordechai's face. "Oh, to some small extent. There are many people in New York City who owe us something who don't mind keeping an eye open. But mostly, this group's notion of computer security is laughable. An eight-year-old with a student laptop could hack their files, and their attempts at encryption are just as feeble. So we know what is in their systems as soon as it is entered." His smile broadened. "Israeli cyber-sleuths are among the best in the world—as noted by the fact that they are seldom noticed, much less caught."

"Huh." Ariel tilted his head as he considered his companion. "I'm still amazed at how well you function in the twenty-first century."

Mordechai shrugged. "The aims, goals, and approaches of espionage and warfare have not changed appreciably in hundreds of years. Only the tools and some of the methods. Just as one does not have to be a talented pianist to appreciate fine music, one does not have to be a cryptologist to appreciate and utilize the work of a master spy."

"But you do some of the espionage work? Like your trip to Turkey?"

Mordechai shrugged again. "Sometimes. I have certain . . . advantages, let us say, that a normal human does not. Advantages which you share, by the way."

"I don't have your experience."

"This is how you gain experience, my friend. There is no substitute for doing the work."

"I guess that's true." Ariel came back to his original topic. "So what's the plan?"

"Both pairs of them work the graveyard shift, as it's called in America. They both take a brief break at different locations in the middle of their shift. You and I will appear at their break spots dressed as a couple of our Chassidic brethren, and serve as bait. I doubt they will be able to resist the temptation."

"Ah," Ariel breathed. "And once they attack, we can respond in self-defense."

"Oh, yes, that could be a factor if we were going to use the courts. But the courts have already served injustice here by not prosecuting them earlier. So we will rely on their own teachings. Mohammed is reported to have said in their own hadith, 'As you would have people do to you, do to them.' It is fitting, after all."

"Indeed," Ariel breathed.

"As they took lives in premeditation, so let their lives be taken." Mordechai's voice was cold.

"You said we would disappear them."

"They will never check in from that patrol. There will be no traces of them. Their leaders and friends and families will be mystified and, just perhaps, will learn something from this." Mordechai's face grew hard. "If not, we will return until they do learn the lesson."

Ariel said nothing, but he felt a certain warmness inside at the thought. Justice—not vengeance, but justice—would be done.

A long moment of silence passed, then Mordechai picked up the broken tablet and stood. "We're about ten hours out from New York. Get as much rest as you can. We'll be very busy once we're on the ground."

CHAPTER 18

THREE NIGHTS LATER ARIEL PULLED HIS OVERCOAT collar up around his neck. It was after 2:00 A.M., and the streets were empty but for the community patrol car that had pulled up to the curb about thirty feet up the street from where he lurked in a very shadowed doorway corner. It was cold, which he acknowledged in a corner of his mind but didn't react to. He wasn't as affected by weather extremes as he was when he was younger—one of many things the conversion had done to or for him. Thankfully it wasn't raining. That could have made the evening's plans a bit more uncertain.

He stepped out of the doorway, hunched his shoulders and bent forward, taking short, slow steps to mimic the shuffle of an older man. Also fortunately, the evening winds had died down, so that the homburg hat he was wearing stayed in place. His head was apparently in between standard hat sizes, so this one was a bit of a loose fit.

The last three days had been busy, almost frenetic. They had locked their Israeli pistols in a discreet locker on the plane before debarking, since they didn't plan on using them in the US and didn't want to have to explain them. Mordechai had even insisted that he leave the glass knife on the plane.

Disarming had surprisingly made Ariel somewhat nervous. He had gotten more used to carrying the pistol than he'd realized.

After clearing customs, they had left the airport and gone to a small, quiet hotel not far away. It didn't have the large sign of one of the major hotel chains, but the parking lot was reasonably full, and their rooms were bordering on luxurious, so it was evidently a well-thought-of place. Certainly it was quiet.

They had reviewed the files again, with the latest up-to-the-minute updates. They had pored over maps and photos. They had even gone out and driven the streets both in late afternoon and at night several times to make sure they had a feel for the territory and the likely traffic for their targeted time. Ariel had been guided by Mordechai's preparations, and felt ready.

Ariel heard the car doors slam behind him. He felt his lips peel back and his fangs emerge. He had chosen the pair of Khamis and Sajid, and he was looking forward to meeting them face-to-face.

"Hey! Old man!" one of them called out in heavily accented English.

"You! Jew! Stop!"

Ariel stopped, listening to the steps that came hurrying up behind him.

"Turn around, old man."

Ariel turned slowly, and faced the two men. He could see them clearly with his night vision, but he doubted they saw him well at all since they were blocking the headlight beams from their car. One was grinning, one was frowning.

"You lost, old man?" That was the grinner, Khamis.

Sajid, the frowning one, snarled, "You're not supposed to be here. This is our street, not supposed to be polluted by the feet of Jews. Get out."

Ariel didn't move.

"Didn't you hear me? Get out!" The snarl was a shout now.

There was a *whisp* sound as they both jerked their nightsticks high. Ariel caught the nightsticks in midstroke and ripped them out of their hands, dropping them behind him. Before the two men could recover, Ariel's hands were locked on their throats, fingers grasping their larynxes, squeezing hard enough to cause serious pain and panic as they felt their breath being choked off.

"Hello, boys," he said. "You don't know me, but I'm a friend of Jonathan Goldberg. Surely you remember him—the young man you basically beat to death several months ago? Well, you may have thought you were going to get away with that one. I'm here to tell you that you're not."

He tightened the grip of his hands a bit, and was rewarded to see them start to choke and their eyes widen to their limits. He ignored the blows they made with their fists as he spread his arms a little and forced them apart enough that the car lights lit his face up. He smiled broadly to show his fangs.

"No, sorry, I hate to tell you this, but Jews are not demons. A few of us, however, are vampires." He tilted his head a little as their blows became even more frantic, and squeezed a bit harder. "I'm here to tell you that justice deferred is not justice denied, and it just caught up with you."

Sajid tore at Ariel's hand on his throat. "You... can't..."

"I can't? Oh, but I can. You will be standing before Allah in a few moments. I hope you're ready to meet him." Ariel drew them closer to himself, ignoring their struggles, and stared them in the eyes. "I'm afraid your prophet will be very disappointed in you. Try not to let it ruin your day." He let them struggle a while longer as he stared at them, then clenched his hands, feeling their larynxes and tracheas crunch between his fingers. He released them and they dropped to the sidewalk, where they struggled, trying to gasp for air that could no longer flow. The struggles weakened, and grew feebler, until they stopped, and both bodies sagged into motionless death.

"Never again," Ariel whispered. He dragged the corpses over against the edge of the building.

He looked up and down the street. The neighborhood had been seriously battered during the Covid year. Most of the small businesses had closed and their windows were boarded up. From what they had seen during their evening drives, a lot of the second- and third-floor residents had also left. Between the cold weather and the patrols, there weren't many of the homeless around, either.

There hadn't been many lights on, but there had been some. A couple more of them came on now, and he could see outlines against the shades moving toward the windows. He stepped over to the driver's side door, where he sat down long enough to shut off the engine and turn off the headlights. He allowed the door to close enough that it barely latched, then he stepped over to a pool of shadow and became motionless. He could see the blinds in the windows being pulled to one side enough for someone to peer out. After a long moment, the blinds swung back to their normal places and the lights went out again. Ariel shrugged. Curiosity got more people into trouble than it did cats, according to Rabbi Mendel.

He eased back over to the car and opened the door long enough to sit and put the transmission in neutral. The street was flat enough it wouldn't roll. He reached up and ripped the dashcam out of its mount and tossed it in the back seat, trailing broken wires behind it.

Ariel exited the car, closing the driver's door. He reached up to grasp the end of the light bar. Unlike many true police cars, it was not an integral part of the car, having just been clamped into the rain channels, so when he applied his strength it popped loose with a small crunch sound. He then walked around and did the same thing on the passenger side, pulling the wires loose as he did so. Opening the rear passenger door, he placed it inside the compartment. Then he picked up the two nightsticks and tossed them into the car. The last thing he did was pull a cheap cell phone out of his pocket and speed-dial the only number in its directory.

The call connected on its third ring, but there was no answer. Ariel simply said, "Done," ended the call, turned the phone off, and tossed it in the car as well.

It only took three minutes for the first vehicle to appear. A battered Ford Econoline with a logo on the side for Overholser Farms pulled up in front of the patrol car. Two burly guys got out, opened the side door, picked up each body in turn and placed them in the van with little sound, then closed the door and left. No words were spoken. Ariel thought there were other dark lumps in the van, but he didn't look closely.

The van had barely turned the corner out of sight when the tow truck pulled up. Its logo said Hurricane Towing. It was one of the platform-style car-hauling trucks rather than a true tow truck. Ariel didn't care.

The guys who got out of this truck were at least as large as the two guys in the farm truck.

"Keys?" said the driver in a quiet soprano voice, which shocked Ariel a bit. He peered closer at the figure, and realized it was a woman.

"In the ignition," he said softly. "It's in neutral."

They didn't say anything more, just moved quickly to get things done. First, the passenger in the truck unfolded what looked to be a bag or cloth or something on top of the car, and in a matter of moments the two of them had it stretched and fitted to cover the body of the car. Ariel realized it was a fabric car cover, but what really caught his attention was that this one had been printed or painted to look like a Ford Taurus. It probably wouldn't have provided much cover in daylight, but at night it readily disguised and covered up the Chevrolet patrol car.

The next part of the operation was not at all noiseless. The driver lowered the back end of the platform and the passenger hooked up the towing chains to the car. Only one light came on this time. Ariel returned to his pool of shadow.

Four minutes later the car was on the platform, the platform was raised back up into travel position, and the chains had the car locked to the platform. The driver and her assistant were back in the truck and it was moving. It turned the other direction at the corner, and was gone.

Ariel sighed, turned, and walked back south. Five blocks into the Jewish neighborhood, he walked up to a waiting Audi sedan, opened the front passenger door, and got in the car. He looked over at Mordechai, sitting at the wheel. "Done," he said.

"Done," Mordechai replied. He put the car in gear, and put it in motion.

Once they were well on their way back to the hotel, Ariel asked a question he'd been thinking about for some time. "Umm, just who were those people?"

"Which people?"

Ariel looked over at Mordechai and saw the corner of his lip curling up a little in the light from the dashboard. "Who are Overholser Farms and Hurricane Towing, and why were they willing to help us?"

"Ah, *those* people." Ariel didn't say anything, and Mordechai's smile grew a little larger for a moment, then faded away. "First of all, they are fictitious. It's amazing how cheap magnetic signs for the sides of trucks are."

"So Overholser Farms and Hurricane Towing don't exist?"

Mordechai shook his head. "Not in New York, either the city or the state." He guided the car around a corner.

"But the people were real."

Mordechai nodded. "Have you ever heard the saying, 'The enemy of my enemy is my friend'?"

"Yes."

"Do you believe it?"

Ariel looked at Mordechai with a puzzled expression. "What?"

"Do you believe it? Do you think it's true?"

"Well..." He hesitated for a moment. "I guess so. It makes sense."

"To use one of your pithy Americanisms, bullshit. The only thing you can count on about your enemy's enemy is that he is your enemy's enemy. The fact that you share a common enemy does not make you friends or allies at all. Think back to your school days—wasn't there at least one kid in your classes that everyone hated—or at least disliked?"

"Yeah." Ariel dragged that word out.

"Did that automatically make you best friends with everyone else in your classes?"

"No. But what does that have to do with—"

"Bear with me. I'm getting there. Having said that, the fact that your enemy has other enemies may be useful to you. You may not be friends. You may not be able to form a full alliance with them. *But*," Mordechai emphasized the word, "you may from time to time be able to cooperate with each other on a mutual project that will disadvantage your common enemy."

Ariel thought about that. "All right, I can see that."

"You should be able to understand that this particular immigrant community, arrogant and obstreperous as they are, has managed to offend, inconvenience, irritate, and to use another Americanism, 'piss off' several other cultural communities in the city. Some of those communities, like our own, have some members who are a bit less than observant of every fine detail of the laws of the land."

Ariel's eyebrows raised. "So Overholser Farms..."

"Under another name belongs to an Irish clan that raises pigs."

It took a moment for the implications to sink in, then Ariel's stomach lurched. "If pork wasn't *trayf* before..." He swallowed hard, and again.

"Indeed. There are stories..."

"I don't want to hear them." It took a few more moments for his stomach to quiet down enough to continue. "And the tow trucks?"

"Italians, and the car-crusher yard that the cars are being taken to is owned by a Polish family that runs it twenty-four hours a day. In about another hour or so, those cars will be crushed and compressed into a couple of anonymous cubes of scrap metal and by tomorrow morning will be loaded on a ship on its way to Japan."

"And we will leave..."

"Never having been seen by anyone in the community, after having seen to it that no one will ever see the drivers of those vehicles again."

"Disappeared."

"Completely. Totally. Without a trace that they will be able to locate."

Ariel settled back into his seat. Justice... with a bit of mystery. He decided he liked that.

CHAPTER 19

IT WAS THE NEXT DAY WHEN ARIEL HAPPENED across an article about events in California while scrolling some news feeds looking for any reports about the community patrol. He paused when he saw the topic, and his eyes opened wide as he read the details.

"Mordechai! Have you seen this?"

He spun his laptop around and pushed it across the table to the older man. Mordechai looked up from the book he was reading. His eyes narrowed as he read the banner, and his hand flashed to the computer to page through the article rapidly. Then he backed up to the beginning and paged through again, slower. Once done, he looked up.

"Six synagogues vandalized or painted with graffiti in or near Santa Carla in two weeks. Even for the times, that's excessive."

"And that last one—Congregation Beth Shalom— that's the synagogue I grew up in. My parents still go there!" Ariel sprang to his feet and stalked over to stare out the window at the night sky. He looked back over his shoulder. "Can we do anything about this?"

"We can. The question is whether we should."

"What do you mean? They're threatening my parents!"

"First, while they may be your parents, you are no longer their son, by your own choice." Mordechai's voice was hard and his face was just as adamant.

Ariel stared at him for a moment. "But..." His voice faltered as he absorbed what Mordechai had said.

"Second, we were sent here to resolve a single situation. We have done so. We do not have the authority to divert resources to make a trip to California rather than returning to Israel.

"Third, there may be something else that requires our abilities even more than this." Ariel stared at Mordechai. He understood his points, and couldn't argue with him, but his heart burned to... to do *something*, although he didn't know what. His fists clenched in frustration.

"That said," Mordechai said, and his face relaxed a bit, "let me make a phone call." He walked over to the closet and pulled out his carry-on bag and set it on his bed. Unzipping it fully, he let the sides flop out flat, reached down and pushed on two points of the rigid bottom of the bag. A panel popped up, and he set it aside before picking a small parcel out of the metal-lined compartment that had been revealed. He unsealed a silvery plastic bag, and took out an object.

"Satellite phone," he said to Ariel, holding it up as he walked over to the window. "For when you want to make absolutely sure you're not being overheard, especially in the US. In a Faraday bag to keep it from being detected by those on the lookout for such devices."

Mordechai flashed a grin at Ariel, then dialed a number on the phone and held it up to his ear, listening. After a moment, he pressed a button on his wristwatch and said, "Zalman 74737Q." He looked at his watch again, and said, "Confirm Alpha Zed 5962." Pause, then, "Report on US, California, Santa Carla, synagogues."

Ariel watched as Mordechai listened for what seemed like a long time (but when he looked at his own watch was less than five minutes), interspersing comments like "Hmm" and "Okay." At the end of the report, Mordechai said, "Right. Pogrom level 3, headed toward 2. We're in New York City right now; we can be in Santa Carla in eight hours, or sooner if the plane is serviced and the pilots are awake. I think we should nip this one now. Approved?" A moment later. "Good. We're on the way. Cheers."

Mordechai turned the phone off, replaced it in its Faraday bag and returned it to its compartment. He then picked up the room phone, punched a number, and waited. "Michael? Zalman here. We have a new commission. We're heading for Santa Carla, California. It's south of San Francisco. I know you can fly into San Francisco or Los Angeles, but I'd rather go into a closer regional airport. Rabbi Mendel and I flew into one a few months ago, close to a year if I recall correctly. See if you can find that flight record and fly to the same one, please. Ariel and I will pack. After you work your magic, call my mobile to let me know when we have to leave. Right. We'll be in the lobby."

He hung the phone up and turned to Ariel. "Go pack, and meet me at the front desk in half an hour."

❖   ❖   ❖

Ariel decided again that he really liked flying by private jet, if for no other reason than not having to mess with the security lines in the main terminals. Thirty minutes after Mordechai had hung up the phone they were arriving at the fixed-base operator building where their jet had been stored, and thirty minutes after that they were taxiing out toward the runways without going through a single security checkpoint. He smiled at that thought.

Once they were airborne, he looked over at Mordechai. "So how long will this one take?"

"According to Michael, it's a bit less than three thousand miles, so somewhere in the neighborhood of maybe four and a half hours. We'll be landing at San Jose International Airport, if you know where that is."

Ariel snorted. "Yeah, I know where it is. We drove by it every time we drove up to San Francisco or Oakland, unless we took Highway 1 up the coast. It's a bit over thirty miles to Santa Carla from there. Good choice."

Mordechai nodded. "Michael knows what he's doing." He put his laptop on the table and opened it up. "Aha. We have some more information from Israel."

Ariel pulled his own laptop out and flipped it on. "Man, I wish I could have gotten this kind of service on commercial flights."

Mordechai chuckled, but didn't say anything further. They both dug into the files that had been sent to them.

There was a surprising amount of information provided, much of which was material Ariel wasn't familiar with, even though he'd been born and raised in the area. He paged through article after article about recent anti-Semitism in California. Nothing much new there, from what he could recall. Then he hit the first article about the apparent rising tide of neo-Nazi speech and behavior among many of the street and motorcycle gangs on the west coast.

He looked up when Mordechai sat back and crossed his arms for a long moment, then nodded. "Him."

"Who?" Ariel asked.

Mordechai turned his laptop around, and Ariel saw a picture of a square-headed white man wearing a leather jacket and with a name displayed: Cord "Snake" Campbell. He flipped to that file in his own laptop, and read through it.

"Why him?" Ariel looked up with a puzzled expression. "He doesn't look any different from the rest of the gang guys."

Mordechai tapped his lips with a finger a couple of times, then said, "Because of how he writes. They all post remarks and diatribes to social media pages. But his are focused manifestos, and of a pretty refined caliber of writing. And where everyone else is mostly blaming the Jews for all the various social justice issues of the last few years, he attacks our very existence. He argues that we don't even have a right to exist. And he appears to be gathering support." Mordechai tapped his lips again, and sat silently for a long moment. "This man is dangerous. Very dangerous."

Ariel read through the articles again. "He's leader of a new biker gang... Los Dracos Negros. That's a Hispanic name, but he looks as white as they come."

"Indeed," Mordechai said. "Most of the motorcycle gangs are white men, although there is one elsewhere in the state that is Hispanic. But his gang is mixed race. That's part of what makes this 'Snake' dangerous. He can apparently attract and bond across social divisions, and in someone with his beliefs and apparent agenda..." Mordechai shook his head.

"So what do we do?"

"Research on the ground, I'm afraid," Mordechai said.

"How?"

"I've sent a few questions back. What answers I get may help with that. Meanwhile, we'll be landing in a couple of hours. You might try to get some rest." With that, Mordechai closed his laptop, reclined his seat, and closed his eyes.

Ariel sighed, and closed his own laptop. He knew Mordechai was right, but his brain was racing, and he didn't think he'd rest much.

He was right.

The next evening they were standing across the street from Congregation Beth Shalom in the shadows of a couple of palm trees, watching as the sun finished setting and night finished overtaking the sky. They were dressed in dark clothing, so were pretty much undetectable where they stood.

The synagogue was an older building built in the 1920s, if he remembered correctly. Synagogue architecture in California was rich and varied from square, blocky neo-industrial brick buildings to Spanish-influenced designs with terra-cotta roofs to small stucco clad buildings with stone veneer fronts, and others. Most of the synagogues that Ariel had seen in the parts of Tel Aviv he frequented, including the one he attended, were relatively modern, many not more than a generation old, with angular lines and rectangular windows in contrast to the preponderance of arches and curved windows in the California synagogues.

Congregation Beth Shalom was an exception to both rules. Ariel knew his father had believed that it was either designed by Frank Lloyd Wright or one of his students. It was larger than many synagogues, because it had also been designed to be a community center as well as a worship center. Tall, with a swooping roofline and a matching swooping great window across the front, it was unique in California—in the world, Ariel suspected. But for all its familiarity, for all its presence in his previous life, this wasn't home anymore. A bit too much art, he feared, and not enough focus on *haShem*. It surprised him to feel a pang of nostalgia for his simple synagogue in Tel Aviv.

The sky was cloudless, and between the streetlights and the quarter moon hanging low on the horizon, they could see very well. Ariel looked up and down the street, but didn't see anything other than a few cars crossing at intersections farther back down the road. The next block over was a dead end, so little traffic came down this road. The synagogue parking lot was empty.

"So, any responses to your questions yet?" Ariel kept his voice low, even though no one else was around.

"No, but they said maybe later tonight. You have to remember they're about ten hours ahead of us. The end of their day will be around dawn here, or a little after."

"Nine hours right now," Ariel said. Mordechai looked at him with lowered eyebrows, and he grinned.

"California's on daylight saving time until early November, remember?"

"Ten hours. So is Israel." Mordechai's mouth twisted. "Daylight saving time," he muttered. "Whose bright idea was that?"

"Believe it or not, Benjamin Franklin is usually credited with saying the idea first, although he didn't call it that."

"Huh. Figures it was an American."

Ariel snickered. He looked up and down the street. Nothing.

"You really think someone will come by tonight?"

"They're starting to do repeat visits," Mordechai murmured. "There's about a thirty percent chance they will come tonight."

"Okay."

Ariel looked at his watch. 9:04 P.M. He looked up and down the street again. Nothing.

The night progressed. Every once in a great while a car would turn onto the street, then turn off again a block or so later. No one was out walking.

11:11 P.M.

12:07 A.M.

1:00 A.M. Very quiet. Only a breeze moving.

2:14 A.M.

"Hist!" Very quietly. Ariel looked over to see Mordechai point down the street. Two figures walking up the sidewalk slowly. They watched as the figures made their way toward the synagogue, eventually drawing even with it, where they stopped. After a moment, they started walking across the lawn toward the synagogue. At that point, Ariel and Mordechai stepped out of the shadows.

They crossed the street and approached the synagogue from behind the intruders. As they neared, Ariel could hear the sound of spray-paint cans being shaken. Just as one of them was raising a can, Ariel tapped him on the shoulder.

"I don't think you want to do that, friend."

The man jerked, then swung around fast, swinging the butt of the paint can in his right hand toward Ariel's head. Ariel grabbed his wrist and squeezed. Something crunched, and the man yelled, then broke into a torrent of unintelligible Spanish. Ariel twisted his wrist, and the man dropped to his knees, dropping the paint can and grabbing for his captive arm with his left hand as he did so. "You bastard..." he hissed. "You broke my arm!"

"I broke your wrist, friend," Ariel said matter-of-factly as he watched Mordechai, "and if you don't want more damage than that I suggest you stay still."

Mordechai had faced off with the other man, who had pulled a knife and was leaning forward, waving it between them, cursing as he did so. After another moment, Mordechai blurred into motion, and they swirled around for a few seconds until they broke apart, only now the knife was standing out from the man's shoulder. "You stabbed me," he moaned, reaching for the knife hilt.

"I suggest you leave that there," Mordechai said in a matter-of-fact tone. "It will slow down the bleeding until you can get someone to bandage it for you." He beckoned to Ariel, who hauled his captive over to stand beside the other. "You two will carry a message for me. Go back to where you came from, and tell your leaders to leave the synagogues alone, and leave the Jews alone. If you don't, you won't like the consequences. Do you think you can remember that?"

Ariel's captive began cursing in Spanish again. Ariel only understood about one word in seven or eight, but it was enough to recognize the probable content. He lightly squeezed the wrist he was still holding. The man broke off in a gasp, but nodded his head frantically.

"How about you?" Mordechai asked the other, reaching out to tap the knife hilt with a finger.

He jerked, and said, "Yeah, yeah, I'll remember," in a rapid tone.

"Good. Now leave."

Ariel gave another slight squeeze to the wrist, eliciting another gasp, then released it, and the two men broke into a shambling run, both of them holding their injured arms. He could hear their footsteps and grunts of pain for quite some distance down the street.

Once they were out of sight and Ariel couldn't hear them any longer, he picked up the sack one of them had dropped. It had another can of paint in it, so he gathered up the two cans they had dropped, and their matching caps, and added them to the bag.

"We done here?"

"For tonight," Mordechai said.

"Think we did any good?"

"At least there's no mess to clean up."

"True. Think they'll listen?"

Mordechai sighed. "If they don't, at least they won't be able to say they weren't warned."

The next day Mordechai had received responses to his questions, and they spent the late afternoon and early evening reviewing those. They had a lot more information now about the various outlaw motorcycle gangs in the area, including Los Dracos Negros. Ariel guessed that was a good thing, although he wasn't sure how they would use it. Whoever Mordechai's source was, they apparently could provide the real scoop.

Somewhere around 9:00 P.M. Ariel closed his laptop. "I'm tired of looking at these four walls," he said. "Let's go to the bar. They've got single malt scotch. I checked."

"Do they, now?" One of Mordechai's eyebrows rose. "What type?"

"He said the best they had was Glenmorangie."

Mordechai's other eyebrow rose, and he stood. "Well, then let us seize the moment."

A few minutes later they were upstairs in the bar and their waiter, a skinny black man named Charles, was delivering their drinks. "Let me know if you need anything else," he said with a smile before he slipped back through the crowd.

Ariel drank some of his Perrier and watched Mordechai lift his snifter to his nose.

"Well, how is it?"

A small smile crossed Mordechai's face. "It's . . . very nice. Different, of course, from the others I've tried. But very nice."

They sat and watched the other patrons in the bar: men ranging from Ariel's age to late middle aged; women ranging from young to ageless, some in groups, some in couples, a few alone. Much laughter and loud conversation, which helped cover up a few intimate conversations that Ariel didn't want to overhear.

"So who should we approach?" Mordechai asked with his glass before his mouth.

"If it's up to me, I'd say The Devil's Legions. They're the biggest gang in the area. For that matter, they're the biggest gang in the state. They've almost got to know what's going on with Los Dracos Negros, and from what I can tell there's no love lost between them."

Mordechai nodded. "I agree. So tomorrow we'll go visit the local chapter and see what we can see."

Ariel looked at him. "Seriously? You're just going to stroll in and expect them to talk to us instead of bust our heads open and throw us out on the street?"

"Trust me," Mordechai smiled. "It will work. You'll see." He took another sniff. "And if it doesn't, you and I will have a nice bit of brisk exercise"—his smile disappeared and his tone dropped—"without restraints."

Ariel nodded slowly. "Good enough."

He looked around the bar again, and his eye was caught by a text banner scrolling across the bottom of a nearby TV screen up on the wall. His eyes widened to read SYNAGOGUE BOMBING—BETH SHALOM. He grabbed Mordechai's arm and pointed at the screen. They watched as the small amount of text said someone threw a bomb into a classroom being used for an evening community class. Numerous people killed and injured, details to follow. They rose in unison. Mordechai threw a bill on the table, and they headed for the elevator bank rapidly, people barely clearing out of their way before they went by.

CHAPTER 20

MORDECHAI DIDN'T DRIVE WITH QUITE HIS USUAL panache in America, Ariel had noted. He assumed it was because he didn't know the streets as well as he did in Tel Aviv. They still pulled up a couple of blocks down the street from the synagogue in what seemed to be a very short amount of time. The street was totally blocked by emergency vehicles with blinking lights. They saw an ambulance pull away as they got out of their car.

"With me," Mordechai murmured. Ariel restrained his urge to sprint ahead and paced alongside the older man as he walked down the far side of the street, sticking to the shadows as much as possible. It wasn't long before they edged up behind a small crowd gathered near a well-dressed man talking to a couple of policemen.

"Could I have your name, sir?" one of the policemen asked, pulling out a notebook.

"Joshua Steinberg," the man replied. "I'm the rabbi here."

"Good," the policeman replied. "I'm Sergeant

Ramirez. We would have been trying to contact you shortly. We need some information please."

"I'll do my best," the rabbi said with a catch in his throat.

"Can you tell us what parts of the building were supposed to be occupied tonight?"

"It . . . it should have just been room 104 in the northwest corner of the building, and room 105 right next to it on the west side. We do a couple of English As Second Language classes every week for new immigrants. We . . ." The rabbi choked for a moment. He took a deep breath. "Sorry."

"That's all right," the sergeant said. "Take your time. Do you know how many people were in the building tonight?"

"Not exactly. Once we can get to the office, we can get on the computer and tell you how many were enrolled in each class, but that may not help a lot. Attendance is usually a bit irregular, but most weeks there are between ten and fifteen people in each room."

"Does that include the teachers?"

"Maybe. Can you tell me what happened?"

"Someone threw a serious bomb in the northwest room. The furnishings were destroyed."

"Oh . . ." the rabbi said faintly. "Is . . . did anyone . . . die?"

"Everyone in the other room survived, although they're all injured, some of them badly. But room . . . 104, did you call it—the northwest room—we didn't find any survivors. They're clearing away the bodies now."

"Oh . . ." Steinberg repeated. "The Caans . . . Moses and Miriam . . . that was their room . . ."

Ariel made a noise, and Mordechai quickly pulled him away from the crowd.

"Your parents?" Mordechai murmured in his ear as he led him back down the street.

"Yes," Ariel whispered. "Mom taught an ESL class the last few years, and Dad tutored with her. They said it was fun, it let them meet new people, and it helped them give back to the community. But it was always on Tuesday nights. It was always on Tuesdays. Why Wednesday this week? Why tonight?" A note of anguish filled his voice. Mordechai wrapped an arm around his shoulder, and hurried him to their car, using the remote to unlock the doors and get him in.

Ariel felt the car rock a little when Mordechai settled into the driver's seat and closed the door. Tears started trickling down his cheeks.

He didn't know how long they sat there in the dark. Eventually he felt the sensation as the tear tracks dried and were not replaced. He scrubbed his face with his hands.

"I'm sorry," Mordechai said. "I made a mistake. I didn't think they would react this fast to our stopping them last night. And I didn't think they would escalate to this level so soon. So this is at least partly my fault."

Anger began to burn in Ariel, first seemingly in his gut, but then in a cold fire in his mind. "No," he whispered. "Not your fault. Not my fault. Not my parents' fault. Theirs. Theirs."

After a moment, Mordechai said, "So what do you want to do?"

Ariel let that thought roll through his mind, through the cold flames of his rage. "As they have done, so let it be done," he finally responded.

"Fitting," Mordechai responded. "But if that's what you want, we'll have to move fast to beat the local police to them."

"Fast works," Ariel said, a snarl in his tone. "I'm up for fast."

Mordechai said nothing more, simply started the car and pulled away from the curb, turning a corner almost immediately to leave the emergency vehicles behind them.

After traveling several blocks, a thought wormed its way through the waves of anger and obtruded into Ariel's focus. His eyes widened, and he said, "Turn right here."

Mordechai made the turn, then said, "You have someplace you want to go?"

"Yes. Home. I have some small things I want to get, and tonight is the best time before anyone else knows about . . . them."

"Ah. Well, put the address in the GPS, then."

Ariel did so, then sat back. He said nothing more during the drive. In fact, he was trying not to think at all, and he did a pretty good job of it until they turned into the neighborhood.

"Nice houses," Mordechai murmured. "Expensive?"

Ariel shrugged. "Most of these houses are what's called Craftbuilt or Craftsman style. They were all built over a hundred years ago. Our home is one of the newest, and it was built in 1920. They're not mansions, but there is something of a status to having one of these, and if they're in good shape they command top dollar, even in the crazy California real estate market. I know Dad turned down an offer of

two million dollars for our home a few years ago."
Ariel waited as Mordechai guided the car around a
couple of corners, then said, "Pull up under that big
chestnut tree there. This shouldn't take long."

"You sure you can do this without causing a problem?"

"I know where the spare back-door key is hidden,
and I know the alarm code. This is my best chance."

"Okay."

Mordechai was shutting down the engine as Ariel
got out of the car. He closed the door quietly, then
walked down to the house he had grown up in. He
skirted around the edge of the yard to avoid the electric
eye that would turn on the front-yard floodlights and
slipped into the backyard, stopping at the back-corner
rainspout long enough to reach inside and remove the
magnetic key holder. A moment later he was inserting
the key in the back door.

Once inside, he closed the door quietly and stepped
over to the alarm keypad. This was the part he was
nervous about. If his father had changed the alarm
code . . . he punched it in quickly. A moment later, the
alarm turned off, and he released his breath.

Ariel heard the *tic-tic-tic* of little nails on the
kitchen's tile floor, and looked down to see his mom's
Shih Tzu approaching. She sniffed his foot, then looked
up at him with a curled lip. She knew who he was,
regardless of what he was calling himself, and she
didn't react much better than she had the last time
she had seen him.

"Hey, Tiffy," he said around the lump in his throat.
"Mom's . . . not coming home, baby. I'm sorry." He bent
over and tousled her ears and her little hair bow. She

put up with it for a moment, then walked away. Ariel made himself stand and move on.

His father had left the foyer light on, which gave Ariel plenty of light to see by as he soft-footed it up the stairs to open the door to what had been his bedroom.

Once inside, as he had expected, nothing had been changed. He'd been certain that his mother still hadn't been able to bring herself to move anything or put anything away yet, even though she thought he was dead. He moved to the dresser and found the kippah he had worn at his bar mitzvah. Folding it and putting it in his shirt pocket, he looked around the room. Mementos, memorabilia, what was left of his books, but nothing really drew him except for his Boy Scout sash with the twenty-five badges and emblems on it, including the Eagle Scout emblem. For nostalgia's sake, he almost took it down from where it hung on the wall, but in the end he only pulled out his phone and took a picture of it.

A moment later he stepped off the last tread at the bottom of the stairs and moved around the corner into his father's study. There, on the front left corner as seen by whoever was sitting in the desk chair, was his father's copy of Tanakh; not the fancy leather-bound edition that he carried to shul on Friday nights, but the worn hardback edition with page edges dirtied by hands turning them during years and years of study and meditating, and with decades' worth of handwritten notes printed neatly in margins and flyleaves. He ignored every other volume on the nearby shelves. This—more than anything else, this was his father's soul.

Ariel's final stop involved a return to the kitchen, where he set the book down on the corner of the breakfast table and approached the china cabinet. He pulled the center drawer open, and there on top of the fancy napkins, just as he knew it would be, was the dark blue velvet drawstring bag that housed his mother's most prized possession. He undid the drawstring and slid the solid silver menorah out onto his hands.

It was old, and very old school by today's standards, of course. Old-fashioned, nine candle holders, slim, slightly tarnished. But it had been part of Ariel's life for as long as he could remember, sitting on the table every Chanukah. It had been made in Lithuania in the late 1800s, two generations before the Holocaust, and had belonged to his mother's grandmother. In his hands, Ariel held the tangible evidence of his mother's faith. He gently slid it back in the bag, drew the drawstrings shut, and equally gently placed it on top of the book.

Glancing into the kitchen, Ariel could see that Tiffy's water and kibble dispensers were full, so she was set for three or four days. He looked over at where she stood watching him. For all that she'd never been his pet, he regretted that she could no longer accept him.

"Sorry, Tiff, I have to go. Uncle Bernie and Aunt Rachel will probably be here tomorrow. You'll be okay until then, and they'll take good care of you."

He swallowed around the lump that was back in his throat, reached down to touch her little black nose with his fingertip, and after a moment was surprised to feel the rasp of her tongue caress it.

It only took moments to gather up the book and

bag, set the alarm, exit through the door and make sure it locked, and restore the magnetic key holder to its hiding place. It was only moments more to retrace his steps to the car, again successfully avoiding the light-sensor perimeter.

Ariel slid into the passenger seat and closed the door. He looked over at Mordechai.

"Let's go."

CHAPTER 21

IT WAS THURSDAY AFTERNOON.

"Are you ready?" Mordechai shot his shirt cuffs from his sleeves and adjusted his coat.

"I suppose so," Ariel replied. He was in a black suit with a collarless dark charcoal shirt. "You sure we need to do this in the afternoon?"

"Yes. We need the extra time, and you need to get some experience moving around in the daylight. Do you have your sunglasses?"

Ariel pulled them from his left inside breast pocket and put them on. "Right here."

"Right. Let's go, then."

A few minutes later they were in the car and headed toward their destination, a slightly run-down bar called Hannigan's on the west side of Santa Carla just east of the river. According to many of their sources, this was the main local hangout for the local chapter of The Devil's Legions. And according to Mordechai's special sources, the man they wanted to contact was usually there in the late afternoon every day. Hence their timing.

Santa Carla's afternoon traffic was relatively thick on the streets, but the GPS system gave them good instructions, and it didn't take all that long to arrive. Mordechai pulled into the small parking lot, and found an empty parking spot near the end of the building. There were half a dozen motorcycles, mostly Harley-Davidsons, parked directly in front of the bar.

Mordechai didn't say anything; just beckoned with his head. They exited the car and headed for the bar's entrance.

Inside, the ambient lighting was dimmer than outside, but neither of them removed their sunglasses. They stood for a moment, taking in the environment of the bar. It was a fairly standard layout, Ariel decided: bar with stools, tables with chairs, and a couple each of pool tables and pinball machines in the back of the main room, all of which were in action with several long-haired and bearded guys with either leather or denim jackets on—all of whom were now looking their direction.

Mordechai headed for the bar. Ariel was two steps behind him, keeping one eye on the bartender and the other on the guys around the pool tables.

"What can I get for ya?" The bartender's voice had a hint of an Irish accent, which fit the name of the place. Whether it was real or not was anybody's guess.

"I'm actually looking for Mr. James McLeod," Mordechai said, resting one hand on the bar. "I was told he's often here about this time of day."

The bartender made a point of looking all around the room before returning his gaze to Mordechai. "He's not here right now. Did you make an appointment? Do you want to leave a message?"

"No and no." Mordechai shook his head. "But I'm very certain he's going to want to talk to us."

The bartender looked back at the bikers, and after a moment one of them gave a slow nod.

"He's most likely next door at the gym," the bartender said.

"Thank you," Mordechai responded with a nod. "We'll go there directly." He turned and headed for the door. Ariel lingered for a moment, looking at everyone in the room. The bikers were all uniformly hard-faced, and they stared back at him. He made sure he remembered what they looked like. Once he had that, he followed Mordechai.

Back out in the parking lot, Ariel felt the tingle of the sun on his face even through his sunscreen. He suspected it would become somewhat unpleasant in short order, and he was very glad for the dark glasses shrouding his eyes. He joined Mordechai in gazing up at a green sign that proclaimed Murray's Fight Club. Looking through the plate glass windows, it looked more like a regular workout gym, with the standard machines in the center of the room, bracketed by large setups of free weights on each side. There was an area of mats at each end of the room, and a couple of guys were desultorily sparring on one of them, so that kind of supported the name.

Mordechai looked over at him. "Shall we?"

"That's why we're here."

Mordechai's mouth quirked, and he led the way into the gym. Ariel remained a couple of steps behind him, keeping an eye on everyone else in the place. It wasn't crowded, but then he didn't expect it to be since it wasn't the kind of place suburban soccer moms would normally visit during the afternoons, and most of the rest of its patrons probably had day jobs.

They were met inside the door by a muscular man not much older than Ariel wearing a green T-shirt with the gym's name and logo on it. "Can I help you gentlemen with anything?"

"I'm told that James McLeod is here today."

The young man looked over his shoulder. "Jake! Couple of gentlemen here to see you." There was a slight emphasis on the word "gentlemen."

There was a momentary pause, then a raspy voice said from the middle of the workout machines, "Send 'em on back."

They threaded their way through the machines until they found themselves facing a middle-aged man wearing gray sweats and a dingy black sweatshirt with the sleeves cut off. He was doing leg presses. His hair and beard were shorter than in the pictures Ariel had seen, and there was definitely more gray in the hair, but the face was recognizably that of one James McLeod, putative leader of the local chapter of The Devil's Legions.

"...thirteen, fourteen, fifteen," McLeod was count-ing slowly as he did his presses, "sixteen, seventeen, eighteen, nineteen, twenty." He let the weights down slowly, and sighed as he sat up and pivoted to put his feet on the floor before he wiped his face with a towel, which he then wrapped around his neck. "Whew."

McLeod looked up at them. "I laid my bike down in some rain a few months ago and messed my knee up. They did a good job of putting it back together, but don't let anyone tell you therapy ain't a bitch, especially past forty-five." He reached out and grabbed a cane propped against the next machine over, and pushed to his feet.

McLeod tilted his head as he looked at them. "Don't believe I know y'all. You cops?" Mordechai pursed his lips and shook his head, and McLeod said, "No, you're not local, or I'd already know you. You're not CBI or FBI—you dress too good for either of them. You're not the type for DEA, and ICE doesn't bother with us. CIA? NSA, maybe?"

Mordechai shook his head again. "No, Mr. McLeod, we're not with any police organization, although from time to time I have been known to assist one or more groups like that."

"Freelancers, huh?"

"After a fashion."

McLeod's rasp got stronger as he said, "So what's your name?"

Mordechai gave his razor-thin smile, and said, "Richard Wolf, and my associate is Joseph Green."

"You got some ID you can show me?"

"Not with me."

"Well, Mr. Wolf"—McLeod's voice got a little harder—"I don't much like talking to strangers when I can't see their eyes, so why don't you and your friend there take off those fancy shades?"

"As you wish." Mordechai took off his sunglasses and put them in an interior coat pocket. Ariel followed suit. At that same moment, the door behind him opened, and he looked around to see the biker that had nodded to the bartender enter the gym. Ariel stepped sidewise a bit to be able to keep an eye on both him and McLeod at the same time. The biker made it easier for him by slipping through the machines until he was behind McLeod, where he stopped and held position.

McLeod looked at them for a long moment, before saying, "That's better. Now, Mr. Wolf," with a sarcastic emphasis on the name, "when people I don't know say they want to talk to me, they either want something from me or they want to sell me something, usually at an outrageous price. Which is it this time?"

Mordechai's razor grin sharpened even more. "A bit of the former and a bit of the latter, actually. I want some information from you that won't generate any risk for you and won't cost you anything. In return, we will resolve a long-term problem for you, again at no risk or cost to you."

"Uh-huh. You really expect me to fall for that? I ain't that big a fool, Mr. Wolf." McLeod's rasp was getting more pronounced.

"Tell me what you know about Cord Campbell."

There was a choked-off sound from the biker behind McLeod, who held his hand up. For a long moment, there was no other movement, no other sound from anyone in their little group, until McLeod started chuckling.

"I must confess I didn't see that one coming. Well played, Mr. Wolf. Well played." McLeod's rasp lightened, and the precision of his speech changed. "Am I correct in assuming that the focus of your question and the long-term problem are one and the same?"

Mordechai said nothing, simply tilted his head a little to one side and a little forward at the same time.

"Very well." McLeod brought his cane before him and rested both hands on it. "I knew Cord Campbell fairly well for most of his life. We grew up together.

His older brother Colton and I were close friends; we enlisted in the Army together, and we served in Desert Storm together, although in different units. I came home, Colton didn't. That affected Cord. He was single-minded about being in the Army after that, even though he wasn't really suited for it. I tried to talk him out of it, but he insisted on enlisting and following his brother into the infantry. His first great disappointment was when he didn't make it into the Rangers, like Colton did. He got a bit sour after that, but he still did two tours in Afghanistan. The second tour, a string of IEDs took out pretty much his entire platoon and left him with a major belly wound and a massive concussion. He lost part of his colon, and most of what made him him. He was a different man when he came back to the States and was released on a medical discharge."

McLeod stared past them for a long moment. Ariel said nothing, simply continued to listen and to keep an eye on everything around them. McLeod finally resumed with, "You have to know that most of the military folks are good people...at least the enlisted ones. Some of the officers are good, too, especially the younger ones. But a lot of the officers are political beasts, and that pulls a lot of them toward the liberal side of things. The enlisted folks, though, mostly come out of the service with a pretty conservative mindset, especially if they spend more than four years in. There are a few of them, though...what I'm trying to say is that most of the military aren't rednecks or white supremacists. But there are a few, and Cord connected with some of them while he was recuperating. He came home a very different man."

Another pause. "I let him ride with us for a few years, and at first he was okay, but as time passed he began drifting more and more to the nutcase fringe, and he kept pushing that we should be doing something about what he called the Jewish Problem." Ariel could hear the capital letters in McLeod's voice as he spoke the label. "Oh, he had names for a lot of other problems we should be dealing with, but that was the number one item on his list. Finally, when the Covid mess happened a couple of years ago, that seemed to push him over the edge. He broke with us right after the vaccine came out, and went out on his own. We probably should have dealt with him then, but we all thought he was a nutcase, and we didn't think he would amount to much on his own like that. Guess we were wrong."

"I daresay," Mordechai said in a chilly tone. "He seems to have attracted several kindred spirits." McLeod nodded without saying anything. "Who does his explosives work?"

"From what we can tell, he does. Nobody else in his group has military experience."

"Can you tell me where they meet? Do they have a single lair or hiding place?"

"Before we go any further with this," McLeod said, "what's your concern here? Am I going to find you digging into our business? Are you going to be digging up information on us and interfering with our operations?" McLeod's eyes had narrowed and his voice had gotten raspier again.

Mordechai sighed. "Mr. McLeod, I am here to deal with a single, very specific issue. What you and yours do here in your own area, your own 'turf' I think they call it, doesn't concern me at all. I'm not interested in it. It's not my business, frankly, and I don't want it to be my business. Your operations, as you call them, are safe from me and my associates. Bluntly, I don't care about you and yours, and trust me, you don't want me to care about you and yours...you really don't. Let me go on to say that you can say or do anything you think you can get away with or anything your law enforcement and courts will permit you to get away with, and I won't even think about it. *But*," he emphasized that word, "there is one exception: the Jews. You can even blame the Jews for all of the ills of society and the economy, and you'll be officially ignored. They've dealt with those lies for thousands of years; they can continue to do so. However, if you begin inciting people to *deal with* the Jews, or should you actually lay a finger on one, then it becomes, shall we say, my business. And you really don't want that, Mr. McLeod. You really don't. Despite it sounding like a bad movie cliché, I really am the stuff of nightmares."

Ariel had to suppress a shiver at that last. Mordechai's voice was pure steel, and cold—so cold. He could see that McLeod's eyes had widened. He didn't blame him. He wouldn't have wanted to be on the receiving end of that statement.

"So, Mr. McLeod"—Mordechai's voice had warmed marginally—"might we have the location where we can find Cord Campbell?"

McLeod opened his mouth, then had to clear his throat before looking over at the biker. "Slick?"

The biker said nothing for a long moment, until McLeod frowned at him. "His pack has been staying at that old warehouse he bought a few months ago."

"Address?" Mordechai's voice wasn't any warmer.

"1206 Fairway Avenue."

Ariel pulled his phone out and made a note, nodding at Mordechai when he looked his direction.

"Very good," Mordechai said. "My thanks." He started to turn away, but stopped. "One last bit of advice, Mr. McLeod. If I were you, I would give serious consideration to telling your groups to leave the Jews alone. It will avoid the possibility of mis-understandings, you see. As I said earlier, you really don't want to attract my attention."

"I don't take well to threats, Wolf," McLeod rasped out.

"Not a threat, my friend, not at all. I don't do threats. That was simply a piece of sound advice. One last thing..." Mordechai pulled a card case out of an inner pocket, extracted a business card, and held it out to McLeod. "I doubt we'll meet again, but on the very remote chance that you might need to contact me at some point in the future, send an email to this address. Someone will contact you after that." He held it out until McLeod slowly reached out to take the card. "Good day, gentlemen."

With that, Mordechai gave a short nod and turned for the exit. On his way out, he detoured slightly to pick up a loaded barbell from the floor with one hand and hoist it onto a nearby rack. Ariel could see both McLeod's and the biker's eyebrows lift in surprise.

Ariel lingered for a moment, looking at McLeod and the biker Slick. McLeod turned his head toward Ariel. "You need something?"

Ariel shook his head. "Keep an eye on the news," was all he said before he pulled his sunglasses out again and followed Mordechai out the door.

Once he was in the car, Ariel was surprised to see Mordechai looking at his mobile phone. Mordechai's usage of the phone was usually as just a phone, so to see him doing something else with it was remarkable. Before he could comment on it, though, Mordechai held up a finger, so he sat back and waited.

It took a few minutes, but eventually Mordechai laughed and tapped a control, then tapped another one before he started the car and backed out of the parking spot. Ariel could hear a hiss, and then voices started speaking. The sound wasn't great, but it was good enough to make clear it was McLeod and the biker Slick talking.

Slick: "Well, that was weird as shit."

McLeod: "Yeah."

Slick: "Want me to get a couple of guys and tail them and convince them to stay out of our business?"

McLeod: "No. I don't know who they're with, but they're some kind of special forces—something foreign, based on the old man's accent. The kid would waste all of you, and I don't want to think about what the old man would do to you."

Slick: "You're shittin' me, right?"

McLeod: "Slick, you know that T-shirt you like to wear, the one that says 'Beware the old man in a land where men die young'?"

Slick: "Yeah, what about it?"

McLeod: "That old man is the old man in the shirt. He's the real deal. I saw it in his eyes. He's seen more death than all of us put together. Hell, he's probably done more death than all of us put together have seen. He's right...I don't want to see him again, and I don't want to do anything that will bring him back to town. So pass the word to everyone: as of now, back off the Jews."

Slick: "You can't be . . ." There was the sound of a pistol action chambering a round. "All right, man, all right! Take it easy!"

McLeod: "Yeah, I'm deadly serious, Slick. Serious enough to leave anyone who screws with me on this out in the desert with a nine-millimeter headache pill. Clear?"

Slick: "Yeah, Jake . . . clear."

After a couple of seconds the hiss ended, and Mordechai put his phone back in his jacket.

"Looks like you sold him," Ariel said.

"Indeed. That, as they say, is a good thing."

"So where did you put the bug? On one of the exercise machines?"

"No. I could have, but they would have found it sooner or later, and they would have guessed where it came from, which would have caused other complications." Mordechai smiled. "No, you saw me hand it to them."

Ariel thought for a few seconds. "The business card? Really?"

"Not very sophisticated, good for only a few minutes of transmitting, short range, but almost never detected and easy to leave in a place. And once the power runs out, it really is just a business card."

"Huh. Do I need to worry about playing poker with you?"

Mordechai laughed.

CHAPTER 22

THEY SPENT AN HOUR OR SO INVESTIGATING THE warehouse at 1206 Fairway Avenue and its environs. It was an older building, wood-clad outside with a steel roof. The few windows in the building were small, high on the walls and covered by iron grates. There were single entry doors on the front and rear of the building, plus a large roll-up door for deliveries. It wasn't all that large, maybe twenty meters deep and thirty meters wide—call it sixty-five feet by almost one hundred feet. It would be somewhat smaller on the inside, of course. There was a small parking lot out front and an alley behind it. There was no signage on the building or on the street side, just the address number. As anonymous as a building could be.

"Nothing unusual on the surface," Mordechai concluded after their final drive around. "It has standard utilities: electricity, gas, and I assume water and sewage. Limited access: doors are normal types, locks appear to be normal as to types and quantities. We can get in easily enough, and as long as the big door remains shut, we can control the exits. I go in the front, you go in the back, the electric meter is right by the door so their master panel should be at about the same spot on the inside. Once the action starts, you turn off the electricity, they're in the dark, or mostly dark even if they have emergency lighting. Twelve, maybe fourteen of them, two of us. We'll be done in five minutes, even if they've built-out rooms inside."

"Weapons?" Ariel asked.

Mordechai's razor smile appeared. Seen from the side it was even more ominous than seen full-on. "We'll have a couple of pry bars in case the doors are locked, but we won't need more than our hands otherwise. Even if they are armed, in the dark they won't be able to see well enough to target us, especially if we keep moving."

Mordechai looked directly at Ariel, and his eyebrows lowered. "You have to understand, Ariel, that in the normal course of things, you would not be participating in this operation."

"If it's about my parents—"

Mordechai cut him off. "No, it has nothing to do with your parents . . . or very little to do with them. We in Israel are a small people, and connections are widespread. It's hard to get operatives for something like this without someone knowing someone either in the cause or in the operation. No, this is about the fact that you are about as raw a recruit as there is. Yes, you have been converted. Yes, you are now stronger and faster and tougher than any three humans now alive. But that's your body, not your mind. Yes, you're now a young journeyman in Krav Maga. But again, that's your body, not your mind. You have skills and training, but you have no experience in this kind of operation. You're more of a liability than you are a help, and you will be for some time to come."

"But—"

"No 'buts,' Ariel." Mordechai's voice was harder. "Skill and training will only take you so far, and that's not very far at that. You need experience to learn the things that all the training in the world cannot teach you, the things that will help you survive as a vampire and as an operative."

"But if you don't want me involved in anything until I am experienced, how do you expect me to get experience?" Ariel was a bit surprised that Mordechai had allowed him to finish that sentence.

Mordechai sighed. "And there's the rub, to quote Rabbi Mendel's favorite goy, Shakespeare. You need experience to get experience. So we're going to do what leaders and planners have done for centuries: use green, raw, inexperienced troops in operations in the hopes that enough of them survive long enough to become experienced. Experience always comes at a price, Ariel, remember that. Sometimes your opponent pays it, sometimes your companions pay it, and sometimes you end up paying it yourself, but the price is always paid."

The older man's face relaxed, and his vocal tones shifted from authoritarian to businesslike. "There is actually one good thing about you coming along tonight."

"What's that?" Now Ariel was curious, after Mordechai had spent so much time telling him why he shouldn't be involved.

"Understand, Ariel, I could do this by myself. Twelve, fourteen of them, I could take them all out. Oh, it wouldn't be simple or easy, and I'd probably take some injuries from it, but I could take them. I have the experience you lack, you understand: I'm fifteen times your age, and a thousand times more experienced. I might be only a child compared to Methuselah, but I'm significantly older than Torah says Abraham was when he passed. But just because I can do something alone, doesn't mean I should. Solo operatives are bad strategy and even worse tactics. There should always be a backup.

"Tonight, you're the backup. Your main responsibility is to survive. You're not Jackie Chan or Jet Li. You're not to try and take down as many of these guys as you can. Your job is to survive the encounter. That's your priority. If you happen to take down one or two of these men, fine, but that is a secondary priority. Do you understand?"

Ariel nodded, but said nothing.

"You've never been in real combat. You've never experienced a mob scene. This is going to be very confusing to you. Just stay by the back door and try to keep them in front of you. This is not sparring, Ariel. This is the real world. This is for all the shekels, understand? No restraints, Ariel. No hesitation. Our goal, our purpose, is to eliminate these people. We move at full speed and full strength until it's over."

"Right." Ariel felt resolve. And a certain anticipation at facing his parents' murderers.

Mordechai looked at him sternly again. "What's your job?"

"Survive." Ariel kept his voice level.

"Remember that. Now, let's go prepare."

They made one stop on the way back to the hotel.

Mordechai pulled into the parking lot of a big-box hardware store and parked near the exit.

"You wait here," he said. "We don't want you appearing on any security recordings." With that, he was out the door and striding toward the entrance. Ariel leaned back and closed his eyes. After a moment, he leaned to the left to shift the side of his face out of the direct sunlight. He mused on the thought that had just become real to him a few minutes ago, that he might actually someday reach Methuselah's age. The implications were somewhat staggering.

It wasn't long before he heard Mordechai's steps approaching. When the back door opened and a couple of items thumped and clanked on the back seat, he opened his eyes.

"Pry bars?"

"Yes," Mordechai said as he slid into the driver's seat. "Paid cash, of course."

When they entered the hotel, Mordechai checked at the front desk for messages. Ariel was surprised to be handed a fairly good-sized box of moderate weight. "What's this?" he asked on the way to the elevator.

"You'll see in a moment."

When they arrived at Mordechai's room, the box was opened to reveal a couple of black leather motorcycle jackets. Mordechai checked them both out. "Here. Even though we're vampires, prudence would dictate wearing body armor. No sense in taking unnecessary injuries, after all. However, getting body armor right here and now would have possibly attracted too much attention, so I had these shipped to us. This is stout leather, so it will offer almost as much protection against blades as body armor would have. Won't help a lot against bullets, but we'll have to take our chances there. Go get dressed."

Ariel went to his room, stripped off his suit, and put on black jeans and a black T-shirt. For shoes, he went with his favorite Doc Marten boots. He'd practiced with them enough with Gil that he was pretty comfortable wearing them, even if he was going to be in a fight. He put on the leather jacket, and checked the fit, snapping the fasteners on the front and sleeves and swinging his arms around. Other than the fact that the sleeves were a bit shorter than he would have liked if he was buying it, it was fine. It certainly didn't bind his movements any.

When Ariel went to Mordechai's room he found the older man dressed in midnight blue, carrying the jacket. Mordechai didn't favor black for night work. He had told Ariel that it wasn't as stealthy as people thought.

Waiting, Ariel checked his tablet, and discovered that the police had officially released the names of the fourteen people who had been killed by the bomb blast. At the top of the list were Miriam Caan and Moses Caan. He knew that, but seeing it in the announcement just made it more concrete, somehow. He felt his jaws clench and his muscles tense, felt his fangs begin to extend.

"When did you last feed?"

Ariel looked up. "What?"

"When did you last feed?"

"Two days ago. Why?"

Mordechai walked over to a small case that was plugged into the wall, unlocked it, and took out a bottle that he handed to Ariel. "Here. You're getting ready to do some serious work. Drink it now, so you're ready."

Ariel looked at the bottle of blood, quirked his mouth, removed the bottle cap, and raised it to his mouth. Moments later, he lowered the empty bottle, put the cap back on it and handed it back to Mordechai.

"Israeli blood," he said with a small smile.

"Indeed." Mordechai put the empty bottle back in the case and locked it, then pulled a bottle of sparkling water from the room refrigerator. "Here."

Ariel downed that pretty quickly. As he tossed the empty bottle in the trash, Mordechai pitched a bag to him. It landed in his hands with some weight. He opened it to find a pair of black leather gloves much like the ones he usually used to spar with Mordechai. Ariel put the gloves in the jacket's pockets. He looked at Mordechai and raised his own eyebrows. Mordechai waved at the door, and they left.

Mordechai pulled the car into a parking spot on the street about a block away from the warehouse. The streetlights were on the other side of the street, so there were some shadows on the side where they parked, which was good. The block they had parked in was a mixture of small businesses, almost all of which were closed except for the check-cashing outfit on the corner behind them. There wasn't a lot of traffic, and no panhandlers or drunks wandering around. It was as quiet as they could have wanted it. Ariel was glad.

After turning the engine off, Mordechai sat with both hands on the steering wheel for a moment. He sighed, and turned toward Ariel. "Your last chance to walk away from this," he said. "The event in Tel

Aviv was mostly impromptu and reaction to what the terrorists did. Even throwing the girl on the grenade was basically caused by her. New York was precisely targeted and a very clean operation. But this—if you get out of this car and walk down the street with me, your hands will bear as much blood as mine. This is your last chance to turn away from that."

Ariel shook his head, but took his time in answering. "I'm not walking away from this one. They killed Jews. They killed my parents. I stand with Ehud ben-Gera."

Mordechai gave a small smile, picked something up from the car console and placed it in his ear, then handed one to Ariel. "Put that in your ear. Short range, low power, but enough for what we're doing tonight."

Ariel inserted the bud in his ear, then pulled on his gloves. Mordechai reached into the back seat, picked up the pry bars and brought them to the front seat. "Just in case we need them for the doors."

Ariel took one and hefted it as he got out of the car, then swung it up so it was riding along the back of his arm.

"*Test*," he heard in his earpiece.

"Test," he muttered back.

"*Clear.*"

They walked in silence until they reached the block the warehouse was in where they separated. Mordechai continued walking toward the front of the building, while Ariel jogged down the cross street to the alley that cut in behind the buildings. The light was very dim in the alleyway, but Ariel had no problems seeing what was there. He arrived at the back door to the warehouse without incident, and placed his back against the wall on the other side of the door from the electric meter.

"Here," he whispered. He tested the door handle. It turned, but the door didn't move. "Locked."

"Here. Front not locked. Count five from mark and come in. Turn the power off at the second mark." About two breaths passed. *"Mark."*

Ariel counted to five, set the flat end of the bar in the space right above the lock, and pushed with all his strength. There was a *creak-crunch-pop* sound, and the door swung free. He stepped through, pulling the door back to the jamb as he did so.

The building was one large open bay—no interior walls anywhere. There were some cabinets along one side of the back wall, and there was a gun rack over on the side wall to his right. A large swastika flag hung on the opposite wall. The walls must have been pretty thick, because the inside was smaller than he expected—maybe fifty feet by ninety. Still a good-sized room, but the men standing in it had room to move around.

The spot he was in was shadowed, but there were bright lights farther out. He looked quickly, and determined that the power panel was immediately to the left of the door, as they had expected it to be. There was a master cutoff lever there. He hefted the pry bar and edged that direction.

There were a number of men in the building, all looking toward the front door. Ariel did a quick head count, and came up with thirteen. Most of them were wearing jackets with black dragon heads on the back. So, it looked like everyone in the gang was there.

"Who the hell are you?" a guy in the middle of the crowd snarled at Mordechai. "What makes you think you can just barge in here?"

"Ah, Mr. Campbell," Mordechai said. "How nice of you to identify yourself right away. That will save us some time later. As for who I am"—he raised his voice to talk over the growing shouts and curses—"I am Retribution."

"That's the guy that stabbed me!" shouted a guy with an arm in a sling.

"And this is the guy that broke my arm!" came from a guy at the back of the crowd who was pointing at Ariel.

The noise redoubled, and one of the crowd broke for the gun rack. Mordechai's arm blurred into motion, and his crowbar speared through the man. He contorted and fell, several feet from the wall, and blood began pooling on the concrete floor under him.

There was a moment of stark silence, which Mordechai broke. "Last night one or more of you threw a bomb in a synagogue window." His voice was cold and hard, more so than Ariel had ever heard before. "You all approved and condoned intentionally murdering fourteen people and wounding a dozen more. Tonight, justice will be performed. Prepare yourselves. Mark!"

Ariel reached up and pulled the electricity master cutoff lever. The lights went out for a moment of almost utter darkness, then a single emergency light above the front door came on, throwing very stark shadows across the room.

Mordechai was already in motion. Ariel saw two men coming his way. He ducked under a swing by one of two men charging him and bashed the other one with the crowbar. The crunch that vibrated into his hand told him that man was done for. He then blocked another swing by the first one and punched him in the throat. Another crunch. Another one down. After that, things got crazy.

Ariel caught a flicker of motion out of the corner of one eye just before a pipe hammered into his lower back. He grunted, then spun to face the wielder, only to have another man slam a baseball bat into the bicep of his left arm. That one hurt. He pushed that guy hard against the wall. He turned again to face the guy with the pipe. Pipe guy backed up, hands in front of him. "I didn't mean it! I didn't mean it!"

Ariel snarled, exposing his fangs, and the man's eyes widened and he froze. The acrid smell of piss filled Ariel's nostrils as a large stain spread across the front of the man's worn jeans. "Too little, too late," Ariel said. He started to reach out, only to have a couple of others come flying back at him from the circle around Mordechai. They knocked him to one side, and the pipe holder screamed and ran the other way.

The two new ones started swinging punches. One landed solidly on his nose, which was just as full of nerves as it ever was, and the blossom of pain from the hit stunned him for a moment. When he focused again, the other two were gone, one of them sucked back into facing Mordechai, and the other to run toward the gun rack. Ariel looked around for his pry bar, and found it just to one side. The gang member was pulling a rifle down and racking the action when Ariel imitated Mordechai's throw. The crowbar smashed the man's head with a spray of blood and gray matter. Not as elegant as Mordechai's throw, perhaps, but it did the job. Three down.

Ariel looked around. The front of the room was almost cleared. One of the gang backed into Ariel while trying to avoid Mordechai. The gang member tried to duck away, but Ariel reached up and twisted his head so he was looking directly behind him, accompanied by more crunching as vertebrae broke.

Four down.

Mordechai dropped his last target at the same moment. They looked at each other, then in unison turned to look at Cord Campbell, who was the last of the gang members standing. Ariel was surprised at Campbell's height—or rather, the lack of it. He was actually a couple of inches shorter than Ariel.

Campbell pulled a pistol from his belt and moved it back and forth to cover first Mordechai, then Ariel, and back again. "What...what do you want?"

"I told you," Mordechai said in his coldest voice. "Justice for the fourteen people you murdered last night."

"You...you can't do this. It's illegal!" Campbell shouted.

Mordechai waved a hand across the floor. "It looks like we've already done it. And it's only illegal if your police can find us. Which they won't."

Ariel slipped a couple of steps closer as Mordechai kept Campbell's attention.

"But why? Why do you care? They're only Jews."

They're only Jews. That statement lit a flame of fury in Ariel's mind. He closed the distance with Campbell in less than a heartbeat, and ripped the pistol out of his hands, breaking fingers in the process.

Campbell screamed in surprise and pain, then was reduced to choked moans as Ariel lifted him one-handed by the throat.

"They're only Jews," he hissed, leaning forward

to stare into Campbell's eyes from less than a hand-breadth's distance. *"They're only Jews!"* He shook Campbell so hard his body flopped under his neck hold. *"You murdered my parents and all you can say is 'They're only Jews'?"*

There was a moment of almost silence as Ariel heaved breaths and Campbell pawed at the hand around his throat, choking. Ariel leaned forward again, and smiled, making sure that his fangs were showing. "Little man," he crooned, "get ready to meet God, knowing that you've failed." His smile broadened. "Get ready to meet God, knowing that you never knew anything about the Jews. We're not demons. We're not trash. But some of us"—he reached up and tapped a fang with his other hand—"some of us *are* vampires, and two of us took down your whole gang tonight. Don't worry, I'm not going to take your blood. I wouldn't pollute my body with it. You're not worth it. Just die knowing that even one such as I find you to be the uttermost filth."

He paused for a moment, lifted Campbell a little higher, and said, "You've cost us enough time. No farewells, filth. Go meet your judge."

Ariel's fist clenched, Campbell's neck crunched, his feet kicked in the air for a few seconds, and then he fell limp. Ariel let the body drop to the floor.

Five down.

Ariel stood for a long moment, just staring at the dead gang leader. He felt . . . he didn't know what he felt. There was no sense of victory, no sense of fulfillment. Just . . . emptiness. A void, where his mother and father used to be.

CHAPTER 23

ARIEL COULD HEAR MORDECHAI WALKING AROUND the warehouse, opening cabinet doors and moving things. "Ah, this will work." He looked around to see Mordechai pick up a can from a cabinet and a hammer from a shelf.

Mordechai walked over to the front door. "Ariel, come help me." He set the can and hammer on the floor, then lifted one of the gang members and propped the corpse against the wall by the door. "Come hold this up. Try not to step in the blood."

Ariel stirred himself to walk over and put a hand on the corpse's chest to keep it in place, wondering what Mordechai was going to do. There was a wooden beam that ran horizontally about five feet above the floor. Mordechai picked up the hammer and pulled a rusty spike about a centimeter thick and twenty centimeters long out of the can. He pulled the gang member's arm up against the beam, and with two blows had the head of the spike flush against the wrist. Another spike, two more blows, and the other arm was nailed to the beam.

"What are you doing?" Ariel demanded, stepping away from the body and letting it sag against the spikes.

"Leaving a message," Mordechai said. "Come on, this shouldn't take long."

And it didn't. Ten minutes later, Ariel looked around the warehouse to see a dozen of the gang members spiked to the walls. The one that had been transfixed with the crowbar still had it projecting from his body, which he had to admit looked weird. He turned to see the body of Cord Campbell still lying on the floor.

"What do we do with him?"

"Well, we've run out of open wall space," Mordechai said, "and we only have one spike left. But there's something we can do. Go rip that filth off the wall." He pointed to the swastika flag.

By the time Ariel had done that and returned to the center of the warehouse, Mordechai had retrieved a bundle of rope from one of the back cabinets. "Here, hold this." Mordechai took the flag from Ariel and thrust the rope into his hands. A minute later, one end of the flag had been tied around Campbell's neck, and Mordechai was knotting one end of the rope to the other end of the flag. When that was done, Mordechai tossed the other end of the rope up through the lattice of one of the roof support beams.

Two taps with the hammer, and the last spike was protruding from the frame around the front door. Mordechai dropped the hammer, pulled on the rope one-handed to hoist Campbell's body so that his feet were hanging four feet off the floor, and tied off the rope to the spike. Ariel joined him where he stood before the door, and they took in the sight. "A worthy job, if I do say so myself," Mordechai said. "Just one more thing to do. Clear everything out from the center of the floor."

It only took a few moments for the two of them to kick the garbage and debris and detritus of the gang's occupancy toward the side walls. Ariel understood what the purpose was after Mordechai picked up a spray-paint can and began shaking it. He watched as Mordechai painted a message in large red letters.

THEY
WERE
WARNED

The air in the warehouse was already becoming noisome with a fetid sewage reek; a number of the bodies had released bladder and bowel contents moments after their deaths. Now the hyper-pungent chemical smell of spray paint began wrestling with it in the air. Ariel blew his breath out and wrinkled his nose. To say it was unpleasant to vampire senses understated the matter significantly.

"Can we get out of here?"

"One more thing."

Mordechai stepped forward one step and pulled his mobile phone out. "Stay behind me," he said as he began a video recording with a slow pan around the room, capturing imagery of all the corpses on the wall as well as Campbell suspended in midair, with a final long shot of the message on the floor. Ariel dwelt on that as well as he pivoted behind Mordechai's turn. The phone light went out, and Mordechai tucked it back into his pocket.

"We're done," the older man said with a certain note of satisfaction in his voice. "Let's go."

They exited through the back door into the alley. Mordechai flipped the master power switch back on as they did so. "The emergency light batteries will only last so long," he said. "We want this to have its proper effect when the police arrive."

Ariel said nothing, only nodded as he took a breath of clean air. They walked together back down the alley to the cross street, then retraced their steps to the car. Once they settled in, Mordechai started the car and drove off. Ariel was fairly certain they weren't done, but Mordechai hadn't told him what the next step was.

Mordechai drove for a few blocks until they were on the main road to the nearest bridge over the river, when he finally spoke.

"There's a burner phone in the console. Call the police and tell them there are bodies at the warehouse."

Okay, that made some sense. No reason to leave a message if it isn't delivered, after all. Ariel opened the console, pulled the phone out, closed the console, and dialed 9-1-1.

The phone clicked, and a brusque matter-of-fact female voice said, "911, what's your emergency?"

"I just saw a bunch of dead people," Ariel said in a breathless high-pitched tone.

"Dead people?" That certainly got the dispatcher's attention. "What location? Where are you?"

"1206 Fairway Avenue," Ariel said in the same tone as before.

"1206 Fairway Avenue," the dispatcher repeated.

"Yeah. You better hurry, there's a bunch of them."

"Are you there now?"

"You better hurry," Ariel repeated, and ended the call.

"That should have gotten their attention," Mordechai murmured. "Well done."

The car slowed down as they neared the crest of the bridge. The river wasn't very wide, so the four-lane bridge wasn't very high, and they were in the outside westbound lane. "Throw the phone in the river," Mordechai directed as the passenger window rolled down. Ariel waited until they were at the center of the bridge, then flung the phone out with a snap of his wrist. It easily cleared the side barrier and dropped into the night headed for the waters of the river.

The window rolled back up, and the car picked up speed. The trip back to the hotel passed in silence.

"Meet me in the bar in twenty minutes," Mordechai said after parking the car.

CHAPTER 24

NINETEEN MINUTES LATER, ARIEL STEPPED ON THE elevator. He'd put the bloodied leather jacket and clothing and the gloves in a plastic bag that he tucked into his main bag, then changed back into slacks and a collarless shirt. He cleaned off his Doc Marten boots and flushed the wipes down the toilet, then slipped into his blazer to complete his transformation into the young businessman out on the town. He checked his image in the elevator mirror, and nodded to himself. He shook his head, remembering who he was only a few months before: a pudgy, nerdy, loner geek who thought vampires were bad fantasy. The word "conversion" applied to him in more than one way, he decided. And if only the high school girls could see him now. His own mother would likely have had trouble picking him out of a crowd. That thought caused a deep pang in his heart, but after a breathless moment he consoled himself with the thought that her murderers were dead.

The elevator stopped and he moved past other guests onto the hotel's main bar floor. It was a little busier than the night before, but not jam-packed. He looked toward the table they had occupied before the news broke last night, and sure enough, Mordechai was there, pointing a finger at him. Ariel began making his way toward the table, slipping through the crowd in the foyer and around the bar. One of the few times when being shortish and slim worked to his advantage, actually.

Most of the patrons he was ducking between were wearing name tags, and he remembered seeing signs in the main lobby about some kind of convention. Funny how quickly the country had rebounded from the alarmism of the Covid year, as most people thought of 2020. Once the vaccines were available in sufficient quantity to allow most people to escape the fear, most of life had fairly quickly returned to something like the pre-Covid normal. And although the modern workplace had been irretrievably changed to allow a lot more remote working and a lot more electronic meetings, there was still a certain urge, a certain need, to have real face time with other people, especially in certain disciplines. A lot of people discovered that remote meetings just didn't satisfy the urge to connect. Studies were beginning to be published based on Covid year social data that indicated that a lot of people simply couldn't empathize with someone unless they actually met them in person in real time. So bit by bit, some of the business conventions were beginning to come back; smaller than they had been, of course, but returning to life nonetheless. Other types of conventions were also flickering back to life.

Some of the people Ariel was moving through had a certain air of desperation about them, as if they weren't sure it was real—that it wasn't a dream from which they would awaken and discover that they were still back in the living nightmare. Ariel could certainly understand that, given the turn his own life had taken in the last year or so.

Ariel had made it most of the way through the crowd when a large man stepped in front of him and bumped him with enough force that in earlier days he might have been knocked down. He just stepped to the side, said, "Sorry," and started to move past the man. A large hand that descended on his shoulder stopped his progress.

"Buddy, you need to be more careful about where you're going," a bass voice slurred. Ariel looked up. He was used to thinking in metric terms after his time in Israel, and he estimated the man was close to one hundred ninety centimeters tall. He probably weighed at least one hundred twenty kilograms, maybe more. His nametag read "Bob," and he was seriously drunk.

Ariel sighed. "Look, Bob, I already apologized. Now if you don't mind, I'm supposed to be over there talking to my boss about our next deal, so I'd appreciate it if you'd let go of me so I can get on with it."

Bob blinked. "Kid, you ran into me and spilled my drink. You need to buy me another one." He blinked again. "And where's your badge?"

Ariel shook his head. "Look, dude, I didn't run into you. You ran into me. And I'm not buying you a drink, because you're drunk. Now let go of me."

Now Bob frowned. "Son, you're not old enough or big enough to play with the real men. Now, get me my drink."

Ariel's voice got hard. "I'm not your buddy, I'm

not your kid, I'm not your son, I'm not your friend, and the reason I don't have a badge is I'm not part of your group. Now for the last time, get your hand off of me."

Bob tried to shake Ariel, but his frown deepened when he found his hand moving but Ariel not shaking. Ariel rolled his eyes, then spun in place and punched Bob right above the belt buckle. The punch only traveled a few inches, but it was powered by vampire muscles.

Bob's eyes opened so wide there was white visible all around the pupils. His mouth opened in an O shape almost as if trying to imitate the eyes, and every molecule of breath in his lungs was expelled as his diaphragm was rudely compressed. Not a sound came out of his mouth. His hand fell off of Ariel's shoulder.

Ariel was watching as Bob's head jerked a bit and his jaw muscles suddenly stood out in relief. From his time at the Urgent Care he knew what that portended and swiftly stepped to the side, giving a forceful tug to Bob's jacket sleeve as he did so. Bob began vomiting profusely before he hit the floor, which caused screams and shouts and curses among the crowd. Everyone watched in horrified fascination as he proceeded to empty his stomach. From the looks of it, Bob had had a lot of shrimp at dinner. Ariel wrinkled his nose as the odor of mingled gastric juices, shrimp, and mass quantities of alcohol began to rise from the floor.

"Charles," Ariel said as the waiter appeared at his side, "it appears that Bob here has had a bit too much to drink. It might be good if his friends—if he has any—would take him to his room and pour him into bed." He looked at the people between him and his table. "Excuse me, please." A wide path opened as he moved around where Bob was on hands and knees, head hanging low, then skirted the noisome pool of ejecta.

"Nicely done," Mordechai murmured as Ariel settled into his seat. "A bit public, perhaps, but nicely done, nonetheless. You moved so quickly I doubt anyone really caught what happened." He lifted his glass of Glenmorangie, and tipped his head before he took a sniff. "Oh, by the way, Charles says they've had a run on the Perrier, so you're drinking San Pellegrino tonight."

"Fine." Ariel twisted the cap off the bottle, poured it into the waiting glass, and took a sip.

Events like Bob's must not have been uncommon, as hotel staff had it cleaned up and the floor mopped and dried in less than seven minutes. In another two the crowd was circulating across the area as if nothing had happened. Ariel's mouth quirked at the observation.

They sat quietly for quite some time. Ariel was looking toward the crowd, but he wasn't really seeing them. His thoughts were occupied with a mental replay of the events earlier in the evening. From parking the car, to walking to the warehouse, to opening the door, and what followed, it cycled through his mind in an endless loop.

The loop broke when Charles appeared beside the table with a fresh bottle of San Pellegrino. Setting it on the table, he leaned over and said in a murmur, "Your tab is on the house tonight. We'd been trying to get that guy to calm down for a couple of hours. He'd been harassing both men and women for most of that time. He's out now, and the bar manager has banned him from the bar for the rest of the convention. I don't know what you did, but thanks."

Ariel finished his drink and opened the new bottle, pouring it into the now empty glass. "I'm not admitting anything," he replied in a low tone, "but for what it's worth, you're welcome." Charles flashed a grin and moved back into the crowd.

For the next little while, they didn't speak. Ariel watched the movements of the people in the bar, and played with the bubbles in his water, all the while thinking about what he had just done.

He had killed five men, and been an accessory to the deaths of eight more. He refused to use the term "murder" in considering the event, because in his mind it was not murder. It was justice. It was illegal—no, extralegal—justice, but it was justice. But before the "conversion," when he was the pale, pudgy, nerdy Jewish almost-prodigy Chaim Caan, would he have countenanced such a thing? Would he have condoned it? Would he even have contemplated it? He wanted to think so. He wanted to think he would have had the courage and the fire in his belly to want to bring justice to killers of Jews—to the killers of his parents. But the truth was, he didn't know. And he'd never know, because he was no longer Chaim Caan, young American cosmopolitan Jew—he was Ariel Barak, soon to be a member of the Israeli Yamam, a vampire, a trained killer, whose system was filled with more adrenaline and anger on a daily basis than poor Chaim had ever experienced in a full year. His physiology had changed, was still changing. His hormones had changed. His brain chemistry had to be changing. Was he even the same person, physically, mentally? And what did it portend if he wasn't?

Ariel snorted, and waved at Charles for a fresh bottle of San Pellegrino. As if it would make a bit of difference either way. He was what he was, and there was nothing he could do about it. He'd drifted into the fine Jewish sport of overthinking his problems and worrying about the results. "Jews are world-class worriers," he'd heard his father say once, "although Russian babushkas will give them a run for their money." That thought gripped his throat for a moment. "It is what it is," he muttered, and resolutely turned his mind away from the matter.

Charles arrived with the new bottle of water, which he delivered with smooth style and another flashing grin. Ariel poured a fresh glass and took a sip. As he set it down, Mordechai said, "Are you ready to talk about it now?"

Ariel looked at the older man. It dawned on him that Mordechai was an atypical Jew in more than one way. In addition to being a vampire, he wasn't driven to fill a silence that lasted for more than three seconds. He was content to wait on the other person to speak, even if it meant he was listening to his own thoughts for a while. How unusual.

Turning the glass around and around in his hands, Ariel sighed. "I guess so." He turned the glass some more, trying to figure out how to say what was in his mind. "Is it always like that?" he finally asked.

"What do you mean?"

"There were thirteen of them, and only two of us, but they didn't really have a chance, did they?"

Mordechai pursed his lips and shook his head. "No. Even if they'd had major weapons in hand when we came in the doors, they probably wouldn't have touched us. We're too fast, too strong."

Ariel stared off at the wall across the way. "I guess I was expecting to have to struggle, to have to fight harder in order to win out. I mean, yeah, it was crazy, and I see what you mean about experience, but still..."

"You were expecting a sense of victory," Mordechai said.

"Yeah. I was. Instead, I feel...I feel like I just stepped on a bug that was in my path."

"Oh, not just a bug," Mordechai said with a small smile. "A scorpion, at least."

"Huh," Ariel grunted. "Yeah, I could buy that. A nest of scorpions, even."

"Indeed." Mordechai lifted his scotch and sniffed it again.

"So is that what it's all about? Pest control? Is that what being one of the *Gibborim* is all about?"

"No." Mordechai shook his head, rested his fore-arms on the table, and leaned forward. "No, it's not. Sometimes you have jobs like the night club, where you rescue hostages and walk away feeling really good about being there and about saving someone's life. Those are usually wonderful days.

"Sometimes you work a commission where you pre-vent someone from executing their plans, and thereby save who knows how many lives. Those are days when you feel a great deal of satisfaction about the work and about your part in it.

"Sometimes, you have things like this, where you're coming behind the event, and you can't undo the dam-age, no matter how much you want to. All you can do is whatever you can do to keep it from happening again."

"Like now," Ariel said.

"Like now," Mordechai agreed. "There is no joy.

There is, perhaps, a grim satisfaction at knowing you have stepped on that particular scorpion, and it won't sting anyone again. Not pest control. Vermin eradication, maybe.

"And sometimes..." Mordechai's face was grim, and his eyes had focused on the wall, "sometimes things don't work, and all you can do is cause as much damage as you can and try to get out alive."

"Like Warsaw?" Ariel asked.

Mordechai sat, motionless, for a long moment, then slowly nodded. "Yes, like Warsaw." After another moment, he shook his head. "But regardless, unless they have unusual weapons, or unless you're in a very dangerous place like a chemical plant, you'll almost certainly survive and usually accomplish your task."

"If that's so," Ariel said, "why did you have me trained in firearms? Why didn't we have firearms here? I would have felt a lot more comfortable going into that building with that Glock under my arm."

"I could have gotten weapons for us here," Mordechai said. "I intentionally didn't, because it was clear we wouldn't need them to accomplish the task. And it would have been a problem for you in this case, in your first operation."

"How so?"

"Because even though you've had the training, at this point it wouldn't have been a tool for you, it would have been a distraction." Mordechai sighed. "And we train with weapons because every once in a while, you will find yourself in a situation where you need to either deal with a lot of targets in a very short period of time, or you need to deal with someone right then who is farther away than you can physically move before it's too late. I find it is better in that situation to have the weapon and the training to use it, instead of discovering you need it but don't have it."

Ariel lifted his drink and downed some more of it. He set it down and stared at it. "I guess..." he said again. "I guess I was just expecting to burn up all my anger and hate in this, and..." He stopped, unable to put words to what he was feeling.

There was a long moment of silence, then Mordechai asked quietly, "In the end, was it righteous?" He pointed a finger at Ariel. "Do you judge it righteous?"

Ariel stared at him. "Me? How would I know? I'm a nineteen-year-old kid. How would I know."

"You're a nineteen-year-old kid who will outlive your contemporaries' grandchildren, and probably their grandchildren as well," Mordechai said sternly, "and you will be dealing with the consequences of your decisions and choices and actions for all that time. You've had your bar mitzvah. You are a man before *haShem*. You need to decide for yourself if what you have done is righteous. The Torah will help. The Talmud will help. The rabbis will help. But in the end, only you are responsible to *haShem* for you and your choices. Decide. Is what you just did righteous?" He lowered his finger.

Ariel felt a surge of anger. "Yes, it was righteous!"

"Why?"

"Because they murdered fourteen Jews, including my parents." Ariel bit the words out in a sharp tone. "Murder is one of the capital crimes in Torah. We invoked justice."

His anger started to rise when Mordechai gave a small smile. He thought he was being mocked, but then Mordechai said, "That is a telling point. It supports your decision that what you did was righteous. But is it enough?"

That shocked Ariel. He sat back, and said slowly, "I think so, but obviously you have another consideration. Don't dance with me, please. Just tell me what it is."

"Do you know why Israeli courts are so reluctant to execute criminals that they've only executed two people in over seventy-five years?" Ariel shook his head, but said nothing. "For the same reason that most Jews are against capital punishment. It eliminates the possibility of repentance. If someone will possibly repent of their actions, all the rabbis say that is preferable to ending his life arbitrarily."

"Okay," Ariel said, his speech still slow. "I guess I can see that. And since you brought it up, you obviously feel that is a consideration here. But how?"

"In his masterwork *Gates of Repentance*, Rabbenu Yonah of Gerona—do you know of him? He was a cousin of Nahmanides—says that the very first step of achieving repentance is to recognize and acknowledge the sin. Until the perpetrator, for lack of a better word, achieves that, repentance will never happen. The door to repentance does not open without that. Now...remember what happened. Remember what those men said, especially their leader, Cord Campbell. Did he sound like he was open to repentance? What were his last words?"

Ariel shook his head. "No," he said through gritted teeth. "His last words were 'They're only Jews.'"

"'They're only Jews.' Does that sound like the mind of a man who recognizes that he has committed a sin and needs to repent?"

Ariel shook his head, not wanting to say anything further.

After a moment, Mordechai said, "Do you know why the Israeli court executed Adolf Eichmann?"

Ariel looked at him with a furrowed brow. "Because of his work in the concentration camps."

"No, that was the excuse. That was the justification. I've read all the documentation of that trial, and you won't find this in the records anywhere, but the real reason why they finally ruled to execute him was he would not acknowledge his sin. He would not acknowledge that what he did was a crime, a personal crime on his part. To the very end, he would not acknowledge it. That is why his execution was righteous, and that is why, ultimately, what we did in that warehouse was righteous. They committed a horrible crime, a horrible sin against the Jewish people, and they refused to acknowledge their crime." Mordechai nodded, and pointed his finger at Ariel. "Remember that, Ariel. It's not just a question of justice. It's never just a question of justice. It never should be just a question of justice."

He dropped his hand and took a sniff of his scotch. Ariel stared at the wall across the room, mind whirling.

After a while, Mordechai said, "We fly out to Atlanta early tomorrow morning. We'll refuel there, and return to Tel Aviv. Once we're there, we'll go to the Western Wall."

"Will I find answers there?"

Mordechai shrugged. "Maybe, maybe not. But it may help you put it in perspective."

Ariel drained his glass and waved a hand at Charles. He stared at the wall.

CHAPTER 25

THROUGHOUT THE FLIGHT FROM CALIFORNIA TO Atlanta, Ariel sat holding the two mementoes of his parents—his father's Tanakh in his right hand, and his mother's menorah in his left. His eyes were closed, and he was remembering everything he could about them.

Ariel thought he had grieved before when he had cut himself off from his parents. The thought that he would never see them again had been very painful. But he discovered that that emotion was but a pale imitation of the grief of knowing they were gone, that he would truly never see them or anything about them again, and of knowing that they had died in such a meaningless fashion. His heart was filled with rage that burned but was yet cold. It was little consolation that their killers were likewise dead. Likewise it brought little balm to his soul to know that he had had a major part in enacting justice on their killers.

Grief, pain, horror, and rage alternately danced within his memories. He kept having to force his hands to unclench from the book and the menorah. With his current strength, he could actually damage them, and he didn't think he could stand that.

By the time Ariel felt the pilots begin the descent, he had wrestled the rage into submission, and the pain and horror were beginning to pale. He knew the grief would be with him for a while, but that felt normal to him. He felt that that was part of the price of being who and what he was. Right then, he felt it reminded him of his humanity. Not that he was a candidate for the new Job, or anything like that. But sorrow was a part of the human existence, as the history of the Jews had proven over and over. It was a mantle he was fit to wear, he decided.

While they were on the ground getting the plane refueled, the pilots got out to stretch their legs and take a meal break. Ariel put his keepsakes back in his bag, and returned to his seat.

"Through sitting *shiva*?" Mordechai asked, looking up from his laptop.

"Not really that," Ariel responded. "Just . . . remembering them."

"That's what shiva is all about," Mordechai responded. "The ritual is just a framework. It's the remembering that's important. Whether it lasts a week, or three days, or just an hour, that's what's important."

"That's not what the rabbis say," Ariel said. "They say immediately, and the full seven days."

Mordechai snorted. "The Orthodox do. There are differences of opinion among the people, of course. We're Jews—of course there are differences of opinion."

Ariel looked at him and raised his eyebrows. "Are you Orthodox, Mordechai?"

"I was reasonably Orthodox before I became what I am. Now, after all these years, I am as Orthodox as I can be. Orthodoxy fits me like an old comfortable suit, but there are times and places where I have to move beyond it. Not to replace it, not to disparage it, but to help it remain a proper fit for the man I am now, as opposed to the man I started out as so many years ago."

Mordechai sighed. "In some ways, you and I, we have moved beyond the labels of Orthodoxy and Conservatism and Reform. We are Jews, yes. We are part of the Jewish community. But we cannot, by the very nature of what we are, be restrained or constrained by labels created by men who did not and do not realize all that haShem has included in his Creation."

Ariel blinked. Suddenly Mordechai's age seemed to weigh on him. It pressed him into his seat, somehow.

After a moment, Mordechai looked at him over the top of the laptop, and sighed. "You do realize this is going to happen again and again, don't you?"

"Huh?" Ariel titled his head, trying to catch up with the topic change. "What do you mean?"

"You're not immortal. But you are going to be longer-lived than anyone you know. Every friend you have or will make will grow up, age, fade, and die before you, sometimes before your very eyes. And there's nothing you can do about it." Mordechai's eyes for the first time showed Ariel deep emotion. "There's nothing you can do about it, but remember them, and pray," he whispered.

For the first time, Ariel really saw Mordechai bearing the weight of his nearly three hundred years. For the first time, he truly understood the price the older vampire paid to be what he was. It awed him. It challenged him. And it more than a little frightened him. He stared at his mentor, wanting to reach out to him, but was void of words.

❖   ❖   ❖

Several hours later they were well across the Atlantic Ocean, almost halfway to Israel according to the flight map on the big screen at the rear of the compartment. Ariel was reading in his father's Tanakh, seeking solace in the Psalms. Mordechai was apparently engrossed in his laptop whenever Ariel glanced up, his finger scrolling the feed.

Ariel was midway through Psalm 47 and had just read the *selah* after the verse describing the fortress of Ya'akov when Mordechai exclaimed, "Ha!" and tapped a few keys. "Watch this!"

The flight map flickered, then was replaced by a video with a banner across the bottom of the screen that read *Blue Lance*. Above the banner was a shot of a studio with two people sitting at a table across from each other. Ariel recognized the man as James McLeod wearing his gang jacket. The other person was what seemed to be a youngish Asian woman in a sleeveless black leather vest and long hair dyed almost an electric blue.

"Hey, and welcome to the Blue Lance blog," the woman said, "where we don't care if you're a left-winger or a right-winger or a wing nut, we're here to burst your bubble and get at the real truth. I'm Azure Wong, and we've got some interesting stuff going down today. In a little while, we'll be talking to some folks about some problems down Bakersfield way in one of the oil fields. Stay tuned for that. But to kick things off, if you haven't heard about it, there was some real heavy action going down in Santa Carla in the last couple of days. Someone walked into the hangout of a motorcycle gang called Los Dracos Negros and executed them all. We're about to show a video which has been an internet sensation for the last few hours. It shows the results of extreme violence, and we suggest you not watch it if you are sensitive or have children in the room."

What followed was the video that Mordechai had shot with his phone, panning around the corpses spiked to the walls of the warehouse and ending with the corpse of Campbell hung with the Nazi flag. Ariel felt a certain warmth at seeing that, nodding his head in some satisfaction.

The picture flipped back to the reporter and McLeod.

"That's what was released by unknown sources," Azure said, "and I don't know about you, but that's pretty damned bloody. To try and get some background and understanding of the gang dynamics in Santa Carla and surrounding areas, we've invited the leader of the local chapter of The Devil's Legions, Mr. James McLeod, into our studio. Welcome."

"Call me Jake," McLeod said with a grin.

"Okay, Jake. Can you tell me what your feeling is about the terrible things that happened to your enemies in the Los Dracos Negros gang?"

"Well, first of all," McLeod drawled, "while it's true that there wasn't any love lost between us and them, they weren't really our enemies." He paused for a beat. "They weren't that important."

"What do you mean?"

"They were a new club, they only had a few members, and they really didn't have the muscle to cut in on our turf, our activities. They talked a lot of trash, but they didn't stand behind it." McLeod shrugged. "More like a gang of wannabes, than anything real."

"So you didn't take them out? You didn't kill them?" When McLeod pursed his lips and shook his head, Azure continued, "Do you have any ideas who did?"

"I can tell you it probably wasn't any of the organized gangs in the valley," McLeod said, "whether bikers or the others. We could have taken them out, sure. So could most of the others. There'd have been a big brawl, blood would have been everywhere, and bodies would have either been scattered around or found in the river. But that's not what happened. You've seen the video."

"So, Jake, you're saying your gang didn't do that?"

"Hell, no," McLeod said.

"And you don't think any of the other gangs did?"

"No."

"Why not?"

McLeod held up a finger. "First of all, it's too controlled. If cops or SWAT or FBI did it, Cord Campbell and his buddies would have been filled with bullets. The cops haven't made an official announcement yet, but the rumors all say they were killed by hand—no gunshot wounds. You have to get up close and personal on purpose to do that."

He held up another finger. "Second, it's too neat. Gangs or cops would have come in with twice their numbers, and would have made a real mess of things. This is like one or two OCD ninjas came in, wiped them out, and then nailed them up on the walls to get them out of the way or something. It's too clean."

McLeod dropped his hand. "Nah, it's nobody from around here. No rumors, no encounters leading up to it, not even with the cops." He shrugged.

"So you don't have any ideas, any guesses?"

Jake grinned. "Oh, I have some ideas about what happened, but there's no way to prove them."

"So what do you think went down in that warehouse?"

Azure's head tilted and she leaned forward a little, showing a little more cleavage to Jake and the camera.

"I think they did something that pissed off someone, somebody important, somebody with a lot of juice."

"Someone in politics or government or organized crime?"

McLeod shrugged again. "Maybe. Who knows? But I think whoever it is has resources like not even the Feds can get. I mean, I'm not sure even somebody like Seal Team 6 could have or would have done this job this way."

"But why?"

McLeod grinned. "That's easy. It's a message."

"What do you mean?"

"Oh, come on, Azure . . . it's obvious. If you do something like this, and you leave a message like 'They Were Warned,' like they did, they're obviously saying, 'Don't do that again, or we'll be back, and we'll really be pissed next time.'"

"So who are they warning?"

"I don't know, man," McLeod sobered. He tapped his chest a couple of times. "Not us. But I'm pretty sure they had a target, and as much airtime as this is getting I'd be willing to bet that the message has been received."

The picture froze there, and Ariel looked over at where Mordechai was sitting, grinning. "Well, if Jake figured it out, I suspect others will as well."

Ariel nodded. "Will they figure out who did it?"

Mordechai shook his head. "That's doubtful. They might guess that someone from outside the country did it. They might even guess Israel was involved somehow. But being able to link it to you and me?" He repeated his headshake.

"Never again," Ariel said.

"Never again," Mordechai echoed.

Ariel jerked awake as the plane's wheels kissed the runway at Ben Gurion Airport. As his eyes flew open, he felt the book shift on his lap, so he made a panicked grab to catch it, which he managed to do.

He didn't know for sure when he'd dozed off. The last thing he remembered clearly was they were still a couple of hours out. He shook his head in an attempt to clear it from the sleep fog, then turned to put the book in his carry-on bag. He gave a big yawn as he zipped the bag shut.

By that time the plane finished what seemed to be a lengthy taxiing process and pulled into a small hanger building rather removed from the main terminals. Once the plane pulled to a stop and the engines spooled down, he and Mordechai arose, grabbed their carry-ons, and met the pilots at the door.

"Great job ferrying us around, Michael, Yonatan," Mordechai said with a pleasant smile. He headed down the steps.

"Thanks, guys," Ariel added as he held his hand out.

"Our pleasure," Michael said with a grin. "Literally. Don't tell anyone, but we'd probably fly this baby for free if it was the only way to get it."

"Speak for yourself," Yonatan said with a snort as he in turn shook Ariel's hand. "I have three kids to feed."

Ariel laughed, and followed Mordechai down the steps.

He was surprised to find Rabbi Avram waiting on them by the doorway into the office and waiting area. Mordechai was standing talking to him, but as Ariel

approached the rabbi turned toward him and held
out his arms. Ariel set down his bags and stepped
into the embrace.

The old man's grasp seemed light to Ariel, undoubtedly because of his age, but also no doubt because of
Ariel's own strength and strengthened stature because
of what he now was. Nonetheless, Ariel welcomed it,
and moderated his own embrace to avoid crushing
what he now knew was an increasingly fragile old man.

"I am so sorry, Ariel," the rabbi said, his whis-
kers brushing and tickling Ariel's cheek as his jaw
moved. "So sorry to hear about your parents." He
went on to murmur, *"Ha-makom yenachem otcha
b'toch she'ar avlei Zion v'Yerushalayim."* Ariel's mind
was still treating Hebrew like a second language,
so the back of his mind translated it as "May God
comfort you among the other mourners of Zion and
Jerusalem," but the front of his mind was so drinking
in the feeling of the embrace and the warmth and
care that the words didn't register deeply at the
moment. He felt like a man parched of thirst who
was being showered with cool water. Standing there
was almost like when his *Zaydeh*, his father's father,
had embraced him after his bar mitzvah.

Ariel wasn't sure how long they stood like that, but
finally Rabbi Avram released his clasp and they each
stepped back a half step. "Thank you," Ariel murmured.

After a moment, Mordechai looked at Mendel.
"Did you get it?"

Mendel nodded, pulled a small wallet-sized folder
out of his pocket, and handed it to Mordechai. He
flipped it open, nodded, and handed it to Ariel. "Here.
This is yours now."

Ariel discovered he was holding an ID card that indicated that he, Ariel Barak, was a *shoter*, or constable, in the Special Police, the Yamam. "This is real?" he asked.

"Absolutely. You're the lowest rank possible, so you have no authority, but you also have no responsibilities. And in their records, you are seconded to Mossad. And in Mossad's very restricted files, you are assigned to . . . me," Mordechai said with a smile.

"So this makes me official, though, right? Do I get a badge?"

"As official as a lowly *shoter* can be." Mordechai grinned. "No badge. You can't give any orders yourself, but you don't have to take anyone's orders but mine. What it does do, however, is make your weapon license a little more official."

Ariel looked at the card another time. The photo looked like the same one that was on all his other documents. He shrugged, closed the folder and put it in his pocket.

"Ah," said Mendel, looking over his shoulder, "there is the rest of your baggage." And indeed, their larger bags were being placed right behind them at that moment. "Come, the car is waiting in the parking lot."

It was only a matter of a couple of minutes to trundle their bags through the office and waiting area to the front door and out into the parking lot, where they found a large Mercedes sedan waiting on them.

Mordechai gave a whistle, then said, "Fancy," with a grin. "Stepping up in the world, are we? Next thing you'll have us flying in and out of the fancy private aircraft VIP lounge."

"*haShem* forbid it," the rabbi pronounced. "And

your sense of humor is going to get you into trouble, Mordechai Zalman."

"Probably," Mordechai said, his grin broadening.

The driver of the car stowed their bags away, and ushered them into the passenger compartment of the car. The rabbi and Mordechai sat in the rear seat facing forward and Ariel sat in the middle seat facing them.

"This *is* pretty fancy," Ariel said. "I know renting one of these in California for prom night would have cost a lot."

"Meh," Rabbi Avram said. "We had someone donate several rides to us for use with important guests. We don't have anyone coming in any time soon, so I decided to use one tonight. It saves you having to drive after a long flight, and it cushions my old bones." He shrugged. "Nothing in Torah says we must be uncomfortable in our work, after all."

"But surely there is something in the Talmud that draws a line between comfort and luxury," Mordechai murmured, looking around the plush compartment with his eyebrows elevated. Ariel grinned and suppressed a chuckle.

The two older men spent most of the ride discussing some aspect of the job they had just done in New York. Apparently the immigrant community's leaders were trying to blame the city government for the disappearance of their patrollers. Mordechai found that to be hilarious, but Mendel was concerned that it could still twist to become a problem for them.

By the time the car pulled into the parking lot of the foundation building, they had agreed to table the discussion for a month to allow time for more developments. "Just leave your bags in the car," Mendel said. "The driver will take you home afterward."

"After what?" Ariel asked, climbing out last and joining the two older men as they walked toward the entrance.

"You need to meet someone," Mordechai said.

"Tonight?"

"You have anything else to do tonight?" There was a hint of a laugh in Mordechai's voice.

"No," Ariel said with a shrug.

"All right, then."

They took the elevator down to the basement. Ariel followed the others down the hall and into what he knew was the door to a small gym and workout room. There he found two older men standing in the middle of the room who broke off a conversation to look at him.

"Ariel," Mordechai said in Hebrew, "let me introduce you to Menachem Aronson"—he pointed to a wiry man about Ariel's height with a full gray-shot bushy beard—"and Eleazar Katz." Katz was shorter than Ariel, and built like a fireplug: short and squat, mostly bald with a fringe of iron-gray hair and full beard and thick black eyebrows that almost met over his nose.

"So you're the new one," Aronson said in a nasal tenor. "Good. In another hundred years or so we might be able to form our own minyan." He emitted a dry chuckle. His Hebrew had a different accent than Mordechai's, but given that he was at least a hundred years younger and was born in a different country, that probably wasn't too surprising.

"I am pleased to meet you," said Katz, bobbing

his head and holding out his hand to be shook. "And while I am glad after a fashion to have another of us, I would not wish this on an enemy, much less a Jew, so I am sorry, as well. I am sorry, too, to hear of the loss of your parents. To lose them so young." He shook his head. "It makes me think of the times generations ago." He stepped forward to place a hand on Ariel's shoulder. "I shall pray for you, young Ariel. And soon—soon we will sit shiva with you."

"Thank you," Ariel murmured. He looked to Mordechai after Katz turned away. "Is there a reason why"—he waved a hand at the gym—"we're here? I thought you said they wouldn't be meeting me?"

Mordechai shrugged. "After word of what we did, they decided they wanted to meet you. It's not every day that someone joins our ranks, after all. Besides"— he grinned—"you need to spar. You need to burn up some of that energy, some of that emotion that is riding behind your eyes."

"And what do they need?" Ariel nodded toward the others.

"They needed to meet you, you needed to meet them, and this will help them get a feel for you as much as you for them."

Rabbi Avram walked over and sat in a chair that was in a nearby corner. "Don't mind me. While you lads play, I'll just take a nap." He sat down, leaned back, and tipped his hat forward over his eyes. That caused snorts and grins from the older vampires, and even Ariel felt the corners of his mouth twitch.

Mordechai took off his coat and tie and laid them on another chair, then began unbuttoning his shirt-sleeves and rolling them up.

"Any rules?"

"No eye-gouging, no biting, no hits to the stones," Aronson said. "Other than that, if you can land it, it's fair."

Mordechai walked out to the center of the mat that covered most of the floor. He turned and beckoned.

Ariel saw that all three of the older vampires were displaying their fangs. He took off his own coat and laid it atop Mordechai's, then followed him to the mat. "No armor, not barefoot?" he asked as he settled into stance.

"Shit happens everywhere, anywhere, anytime. Practice for real. Clothes can be replaced if necessary."

"Heh," Ariel said. "That's what Gil said."

"Gil does get things right more often than not."

"All right," Ariel smiled at Mordechai. "Just wanted to be clear on that."

Mordechai flicked his right hand out, and the sparring began.

Ariel had no idea how long they sparred. He was too busy to look at his watch and the gym didn't have a clock. As usual, sparring with Mordechai was like fighting a machine: it didn't matter how hard you hit him or where you hit him, he just kept coming at you, with blows and kicks that were just hard to block without getting knocked off-balance or to the ground. So the majority of the time he was ducking or evading the older vampire's strikes, while occasionally attempting one of his own. When Mordechai held up a hand and waved Aronson onto the mat, Ariel felt his heart rate elevated and he was breathing through his mouth. He was disappointed that he had only landed four solid hits, though.

Aronson started out as more of the same, but they weren't very far into their bout when he landed a slap on Ariel's left cheek that spun him around. "Guard up, young man," he snapped, before landing a backfist to the other side. "Faster!"

For all that Aronson was about Ariel's size, so therefore was shorter than Mordechai with a shorter reach, that did not mean that Ariel found it any easier to touch him. If anything, Aronson was quicker. Ariel felt as if Aronson's every strike was penetrating, was landing, was punishing him. He finally began to feel a bit of rhythm toward the end of the bout, and managed to land one good fist to Aronson's abdomen.

Aronson immediately held up his hand and stepped back, and Katz charged onto the mat. Where Aronson was a striker, Katz was a wrestler. He was also incredibly strong, Ariel found out the hard way. He managed to evade or block the first three grabs Katz made for him but not the fourth. A couple of dizzying seconds later, Ariel found himself lifted up then slammed to the mat with enough force that even his vampire-strengthened frame was shocked and his mind was stunned.

Katz knelt and touched his fist to Ariel's throat. "You're dead, boy," he said with a chuckle, then stood up and reached down a hand.

Ariel coughed, then reached up to take the hand. "Yeah," he said as he was pulled to his feet, "I'd say so. You guys are tough. And I don't know as much as I thought I knew."

Mordechai laughed from the side of the room. "Now you know who I work out with. They're both better than I am."

"Eh, we started working with Imi Lichtenfeld before you did," Aronson said. "And he's meaner than both of us anyway." He jerked a thumb at Katz, who jerked a different digit back at him.

"Wait a minute," Ariel said. "Imi Lichtenfeld, the creator of Krav Maga? You guys all studied with him? All three of you?"

"Studied with him?" Katz replied. "I'm not sure that's the best word. He was developing things in the thirties. It wasn't very formal then. He was still trying to figure out what worked and what didn't. So study? No. Worked with him, yes. In fact, that's where we met."

"Actually, Mordechai and I had met once earlier," Aronson said. "Before I knew he was a vampire. But yes, working with Imi was when we first met and first realized that we were all vampires. Dark times."

"In more than one way," Katz said. "The thirties were dark, but the war . . ." He shook his head. "That was darker."

"And Warsaw was darker yet." Mordechai's tone was very somber.

"*Zichronam livrachah*," came from behind them. "May their memories be a blessing." Rabbi Avram stepped forward. "And yet, in a way, that time is what led to the establishment of Israel. So there is a good that comes out of even great evil."

There was a moment of silence, then Mordechai responded, "Blessed be *haShem*."

"Amen," the others murmured, including Ariel.

"Now, let me order your sustenance," the rabbi said. He left the room.

"The rabbi is a good man," Aronson said.

"He's a great man," Katz replied.

As they bickered like a couple of very old men whose friendship was also very long, Mordechai stepped alongside Ariel. "So, do you feel a little worked out now?"

"Oh, yeah," Ariel said with a wince as he moved his shoulders. "Very worked out. I guess I should say thank you, but really, we probably need to do this more often. If I'm going to get better at this, I need more than one sparring partner."

"I agree. I was just waiting for the right time to introduce you. As I said some time back, they are very private men."

"I'll meet with them whenever I can, but I don't know for sure what my schedule for the next school session will look like."

Mordechai nodded, but before he could respond the door opened and Mendel entered with a carrier of four bottles of blood and four bottles of water. Ariel allowed the others to make their selections first, then took the last bottles.

Aronson looked to Mordechai. "You are eldest; you say it."

After a moment, Mordechai lifted up his bottle in both hands and said, "Blessed are You, Adonai our God, Sovereign of all, Creator of life."

Aronson, Katz, and Mendel all murmured, "*Omayn.*" Ariel belatedly followed suit.

With that, they all removed the tops from the bottles and partook of the blood.

There was no conversation. Ariel saw that the others did not gulp the blood, but did not sip at it either, so he imitated them. Even when drunk with respect, it did not take a long time to consume a half-liter of the blood.

Once they were all holding their open water bottles, Katz said, "That was good work that you did, Mordechai, you and young Ariel. Righteous work."

"Indeed," Aronson said, holding his bottle up in salute. "So, have you been to the Wall yet?"

"No," Mordechai said. "We came here directly from the airport. Perhaps tomorrow."

"Good," Aronson said. "You spend some time there. It will help. You, too, young Ariel."

Ariel sighed as it dawned on him that he was probably going to be known as "young Ariel" for the next century or so.

CHAPTER 26

ARIEL DRAGGED HIS BAGS THROUGH THE DOOR OF his apartment, wheels rumbling on the tile, and felt his shoulders and back just relax at the thought that he was home. It actually felt a little odd to him that his little forty-square-meter apartment—which he still thought of as being about four hundred square feet—had the whole home vibe for him. Home wasn't that house in Santa Carla anymore—not since this trip, anyway.

He dragged his bags through to the bedroom and tossed them on the bed, then immediately stripped off and took a shower. He didn't sweat much these days, but after the workout he'd just had, he felt the need to sluice off the dirt and dust and the thought of dried sweat.

Fifteen minutes later, dressed in a black tee and a pair of faded black jeans, Ariel padded barefoot around his apartment putting things away. He and Mordechai had unloaded the bloody clothes, jackets and gloves from the California operation at Rabbi Mendel's building to be disposed of as "contaminated" material. Ariel supposed it qualified as that. That had left his bags somewhat lighter and less full. The worn clothes had gone into a bag to be dropped off at the cleaners, his shaver and toothbrush and toiletries had gone back in the bathroom, and his laptop had just been returned to its place on his desk and plugged in to charge, with the glass knife sitting on top. He threw his empty carry-on bag inside his empty clothing bag, zipped it up and stuck it in his closet.

Ariel wandered back to the kitchen and pulled a bottle of sparkling water out of his refrigerator. It was a cheap brand. He didn't buy the good stuff for home use. Plain carbonated water was fine. He twisted the bottle cap off and effortlessly broke the plastic strand that kept the cap linked to the ring that remained in place around the bottle's neck, laughing a bit as he realized that that probably marked him as an unregenerate American. But he couldn't stand having the cap scratching at the side of his face when he was drinking from the bottle.

Picking up his mobile from where he'd dumped it on the kitchen counter along with his keys when he'd come in, he thumbed through the icons until he got to his voicemail. Huh. Only six messages during the whole trip. Usually he had more than that in a day.

Three minutes later he had deleted three spam robocall messages that had made it through his filters, and listened to two short routine messages from the university about the upcoming session. The last message was for real, and it surprised him.

"Ariel, this is Yael. Listen, I know your greeting says you're going to be out of touch for a few days. I'm leaving this kind of just because. Maybe it's nothing, but I'm getting a weird feeling about a guy that's been flirting with me for the last couple of nights at Shaka's club. He's a Russian immigrant, says his name is Gersh Davidoff. I can't say there's something wrong, but he doesn't appear to like a 'No' answer, and he spent most of tonight staring at me from across the room after I told him to leave me alone. So since you work for somebody, I thought I'd leave this with you, just in case something happens."

The message ended. Ariel checked the time it was left: 0045 that morning. No messages since then. His stomach tightened. He looked at his watch: 2315. He hit the return call icon and turned the speaker phone on. Three rings, four rings, five rings. "Hi, this is Yael. Can't take your call right now. Leave a message, and I'll call you back later."

He thumbed the call off. His tension ratcheted up. Did Yael live with someone? Yeah, but who was it? Ab...Abigail Hershkowitz, right. Ariel called up her name in the phone's directory, and placed the call. Three rings, four rings...

"Hallo?" Female voice. A moment of relief.

"Abigail? Hi, it's Ariel Barak. I just got back and I've been trying to get in touch with Yael, but her phone keeps rolling to voicemail. Is she there?"

"No, Ariel. I haven't seen her since yesterday evening. She went to a club last night and didn't come home."

Her voice sounded tense. Ariel's own tension escalated some more.

"Has she done that before?"

"Every once in a while, but never for this long. I'm getting worried. But if I call the police she'll yell at me when she finds out."

"Sometimes we have to do the right thing," Ariel said. "Your call to make. But that doesn't sound normal to me, either. Have her call me if she comes in, please."

The call ended. Ariel moved to the bedroom and crammed his feet into a pair of shoes, forgoing socks, then spent the next few moments putting on his holster and loading his wallet, police card, and keys into his pockets. He grabbed his leather jacket and shrugged it on as he headed for the door.

Once outside, he called for an Uber ride, thankful that Israel had finally allowed Uber to operate there. It was late, and he didn't want to take a chance on a bus. The Uber car showed up four minutes later, and he slid into the back seat.

"Shaka's, right?" the driver confirmed.

"Right."

"On the way."

The car pulled off into traffic.

Shaka's was near the Sarona District, a trendy area of older buildings with numerous clubs and wine bars. It was popular with uni students. Even he'd been there a couple of times when Yael and their usual group convinced him to tag along.

Ariel's mouth quirked as he recalled that "older" in Israel meant much the same as in Europe: not decades, but potentially centuries. That was something that wasn't true in very many places in America.

He thought of something he needed to know, so he pulled his mobile out and called Abigail again.

"Hallo?"

"Abigail, it's Ariel again. Sorry to be calling you so late, but I have two questions. Have you got a picture of Yael you can send me? And does she still wear that sandalwood perfume she likes so much?"

"Yeah, and yeah. It's all she puts on these days, although as much as it costs I'm surprised. Why? You think you can find her?"

"Her voicemail said she was at Shaka's last night, so I'm going to go down and see if anyone remembers her."

"Pic's on the way. Let me know what you find out, please." There was a definite sound of relief in Abigail's voice.

"I will."

Ariel ended the call. A moment later the mobile buzzed, and he pulled up the picture Abigail had sent him. It was recognizably Yael. He nodded at it, put the mobile back in his jacket pocket, then looked out the side window at the buildings going by in the night. He wished Mordechai was driving.

The sandalwood perfume that Yael preferred was distinctive. That might be useful. He wasn't counting on it, but if there was something going on, he'd use anything he could get.

The car pulled up before Shaka's. Ariel added a tip to the charge, and climbed out of the car. He shoved his hands inside his jacket pockets and walked into the club. Thankfully it wasn't a dance club. There was music, and it was loud, but he could tune it out for the most part.

The décor of the club was all surfboards and surfing paraphernalia. That took Ariel aback the first time he'd come in, until it dawned on him that with their long Mediterranean coast, Israelis certainly had to have opportunities to surf. Now it was just kind of nostalgic to him, evoking the California culture he'd grown up in. Several monitors mounted high on the walls were showing surfing scenes, although it wasn't clear to him if they were local shots or were taken from other locations around the world.

Up over the bar was a sign that showed the back of a fist with the thumb and little finger extended out to the sides. He remembered seeing that in California, mostly from the kids who were surfers or skateboarders. He shook his head with a bit of a smile. Okay, so that made the name clear.

The club wasn't huge, but it wasn't tiny, either. It was larger than The Grey Havens, for example. There were enough people there, most of them in their twenties, that the place felt full without feeling crowded. There was a seating area with tables, all of which were taken, and a more open area at one end where there were groups just standing around talking loudly. He wasn't able to get a good head count, but it looked like around eighty people were there, maybe a bit more.

Ariel started moving around the perimeter of the room, looking around. He took his time, moved slowly, running his eyes over the crowd. There were a number of women who bore passing resemblances to Yael, from physical build to shape of face to curly brunette hair, but only resemblances. None of them were Yael.

He ended up at the end of the bar, still looking out over the crowd.

"What'll you have?"

The waitress that had come up behind Ariel almost startled him. It was unexpected because of the ambient noise level. He turned to face her and leaned forward so he didn't have to shout.

"How about a Perrier?"

"Sorry." She shook her head. "The distributor didn't make his run today, and we ran out. I can give you some tonic water, club soda, or seltzer."

"Plain seltzer with ice, no fruit," Ariel ordered. It was his most common drink order.

"I'll have to charge you for a drink."

"Fine." A few seconds later, there was a tall drink glass with bubbling water and a few ice cubes at his elbow.

"Fifteen shekels," the waitress said.

Ariel pulled his money clip out of his front pocket, peeled off a twenty-shekel note, and dropped it on the counter. He took a sip of the drink, but put his fingertip on the bill when the waitress reached for it. She looked at him with a frown.

"Who's managing tonight?" he asked.

"Nick's got the duty tonight." She jerked a thumb over her shoulder at a large blond man at the other end of the bar.

"I'd like to have a word with him, please." Ariel lifted his finger from the bill, which disappeared into her apron pocket as she moved toward the other end of the long bar. He turned and looked back out at the crowd. They were getting a bit louder.

"Whatta ya need, mate?"

The voice that came from behind him this time spoke in English, and was also heavily accented— which took him by surprise, because it wasn't the usual British accent or Israeli/Hebrew-inflected tone.

"Australia?" He faced around to look up at the manager.

The manager sighed. "Yeah, mate. I'm an Aussie."

"So how does an Aussie end up in Israel?"

"Came twenty years ago to try the surfing." The bartender grinned. "Liked the scene so much I stayed."

Ariel took a good look at him. He was heavily tanned, had lines around his eyes, and his full head of short hair was so pale it was almost white. He was wearing shorts and a loud floral pattern shirt that reminded Ariel of the Hawaiian shirts his parents' next-door neighbor used to wear. He remembered seeing the man the last time he was in the club.

"You the manager?"

"Manager, part owner and partner, and general dogsbody, that's me, Nick Lewis. You need anything, ask for me." He stuck his hand out. Ariel shook it. "Now, you told Georgia you needed to talk to me. Either get on with it, or get on, because I've got work to do."

"Nice to meet you, Nick. My name's Ariel Barak. And actually, I do have a question for you. Were you working last night?"

"Yeah." Nick's expression sobered. "Why?"

Ariel pulled out his mobile and called up the photo Abigail had sent him. "Do you remember seeing her?"

"Mate, do you know how many people come in here every night?" He looked at the picture briefly. "She looks like half the girls that come in here. Why? You a cop or a private investigator?" That last was delivered with narrowed eyes.

Ariel held up both hands in a placating gesture. "Yes, I am a cop of sorts, but this isn't official. Her name's Yael Malka, and she's a classmate of mine. I got a voicemail from her early this morning saying she was here and having problems with a guy who wouldn't take no for an answer. Her roommate says she hasn't been home all day, so I told her I would come check here to see if anyone remembered anything."

Nick took a closer look at the picture as Ariel dropped his hands. "Yeah, I might have seen her sitting at a table by herself. I don't remember any disruptions, though." He turned toward the other bartenders. "Hey, Adam, Georgia, c'mere. You remember seeing this girl last night?" They came over and peered at the mobile.

Adam shook his head and went back to serving drinks. Georgia, however, looked at the picture for a long moment, then nodded. "She was at a table in the back corner," she said, waving a hand toward one corner of the seating area. "Sat by herself most of the night, although there was at least one guy trying to hit on her." She looked around. "Haven't seen her tonight."

"Did you know him?" Ariel asked, leaning forward a little.

"Not by name. He's been in a few times. Russian guy, I think."

"Gersh Davidoff, maybe?" Ariel's voice got a bit more intense.

"Sorry, I never knew his name. But whatever he's called, he hasn't been in tonight." She spread her hands. "Sorry." She looked at Nick, who nodded, which sent her back to her work.

Nick passed the mobile back to Ariel. "Sorry," he repeated.

Ariel tucked the mobile back into his jacket pocket. "Mind if I look around?"

Nick shrugged. "As long as you don't bother the customers, feel free. Stay out of the kitchen, though. And if you need anything, come ask me."

"Thanks." Ariel picked up his glass, and wandered off.

He made another circuit of the entire floor, taking another slow look at all the people there. Still no sign of Yael. He paused by the table that Georgia had said Yael had used last night. It was occupied tonight by three girls who were chattering away in Hebrew and laughing, none of whom looked up as he paused nearby.

His last pass was through the crowd, moving slowly between the tables in the seating area and through the standing groups. Nothing caught his attention: no sight, no sound, no words, no smells. Nothing present, nothing missing. Once through the crowd, he took a deep breath, and let it out slowly.

Ariel moved toward the back wall of the room and leaned against it. He sipped his water, playing with the carbonation of it in his mouth while his eyes continued to scan the room almost on autopilot, while his mind considered what to do next. That was decided when he saw several of the crowd walk toward an opening in the wall by the bar, obviously headed for the restrooms. He slid along the back wall, waited for them to pass, then followed them into the hallway.

Pausing just past the restrooms, Ariel stood listening for a while, absorbing what the normal sounds in that area ought to be. He felt the airflow. He took several deep breaths through his nose, smelling nothing pungent or remarkable.

After a couple of minutes, he moved farther down the hallway toward an exit door with a security camera mounted above it. There was a green light on the camera housing.

Several doors were on the right side. He tried the handles as he passed. All were locked.

An open doorway appeared on the left, leading to

the small kitchen. He could see and hear a couple of people working in it. Abiding by Nick's instruction, Ariel didn't enter.

The next door on the right, when he tried the handle, it turned in his hand. Drawing the door open, he saw another hallway, short this time, with two doors to the left and a door at the end. There was a security camera above the end door, also showing a green light.

He closed the door and stood there, listening, breathing, smelling. At his third inhalation, he got a tiny whiff of something . . . it was so light, he could barely smell it, but it smelled very much like Yael's sandalwood perfume. He wasn't absolutely sure . . . but it could be.

Ariel stepped to the first door. He tried the door handle. Locked. He placed his nose against the crack between the door and its frame, and inhaled deeply. He held his breath, letting his brain process what he had drawn in.

A faint disinfectant smell.

He moved to the second door. That handle was also locked. He repeated the attempt to smell what was behind the door.

A faint hint of mildew.

Now the end door. That it was also locked came as no surprise. Ariel stood next to the frame, bent forward, and inhaled.

Not disinfectant or mildew. That faint, faint hint of sandalwood, and a slightly stronger hint of . . . blood.

Ariel didn't run, but it didn't take long before he was standing at the end of the bar again.

"Nick!"

Nick responded to his almost shout and forceful beckon. "What?" He didn't look happy.

"I need you in the back hallway, now!" Ariel didn't shout, but his voice was very intense.

"What is this about?"

"Now! Or I'm calling my boss and you can explain yourself to him."

"All right, all right, I'm coming. I'll meet you by the kitchen."

Ariel was standing there, arms folded, when Nick came through the doorway. He yanked open the other hallway door and said, "What's in these rooms?"

"Storage. This one"—he pointed to the first door—"is cleaning supplies. This"—he pointed to the second door—"is a small closet for brooms, mops, and such."

"What about that one?" Ariel pointed to the end door.

"Seasonal holiday decorations, and old business records."

"When's the last time you were in it?"

Nick thought for a moment. "At least two weeks ago."

"Open it."

"Why?"

"Something doesn't smell right with it."

"Are you serious?" Nick was frowning.

"Open it, or I'll pull that door off its hinges." Ariel made his voice as cold as possible.

"All right, all right. Keep your knickers on." Nick was looking very put out, but he pulled a small ring of keys from his pocket and flipped through them until he found one that he inserted in the lock. He turned the key, then turned the handle and pulled the door open.

Ariel's heart fell when the lights in the room came on and revealed Yael lying on the floor, limp, contorted, disheveled.

CHAPTER 27

ARIEL SHOVED PAST NICK AND KNELT, SETTING TWO fingers against Yael's neck. He looked up. "She's still warm, she still has a pulse. Call the police now! Call for an ambulance now!"

"Right!" Nick backed into the main hallway, pulling a mobile out of his hip pocket.

Ariel knew enough not to touch the crime scene. Yael was unconscious, it had been a long time since he had qualified for his Boy Scout first aid badge, and he had no supplies, so there was really nothing he could do for her. And it would likely only be a few minutes before the ambulance arrived. If she had survived this long, she should make it until then.

He closed his eyes and inhaled—once, twice, three times. Sandalwood, blood, both stronger now that the door was open. Dirty oily body, and an acrid musk smell. Inhaling again, he concentrated on those last two, which certainly weren't Yael's markers. He thought he would recognize them again if he ever encountered them.

Ariel looked around. Across the doorway space from him were some filing cabinets. There were shelves mostly filled with boxes stretching from each side of the doorway. No first aid kit or anything else.

Nick showed up behind him as he put his mobile away. "Ambulance called, they don't have far to come, maybe two or three minutes. Georgia is out front waiting on them. Police have to come a little farther, probably almost ten minutes for them." He looked down. "That the bint you're looking for?" His Aussie accent was thicker, and he'd reverted to his native slang.

"Yeah," Ariel said through gritted teeth.

Nick shook his head. "Someone's had at her, and no mistake." He caught the glare from Ariel, and held up his hands. "Look mate, I was a driver for a volunteer ambo service in the outback. Not the first time I've seen such. She'll probably survive it, being as she's made it this long. But it's going to be a long hard go of it for her coming back, and she's going to need every cobber and pard she's got to do it. Y'see?"

"Yeah," Ariel muttered. "Got it."

There was a clatter out in the hallway, and in a moment two ambulance attendants in emergency vests parked a wheeled stretcher outside the hallway door and came toward them carrying cases. "What's the problem?" they said first in Hebrew, then in English.

Both men stepped out of the way to reveal Yael's body. "Assault and probable rape," Ariel said.

The two medics moved past them to attend to her, one on either side. The female took a couple of quick pictures of Yael's body and its position, then they knelt beside her and got to work. In moments, the medics had a blood pressure cuff on her and were taking her temperature. The male looked up. "This isn't fresh. How long has she been here?"

"What time did you close last night?" Ariel asked Nick.

"Two o'clock, just like always."

Ariel looked at his watch. It was a bit after one o'clock now, the next day after. "Based on when she left me the voicemail last night, probably about twenty-four hours." Both of the medics looked up at him with hard expressions. "Look, I'm a friend of hers, and the only reason we found her now was because I came looking for her."

"Bloody honest truth," Nick averred.

The female medic pursed her mouth and focused back on Yael. The male medic nodded before he, too, turned back to his work. "You want to get out of our light?" he muttered.

Ariel and Nick moved back out into the main hallway, stepping around the stretcher as they did so. "Hang on a moment," Nick said. He unlocked one of the side doors and pulled out some posts with the thick velvet ropes that restaurants sometimes used to set up barriers. He relocked the door. "You lot move back," he growled at the people that were starting to edge down the hallway trying to see what was going on, then made a barrier across the hallway just on the inside of the restrooms. "There, that should keep people out of the way."

"Good idea," Ariel said with a nod.

Nick quirked his mouth. "Not my first dance on this floor." He gave a sharp nod, then said, "I need to go check the bar. I'll come back when the police get here." He vanished into the kitchen.

Pulling out his mobile, Ariel called Mordechai. It rang three times before Mordechai answered.

"Hallo." Mordechai sounded a bit weary.

"It's Ariel. I may need some help."

"What with?" Mordechai's voice sharpened.

"The short version is that I got a voicemail while we were gone from early yesterday morning from one of my classmates saying she might be in trouble. After I got it, I called, but it rolled to her voicemail. I called her roommate, who told me she hadn't come home last night or all day. I came down to the club she called me from, and after looking around, I found her. The ambulance medics are with her now. I have a feeling I may have some trouble explaining this to the police."

"Where are you?"

Ariel read him the address from the Uber reservation on his mobile.

"I'll be there in fifteen minutes. Don't leave."

The call ended. Ariel leaned back against the wall beside the kitchen opening so he could look down the short hall, and rubbed his hands down his face. The long day was starting to catch up with him, as was the stress and anger of finding Yael had been hurt after she had called him for help and he hadn't heard about it. All the rage he thought he had tamped down and cooled off from the California experience reignited, and he found himself flexing his hands as he inhaled and exhaled long breaths through his nose.

Ariel heard steps in the short hallway, and looked up to see the male medic coming toward him.

"We're about done with the initial treatments," the medic said, looking down at his tablet. "We'll be transporting her shortly. You said you were a friend?"

"That's right."

"What's her name, and do you know her address?"

"Yael Malka." While the medic was putting that into his tablet, Ariel pulled out his mobile again and called up Yael's contact information. "Here's what I have for an address." He held the mobile out for the medic to copy the information.

"Do you know any of her medical history?"

"No, but she spent a couple of years in the IDF, so maybe you can get something from them. She's also a student at Tel Aviv University."

"We'll see. Do you have any next of kin information for her?"

"No, but her roommate might." Ariel called up Abigail's contact information and held the mobile out again. The medic dutifully entered that as well. "And what's your name, address, and mobile number?"

"Ariel Barak." He recited his address and number. When the medic finished entering that, Ariel asked, "How is she? What can you tell me?"

"Not a lot. She's been badly beaten, but you could see that. She's almost certainly been raped. There's evidence of what looks like semen on her skin and on the floor. We've got an IV started, and we've got her mostly stabilized. She's obviously a strong woman, or she wouldn't still be with us, but it's very worrying that she's unresponsive. We're going to take her to the hospital, and it's probable that they're going to order a CT scan and an MRI. Treatment will depend on what they find. Now excuse me, we need to get moving."

He threw the tablet on the stretcher and wheeled it down the short hallway to the room. Ariel watched as they pulled a spinal board out of the stretcher structure, gently moved Yael onto it, and strapped her down. They equally carefully lifted the board and strapped it to the stretcher, raising a short arm to hang the IV bag from.

Just as the female medic kicked a lever with her foot to unlock the stretcher wheels, Georgia led three policemen up to the barrier, unhooked one end of the rope to let them through, then followed them through and re-hooked it. She stood there, waiting.

Ariel checked the policemen out. Two were younger men, mid-twenties, maybe, one with no rank insignia and one with a single chevron. The third man looked as if he was maybe thirty, wearing two chevrons, which made him a *Samal Sheni*, or lowest-ranked sergeant.

"What do you have?" he demanded of the medics.

"Physical assault, probably sexual assault, as well, *Samal*," the female medic said. "We're transporting her now."

The male medic held up his tablet. "I've got the incident report ready to send. We've already notified the crime scene team."

The *samal* held up his own tablet, the medic tapped his, and a moment later the *samal*'s tablet beeped. He looked down at it and tapped a corner. He read what came up on his screen, and nodded. "Got it. I'll call you if I need more."

The medics headed toward the barrier, and Georgia unhooked the rope.

"Wait!" Ariel called. "Where are you taking her?"

"Ichilov Hospital," the male medic called over his shoulder.

Ariel committed that to memory.

"I am *Samal Sheni* Gabriel Klein and this is *Rav Shoter* Elon Spira and *Shoter* Dvir Sasson. And you are?"

"Ariel Barak."

"Ah." Klein looked at his tablet again. "You are the friend of the victim?"

"Yes."

Klein handed the tablet to Sasson. "Take notes." He looked back at Ariel. "ID card, please."

Ariel pulled out his wallet. "ID card," which was followed by, "weapon license," and after pulling the folder from another pocket, "and my Yamam card."

By the end of the recital, Klein was frowning darkly. "Is Yamam involved in this?" He passed the documents to Sasson. "Do they have responsibility?"

Ariel shook his head. "No. Yamam is not officially involved in this at all. I am involved in it personally, not as a Yamam *Shoter*, and only because Yael left me a voicemail last night indicating she might be in some kind of trouble. I was out of the country when she sent it, and I didn't get back until late this evening, but when I got it, I called her roommate, who asked me to look for her."

Klein's expression indicated he didn't necessarily believe Ariel. At that moment, Sasson passed the documents back to Klein, who spent some more time examining them in detail. While he did so, Ariel looked at Georgia and mouthed, "Go get Nick." She skirted around them and entered the kitchen just as Klein passed Ariel's documents back to him with visible reluctance.

"So who's the manager of this place, anyway?" Klein snarled.

"That would be me, *Samal*." Nick stepped out of the kitchen. Ariel turned a little, and could see Georgia hanging back inside the doorway.

"Name? ID?"

"Nick Lewis." Nick fished his card out of his wallet and handed it over. Klein read through the card, then handed it to Sasson to enter into the investigation report.

"So tell me what happened." Klein bent a glower on Nick, who didn't seem to be affected by it at all.

"He walks in somewhere around midnight"—Nick jerked a thumb toward Ariel—"says he's looking for a woman who was supposed to be here last night, shows us a picture, asks if we've seen her. She looks sort of familiar to me, but we see so many women in here, I don't recall. Georgia"—he beckoned to her and she edged into the main hallway—"said she thought she saw her here last night. She's not here tonight. He"—he nodded toward Ariel again—"asks if he can look around, and next thing I know he's telling me that he smells something funny down that hall and gets me to open that door. We found her, called you and the ambulance. That's all I know."

"Smelled?" Klein's expression as he turned to Ariel could only be called incredulous.

"Yael wears a rather strong sandalwood perfume. It's very distinctive. I know what it smells like. So when I got a hint of it outside of that door, I went and got Nick to open it. That's when we found her."

"So why were you looking for her? What's your relationship with her? She your lover?"

"No." Ariel realized that had come out a little stronger than he'd wanted when Klein's eyes narrowed. He moderated his tone as he continued with, "Yael and I were in a couple of classes together last term at Tel Aviv University. We're friends and classmates.

That's all. As for why I was looking for her, like I said earlier, she left a voicemail on my mobile about 0045 last night, saying she was here and was having some trouble with a guy who wouldn't take no for an answer and she wanted somebody to know about it."

Klein turned to Nick and Georgia. "Did she say anything to you about it?"

Nick shook his head. Georgia replied, "I saw a guy trying to connect with her late last night, but she never said anything to us about it."

Klein turned back to Ariel. "So she called you late last night, but you didn't come down here until tonight. Why?"

"I was out of the country and had my mobile off. My plane landed at the airport about 1800 today, I got back to my apartment a bit after 2200, and I didn't check my voicemail until about 2315 or so. When I heard her message, I called her roommate, who told me she hadn't come home at all last night, and she was worried. I told her I'd come down here and look for her. I called a ride, and got here a bit before midnight. After that, what he said." He motioned in Nick's direction.

"Out of the country? Where?"

Ariel shook his head. "I can't tell you that, but I can tell you that it has nothing to do with this."

"Not acceptable," Klein said, the frown returning to his face. "Answer the question."

Ariel drew himself up and stared Klein in the eyes. "No."

Klein's jaw muscles bunched and his neck reddened. "I'm getting tired of you Yamam types acting like you're above the law and above the regulations. I'm a

Samal Sheni, and you are a simple *shoter*. I outrank you. Now I'm ordering you to answer the question."

"Don't answer that," came from behind them. Ariel turned in relief to see Mordechai stepping past the rope barrier, accompanied by a fairly tall, strong-featured woman with short black hair. Ariel guessed she was a cop by her mannerism and her forthright stride, but she was in a well-tailored pantsuit rather than uniform. Her male companion, who was refastening the velvet rope, was also in plain clothes. In a moment they had joined the group, making the hallway feel a bit crowded.

"I'm Zalman," Mordechai said, handing an ID folder to Klein. "Barak is mine," he added, forestalling a complaint from Klein. He turned to Ariel. "What have you told him?" Ariel went through the short version of the story one more time.

Mordechai held out his hand for his ID. A wide-eyed Klein returned it to him, and he slipped it into an inner pocket of his suit. "Barak is correct. He has told you everything you need to know. He was with me, and we were indeed out of the country, as he said. I and two pilots can testify that he was not back in the country until approximately 1800 hours yesterday. Where we were and what we were doing is not at all connected with this matter, therefore you have no need to know."

"But..." Klein began.

The woman pulled out an ID folder of her own and presented it to Klein, saying, "I am *Pakad* Rivka Dayan." An inspector, Ariel realized—equivalent to a captain. Wow. Mordechai must have pulled her in as soon as he'd hung up from Ariel's call. "Let's you and I go have a talk, *Samal*." She gestured toward the short hallway, and they moved several steps into it.

Once they stopped, beyond what they thought was range of Mordechai and Ariel's hearing, they faced each other. Klein started to say something, but Dayan cut him off. "Shut up and listen"—she peered at his name badge—"Klein, is it? I'm here to keep you from digging yourself into a hole you can't get yourself out of. You don't know who you're dealing with here, do you?" She was whispering. Ariel could still hear every word.

"What do you mean?" Klein's responding whisper had a bit of a surly tone to it.

"Zalman."

"Other than he's got a high-powered ID, what's so special about him?" Klein's tone grew darker, even in the whisper.

"He's the oldest old-timer around. All the other old-timers call him Sir to his face and The Colonel behind his back. He's on a first-name basis with all of the police commanders. He consults on a regular basis with the police commissioners. The directors of Mossad and Shin Bet have him on speed dial. He's one of the three deadliest people I know of. You do not want to get in a pissing contest with him—he'd crush your stones without thinking twice about it. And if you really pissed him off, they'd never find your body. If he tells you something, you accept it. If you're involved in one of his operations and he gives you an order, you do it, no questions asked. If he tells you to jump, you jump, and ask how high on your way up. Got it?"

Klein nodded.

"Is all that true?" Ariel whispered to Mordechai, who had a slight smile on his lips.

"Making allowance for a slight amount of hyperbole, yes," Mordechai responded. Ariel nodded, tucking that all into his memory.

After a moment, Dayan whispered, "Are we clear on this?"

"Yes." Klein's whisper sounded weird. Ariel never realized before that it was possible for someone to grit their teeth in a whisper. "*Chara*," Klein cursed. "Does he walk on water, too?"

There was the sound of a suppressed snort. "I haven't heard that he does"—Dayan's whisper had a hint of a smile in it—"but if anyone can, it would be him. I wouldn't suggest asking him about it, though. Now, we go back out there, and you follow my lead, okay?"

Klein nodded, most of the resentment gone from his face.

They turned and came back out to the main hallway. Dayan stopped by *Shoter* Sasson and held out her hand. "Tablet." He immediately thrust it at her, and stepped back a half step after she took it. She paged through all the documents in the investigation file and medical report. "I want your mobile, *Shoter* Barak."

"No." Zalman sounded almost bored.

"There are documents on that mobile that pertain to this investigation."

"No."

Dayan didn't look surprised or upset when she looked up from the tablet. "Then at least send copies to us of that photo of the victim and the voicemail she left with Barak. Those are indeed pertinent."

Mordechai looked to Ariel and nodded. He pulled

his mobile out, searched to find the tablet locally, linked to it, and copied the files and pushed them to the tablet. An instant later, it pinged. Dayan tapped one corner of it, and after a moment nodded.

"We reserve the right to do further interviews with *Shoter* Barak if we develop additional leads or questions."

"Clear it with me first," Mordechai responded.

Dayan nodded. "We can do that." She looked up at an increase of noise as more police appeared at the velvet rope. "Ah, the crime scene team is here. Good."

"We'll be on our way, then," Mordechai said. "Good evening, Dayan." He nodded at the others.

"Good evening, Zalman."

Ariel nodded to the police, carefully including *Samal* Klein in the circle of that gesture, then gave a separate nod to Nick and Georgia, collecting a wink in return. He turned and followed Mordechai out of the hallway and out of the club.

Once outside, he stopped. "I need to make a fast call." Mordechai stopped and waited.

Ariel pulled his mobile out again and tapped Abigail's number. He looked at his watch while it was ringing. After 0200. Oooh, she wasn't going to like this call, for more than one reason.

"Hallo."

Abigail sounded groggy, which didn't surprise Ariel at all.

"Hi, Abigail, it's Ariel."

"Do you know what time it is?" That was an absolute snarl.

"Yeah, and I'm sorry to be calling so late, but I figured you'd want to hear this now. I found Yael."

"You did?" Now Abigail sounded wide awake. "Is she okay?"

"No. She was assaulted, and left locked in a closet. We found her tonight. She's alive, but was beat up pretty badly. She's in serious condition, and they're taking her to Ichilov Hospital. I gave them what information I had, but I don't know anything about her family or next of kin, so either the hospital or the police or both will probably be contacting you before long."

"Oh, crap," Abigail breathed. "I'll get dressed and get down there right away. Wow." There was a long moment of silence. "I've got to go. Ariel?"

"Yeah?"

"Thanks."

"You're welcome."

The call ended. Ariel slipped the mobile back into his jacket, and sighed.

"Want a ride home?" Mordechai asked.

"Yeah."

Mordechai drove with what amounted to control and deliberation for him. They didn't talk. Ariel was glad of that. His mind was churning, and he wasn't at all sure he could have a civilized conversation at the moment.

They pulled up in front of Ariel's apartment building.

"We'll talk tomorrow," Mordechai said. "Get some rest."

"Right. Thanks." Ariel got out of the car and watched as Mordechai pulled away in the darkness.

Once inside his apartment, Ariel unloaded his pockets on the desk, then tossed his jacket on the sofa. He kicked his shoes off, pulled a small bottle of sparkling water out of the refrigerator, and guzzled it as he walked over to the sliding door that led to his tiny balcony. He opened it, and stepped out into the night. The cool breeze tousled his hair. He put his hands on the iron railing, and just stared across the street at the streetlight.

Standing there with nothing to distract his thoughts, the image of finding Yael in that closet took frontal position in his mind. Damaged, broken, and hurt at a time when he should have been there to protect her. Other images began alternating with Yael's—at first, glimpses of Elena, first at school, then at the prom, then in the hospital, then her casket at the funeral. That was followed by the face of the female vampire that had converted him, which brought to mind pheromones which melded to the smell of an unholy mélange of sandalwood and blood and musk.

The anger that he had been suppressing ever since they found Yael picked that moment to surge and break free. His hands clenched. There was a crack, and he looked down to see that the empty glass bottle that he had been holding in his left hand had shattered. Most of the shards and chunks of glass were either lying on the balcony or held in his hand, thanks to the toughness of his vampire skin, but there were a few pieces of glass now implanted in his palm and fingers with dark blood oozing around them.

"Well, shit," he muttered. The perfect end of a perfect evening. He sighed, and went back inside to find a towel and the first aid kit.

Afterward, he pulled out his chair and turned his laptop on. Time to do some hunting.

CHAPTER 28

ARIEL DISMOUNTED FROM THE BUS AND LOOKED up at the hospital. It was late afternoon, and he was thankful for the shadows cast by the tall buildings. Even with heavy-duty sunscreen and the ultra-dark glasses, he was thankful for anything that kept him out of direct sunlight.

Ichilov Hospital was oddly shaped—it looked like it was at least twelve stories high, with more of a parallelogram footprint than the usual rectangle. There was a large, round helipad on the roof that hung over the edges in a couple of places. He shrugged, having seen stranger buildings in California, and headed for the main entrance.

He caught a glimpse of himself in some of the large window glass as he approached the door. Leather jacket, collarless black shirt, black jeans and his favorite Doc Marten boots instead of running shoes. He was impressed, for a moment, at how cutting edge he looked. The vampire metabolism had left him with a certain "lean and hungry look," to quote a line of Shakespeare that his senior-year English teacher had hammered into him. He was still getting used to that. This was strengthened by the fact that he hadn't slept well due to confused and turbulent nightmares. He could see the effects in his face. He gave his head a shake and reached for the door.

Once inside, it took a few moments to find a help desk, and a few more moments to convince them to tell him where Yael was. The good news was he didn't have to go far. She was on the second floor. The bad news was that was where the intensive care unit was.

Ariel exited the elevator and turned in the direction the signs pointed toward ICU. Someone was standing at the control-station desk. She looked over her shoulder as he approached. It was Abigail. "Ariel!" she exclaimed, before she rushed the three steps separating them and threw her arms around him. "Thank you!" she said, her voice muffled by his neck.

He put his arms around her for a moment, then put his hands on her shoulders and pushed her back. "How is Yael?"

"Better, but they're still keeping her in ICU." Abigail grabbed Ariel by the arm and tugged him into a waiting room where they sat knee to knee in a corner, and she told him everything.

"First, she finally woke up about 0600 this morning. That was a relief to everyone. The doctors were very concerned that she had been unconscious for over twenty-four hours. They were afraid that she had brain damage from the beating. So she woke up, and then not long after that they got the results of the first urinalysis. They found evidence of Rohypnol, so..."

"Wait," Ariel said. "Rohypnol? The date rape drug? So she was raped?"

Abigail nodded. "Rape was confirmed. And, yeah, Rohypnol is one of the date rape drugs. And for her to be out that deeply and for that long, it must have been a really large dose of it. She's-lucky-she's-still-alive kind of dose."

Ariel's anger began to burn again, and increased with every word that Abigail had said.

Abigail continued, unaware of what Ariel was feeling. "Once they knew that, they were able to give her some treatments to help her come out of that. Last time I got to see her, she was more like normal."

"So what else is wrong?" Ariel asked. "She's still in ICU!"

"They did both an MRI and a CT scan on her," Abigail responded. "So far they've found a couple of hematomas in her abdomen, three cracked ribs, and her left ulna is broken near the wrist. Lots of bruising on her arms and legs. The guy must have worn some pointed-toe shoes, from the way the docs talked. But the biggest problem now that Yael's awake is she can't see out of her left eye."

Ariel stiffened. "Is her eye damaged?"

Abigail shook her head. "No, or at least, they don't think so. They don't see any damage. The eyeball itself seems to be fine. The iris is normal. They've added an ophthalmologist to the team, and his exam didn't show any evidence of retinal problems. But she has absolutely no vision out of it. None. No light perception, no blobs, no fuzzy shapes. Nothing. Zilch. So whatever the problem is, it's got to be in her head. They've got her back in the MRI room right now doing another skull series."

Ariel's heart sank. "Oh . . . my . . . God," he whispered.

Abigail's face got a really concerned expression. "What...what is it? What do you know about this?"

Ariel took a deep breath, then let it all out. "I've studied the physiology of the vision system. I had a professor in the US who was a nut about eyeballs and associated stuff." He swallowed heavily. "If there was no damage to the eye itself, then something has gone wrong with the optic nerve. Because she's been beaten, the two most likely possibilities are either internal bleeding in the skull causing enough pressure on the nerve to shut it down or a small blood clot forming in the brain's circulatory system and lodging in the blood vessel next to the nerve. Either one can put on enough pressure to shut the nerve down, and if that happens the nerve will die in less than twenty-four hours unless they can relieve the pressure somehow. If it was the internal bleeding issue, that should have been very evident on the earlier MRI. But if it's the blood clot, it would be very small and it might not have been picked up when they read the MRI. Even if they find it now, it's been so long that..." He choked off.

"That she might be blind in that eye forever?" Abigail whispered.

"Yeah."

Ariel felt his hands start to clench. He put his hands in his lap, lacing the fingers together and clasping them so tightly even his vampire bones creaked. He put his head down and took deep breaths in and out of his nose, staring at his feet, trying to channel his rage. He wasn't sure how long it took him, but at length he did get it damped down enough that his jaw would loosen enough to talk.

Abigail was looking at him, wide-eyed.

"Sorry," he whispered. "Just . . . I wasn't expecting that." After a moment, he looked at her. "I'm not a guy who chases girls," he said with a wry twist to his mouth, "but I know you all know about certain guys in the dating pool. Who could have done this?"

Abigail shook her head, but before she started to speak, Ariel lifted a finger. "Abi, someone she knows did this, even if she only knew him from the clubs. What can you tell me?"

She bit her lip for a long moment, then murmured, "There are two or three guys that the uni girls have put the word out to avoid, yeah."

"Any of them speak Russian?"

"One, I think so." Her voice was fading.

"Do you know his name?"

"I don't remember, but it was a European-sounding name, not Hebrew."

"Could it have been Gersh Davidoff?"

She looked uncertain. After a moment she shrugged and said, "Could be, but I really don't remember."

"Is he a stalker? Does he hunt them down when they're alone?"

She shook her head. "He comes and goes. Whoever he is, he'll be gone for a couple of months, and then be back in town for a week or two. We never know when he's going to be around."

"Anything unusual about him?"

She started to shake her head again, then paused. "Boots. Cowboy boots."

"Boots?" Ariel knew he sounded surprised. That was because he was. Cowboy boots . . . in Israel?

"The rumors say that he likes cowboy boots. But that's not a lot of help. There are several stores in

Tel Aviv that sell them. And most girls don't look at a guy's shoes if they're being harassed. I wouldn't."

Ariel's mobile buzzed with a message. *Where are you?* It was from Mordechai.

Hospital, he typed back.

Be there in 10. Be ready.

"Crap," Ariel muttered.

"What?" Abigail sounded confused.

"Oh, I called in a favor to help find Yael, and now I have to go deal with it. How late is visitation?"

"They allow ICU patients to have visitors every two hours for fifteen minutes. Next time is at 2000. And they only allow one visitor at a time for ICU."

Ariel looked around. "Does Yael have any family here?"

"Her parents were both *olim* from Canada, so she had no other family but them and her older brother. Her brother was in the Border Police and was killed in the West Bank three years ago. Her parents died from Covid two years ago. We're—the group at school—we're all she's got."

Ariel didn't have words to describe how that made him feel. He reached out and took Abigail's hands. "Listen, you tell her that I was here, and I'll be back to check on her as soon as I can. Okay?"

Abigail nodded.

"I have to go now." Ariel stood. "Let me know if anything changes or if you find out anything more. I'll try to be back tonight, but I can't promise it."

"Go," Abigail said. "I'll tend to her tonight."

Ariel wasted no time in getting to the elevator. He didn't run or trot, but his feet were moving quickly and the Doc Martens were thumping the floor with some authority. The elevator door opened as soon as he hit the button, and moments later he was in the lobby, striding toward the front door with people moving out of his way.

Exiting the doors just as Mordechai arrived, Ariel didn't even break stride, just moved to the car and slid into the passenger seat.

Mordechai looked at him. "Well?"

"She was fed a date rape drug, she was raped, and she was severely beaten either before, during, or after the rape. She was apparently kicked several times with pointy-toed shoes or boots. As a result of the beating, she appears to have lost the sight in her left eye. She has no family. I'm going to hunt this scum down."

Mordechai pulled out into traffic. His next question caught Ariel off guard. "Do you love her?"

"What?" Ariel didn't know how to respond to that one.

"Do you love her? Do you think of her as a lover, or a sister, or the Platonic Ideal?"

Ariel snorted. "Not the Platonic thing, that's for sure. Before this"—he laid his hand on his chest—"I would have certainly had a crush on her. She's not beautiful, not in the California sun-and-fun way, but she's intelligent, she's got a wicked sense of humor, and she's somewhere between cute and handsome." He paused for a moment. "I've been resisting her and all the other girls in our group. I can't give them what they need, so it wouldn't be fair to start anything with any of them. So, no, not a lover. Sister?" He shrugged. "I was an only child. I don't know what having a sister feels like." After a moment, he continued, "But she's important to me. I don't know why. She just is."

Mordechai guided the car around a corner onto a

major street, and picked up speed. "All right. I think I can understand that. Especially after what happened in California.

"First, understand that there will almost certainly be people that you connect with in spite of your good intentions. That's actually a necessity, for you to remain sane. Being a vampire has changed your body. It has not changed your mind and soul and spirit—or at least, not that much. You are not a machine. You will continue to need friends, and there aren't enough vampires around to fill that need. Accept that.

"Second, unless someone manages to kill you, you will outlive all of them. Accept that. Deal with that.

"Third, there will be times, like this one, where you will want to defend or provide retribution for someone you have connected with. But if you choose to do so, you'd best be very certain that you're right. Because if those you serve catch even a small hint that you are being unjust, unrighteous, arbitrary, or capricious, you will discover that your life can indeed be terminated. And if I am still around, I will help. Understood?" Mordechai's voice had grown increasingly colder as his monologue had progressed.

Ariel took a deep breath. "Understood."

"So where do you want to begin?" Mordechai's voice had returned to its normal warmth.

"Take me home, first. I'll need to prepare. But after that? I'm going bar-crawling."

Mordechai nodded.

A few minutes later, they pulled up in front of Ariel's apartment complex. Ariel put has hand on the door latch, but paused and looked over at Mordechai. "Where can I buy a reliable cheap mobile?"

"You're thinking a burner?"

Ariel nodded.

Mordechai's mouth quirked. "So you've learned that much of the craft. Good. Actually, you can buy cheap ones just about everywhere. But reliable cheap ones, when I need one of those, I go to The Lucky Star convenience store, the one about three blocks from Shaka's. Mr. Li, the owner, stocks a good grade of anonymous mobiles."

"I'll keep that in mind," Ariel said. He paused for a moment. "Is that just random knowledge, or do you and Mr. Li have some kind of relationship?"

Mordechai's smile returned. "Good question. You're starting to think like an operative. No, he doesn't work for me or the police. But doing what he does, he hears things. He never calls me, but occasionally I'll go ask him a few questions."

"An informer?" Ariel's brow furrowed.

"Not in the American TV cop show sense, no. But he knows his neighborhood, he knows his neighbors and clientele, and sometimes he hears things. So..."

"You occasionally stop and ask him a question or two."

"Exactly."

"Is this your way of telling me I need to start building my own network?"

Mordechai shrugged. "A hint, perhaps."

"Should I talk to him tonight? Should I ask him about Davidoff?"

"It can't hurt; it might help."

"Huh." Ariel chewed on that thought for a minute or so.

"Do you have much cash?" Mordechai asked, interrupting his train of thought.

Ariel thought. "Four, maybe five hundred shekels."

"That's not enough. Here." Mordechai reached inside his suit coat and brought out a long, thin wallet, from which he extracted a thickish stack of what looked like two hundred shekel notes, the largest cash note Israel issued. "Here's four thousand. Call me if you need more."

"I can't take that. I'll draw from my own account. I've got a fair amount stashed away. I don't spend much, living here."

"You won't draw from your account. Don't leave any kind of tracks. Nothing that can be traced. Just in case things go wrong."

Ariel froze for a moment, and realized Mordechai was right. He needed to start thinking like that. "All right," he said slowly, reaching for the cash, "but I'll pay you back later."

"Later is time enough to be worrying about that. And you call me if you need more. You call me if you get into trouble. You call me if you need help. And you call me when you find him."

"Yes, Mama," Ariel joked.

"Not a joke, Ariel. Solo operators don't last long. You need someone watching your back now, just like I did in Santa Carla. I won't insist on walking with you—you will hunt better alone—but I will be in the area. You will keep me advised as to what's going on. Understood?"

Ariel nodded. "Understood."

"Good. Now let's go in and get you prepped."

A quarter of an hour later, Ariel threw the body armor on the bed. "No. It's too big, too bulky, it won't fit under my jacket. And I have to have my jacket to hide the gun and the magazines."

"You could get another biker jacket. There are bikers in Israel, you know."

Ariel caught the small smile on Mordechai's face, so his response was more measured than it otherwise might have been. "What part of 'not wanting to attract attention' is unclear to you?"

Mordechai chuckled at that.

"Seriously, though, you'd best think about getting a larger size jacket to wear for those times where you want to be unobtrusive but will need the armor."

"Yeah, yeah." Ariel waved a hand. "That will be then, this is now." He turned away from the bed and slipped into the black leather jacket he always wore when he wanted to be serious. It dawned on him that he was becoming monochromatically predictable. He pushed that thought aside for later consideration, and started going down his checklist:

"Pistol." He picked it up from the bed, inserted the magazine, and put the pistol in the shoulder holster. He looked up at Mordechai. "Yes, the chamber's empty. I'm being good."

He pulled his coat up and slapped his left hip. "Three magazines fully loaded with hollow points. With what's in the pistol, that's sixty rounds."

Next tap went to his hip pocket. "Wallet with IDs and weapon card."

Ariel moved away from the bed and back into the living room. "Flashlight." He picked a slim flashlight up from the desk and placed it in his inner-right jacket pocket.

"Mobile." That went into his inner left jacket pocket.

"Earpiece." He put it in his right ear, and pulled out his mobile long enough to make sure they were synched.

"Leather gloves." He pulled those out of the outer jacket pockets and held them up, then put them back.

Ariel looked around. "I think that's it."

Mordechai stirred from where he'd been leaning against the bedroom door doorframe. "Not quite. First, heavy zip ties for restraints. Much better than trying to tie someone up with their belt or clothes. Second, heavy cloth tape to cover mouth and maybe eyes. Third, nitrile gloves."

Ariel felt disgusted with himself. Obvious stuff that he should have considered. He now understood why Mordechai kept harping on experience. "None of which I have."

Mordechai grinned as he walked by him. "I have some in the car. I always have some there. Never know when you're going to have to take someone down, you know." He stopped on the other side of the desk. "One more thing. Take this." He picked up the glass knife and handed it to Ariel. "I know you're not a knife guy. But I have a feeling that having the edge of a blade available may prove useful."

Ariel took it after a moment and tucked it into the pocket with his flashlight.

CHAPTER 29

THE LUCKY STAR CONVENIENCE STORE WAS SMALLER than Ariel had expected—maybe five meters by seven meters. It occupied a choice location in a corner space on the ground floor of what looked to be a very prosperous office building. Once he stepped inside, it was obvious that his California expectations didn't match the reality of what he was looking at. No groceries, no household staples, no hardware, no fresh food other than a little bit of fruit. Just a big rack of candy and snack bars, a couple of big cases of cold drinks, a plain coffee and tea station, and a newspaper rack with *Wall Street Journal* and *Jerusalem Post* copies, with the top rack containing several paperback novels. Ariel's eye got caught by the books—all science fiction—which included copies of the latest novels by David Weber, Eric Flint, and Larry Correia. Huh—he hadn't seen the Correia book before. Must be brand-new. He made a note to himself to come back and pick one of those up.

Flanking the register were display boards with loads of small bits of technology. On one side were mobile chargers, various types of connector cords, headphones, and batteries. On the other was a rack of cheap mobiles, all of which had brand names he didn't recognize.

Behind the register was an old Asian man whose face was so wrinkled his eyes seemed to be peering out from a couple of slits among all the folds of skin. The wall behind him was covered with all manner of things from chopsticks to oriental fans to little packages of teas and herbs. Incongruously present were a couple of boxes each of surgical masks and nitrile gloves on the counter below all that. A small monitor on the side wall was displaying an American baseball game, of all things.

"Are you Mr. Li?" Ariel asked in English.

The old man shrugged. "You see anyone else here?" His accent was minimal, which was surprising.

"Mordechai Zalman said I should ask you for a good cheap mobile."

Li tilted his head a little, obviously evaluating Ariel. "Where do you know Mordechai from?"

"I work for him."

The old man tilted his head slightly to the other side. "Can you prove that?"

Ariel tilted his own head a bit, and considered Mr. Li before responding. "Not that it's any of your business, but . . ." He lifted the left lapel of his jacket and revealed the butt of his pistol in its holster.

Li straightened with a slight smile. "That'll do. A good cheap mobile, you said."

"Yeah."

"Most places that would be a contradiction in terms, an oxymoron. However"—he held up a forefinger—"at The Lucky Star, you're in luck."

Ariel's expression twisted. "Oog. Is that the best you can do?"

"Sorry." Mr. Li didn't look sorry at all. "Dad jokes are my specialty."

Ariel shook his head, then stepped over to the mobile display rack. "Which one of these would you recommend?"

"None of that crap. Here." Ariel turned at Mr. Li's voice to see a black phone lying on the counter by the register. "Better phone. Made in India. Cheaper price, not loaded with crap Chinese operating system. And it's charged."

"How much?" Ariel pulled his wallet out.

Mr. Li's fingers tapped the screen of his register as if he were chasing small insects. They stilled, and he looked up.

"Two hundred shekels."

That was actually a bit less than the display prices for the "crap" phones. Ariel extracted a two-hundred-shekel note from his wallet and placed it on the counter. Mr. Li made it disappear so quickly that Ariel blinked, leaving a store card in its place. Ariel wondered if there had been some sleight of hand involved.

He picked up the phone, stripped off the packaging, turned it on, checked the charge, and put it in his front-left pants pocket. "So, why don't you have more fancy foods and drinks in here? I'd think you'd make a killing with this location."

"Not so," the old man responded. He pointed over Ariel's shoulder. "Good sushi place next door there." He jerked a thumb to his right. "Good bakery and coffee shop next door there. No profit in it." He shrugged. "I have a steady consistent patronage, and a few new faces like you every week. I don't need to be greedy."

"Ah," Ariel said. He looked around the empty store. "Quiet tonight."

The old man shrugged again. "Often is, often isn't. Tonight it is." He made the trash from the phone package disappear as easily as he had the shekels. At that moment, there was a sound of muted cheering from the monitor. Mr. Li looked over at it. "All right," he enthused. "A home run!"

Ariel's eyebrows rose. "You're an American baseball fan?"

"Third generation Red Sox fan."

"Boston? So you're from the US?"

"Yep. Third generation, like I said."

"So how did you get here? There's got to be a story behind a Chinese man running a shop in Tel Aviv."

The old man laughed, then shook his head. "Not really. Chemical engineer, me. BSc and MSc from Boston University, PhD from MIT. Forty-five years ago, after the BSc, I married a Boston Jewish girl. When her whole family made aliyah, I came along for the ride. Got a good job with Israel Chemicals Ltd, and settled down and settled in. Had three kids, and her brother and sister added seven more. They're all smart—except for one of my sister-in-law's boys—and most of them have got good jobs in different parts of Israeli society—my son's in banking, for example—although my sister-in-law's two youngest are still in uni or master's programs."

"So if you have a PhD in chemical engineering, why are you running a convenience store?"

Mr. Li's face fell. "I retired nine years ago, but then my wife died of cancer the following year."

"I'm sorry to hear that," Ariel said.

Mr. Li shrugged. "Eh, life happens. After a year of sitting at home grieving, I wanted something to do. This was my favorite little stop, and when the owner mentioned to me that he was looking to sell it, I decided to buy it. So far, I've enjoyed it. I don't sit at home anymore. I get to see my regular customers frequently and talk about what's happening in their lives, I get to meet a lot of new and interesting people"—his smile reappeared and he nodded at Ariel—"and I occasionally get to help people. I've done well enough that I've bought four more independent stores. My niece runs them all, and does a good enough job that I can sit here, read my books, and talk to my friends. Except for when my idiot nephew, her brother, tries to help and usually messes something up. A good kid, but as clueless as they come. Eh, but he's family."

Mr. Li sounded so Jewish right then that Ariel had to laugh.

Ariel caught a glimpse of the clock on the wall behind Mr. Li. "Time to go," he said. He raised his hand in farewell, but before he could say anything, Mr. Li cleared his throat.

"So, you work for Mordechai, right? You working now?"

"Yes."

Mr. Li looked at him sidelong. "Mordechai talk about me?"

"A little."

Mr. Li nodded. "Well?"

"I'm looking for a rapist that preys on uni girls."

Mr. Li's face turned to stone. "New or old?"

"Old, I think."

"Him." Mr. Li shook his head.

"How do you know anything about him?"

"Uni kids come in here and talk a lot. Not to me, to each other, but I hear it. I have a niece and two nephews still in school. They talk to me, tell Uncle Greg things they'd never tell their parents. This guy comes and goes. But when he's here, he's always cruising the clubs in this area. He never takes more than one in a season, and then he moves on somewhere else. But so far he's always come back here. Nobody knows who he is, but they get a feel for when he's around."

Ariel's face tightened as his anger began to rise. He throttled it down, somehow. He didn't need to reveal himself here.

"Is this personal or professional for you?" Mr. Li asked.

"Both."

"How will you find him? You know what he looks like?"

"I know what he smells like."

The old man's eyes narrowed, but then he nodded slowly. "Good hunting."

Ariel walked in the front door to Shaka's. The place was crowded and noisy. He looked around, then headed for the bar. Nick was working and saw him coming, and met him with a glass of sparkling water. "On the house, mate."

"Thanks." Ariel took a sip. "What happened after I left last night?"

"Oh, the crime scene blokes took photos, sampled and swabbed everything they could see, and tried for fingerprints. Not sure they had much luck with the last. They were here until 0500. We were late opening because we had to clean up the mess they left." Nick grinned at that. "The inspector kept Klein under control, which is good. He's got a local reputation of being aggressive in his work, and sometimes he gets aggressive all over people. I wasn't happy to see him come in the door last night."

"It's a good thing he didn't try that with my boss."

"You mean it's a good thing the inspector shut him down." Nick's grin got wider.

"True." Ariel put his glass down and looked up at Nick. "Listen, you have security cameras back there, right?"

"Yeah, but something went south on them. They both quit working a few days ago."

Ariel frowned. "That's weird. So you don't have any security video of the guy dragging Yael back there."

"Nope." Nick sobered. "Just a couple of brief images of a guy pointing a laser at the cameras right before they went down. That's a real problem these days. The boys in Hong Kong figured out that if you amp up the power to a laser pointer you can burn out a security camera. Or someone's eyes, for that matter. This is the second time our cameras have been burned out, and according to our security company, it's happening frequently all over Tel Aviv. Anyway, that inspector woman asked about the cameras as well, so she would have taken any security videos if we'd had any."

"Yeah, she would have, but damn!" Ariel frowned. "I really wanted to see those. That would have been some help." He looked up at Nick. "You going to replace the cameras?"

"Oh, yeah. Insurance requires it. Fortunately, these days security cameras are usually pretty cheap. I'm going to talk to our security guy to see what high-resolution color cameras would cost this time around. I think the prices have been coming down."

Ariel pushed his empty glass back across the bar. "Thanks for that."

"Anything else you need?"

"One last question—did you ever figure out how he got into the closet? Did he pick the lock, did he get a key, was it left unlocked by mistake?"

Nick's expression turned sour. "Cops had the same questions. We didn't have any answers for them, either. But I fired a bartender a couple of nights before then for harassing sheilas, and it looks like he got away with his keys when he left. I've changed the locks today, needless to say. Cops are looking for him now."

"What was his name?"

"Yakov Abragam. And yeah, that's another Russian name, so the cops are trying to put that picture together as well."

"Ah." Ariel nodded. "I'll keep that in mind."

"I take it you didn't have any luck with the name either." Nick raised one eyebrow.

Ariel didn't deny he'd tried. No sense to, since he'd mentioned the name to them his first night there. "No. I was unpleasantly surprised to find out how many Gersh Davidoffs there actually are in Israel."

"Heh." Nick thumbed his nose. "Not quite a Murphy's Law issue, but not far from it, either."

"Too right." Ariel straightened. "Time to get on with it."

"On with what?"

Ariel gave him a tight-lipped smile. "Hunting."

CHAPTER 30

AT 0330, ARIEL STOOD ACROSS THE STREET FROM the Palmyra Club. It had amazed him when he first arrived in Israel that the bars and clubs stayed open so late almost every night. Some of the clubs were open twenty-four hours. Even now, after being in Israel for a few months, that just seemed unreal to him.

"You ready to move in?" He heard Mordechai's voice over his earpiece. He knew that the older vampire was parked around on the other side of the club.

The anger that had erupted within him when he had found Yael and found out what had been done to her was still present in him, growing harder and hotter with each passing hour. It took much of his strength to keep it under control.

The club sat on a corner, and there was a neon palm tree on the front of the building behind the outside seating area. Torch fixtures cast flickering light and shadow across the large group of mostly young people, some of whom were seated, some of whom were milling around, all of whom were talking loudly.

Ariel leaned up against the building he was standing in front of. He was in a pool of shadow, so he was fairly certain he couldn't be seen from the club. He just watched for a while, getting a feel for the crowd, restraining his wrath.

"I guess." Ariel muttered, anger smoldering under his words. "I'd really hoped we'd find him before now. We've hit most of the bars in the area."

"Is this number four or number five?"

"Five, and no luck so far."

"That happens. Patience is a requirement. At least you have two solid clues: his name, and his odor. I've waited much longer with much less in my hand to help find the target."

"Patience," Ariel said in a controlled tone. "I'm a Generation Z-er. I don't have time for patience."

"You ready to move in?" Mordechai repeated. "You're burning moonlight."

Ariel snorted at that one. "Okay, okay, I'm moving." He closed his eyes, placed his hand over the medallion that was under his shirt, and whispered the *Sh'ma*. After a moment of motionless silence, he dropped his hand and straightened. "Time to do this," he snarled.

He crossed the street, dodging traffic, feeling almost like a matador in a bull ring. One of the things that had been a major culture shock when he'd moved to Israel was that pedestrians would cross anywhere, not just at crosswalks. The flip side was that vehicles very seldom would yield the right-of-way to pedestrians, even in crosswalks. Even at this early hour of the morning, crossing a major street in this area sometimes seemed to require speed, agility, and even a definite touch of foolhardiness.

Arriving at the other side, Ariel was greeted with cheers and a couple of bold souls who offered high fives, something that had fallen out of favor during the Covid years but was now making a comeback. He slapped palms with them and slipped into the crowd.

He went to the bar inside, bought a bottle of Perrier, and began quartering through the crowds, first inside, then outside. Nothing. No sight, no scent, no sound. Nothing.

Ariel had to remind himself that this was a hunt, not a game, and that he shouldn't expect to find his quarry right away. He wasn't playing hide-and-go-seek—he was searching for a dangerous man. He felt his rage move from hot to cold, a coldness that entered his spirit. His mind settled, and his vision seemed to sharpen. He started moving again, focused, intent.

It was during his second circle through the outside crowd that Ariel caught a hint of what he thought was Davidoff's scent. Just a hint—not even a whiff. He stopped stock-still, and inhaled very slowly, very deeply. Yes, there was that wisp of scent.

Ariel closed his eyes and tried to judge which direction it was coming from. He turned his head first to the left, then to the right, in a very slow motion. The scent seemed to be stronger to the left. He opened his eyes, turned his body, and began moving in slow steps, inhaling slowly, exhaling quickly, following the scent.

The scent was getting stronger, so he was going in the right direction. The tang of oily body overlaying acrid musk was now unmistakable. Ariel's nostrils flared as he followed it. He licked his lips, anticipating. Step by sliding step he moved through the crowd like a knife through water, leaving no ripple or eddy behind.

Ariel kept his eyes moving from side to side. The scent was getting stronger, true, but there were still a lot of people in the area he was moving through, most of whom were men, which made his task more difficult. Based on odor alone, a number of the men before him hadn't bathed in some time. Normally he could ignore it, but he couldn't tonight because he was concentrating on scent. It made him want to spit. But even so, the redolence of his quarry's odor was even stronger. Why other people couldn't sense it, he didn't know.

Now the scent was weaker. He slowed, and turned his head slowly to the right, then back to the left. Stronger to the left, so he curved his steps that way, still sliding through the crowd slowly, step by step.

The circle he traced was large, thirty feet or more in diameter. He made two circuits of it, and even though there was some movement of people in and out of that crowd, the spoor remained in it. "Potential hit," he murmured into his earpiece.

"Take it slow," Mordechai cautioned.

Ariel didn't respond, but after a moment, he took a chance. He paused, did a slow pivot, and started edging straight through the circle. He had no idea what to look for, but with each step the odor, the spoor, grew stronger. As he neared the center, he slowed his steps even more, ostensibly because the crowd was thicker there, but actually so he could spend more time testing the air.

He turned his head to the right as he inhaled, and got a strong draft of the scent that was almost enough to start him coughing. He paused, leaned a bit to his right, and took a short sniff. An almost overpowering musk, it seemed to him, even though no one else was reacting to it.

Ariel's gaze shifted up. He couldn't get a glimpse of the profile, but on the back of the man's head was a beanie knit from black and white yarn in a pattern of white lightning-bolt symbols on a black background.

Okay, that was distinctive. That would help track him.

Excitement surged, elevating his wrath along with it. He bowed his head for a moment, fighting for calm. He caught his hands clenching, and forced the hand holding the Perrier bottle to relax before the bottle shattered. Having already had that experience recently, he had no desire to repeat it.

He was two steps past the target. He started curving back to the right again, trying to catch a frontal glimpse of the man out of the corner of his eye. Someone else moved out of his way, and gave him a split-second view. His quarry appeared to be wearing a long-sleeved T-shirt in a checkered pattern of gray and green. Jeans of course. Those were ubiquitous in this crowd, especially given that the weather was a bit cool after dusk. Large, if a bit soft around the edges. His facial features were heavy and coarse, and were unfamiliar to Ariel. A fringe of dark hair stuck out from under the edges of his beanie.

Elation danced with rage in Ariel's heart. He could now identify his prey. But he couldn't take him now—not in the crowd. So he choked down the rage yet again. "Found him. Know what he looks like," he reported to Mordechai almost sotto voce under the buzz of the surrounding conversations. He started circling toward a place where he could observe the beanie wearer head-on. In less than a minute Ariel had his desired vantage point.

The crowd had thinned enough that Ariel had a good look at his quarry and the two men he stood between. He edged through the crowd at a tangent, always keeping at least one eye on the man he was increasingly sure was Davidoff. His attention was rewarded when the crowd parted for a few moments and gave him a clear view of Davidoff's feet.

Ariel couldn't believe what he was seeing. One of Davidoff's pants legs was rucked up and the cuff was sitting on top of . . . a cowboy boot. When Davidoff turned a bit to look at the guy to his right, Ariel realized that it was an American-style cowboy boot as big as life. Double confirmation that this was his target. He suppressed a shake of his head at the sight of a *magen* symbol inset into the outside quarter panels of the shaft of the boot. In blue on a white field, even.

The next moment Ariel remembered that cowboy boots had very pointed toes—which brought to mind some of Yael's injuries. He spent the next minute staring at Davidoff as he forced the rage down yet again. He sighed once he accomplished that, not at all certain as to whether or not he could continue to do so much longer.

He couldn't take Davidoff in public. That would cause too many problems, and would likely make trouble for Mordechai as well. Davidoff needed to leave. The question was, could Ariel somehow maneuver Davidoff into leaving? How could he provoke him to leave?

That thought rolled around in Ariel's mind as he stared at Davidoff. Before he reached any conclusion, Davidoff shifted his gaze in Ariel's direction. He happened to lock eyes with Ariel, and frowned as he registered that Ariel was looking at him.

That gave Ariel an idea. He gave his best imitation of Mordechai's razor-edged grin and leaned forward a bit. Davidoff's frown grew deeper. Ariel then placed the tips of his left index and middle fingers below his eyes, then pivoted his hand to point them toward Davidoff. Finally he dropped his left hand down to pull the left side of his jacket back enough to just reveal the handle of his pistol in its shoulder holster. That caused Davidoff's eyes to go wide, and he grabbed for one of his friends.

At that moment, someone moved between them and blocked the line of sight. Ariel moved with that person, thankful for once that he was a bit smaller than average. It made it easier to lose himself in the crowd. He wanted Davidoff to see him, but to reveal himself in unexpected ways. He wanted to amp up Davidoff's uncertainty to the point that he would leave the club.

Ariel shifted to his left about a meter while moving forward about a half meter before moving to clear the crowd. Then he adopted a pose, left leg advanced a half step, weight on his right leg, left hand holding the Perrier bottle in front of his sternum and his right fist propped on his hip. The crowd had thinned enough that they mostly passed behind him. He pasted the razor grin back on his face.

Davidoff was looking around now. He seemed uncertain and disturbed. The next time that Davidoff looked toward Ariel, he moved the bottle slightly, which caught the other man's attention. Davidoff's frown returned, a little darker. He stared at Ariel for several seconds, then turned to his friends and said something. They looked toward Ariel as well. Ariel tilted his head to one side and broadened his grin. They all stiffened.

A moment later, an eddy of the crowd broke the line of sight again, and Ariel moved. This time he shifted to his right about a meter and a half, not drawing any closer. Unpredictable. He half turned, pointing his left shoulder at Davidoff, shifted the Perrier bottle to his right hand, holding it almost horizontal so that the mouth of the bottle almost resembled a muzzle opening, while he let his left arm just hang and turned his head to look down his left shoulder at Davidoff, his grin approaching mockery.

Davidoff was definitely looking around nervously, and it didn't take long for him to find Ariel again. His resulting frown in reaction to Ariel's stalking him was thunderous, and Ariel could see him start forward as if to force a confrontation. But one of his friends grabbed an arm and talked to him until he stepped back. He did, however, point a finger at Ariel before he turned away. Ariel chuckled at that.

Ariel's next move was back to the left about the same distance and another half meter forward. This time he faced fully frontal with his arms folded across his chest, holding the Perrier bottle up in his right hand. No smile this time. Just a serious, straightforward glower. This time when they locked eyes, he mouthed the words, "You're mine," and gave a definite head nod.

It took both of Davidoff's friends to hold him back this time. Ariel could imagine the things they were saying to him, because he eventually threw their hands off of him and snarled at them before turning and stomping away, pushing through the crowd toward an exit on the side street.

Ariel was able to track the beanie as it moved through the crowd. He finished the contents of his bottle and dropped it in a nearby trash can as he headed toward that same exit.

"Got him," Ariel murmured. "He's leaving the club with two friends. Other side from you."

"Be careful."

In full hunting mode, a snarl on his lips, Ariel exited the club, rage pushing to the fore, feeling like a predator for the first time.

CHAPTER 31

DAVIDOFF AND HIS FRIENDS WERE ABOUT HALFWAY down the block by the time Ariel was out of the club. It surprised him a little to realize that the other two men were actually taller than Davidoff, if perhaps not as broad. They were yelling back and forth to each other, although there was enough noise from the club behind them and the cars passing on the streets that even with his vampiric hearing he couldn't understand much of what they were saying, at least partly because they were using what Ariel guessed was Russian mixed in with their Hebrew. Davidoff was unhappy, and appeared to be blaming something on one of the others was all he could tell at the moment. The other man pulled a mobile out of his pocket and started a call.

Ariel hung back while he pulled the leather gloves from his pocket. He didn't want to leave fingerprints or traces of blood or skin cells around for a forensics person to find. He tapped his gun, the knife, and the burner mobile to make sure they were all still in place. Then he sped up his pace a bit to move closer to the trio.

It amazed Ariel a bit that none of them had looked back yet. That was fine with him. It gave him just that much more time to get closer.

He trailed them as they reached the end of the block and turned the corner. Once they were out of sight, he sprinted forward until he reached the corner. He peered around the edge of the building and saw them not too far down the block. "Turning onto Joshua Place," he murmured. "I think I can take them here."

"Got it," Mordechai replied.

This block was less well-lit than the one the club was on. The street was all small businesses that were closed for the night. The streetlights were dimmer, and the shops had few lights on, external or internal. He checked his watch—it was only 4:00 A.M., so the chances of anyone being in the shops yet was small. Ariel was fine with that. It would be more to his advantage than theirs.

Ariel looked around. They were the only ones visible on the block. He smiled in anticipation.

By now Ariel was close enough that he could hear one of the friends talking. "I'm telling you, Gersh, you need to talk to Levchin about this. He can find out if this guy is police."

"I'm not bothering Arkadi with this," snarled a bass voice that had to be Davidoff. His Hebrew was rather accented. "I never saw the guy before tonight. He could be Baba Yaga's son, for all I know."

Arkadi Levchin—Ariel made note of that name. It sounded Russian, which made sense if it was connected to Davidoff. But more importantly, it sounded like it might be someone important to Davidoff, and anyone that was important to someone like him might be important to know about. Mordechai, for example, might be interested in that name.

"He sure seemed to know you, though, Gersh."

"Shut up, Abragam," Davidoff muttered. "If I don't know him, he can't know me."

Ariel nodded at that name. That almost had to be Yakov Abragam, the bartender Nick had fired. If he was one of Davidoff's friends, that would probably explain where the missing keys to the interior doors at Shaka's went to.

The third guy in the trio, the one Ariel didn't have a name for yet, turned his head to look behind them. Ariel didn't try to duck and hide, just kept walking after them.

The third guy froze. "Uh . . ."

Davidoff and Abragam walked a couple of steps farther on, then stopped and turned when they realized the third guy had stopped. "What are you doing, Fridman . . ." Davidoff began, only to trail off when he saw Ariel walking toward them. "You! What are you doing here?"

"Hunting you, Gersh Davidoff." Ariel's voice was as cold as he could make it, for all that he was smiling.

"Why? I don't know you. I haven't hurt you, although that may change here in a minute."

"That's right, you don't know me, and I never saw you before tonight." Ariel's rage was no longer surging—it was slowly building, rising, coalescing into an icy tor that he could almost see before him. "But night before last you raped a friend of mine. You beat her nearly to death, and left her broken and half blind in a back room at Shaka's. She gave me your name."

"She lied! I wasn't at Shaka's that night. Yakov and

Leon will swear to that." Davidoff flung a hand out in a hard gesture.

"I'm sure your friends will perjure themselves for you," Ariel said as he took a step forward. "But unfortunately for them, I smelled you on her. I smell you now, so you can all save your lies. I know it was you." He shook his head, still smiling. "Besides, Yakov Abragam has his own problems to deal with, since he gave you the key to the storeroom." The man to Davidoff's left stiffened and his eyes widened. "Oh, yes," Ariel almost crooned, "the police have your name, Mr. Abragam. They will catch up to you soon. I suggest you tell them the truth. It will be easier for you."

"Dog-raping chazzer!" Davidoff cursed, using a vulgarity for a policeman.

"Oh, I'm not police." Ariel's smile broadened. "But you're going to wish I was. I'm not bound by their rules in this. I'm very old school, I am." He felt his fangs extending and dropping down, and the coldness of his rage seemed to expand.

"Not very smart, either," Davidoff snorted. "One little man like you against the three of us?"

"As the Americans say, 'It's not the size of the man in the fight, it's the size of the fight in the man.'" Ariel shrugged. "One of me against the three of you? I'd say the odds are about even." He leaned forward a bit, flexing his hands. "Enough talk. Time to end this."

Davidoff looked surprised as Ariel took another step forward. "Yakov! Leon! Get him!"

The three men spread out a little and started to encircle Ariel, Davidoff in the center. Ariel let them get set, waiting until they had almost settled into their stances before bursting into motion. *No restraint. No mercy.* Those thoughts ran through Ariel's mind. *Full speed, full force.* His mouth moved to a snarl the last split second before he moved.

In the first breath of the attack, Ariel leapt to Fridman, slapped his hands aside, and hammered a blow to his solar plexus.

Before the second breath began, he was standing before Abragam, delivering the first of three fast jabs to the face before demolishing his right knee with a side kick.

Davidoff's eyes had widened at the sight of his friends suddenly lying on the pavement, and his hands started rising from his chest to his face. Ariel slapped his hands a couple of times, then delivered a moderately heavy punch to his abdomen. Then he stepped back a step and stood flat-footed, hands moving in midair, practically begging Davidoff to throw a punch at him.

The big man made a couple of feints, which Ariel evaded, before finally throwing a left-leg front kick for real followed up with a roundhouse right, which was what Ariel was waiting for. He grabbed Davidoff's wrist and did an arm-wrap takedown just like he'd done to Gabe that evening in Chattanooga.

Ariel let Davidoff hit the concrete and start rolling before he came behind him and applied a rear naked choke hold. He could feel Davidoff start to panic as the strength of his vampire muscles sank his arms deeply into the tissues of Davidoff's neck.

Davidoff tore at Ariel's arms, but was unable to get any kind of grip or leverage. In just a few more seconds, the pressure on his carotid arteries blocked enough of the blood flow to the big man's brain that he was unconscious. Not letting up on the pressure yet, Ariel dragged the big man back up to a cul-de-sac in the row of shops with several trash dumpsters in it. Even for his strength, it wasn't easy, but it was only a few seconds before he had the big man where he wanted him. He looked at the front of the nearest dumpster to verify there was a large metal ring on each top corner. Dropping Davidoff, Ariel quickly stripped off the leather gloves, turning them inside out as he did so and shoving them back into their pockets. A moment later he had the nitrile gloves on. He smiled to himself as he finished double-gloving, finding it both ironic and humorous that one of the skills he'd picked up at the Urgent Care was coming into play. He reached into his inside jacket pocket and brought out two of the long zip ties.

It didn't take long for Davidoff to rouse back to full consciousness, but by the time he arrived there Ariel had zip ties around his wrists and through the rings such that his arms were outstretched. In fact, he was applying a piece of wide black tape across Davidoff's mouth when his eyes fluttered open.

"Ah, there you are," Ariel said, a cruel smile on his face. "I'll be back in a moment. Don't go away."

He turned his back on Davidoff and trotted over to Fridman, who was staggering to his feet after recovering somewhat from the solar plexus punch. "Sorry, man, but this won't do." Before the groggy Fridman could grasp what was happening, he was dragged into the cul-de-sac and his right wrist was zip-tied to a utility conduit and Ariel was using multiple zip ties to tie his left wrist to his left ankle.

"Hey! What . . ." Fridman's objections were interrupted by a slap that rocked his head.

"Shut up," Ariel said calmly as he ripped a length of tape off the roll and covered the other man's mouth with it. He then held Fridman's head motionless and stared him in the eyes. "I'm tying you up to keep you out of trouble. You'll probably come out of this okay, because I don't have anything against you except your deplorable choice in friends. You really need to do better than this bunch. I mean, really. Hanging out with Davidoff is going to get you killed. Seriously. Do better than that. Got it?"

Fridman nodded his head frantically.

Ariel ripped another length of tape off the roll. "Close your eyes. You really don't want to see what's going to happen next, for more than one reason." Fridman's eyes almost bugged out. "I mean it. Close your eyes, or you won't like what this tape will do to you."

Fridman slammed his eyelids shut and squinched his eyes. Ariel snorted, and ran the tape from Fridman's right temple across his eyes to the left temple. "You're good," he said, with a pat to the other man's shoulder.

A moment later Ariel was standing looking down at where Abragam was lying curled holding his knee, moaning. He shook his head. "Now you I don't feel sorry for. You helped him."

Abragam looked up, tears running down his face from the pain. "I didn't do anything to her. I just let Gersh take the keys. I didn't even give them to him."

"Sins of omission are as bad as sins of commission. A court would call that aiding and abetting, and would rule you just as guilty as he is. I suggest you spend the next little while thinking about that, and deciding what you're going to tell the police when they find you. Meanwhile, let's get you fastened up as well."

Two minutes later Abragam was in the cul-de-sac as well, right wrist zip tied to a signpost at the other end from Davidoff and left wrist and left ankle tied together. Ariel pulled Abragam's shirt up and wiped tears and snot and drool off before applying tape to his mouth and eyes as well.

Ariel stood and put the tape back in his pocket. He took a deep breath, taking the leash off his anger. His face grew harder; he could feel it.

His pace back to where Davidoff was standing was slow, almost languid, but it wasn't long before he stood before Davidoff, smiling, arms crossed.

Davidoff was grunting and trying to scream behind the tape. Ariel just let it happen, until the big man ran out of oxygen and sagged against the dumpster, head hanging, inhaling and exhaling rapidly, large breaths, with his nostrils flared and distended with each breath in.

Once Davidoff's breathing had slowed some and he looked up again, Ariel smiled and said in a quiet tone, "Oh, if looks could kill. But then, your looks aren't any more effective than your hands against someone who can stand up to you. Big tough man, drugging a girl, raping her, and then beating her with those big strong hands. Didn't do so well against me, did you?"

Ariel stepped closer. "I lied. It wasn't even odds, you three against me. Even if the three of you knew what you were doing, you couldn't have begun to match me. But after what you did, it was fair."

Another step closer. Davidoff tried to kick Ariel, but he caught the leg. "Uh-uh," he said, and delivered three deep knuckle punches to the thigh. Davidoff screamed again behind the tape as Ariel dropped the leg. Davidoff sagged as that leg folded under him.

Ariel slapped Davidoff lightly—at least, lightly for him. It still rocked Davidoff's head to one side. "Pay attention, stud. You think you're big and tough. You think you can beat up on women without it catching up to you. Well, maybe you can." He stepped closer and reached up with his right hand to clasp Davidoff's right hand. There was enough space in the zip tie holding it that Davidoff had some room to move his arm within the circle of the zip tie. "If you can hurt my hand—I mean, really hurt it—I'll cut you free and you can walk. Seriously. You hurt me, you're free. Go for it. What have you got to lose?"

Ariel had let his hand just rest in a loose clasp around Davidoff's. After a moment, Davidoff's hand suddenly clamped hard on his. Ariel could feel the tension that Davidoff was applying, and could see the muscles in his arm and shoulder shift under his shirt as he squeezed as hard as he could, trying to crush Ariel's hand in his own.

It wasn't enough. Ariel tensed his hand enough to resist Davidoff's pressure, but did nothing more for a long moment. When Davidoff's breath broke and he grunted behind the tape, Ariel smiled at him, and began increasing his own hand's pressure slowly, bit by bit, finger by finger, until he felt Davidoff's clench fail and his knuckles and metacarpal bones begin to grind against each other.

Davidoff began to grunt and moan. Ariel's smile grew, and he suddenly increased the clench of his own hand to the point where the bones began to crack and splinter. Tears flowed from Davidoff's eyes, and mucus flooded from his nostrils as he tried to scream. Ariel held his grip for a long moment, then released it.

"Not so tough as you thought you were, are you?" he whispered in Davidoff's ear. "The hands that you beat her with, that you broke her with ..." He stepped to Davidoff's left, took Davidoff's left hand in his, and crushed it in one sharp motion.

Davidoff did scream this time, but the tape muffled most of it. He sagged against the restraints, and more mucus carried clots of snot out of his nose to run across his taped mouth and drip from his chin onto his shaking chest.

Ariel leaned in to whisper in his left ear, "The hands that you broke her with are now broken. And me—I'm not Baba Yaga's son—I'm her brother."

He stepped back, and let Davidoff suffer for a couple of minutes. When his breathing began to slow down a little, Ariel stepped back in, grabbed Davidoff's right leg, pulled it up, grabbed the top of his cowboy boot with both hands, and pulled so hard it ripped the stitching apart and the pieces of the boot fell on the pavement. He then repeated the process with the left leg and the left boot.

"Eww. No socks?" Ariel wiped his gloved hands on his pants. "I mean, I can see that with loafers or athletic shoes, but boots? Nasty."

He said nothing more, just stepped close and turned before delivering five precise heel kicks with his boots to each foot: two kicks to crush the toes and three to crush the metatarsal bones.

More tape-muffled screaming. Ariel was surprised at how much mucus a human head could apparently hold.

Ariel moved back, and let more time pass. This time

it was over five minutes before he stepped in again to whisper in Davidoff's right ear. "The feet that you used to kick her and nearly kill her are now broken."

Davidoff's beanie had left his head sometime during the brief fight. Ariel pulled the knife from his pocket and drew it from its sheath, then grabbed Davidoff's hair and pulled his head back to hold the knife up in front of his eyes. "You raped her. I should castrate you." He lowered the blade and brought it up under Davidoff's crotch, turning the blade so that the flat of it made contact. The big man shook his head violently and moaned.

Ariel stepped back one step, then delivered three full force kicks to Davidoff's groin. With vampire muscles in play, he might have broken his pelvic bone. That thought didn't bother him. "You raped her." He laid the flat of the blade against Davidoff's neck. "You should thank *haShem* that I don't kill you." He wasn't sure Davidoff heard him.

He re-sheathed the knife, put it away, and watched as Davidoff shook and cried. His shirt was sodden with mucus and now blood was flowing from his nostrils. His bladder had released, and another odor was on the air indicating that he'd shit himself as well. Ariel waited.

It was some little time before Davidoff raised his head again. Ariel grabbed Davidoff's hair and pulled his head back.

"You hear me, Davidoff? Can you hear me?" He stared directly into Davidoff's eyes.

A weak grunt sounded.

"If I hear of you doing anything like this again, I'll hunt you down and finish you." He bent forward and looked into Davidoff's eyes, shining his flashlight on his face, where his fangs were still prominent. "I found you now, I can always find you. If I come after you again, you'll never know it. You'll never see me coming. You'll just disappear, and no one will know why, or where you are, or what happened. You'll just be gone. Painfully. Understand?"

Davidoff made another grunt and tried to wave his hands.

Ariel turned the light off. "Good. I always like it when we can have a meeting of the minds. Just remember, I know everything, and I can always find you. I suggest you turn to righteousness. You'll live longer."

He stared at Davidoff for a moment longer, then turned and walked away.

After he turned back onto the street that ran by the Palmyra Club, Ariel pulled out his burner mobile and dialed the police number. "State your emergency," the operator said.

"If you want the guy who assaulted and raped Yael Malka," Ariel said in a really high-pitched falsetto, "he's tied to a dumpster by Trochta's Flowers. If you hurry, he might still be alive when you get there."

He terminated the call, and immediately took the mobile apart, dropping the battery in the first trash can he walked by and pulling the SIM card and putting it in his pocket. He stopped by the third trash can he walked by, broke the mobile case and circuit board into pieces and dropped them there.

When he got back to Palmyra, the gloves went back in his jacket pockets. He took a deep breath and muttered "Done" to his earpiece.

"Where are you?"

"By Palmyra again. West side."

"Stay there."

A couple of minutes later Mordechai pulled up across the street. Ariel walked over and got in the car.

Mordechai looked at him. Ariel looked back at him and shook his head. "It's done, and I don't want to talk about it right now."

Mordechai nodded. "You need to come down from that mountain first. We'll talk later. Where do you want to go?"

"The hospital."

Ariel got to the hospital a little before 0500. He walked in the front door, had a brief discussion with security where he had to show them his Yamam card, and rode the elevator to the second floor.

The visitor's area was empty, which wasn't too surprising, given that it was just now dawn outside. He walked past it, and was stopped by a male nurse.

"Can I help you?"

"If it's possible, I'd like to see Yael Malka."

"Are you a relation?"

"Not by blood, but I'm a friend. I'm the friend who found her."

The nurse nodded, and said, "She's probably asleep, but come this way."

He led Ariel down the hall several meters and pointed to a room. "She's in there. She hasn't been sleeping well, so don't wake her up if she's asleep."

"Thanks."

The nurse headed back up the hall, and Ariel slipped into the room. The lights were dialed down to very dim, but with his vision that wasn't a problem. He stepped to the side of the bed and rested his hands on the railing, looking down at her.

Yael's face was very bruised, and she had an IV in her right elbow. He couldn't see her body, but that was probably a good thing.

Ariel wanted to touch her, but was afraid to, for more than one reason, so he just stood there looking at her. Something reached her, nonetheless, because her eyes opened and she looked over at him. She frowned.

"It's me—Ariel," he whispered, glad that he was on her right side.

"Ariel?" she whispered back. "You came."

"Yeah."

Yael reached her hand up, and he gently took it in his. She smiled, and closed her eyes again, but didn't let go.

Ariel stood there for a long time. Even though there was a visitation time limit for ICU patients, the male nurse who came in from time to time didn't ask him to leave. It may have had something to do with Yael sleeping soundly while he was there. He didn't care. He was there. That was enough.

CHAPTER 32

ARIEL SIGHED AS HE WALKED IN THE DOOR OF HIS apartment. It was well past dawn outside. Time for all good vampires to be home with the drapes and doors closed. The last seventy-two hours had been very intense, and he was exhausted.

He unloaded his pockets onto his desk and draped his jacket on the chair before heading for the refrigerator. He came back with a bottle of water, but before he could sit down, his mobile rang. He looked at it, and saw that it was Mordechai calling. He answered in speaker mode.

"Hallo."

"Where are you?" Even through the mobile's tinny-sounding speaker Mordechai sounded serious.

"Just got home."

"Good. Stay there."

While he waited, Ariel took a pair of metal tweezers from his desk, picked up the burner mobile SIM card, and carried it to the kitchen. He rooted around in his kitchen junk drawer until he found the butane lighter he was pretty certain he had, then pulled a pottery saucer out of the cabinet.

When the knock came at the door, Ariel was holding the SIM card over the flame of the lighter. "Come on in," he called out. "It's not locked."

Mordechai entered, shut the door behind him, and looked at Ariel. "What are you doing?"

"Just flambéing a SIM card." Ariel looked up with a grin.

"The prophets tell us that fire purifies," Mordechai said with a small smile. "Let me not interfere with your righteous work."

Ariel snorted at that, but continued to hold the card in the tweezers over the flame for another minute or so until all the cardboard and volatile components were burned away and all that was left was the tiny soot-blackened piece of silicon that was the core of the card. "Just to make sure," he muttered. Afterward, he released the lever of the lighter, and the flame died. "There. That's done." He set the silicon on the saucer and laid the tweezers and lighter on the counter beside it. "Sorry, I don't have any scotch. Want some water?"

Mordechai nodded, so Ariel pulled a bottle out of the refrigerator and handed it to him, then waved him toward the small living area his apartment boasted. "Sit, sit." He picked up his own bottle and plopped down at one end of his sofa, while Mordechai sat in the only chair available and set his bag on the floor.

Mordechai stared at him for a long moment. "You did well. The investigators have all three men in custody, and have absolutely no evidence that will point to you. Outside of that"—he pointed toward the saucer in the kitchen—"do you have anything here that could implicate you?"

"The only things that had major contact with them were my gloves."

"I'll take them with me. Get your clothes laundered today, get that jacket and your boots professionally cleaned. After that, you should be clean."

Ariel nodded.

"Are you done with him?" Mordechai's gaze was direct, his voice was level. There was no doubt in Ariel's mind what he meant.

Ariel sighed. "Yes, unless he comes back."

"Oh, I doubt that he will," Mordechai said. "In addition to the physical damage, you may have broken his mind. From the reports, when they can get Davidoff to talk at all, he just raves about being attacked by a monster—by Baba Yaga's brother, in fact."

Ariel snorted. "That's his own doing. He called me Baba Yaga's son to one of his friends. I simply corrected his perception."

Mordechai's razor grin flitted across his face. A moment later it sobered again. "You trod very close to the line, but I judge you didn't go over. You got your revenge. How does it feel?"

"Revenge? I was striving for balance, for equity, for justice."

Mordechai shook his head. "When that which is taken or destroyed cannot be restored, there is no balance or equity possible. There is merely causing equal pain to try and prevent more. And justice? Justice is the right and privilege of *haShem*, of the Most High. What we call justice is only a crude imitation, and is all too often misapplied, miscarried, or misbegotten." He shrugged. "It seems that all we can do is do what is right where possible, and endure the wrong where it's not. That is the history of the Jews in a nutshell, I'm afraid."

They sat in silence for a while. Ariel took a swig from his bottle, and turned it around and around in his hands.

"How does it feel?" Ariel finally repeated the question. "With both the gang in California and with Davidoff here, it feels . . . empty. There is no sense of right being restored. There is only a grim satisfaction that they were hurt as much as they caused hurt, and they will not cause that hurt again. You say I almost crossed a line. I wanted to. I wanted to make him and his friends hurt more than Yael was hurt. *That* I could have enjoyed. That"—he swallowed—"that I *would* have enjoyed."

"And that is why the Lex Talionis tells us that vengeance is the Lord's, not ours. What you did was righteous. If you had enjoyed it, it would have been unrighteous."

"I don't feel righteous," Ariel muttered.

"Hah," Mordechai said. "If you felt righteous, I'd be worried about you. It's my experience that all too often those who most feel righteous are in actuality the least righteous."

"Heh." Ariel thought about that. "I can see that."

They sat in companionable silence for some time, then Mordechai chuckled.

"What?" Ariel asked.

"Your restraint with the other two was good. They have been most cooperative with the investigators, including giving very detailed descriptions of you."

"What?" Ariel sat bolt upright in shock.

"Oh, yes. Did you know that you are at least a

hundred and ninety-five centimeters tall, weigh at least a hundred and ten kilograms, and you're some kind of super-ninja?"

Ariel slumped in relief. "Oh, really? That's good to know. I guess I need to buy a new wardrobe, huh?" He took another swig from his bottle. "Is that all they're saying?"

"No. Hopefully they're being a little more accurate with what they say about Davidoff, though."

"Ah"—Ariel snapped his fingers—"they were talking about being connected with some guy named Arkadi Levchin. I don't know the name, but I thought you might."

Mordechai nodded. "Oh, yes, I do. If they are connected with him in any way, that explains some things. Levchin apparently left St. Petersburg in the early nineties just ahead of what promised to be some uncomfortable conversations with both the police and the local mafia bosses. Here, he's reputedly connected with black markets, smuggling, and occasional flirting with outside forces, but he's kept a low profile and hasn't done anything big enough or splashy enough to warrant serious attention from Shin Bet or Yamam."

"What my dad would have called a two-bit hood, then?"

"If I understand the idiom, yes. But it's still useful information, and I'll see to it that it makes its way to the investigators—suitably anonymized, of course." After a moment, Mordechai asked, "And how is the young woman?"

Ariel took a deep breath, then released it. "Considering what she's been through, she seems to be doing rather well. Physically she's pretty much recovered from the Rohypnol, and the worst of the bruising is starting to heal. The broken bones will take time, but should heal fine. Losing the sight in one eye, though...that's going to be rough, for sure. She'll need some therapy to adjust to the new limits to her field of vision and compensate for the changes in depth perception. But she's tough. She's been in the IDF. She'll adapt. I'm more concerned about the psychological impacts."

"That will be hard, but don't short-change her," Mordechai warned. "As you say, she's tough. Let her lead her life—support her, but don't patronize her. First, be the friend she needs. If something grows from that"—he spread his hands—"then that will be as *haShem* wills it."

"From your mouth to His ear," Ariel murmured.

"Indeed."

Mordechai chuckled again. "She wouldn't be the first IDF soldier with an eyepatch, you know, if she wears one. May she become as famous as Dayan, and a better officer."

Ariel lifted his bottle in a toast to that thought, then finished his water and got up to put the empty bottle in the recycling bin. He leaned back against the kitchen counter. "She's supposed to be transferred to a regular room this morning. They want to keep her for a couple more days to run some more tests. At least one more MRI, I think. She'll get to go home after that."

"Is she the one?"

"The one for me?" Ariel crossed his arms and stared at the wall above Mordechai's head. "I...maybe. But whether she is or she isn't, she's important to me."

"Then be there for her."

❖   ❖   ❖

Later that day, Ariel returned to The Lucky Star store. It was late evening. The sun had set and twilight was progressing. Mr. Li looked up from the book he was reading as Ariel entered.

Mr. Li nodded. "So, was your hunt successful?"

Ariel sobered. "Yeah. It was."

Mr. Li showed a very slight smile. "So I heard."

Ariel's eyes widened. "How?"

The smile grew a bit. "My brother-in-law's son is in the police. What you did has them all buzzing."

"Wait a minute...your son works for the bank, your niece runs your businesses, and your nephew works for the police?" Ariel shook his head. "Is there some kind of Chinese tong running things here in Israel?"

The old man laughed, then shook his head. "Not hardly. Just a family doing well while doing good."

They both shared a laugh over that.

"So, you going to bring this girl by to let me meet her?" Mr. Li asked.

Ariel nodded. "Once she's out of the hospital, sure."

The old man's smile turned gentle. "I'd like that."

Ariel paused in the doorway, and watched Yael talking to Abigail. She looked good, looked almost normal—well, that is except for the fading bruises, the large Band-Aid on her left cheek, and the cast on her left arm. He sighed, and a smile curved his lips.

Abigail must have heard something, because she looked up and smiled and waved. "Ariel! Come in!"

Yael turned toward him, and the smile on her face seemed to light the entire room up for Ariel. He felt almost like he was standing in direct sunlight, he was so jazzed by it.

She held her hand out to him, and he crossed the room to take it. Neither of them said anything for a moment. They just smiled at each other, and Ariel drank from her gaze.

Abigail coughed, and Ariel came to himself. "I see, uh, I see they took your IV out," he said lamely.

"Oh, yes, and I'm so glad they did," Yael said. "I hate those things."

"Nobody likes them." Ariel nodded. "So, how do you feel today?"

"Like I was in a big fight, and lost." Yael's smile turned crooked.

"I'm sorry," Ariel muttered. "I'm such an..."

"Shut up," Yael said as she squeezed his hand. "If it wasn't for you, I probably wouldn't be alive. You found me, when no one else was even looking. You can say anything you want to me, okay? I reserve the right to call you an idiot if I need to, but you can say anything to me. You've earned that."

Her smile brightened up again, and Ariel had to smile in return.

"Well," Abigail stood and picked up her bag, "I need some better coffee than the instant sludge they serve in the waiting room, so I'm going to go find some while you keep her company, Ariel."

"Bring me a large cup of Turkish when you come back," Yael called out as Abigail headed for the door. She got a hand wave in response.

Yael took her hand back and used it to hit the control to make the head of the bed rise more so that she was sitting up straighter. "Come closer and bend down so I can kiss you." Ariel swallowed, but did as he was commanded, and she kissed him on the cheek. "Thank you, Ariel. You didn't have to do that, but I'm so very glad that you did."

"I'm sorry I couldn't get to you any faster." He ducked his head, feeling flushed.

She put her hand under his chin and lifted his face up. "Bullshit," she said, reminding him that she'd spent time with the soldiers of the IDF. "I knew you were out of the country when I left you that voice-mail, and I really didn't think I was in trouble. Boy, was I wrong."

"But what you went through..."

Yael shook her head. "Ariel, you couldn't have stopped it. Yes, I got raped. I'm not the only woman that's happened to, even in Israel. But I was given such a large dose of the drug that I really don't remember it. And I refuse to let this one event shape my life. Not your fault, got it? And don't you dare pity me."

The glower she fixed on Ariel reminded him of his maternal grandmother. Remembering Mordechai's comments, he mustered a smile, and said, "Yes, ma'am."

"Besides," she carried on, "you found me within three to four hours of when you started looking. That's crazy fast. You're a freaking miracle worker, Ariel. If it wasn't for you, the police would still be looking for me."

"Okay, okay," Ariel said with a laugh. "Stop already. You're going to blow my hat size up if you don't quit that."

Yael reached out and took his hand, and they just smiled at each other for a while.

"So, do you know yet when you'll get to go home?"

"Unless something ugly shows up on today's MRI, they say I can go home tomorrow," Yael said. "I am so ready. I miss my bed, and I especially miss my pillows." She pulled a flat specimen of pillow out from behind her and held it up before him. "This thing is pathetic."

They traded quips and insults about the pillow for a few minutes, then he helped her put it back. "After all," he intoned as he helped her slide it behind her head, "even a pathetic pillow is better than no pillow."

"Barely," she muttered as she laid back and sighed.

"I'll try to come check on you tomorrow," he said, "but I may be in Jerusalem. I'm supposed to go to the Western Wall with a friend soon, and it may be tomorrow."

Yael's eyebrows rose. "Would it be possible for me to tag along? I need to go visit. It's been quite a while since I last went. Not tomorrow, of course," she hastened to say, "but maybe the day after?"

A warmness formed in Ariel's heart.

"I think so. Let me talk to him tomorrow."

Her smile increased, if that was even possible, and Ariel felt like a tree drinking in the light of the sun.

The door to Yael's apartment opened, revealing Yael standing there wearing slacks and a hoodie, with Abigail standing behind her, both wearing big smiles.

"You ready?" Ariel asked, then immediately chastised himself for saying something so inane.

"Of course," Yael replied. "Let's go." She pushed past him, then looked back at Abigail. "Don't wait up this time. I think I'll be safe."

Abigail laughed, and shut the door.

"Elevator or stairs?" Ariel asked as they started down the hall.

"Elevator," Yael said. "I'm supposed to do as much walking as I can stand, but stairs are kind of difficult right now. And it's not the going up part that hurts as much as the going down part, for some reason I don't understand. You'd think it would be the other way around. Maybe we'll cover that in one of our physiology classes."

"Could be," Ariel said. "That reminds me. The next session starts in a week and a half."

"Don't remind me," Yael groaned. "I need another break to get over this break."

Ariel laughed.

"So tell me again, why are we going so late in the evening?" Yael asked.

Ariel shrugged. "The rest of us tend to have evening schedules, so it was easier for us to go now than during the day." Not the first time the vampire aversion to sunlight had caused awkward explanations. This time, thankfully, Yael seemed to accept the explanation.

He opened the door for Yael to carefully seat her stiff and bruised body in the back seat, then hurried around to get in on the other side.

"Gentlemen," he said, leaning forward a little, "this is Yael Malka, one of my fellow students at uni. Yael, these are my mentors Mordechai Zalman, who is driving, and Rabbi Avram Mendel. They are the reason why I am in Israel today."

"Pleased to meet you," Yael said.

"The honor is ours," Mendel said, tipping his hat as he turned to look at her. "Any friend of Ariel's is a friend of ours."

"Fasten your seat belts," Mordechai said. "This may be an interesting ride."

"He's not kidding," Ariel murmured to Yael as he fastened his own belt.

Officially it was only fifty-four kilometers from Tel Aviv to Jerusalem, but what with getting out of Tel Aviv and getting into Jerusalem and finding parking, the trip took a bit over an hour. Most of the conversation during the trip was carried on between Yael and the rabbi. He questioned her about her training so far and about what her plans were, and she was delighted to find that not only was he medically knowledgeable, he also had a fine sense of humor. By the time Mordechai parked the car, they had managed to reduce Ariel to tears of laughter more than once.

Ariel exited the car and hurried around to the other side. Sure enough, Yael had stiffened up while sitting in the same position for an hour, and needed a hand to get herself extricated from the back seat and straightened up to walk. She took his arm to steady herself, and they started moving slowly, following the two older men who had gone ahead.

"I see what you mean about 'interesting,'" she murmured to him. "Does he always drive like that?"

"Oh, no," Ariel said matter-of-factly. "Usually he drives faster."

She looked over at him. "You're not kidding," she said after a moment of examination.

"Not even," Ariel said. "Honest truth."

"The intercity buses don't run at night, do they?" she muttered. "Too bad."

Ariel laughed.

By the time they reached the plaza facing the Western Wall, Yael had loosened up enough that she was walking normally. She still held onto Ariel's arm. He didn't mind.

It was after 2100 hours, and was full night outside,

but there was a great deal of artificial lighting in the plaza. It wasn't quite equivalent to daylight, but Ariel had no trouble seeing.

Mordechai and Mendel had stopped outside the security checkpoint to wait on them. "Ariel," Mendel said with a pat on his shoulder, "this is your first visit. Go, find a place, and pray. Take as long as you need."

Yael dropped her hand. "Go on," she whispered.

Although it was night, once they were through security, there were quite a few people in the plaza, maybe a hundred or more, men separated from women by a light partition. But there were clear spaces along the wall. Ariel pulled his bar mitzvah kippah from his pocket and put it on, then began walking toward the wall, aiming for one of the sections currently free of people. As he walked, as the stones in the wall grew in size and in proportion as he drew closer, the scale of the structure and the sheer antiquity of it impressed itself on him. This had been here for over two thousand years. It had been built by Jews, for Jews, as part of the complex devoted to worshipping the God of Abraham, Isaac, and Jacob. Emotion began to well up inside him.

Arriving at the wall, Ariel hesitated, then raised both hands and placed his palms at shoulder height on a single stone. He felt the rough texture of the limestone against his skin. There was almost a sense of electric shock at touching it. He closed his eyes, and murmured, "*Sh'ma, Israel, Adonai elohenu, Adonai echod.*"

Hear, O Israel, the Lord our God, the Lord is One.

Ariel's throat closed. His mind filled with keening. He knew the prayers he should be praying, the ones from the siddur, but he couldn't call them up. His mind was filled with grief.

He leaned his head forward until his forehead rested against the stone. His heart ached. His soul ached. His throat was so closed he almost couldn't breathe.

A single tear trickled from his left eye. As if a dam had broken, Ariel began to weep, silently, motionlessly.

He wept as he grieved for his parents, taken before their time. He wept as he grieved for poor Tiffy, taken from the only home she had ever known and now having to learn to live without her family. He wept as he grieved for Yael, for what she had been through and for the road ahead of her. He wept for as he grieved for Mordechai, for Menachem, for Eleazar. He wept as he grieved for himself, for Chaim, whose life had been so drastically changed and whose memories seemed to be fading in the light of the life he now lived. And he wept for Israel, that she needed such as him to be her defender.

Ariel had no idea how long he stood there, how long he wept, but eventually the tears ceased to flow. He took a deep breath, straightened, and brought the *Gibborim* medallion out from under his shirt to kiss it.

"Lord God of Hosts," he whispered in Hebrew, using the ancient name that a warrior would have sworn by and sworn to, "I am your man. I am your warrior, unworthy as I am. Sustain me as I fight Your fights. Help me to do that which is right. Help me to endure that which must be endured. Let me stand in the gate for as long as I am needed. *Omayn.*" The thought that he was now capable of standing in the gate for a very long time indeed lingered in his mind.

Ariel kissed the medallion one more time, then

tucked it back under his shirt. He straightened, throwing his shoulders back, and wiped his hands across his face. He touched the stone one last time, promising himself and the wall that he would be back.

He could see his three friends standing together. It was only a matter of a few steps to join them. No one said anything. Mordechai nodded, a solemn expression on his face. Rabbi Mendel patted his shoulder a couple of times. Yael moved to stand beside him and put her good arm around his waist. He put his arm around hers, careful to avoid the wraps around her ribs, smiled at everyone, and said, "Let's go home."